'I loved it. C... ...real deal'
Marian Keyes, ... ...*... ...Stole My Life*

'Throws a chilling light on how brazenly power can be abused at the top echelons of society, and the suffering it can bring down on the most vulnerable – packaged up in a brisk and imaginative plot' *Sunday Times*

'Colette ... ... twisty, clever novel, she's guaranteed to win more fans' *Red*

'A tense thriller . . . beautifully written and perfectly paced. Her best book yet' Fiona Cummins, author of *Rattle*

'The complex nature of family relationships is portrayed with clarity and heart . . . A taut thriller' Ali Land, author of *Good Me, Bad Me*

'Dazzling. Political intrigue, echoes of Savile, with a troubled mother and son relationship at its heart' Tammy Cohen, author of *When She Was Bad*

'An intelligent psychological thriller with a new twist on the genre. A thrilling read' C.L. Taylor, author of *The Missing*

'Vivid characterisation, great plotting, and a denouement to freeze the blood. I loved it!' Liz Nugent, author of *Lying In Wait*

'Thoroughly gripping, clever, beautifully written crime fiction' Jane Casey, author of *After The Fire*

'I inhaled it – literally reading it in one sitting. A beautifully written, gripping and thought-provoking book' Emma Kavanagh, author of *Falling*

'Fiendishly impressive structure; taut, evocative prose; gripping plot' Sarah Vaughan, author of *Anatomy of a Scandal*

'Colette McBeth just gets better and better, but this was something really special' Holly Seddon, author of *Try Not to Breathe*

# Colette McBeth

# AN ACT OF

# SILENCE

**WILDFIRE**

The right of Colette McBeth to be identified as the Author of
the Work has been asserted by her in accordance with the
Copyright, Designs and Patents Act 1988.

First published in 2017 by WILDFIRE
An imprint of HEADLINE PUBLISHING GROUP

First published in paperback in 2018 by WILDFIRE
An imprint of HEADLINE PUBLISHING GROUP

2

Cataloguing in Publication Data is available from the British Library

ISBN 978 1 4722 2671 6

Typeset in Bembo by Avon DataSet Ltd, Bidford-on-Avon, Warwickshire

Printed and bound in Great Britain by Clays Ltd, St Ives Plc

MIX
Paper from
responsible sources
FSC® C104740

Headline's policy is to use papers that are natural, renewable and recyclable
products and made from wood grown in sustainable forests. The logging and
manufacturing processes are expected to conform to the environmental
regulations of the country of origin.

HEADLINE PUBLISHING GROUP
An Hachette UK Company
Carmelite House
50 Victoria Embankment
London EC4Y 0DZ

www.headline.co.uk
www.hachette.co.uk

To everyone who hasn't been heard.

# PART ONE

PART ONE

# Monday, 17 November 2014

## Linda

Say yes.

One word, all he wants to hear.

*Yes, I believe you. Yes, I will help you.*

That look of his, brimful of need, stirs in me the biological instinct to protect, make safe, put things right.

I am hardwired to give him what he wants. That is love, I suppose.

But here's a thought: what if I had resisted, left him to deal with his own mistakes, learn his lessons the hard way; would he be the same man, sitting here recounting this story?

The truth is I'll never know.

We are where we are.

It is early, night is fading but dawn has yet to crack open the day. These are what I call the never hours. Suspended between dark and light when the world's eyes are firmly shut and only the few night owls and early birds among us get to glimpse secrets unfolding. Five minutes ago I woke with a jolt; a noise, a movement, an overactive imagination tore through my sleep. I descended the stairs, fearful there was a secret waiting for me in the shadows, behind a door or hidden in a cupboard. I reached the kitchen, flicked on the light and his voice shattered the morning silence with a simple request.

'Milk, one sugar, please.'

The fright found an echo in my heartbeat, galloped through

my body. Another break-in, that was my first fear. My second? That it was me they wanted this time, not simply an old laptop. I swung around to match the voice to a face and found him.

I waited for relief to flood me. It didn't arrive. Instead, my fear was replaced by dread.

It wasn't him.

He could have been a stranger, this man. The familiar gloss of wealth and success and fame scoured away to reveal a bleaker version, one with a film of dirt thick on his skin, dark oily eyes that hadn't found sleep in a long time. He was broken, that much was obvious. Something had happened and seeing him like this broke me too.

'What have you done?' I asked.

He caught me in a stare. The swell of tears in his eyes quickly rubbed away with the back of his hand.

'Oh, Gabriel.' I held my son as tightly as I did when he was a baby. 'Tell me,' I said. 'There's nothing that can't be fixed.'

Now we sit at my kitchen table where he used to inhale one, two, three Weetabix as a boy each morning. And he tells me.

A woman.

She is called Mariela. Pretty name. About mid-twenties he thinks but apparently it's hard to tell these days.

'Was she your girlfriend?'

'It was just sex.'

I don't bite. Gabriel's casual approach to intimacy has long been the cause of my disapproval. Now is not the time for lectures.

'I see. And when was this encounter?'

'Two days ago. Not last night, the night before.'

'At your house?'

He nods, rolls his eyes at his own stupidity.

'And then what?'

He covers his mouth with his hand, the words sting as they come out.

4

'Then they found her.'

These are the facts I collect.

My son Gabriel met a woman called Mariela in a sushi bar two nights ago. She went home with him where they had sex. The next morning she was found in an allotment.

Mariela is dead.

The allotments back on to his house.

Gabriel has been asked to report to Camden police station in six hours for questioning.

'You believe me, don't you?'

'I . . .'

I'm not fast enough and he can't slow down now he has started. He races on with his monologue. My mind is stuck, terrified of following him because it knows where this ends.

He wants me to help him. Give him some time to get his head straight. Provide my car, that's all really, not a lot to ask, and cash too. And if anyone asks if I have seen him, the answer is no. He's not running away, just giving himself a bit of space.

There's an intensity to his argument that is impossible to ignore. Wasn't it always the way? My boy is nothing if not persuasive; one of his many qualities, but dangerous at times too. 'Someone is trying to frame me,' he says. I want this to be true but it doesn't stack up, all I can think of is, *Why, why, why would they do that?*

'You're my mother. You know I couldn't have done this. And you know how it looks, it'll be all over the papers by the morning. They'll be judge and jury and I'll . . . I'll be fucked. I've never begged you for anything before but I'm begging now.'

His desperation spins out a fierce, kinetic energy that drags me along. He is falling apart and it is agony to witness. I need to hold him together, I have to do something to help. He is right about the press, they'll crucify him. He won't be treated fairly.

He is well known, a famous face, all the better to sell newspapers. They'll rake over every detail of his life, cook up a dark side. And my name will be dragged in to damn him further: disgraced politician's son. He's in for a public mauling, no doubt, and having been there myself I wouldn't wish it on anyone, least of all my son.

I have to do the right thing, but it wears many guises and at the moment I can't tell it apart from wrong.

Time. He's not the only one who needs time to think. The world has slipped out of sync, sent me freefalling into a terrifying darkness. I close my eyes, praying that when I open them again, order will be restored.

'Mum, please.'

His words go to my core, to who he is, who I am. He is a baby in my arms again, the midwife handing him to me for the first time, a tiny wet being writhing against my skin. And me, his mother, drunk on fear of the past, hope for the future.

'Gabriel,' I said. My very first word to him, to his father. 'We'll call him Gabriel, like the angel.'

*Yes, I'll help you.* I'm about to give him what he wants because what else can I do, he's all I have. He needs me and above everything else I know this: my son is not capable of murder.

But.

I open my eyes and I see it, a red line gouged out of his neck like a warning.

'What is that?'

He runs his index finger along its trail. Surprised. Hesitates long enough for me to catch the lie that flashes on his face.

'Oh that. I did it on a branch.'

It is only a scratch but it rips through my belief. It is doubt and fear and dread.

'Don't do that,' he says.

'What?'

No answer. He's stopped making sense now.

'If you haven't done anything wrong,' I say, 'you have nothing to worry about.'

'If?'

'What?'

'You said, *if* I haven't done anything wrong.'

'Did I?'

'You think I could have done this?'

## Gabriel

It's her house. My subconscious is playing tricks, has lured me here knowing that if I was in full control of my faculties this is the last place I would have chosen. The vision of it rearing up in front of me, half lit by a stuttering streetlight, produces a violence in my gut. Why here? Why not a friend's house, or Palab's? Anywhere.

A deep phlegmy laugh crackles through the night air. Someone's been smoking too many Marlboro reds. But there's no one else around. It is my laugh. And suddenly I know what's so funny. The truth, that's what. This is the place. The only place. Who else was I going to turn to? She knows who I am, underneath the bullshit and the expensive suits and the fame. That's what everyone else wants, my so-called friends, my manager, the women. She loves me despite it. Another truth, they're coming thick and fast tonight. Maybe that's why I avoid her. She can see right through me.

She's my mother.

I have to tell her. That's why I have come here. I need her to look at me and see beyond the state I'm in and know, absolutely, no shadow of a fucking doubt, that despite everything I am still her son. I'm her boy, not faultless, far from it, but good at my heart.

I am not a murderer.

I need to hear her say the words: I believe you.

If I don't have that, what else is left?

I let myself in. The blue numbers on the oven say 5.01. I want to wake her but then I always was a selfish bastard so I fight the urge, sit on my hands and let her sleep. As it happens, I don't have very long to wait until her footsteps creak on the stairs. A warmth spreads through my veins, travels the length of me from my big toe to my fingertips and up through my head. It is hope. She is my hope and she's here in the kitchen, flicking on the light. She hasn't seen me, so I keep it casual and say, Milk, one sugar, please.

You'd think it is a fairly harmless request, but it doesn't go down well.

She emits a scream. I hadn't entertained the possibility that my presence might give her a fright, it certainly wasn't my intention. I should have thought it through, planned my arrival more carefully, but my cognitive abilities aren't functioning at their peak right now, and I can't turn back the clock.

We are where we are.

Her first words take a while to come out because after she recovers from the initial shock she spends a good while staring at me with a look of abject horror. It produces a sweat that beads on my forehead and chin and slides like worms down my back. I know I'm not looking my best but, to be fair, neither is she. Her hair would put Medusa to shame and her dressing gown, well, that should have been retired years ago. So I'm on the verge of saying, Shall we call it quits, when she beats me to it.

'What have you done?'

I rerun her question in my head. *What have you done?* I heard it right first time. Why would she assume, before anything else, that I had done something wrong?

*Because she always does.*

8

My eyes tear up. The hope that had been kicking out so much heat fizzles to nothing.

I'm a grown man, universally acknowledged to be a success – though granted this current shitstorm isn't my golden moment – but I need her trust, her love. Belief. I still need her.

She sees my tears. I wipe them away, embarrassed.

'Oh, Gabriel,' she says and holds me in a squeeze. 'Tell me. There's nothing that can't be fixed.'

BOOM!

The hope ignites again.

I tell her about Mariela, as best I can; the details are a little sketchy even in my mind. I wasn't exactly sober on the night and thirty sleepless hours have not improved my recall.

As I'm recounting the story and trying to gloss over the sex bit (there are things no mother needs to know about their son) it occurs to me that I can't turn up at the police station in my current frame of mind. How can I sit in a room for hours and answer question after question? Christ, I don't have any answers, none of it is straight in my head. I need a bit of space. Time to straighten myself out and collect my thoughts.

I ask her if I can borrow her car because this, it seems to me, is the obvious solution. She mutters something about needing it for a trip to Scotland. I ask for a bit of money too. It's not like she won't get it back. I have plenty, but walking to the cashpoint right now could be problematic. Someone would recognise me and, even if they didn't, the police could trace my whereabouts. That wouldn't be good for either of us.

I wait for her response. I'd settle for a simple nod of her head. Something. Now is not the time for the silent treatment.

In the absence of a reply, I up the ante. 'Someone is trying to frame me. You're my mother. You know I couldn't have done this . . .'

*Say you believe me.*

She closes her eyes as if she's trying to summon sleep and the anger swells inside me.

'Mum, please.'

Her eyes are open again, staring at something on my neck.

'What's that?'

I run my finger over the area in question. It's a scratch, more of a gouge. Mariela and her nails. She wanted it rough. Don't they all.

'Oh that. I did it on a branch.'

She stares at it too long and I know what's happening, her dedication to root out the worst in me is currently fastening itself to this cut on my neck.

'Don't do that,' I beg. I sound pathetic. Can't help it. She's making my insides shrivel. I need her to hold me, kiss my head, tell me not to worry, *It's a mistake, I know you couldn't have done it.* I search her face for love but instead I read **disappointment, disbelief, distrust**.

'If you haven't done anything wrong, you have nothing to worry about.'

*IF.*

The word goes off like a siren.

'You said, *if* I haven't done anything wrong.'

'Did I?'

'You think I could have done this?'

My own mother doesn't believe me. She sees right through to my soul and finds only dark, putrid matter inside. The hope is snuffed out. She was it. It all comes down to her. Always has. Her trust. She won't give it. Can't. I look to her for answers but all I find are more words: **disdain, disapproval, disgust**.

## Linda

A phoney calm descends. We sit with each other, me trying to go over his story, but his facts are jumbled and he grows weary and angry at my questioning. I offer to cook him an egg, some toast, whatever he fancies. He doesn't fancy anything apart from a third cup of coffee. I'd caution against it, but a caffeine overdose is the least of my worries. Besides, it is clear I need to choose my battles carefully.

By the time the winter sun rises and fills the kitchen, the air is thick with panic, mine more than his. He should be showering, preparing to go to the police station, but exhaustion and delirium have taken hold. He is hunched over his mug, head jolting as he bounces in and out of sleep. Gabriel is not going anywhere.

One shoot of hope; there is a chance none of this is real. Gabriel's life is one of excess, late nights, partying, drinking too much. No good can come of that. Fame has feasted on him; the women who sell their stories, the so-called friends who party on his tab, and don't even get me started on that awful manager, Palab. He'd sell his granny if he could resurrect her from the dead. Even I struggle to find my son behind the façade. Perhaps this is the result. Paranoia has taken hold. Drugs can do that, can't they? Lord knows he's had more than his fair share of them. Last year he was pictured in the newspapers snorting cocaine off a woman's breasts. The mind boggles.

I move to the living room to escape the burn of his attention. Outside, buses stream past, helicopters whir in the sky (searching for him?), the sounds of everyday life divert around us. I locate my laptop and log on, hesitating before I run a search for the story. My disbelief is the only thing keeping me afloat.

I type MARIELA and ALLOTMENT.

I open the BBC News website. It is here.

The headline crushes my hope. Crushes me. Mariela Castell. A dancer. Past tense. A picture of the allotment where she was found.

I start to shake, uncontrollably. Pain flashes across my temples. She is dead, this poor woman. Who would do such a thing? Not my son. Gabriel could not take a life and destroy it so callously, leave her all alone and open to the elements. Whatever happened to her, he is not responsible.

'You thought I was making it up.' I jump. I didn't hear him creep up on me. He is hanging over my shoulder now. The tang of his breath makes me wince.

He whips round, kneels down in front of me, face an inch from mine. 'I didn't do it. I don't understand what is happening. Someone is out to get me. You don't think I could have killed a woman do you? Say it.' He has grabbed hold of my shoulders and is shaking me, gently at first but then harder and harder and it hurts. It hurts. His fingers press deep into the nubs of my shoulders and I grow dizzy as my head is forced to and fro. My vision blurs. I stare at this man in front of me, desperately trying to find my son, but I can't. He is gone, vanished, replaced by a stranger with eyes that are deep pools of rage.

Finally, he stops.

He removes his hands from me and they hang suspended in the air for a moment giving the impression he is not in charge of them.

My body is light, floating away from me, as if I've been unhooked and can't tie myself down again. 'Gabriel,' I say. I need to touch him, to feel his body, to know that he is real. Too late. He kicks the side table on his way out. It topples, taking a cup of coffee, a plant, and the laptop with it.

I sit, allow tears to track down my face unchecked. My world seems so fragile, so finely balanced that I fear a single movement, the tiniest disturbance in the air, is all that is needed to crash it completely. And yet, when I finally summon the courage to rise from my chair, nothing happens. The world is oblivious to my pain. To any pain. It waits for no one, casts us aside as flotsam. I see the familiar dark clouds collecting on the horizon, pressing in on me. This time I push back against them. I won't succumb.

Too much at stake. I seek out Chopin, his uncanny ability to restore my equilibrium. I let the sound waves flood and bolster me, clear a space in my head to think logically.

It works, at first. The most likely explanation, I tell myself, is that the poor girl left his house and was attacked on the way home by a maniac. Coincidence has put Gabriel in the frame, nothing more.

And yet.

Sex. My mind stumbles over this and it splits. His reputation as a womaniser is well documented, my son is almost as famous for his sexual exploits these days as he is for his comedy. What if it was rough sex gone wrong? What if he panicked? Had she said no? Were her pleas drowned out by his desire? He's a man who gets what he wants. Has he forgotten he can't have *everything*? What if anger got the better of him, just as it did when he was a boy, possessed him until he spun out, exhausted on his bed. The same rage that twisted his face and shook me by the shoulders only a few moments ago?

What if he hurt her?

What am I to do?

He hasn't made a sound for over an hour, which makes me think he might have gone, slunk out as quietly as he crept in. Inching upstairs, I'm careful to avoid the squeaky floorboards. If he's still here, I don't want to rouse him. I check the rooms, one, two, three and finally I find my son lying on his old bed, curled up, fists in a ball, exactly how he slept when he was a child.

This vision of him overcomes me. Since morning I've tried to dampen my love, make space for logic and reason, but it bubbles up now, comes to the boil, overflows and burns my insides.

I hear the suck of his breath, watch the involuntary twitches of his body. What has happened to us? How did we get here?

We are not the people we were supposed to be. I stare back into the past and see the many versions of us, ghosts of who we should have been. And I can't shake the sense that everything that has gone before has built up to this, that all our decisions, our mistakes, the paths we chose to travel, one instead of another, have brought us to this point.

I reach out and touch his hair just as I did when he was a boy.

It is still soft.

My decision is made.

I retreat to the hallway, pick up the phone. My hands shake in defiance. I get the answerphone, a man's voice. 'I need to speak to you about Gabriel . . .'

And then.

It happens quickly, much too quickly to explain or help myself. His presence unsettles the air and the last words, the only words I hear are, *You fucking bitch*, before my head makes contact with the wood of the bannister. Cracks.

My body finds the wall, slumps down against it. Above me he towers. I can see three of him, each one blurred at the edges, none of them real.

He pulls me upright. My eyes find his, find hatred in them. I lift my hands to protect myself from further blows but nothing comes. Instead he presses something to my head. Soft, to soak the blood.

'Gabriel.'

His footsteps on the stairs grow fainter before they fade to nothing. I look down at the red red blood on the cream carpet. Always a mistake, that colour. Looks worse than it is. Not to worry, I think.

My son is gone.

It is only blood.

# Gabriel

I lie on my old bed, push my face into the cold soft pillow. It smells like childhood. That helps a little, quashes a portion of the anger that's solidified in my gut, but most of it remains. I hate myself for what I have just done. Since when was I a man who shakes his own mother until fear bleeds out of her? Someone else has taken hold. I don't recognise myself. I've become a monster.

The clock has ticked beyond midday and I am clearly not where I should be, sitting in front of a copper incriminating myself with every word I speak. They'll come for me soon, no doubt, but right now I can't summon an atom of energy to do anything about it. Plan A was my mother, and look how well that's gone. I don't have a Plan B. Foresight has never been my strong suit.

Exhaustion tosses me to sleep, where I'm swamped by unwelcome images: Mariela, her red lips, black hair swirling around her face, the sensation of her nails scratching a path down my back. My mother, beaming out her disgust. And something else; a walk through the darkness, muddy boots, cold slapping my face, a scream that pierces my dreams and jolts me awake.

My mum is tiptoeing across the hallway, tiny footsteps loath to make a noise. The sound haunts me for what it reveals, that she is scared in her own house, afraid of disturbing me, of facing the consequences. This is what I have done, driven her away, when all I wanted, needed, craved, was to have her close. She creeps to my room, pushes open the door and waits before she moves a few steps closer to the bed. The current hits me like a shock, the heat that beats out of her is so pure and raw and fierce. Love, no question. It drenches me in remorse. Sorry. That's all I want to say. Sorry for who I am. Sorry for what I did. Sorry. But the energy in the room is so perfect, it's almost chemical. I don't want to do a thing to break the spell. I keep my breathing sleep-heavy as her hand brushes the top of my head, light as a feather. My tears, soaked up by the pillow, hidden from her.

Then she goes.

I count to ten before I swing myself out of bed. A sweet clarity has descended, cleared the silt from my head. There's an urgency to my movements, I don't have much time, a small window of opportunity to put things right. I remember the reason I came here. Not for the car or money or help. Those are sideshows. I came because I want my mum to know that whatever happens, whatever people say about me, I am not that man. I want her to believe me.

Anything else I can deal with.

It's then I see her.

Standing at the top of the stairs by the bannister, talking into a phone. I'm hit by a wall of confusion, but when I hear her words, muffled thanks to her hand being placed over her mouth, the picture becomes so sharp it cuts me.

'I need to speak to you about Gabriel . . .' she says.

The resolve, the remorse, the tenderness that had bloomed inside me a few minutes ago, reforms into cold hard fury.

My own mother.

Talking to the police.

I have to get out. Unravel myself, go back, find the good me, work out how it came to this. Her disbelief compresses my neck, harder and harder. I can't breathe here, can't be around her a second more.

I run for the stairs, she turns around, sees me coming.

'You fucking bitch,' the words are out. Don't make me feel any better, but true. The truest words I've ever spoken.

She's in my way.

I don't mean to push her.

But I do, and I hear a crack before she falls. I look down and her head is oozing blood.

I grab a towel from the bathroom, pull her to a sitting position, press it to the cut. It's just a cut. I should stay and help, but I'll die if I do.

She's killing me. All my life she's been killing me. Making me bad when I wanted to be good.

I'm her son. Stupid me to think it mattered.

It's only blood.

# PART TWO

After and Before

# Monday

## *Linda*

I can't pick myself up. Can't. Won't. Too much has happened. Been lost.

I used to be someone: a mother, a politician, the Home Secretary, with power and influence.

Now look at me. This is how far I have fallen.

Slumped on the floor, blood bubbling out of a cut, head throbbing with failure.

Alone.

Who is going to come and help me now?

Anyone?

*Didn't think so.*

My name, shouted, one, twice. Again.

'Linda?'

'Linda?'

It is not Gabriel. He has gone. My son is not coming back. This is a woman's voice. Anna, my housekeeper.

My head is sticky with blood and perspiration, although I'm cold, not warm. Ice for fingers, body shivering. I'm relieved to hear another voice, but humiliation swims close to the surface. What will I tell her? Anna is nobody's fool.

'Up here.' I can't shout, my voice is too thin, the words come out strangled. Her footsteps thump on the stairs and then she finds me. I make a pre-emptive strike, attempt to diffuse the shock before it hits her. 'It looks worse than it is,' I say. I try to

21

form a smile but abandon it when the pain around my eye spears me.

'Jesus, Linda, are you OK?'

'Just a fall.' The reflex to protect him is still strong.

'Well, from where I'm standing it looks bloody horrific. Is anything broken?'

*Everything.*

'I don't think so.'

'Come on then, you can't sit there all day.' She heaves me upright and I sway towards the stairs. She grabs me, pulls me back; her strength, the only thing between me and a tumble down the stairs.

'Let's clean you up and after that you can tell me what the hell happened.'

I sink into the bed. My eye throbs to a drum beat, puffed up so much it's practically closed over. Anna works her way around the cut, reporting on the size of the injury, its depth and severity. I could do without the commentary but at least it prevents her from asking questions. 'You might need a few stitches, you know.'

'Absolutely not. A trip to A&E would finish me off.'

'If you say so. It's not too deep, could have been worse, although the carpet will never recover. It looks like someone's died out there.'

I miss my cue to laugh.

She disappears to the kitchen, returning with tea, a mug for each of us, Digestive biscuits, an anxious air. She sits on the armchair next to the bed.

'Now,' she says, 'are you going to tell me what really happened?'

A fall, I repeat the lie. This time she doesn't accept the explanation. She's seen the upturned table in the living room, along with the coffee cup on the carpet and the soil from the plant pot. I've been caught out by my slovenly ways, should have cleared up when I had the chance. I consider claiming responsibility for the mess, blaming it on a dizzy spell, when Anna tells me there are several bloody footprints on the stairs.

'I should call the police.'

'Please don't.'

'Who did this?'

I'm backed into a corner and I have to give her something if I want to find a way out.

'Gabriel,' I say. 'It was an accident.'

More questions. I don't want to give the answers away, but she's going to find them anyway. If I don't tell her my version, the press will deal her another one very soon.

Besides, I believe in Anna and I can't say that about many people in my life. Something in her I recognised from the very first day she turned up for an interview; determination, a damaged soul. Takes one to know one. This is why I offer her a basic outline of Gabriel's story; Mariela's body found close to his house, his relationship with her, if I can call it that. I omit the dramatics, him shaking me, *you fucking bitch*. No need to give him more bad PR.

'He thought I was calling the police, you see. He wanted to get out, pushed past me, that's all.'

'Why aren't they here then?'

I rub my eye and a charge of pain shoots through me. 'He's my son,' I say, and wait for my confession to register. 'I was calling a friend first. I wanted his advice, but the damn fool never switches on his phone. Not that I would cover for Gabriel if he had really done something wrong but I just don't believe it.' Anna feeds me disbelief.

'This isn't him, he's not a monster,' I say, pointing at my face. 'You won't call them, will you – the police? Not right now, anyway. I'm not asking you to lie, it's just . . .'

'If that's what you want. Do you know where Gabriel is now?'

I shake my head. 'He wanted to take my car. It was parked outside.'

Anna pulls back the curtain and scans the street. 'Well, it's not there any more.

'You should rest,' she says. 'Decide what to do when you wake up, but I guess you won't be needing this today.'

Out of my good eye I spot her moving my suitcase into a corner. It's all packed. We were supposed to be travelling to Scotland this evening. Tears find their way into the cut, sting like acid. Everything has been planned, the journey, the accommodation, the interview I've secured for the book I'm writing. Anna thinks it's about female politicians of the twentieth century, and that the woman I'm meeting is a political historian. I'm afraid to say neither is true. I'm no advocate of lying, but in this case, it is a small deceit to protect a bigger truth.

'We can send an email,' Anna says. 'Postpone it. Unforeseen circumstances. I'm sure she'll understand.'

*I'm sure she won't.*

I give her the woman's contact details and dictate an email explaining I have had an accident and am incapacitated. I apologise profusely (*That's four times you've said sorry, Linda*) and ask for an alternative date in a few weeks' time.

My head feels heavy and full, overloaded with the day. 'You should get some rest,' Anna says. I don't argue. I'm gone in seconds.

She promised, didn't she? But now she is shaking me gently, telling me the police are here, want to speak to me.

My eyelids are glued with sleep and when I finally manage to open one I see Anna's hands held up in surrender.

'It wasn't me. I didn't call them. They just turned up.'

They are searching for him.

It is real.

I find Detective Sergeant Jay Huxtable, plain-clothed and casual, studying the mess in the living room.

'I would have tidied if I had known you were coming,' I say. The joke is awkward, misfires.

'Mrs Moscow,' he shakes my hand. 'Has your son been here?'

'This morning,' I say. 'But he didn't stay for long.'

'Did he do this?'

I'm unclear whether he's referring to the overturned table or my face, and decide to hedge my bets.

'It was an accident, low blood pressure, it's a bugger. I passed out.'

'You should get it seen to.'

'Anna here has taken good care of me already.'

'Do you know where your son is now?'

'I'm afraid I don't.'

'We want to question him in relation to the death of a young woman. He was supposed to report to the police station at midday. We'll do our best to find him but in the meantime, it's not advisable for you to stay here.'

'I'm not scared of my own son, if that's what you're suggesting.'

*But the man who appeared today? I was scared of him.*

DS Huxtable doesn't let up. I escape to the loo when his badgering reaches a pitch I can no longer bear. He wants me out of here, my own home, says he can't leave until he knows I'm safe. Gabriel has made it hostile. I don't want to go. Despite everything, I want to be here for him in case he comes back. In case he needs me. And yet, there's another voice in my head, the rational, thinking one that tells me enough is enough, begs me to take a look in the mirror and ask: how much longer can I protect him?

I stare at my face and find my answer. Cheek inflamed, one eye closed to a slit. Pitiful. Me.

This is what he has done.

Anna intercepts me in the hallway to let me know my interviewee, Naomi Parkes, has replied to my email. 'Well go on then, break it to me.' The day has already done its worst, I'm of the opinion it can't drag me down any further.

I am wrong. It transpires that Naomi Parkes, whose personal account is crucial to the success of my book, was already having second thoughts, questioning the wisdom of digging up the past. She's sorry I've had an accident, but these last few weeks, mentally preparing herself to talk to me, have taken their toll. She's not sure she wants to schedule another date, what with the kids and work; after this weekend she has school plays and Christmas parties coming out of her ears. And what's she going to tell her husband? He's away this week so she didn't have to explain where she was going, who she was going to talk to. Lying doesn't sit well with her and she's not prepared to do it.

It is this week or not at all.

'We could still go,' Anna says. 'If you felt up to it. You could rest for a few days before you meet her.' She motions to the detective in the living room. 'It would keep him happy, at any rate.'

The prospect of travelling hundreds of miles, putting endless roads and hours between me and my son, wherever he turns out to be, makes me light, shapeless, terrified.

'I don't think I can.'

'Don't let him ruin it. Isn't this what you've been working for?'

She's right. Years I've been trying. I can't let it slip from my grasp again.

Otherwise everything is lost.

# November 1991

## Gabriel, aged 7

I'm seven years, four hours and thirty-three seconds old . . . correction . . . thirty-five seconds . . . thirty-six. I can watch the seconds of my life tick away on my new digital watch.

I can also tell you I've been out in the cold for one hour and fifteen seconds. No one can see me in my hiding place behind the shed, which is good. What's not so good is the cold, the way it bites my bum on the stone step and makes my teeth smash together.

The sky is black but that doesn't mean it's late. It's only dark because we're in November and the nights get greedy and swallow up the days. The air smells like it did when I blew out my candles this afternoon.

*I wish that . . .*

'Don't tell us what you're wishing for,' my mum said. But she was the one person who could make the wish come true. How else was she going to know I wanted her eyes to stop following me everywhere?

'She loves you, that's all, doesn't want you to come to any harm or get into trouble,' my dad said when I complained about it last week.

There must be different ways of showing your love because Tommy's mum lets us play upstairs for hours and her eyes don't interrupt once.

Her love is muddy fields and dirty footprints on the kitchen floor. 'It's only mud,' she'll say. She doesn't even count the number of cookies we have or ask us to wash our hands.

When I blew out my birthday candles I wished for my mum to have Tommy's mum's eyes, although not a direct swap because that wouldn't be fair on Tommy, would it?

The funny thing is, I wish my mum had seen what happened this afternoon. Then I wouldn't be in trouble, and I wouldn't be out here in the cold trying to teach her a lesson.

She said I don't deserve any presents, and my dad said calm down, it's not that bad.

'He does this all the time, Hugh.' She said his name like he was in trouble too. 'And he refused to apologise, do you know how that makes me feel?'

'I didn't do it,' I said. 'Laura tripped.'

'See? It's the lying I can't stand. Bernadette saw it happen.'

'Bernadette is a witch.'

I said this because, a) it's true, and b) because it's about time my mother knew her friend isn't really very nice, and c) because it's not fair that a horrible witch and her moaning daughter get to spoil my day, and d) because it was already out there, like a burp after a glass of lemonade before I had a chance to think of the consequences. And e) my mum's following eyes are Bernadette's fault. She's always telling Mum to keep them on me.

'Gabriel! That's quite enough.'

Bernadette thinks I am a sly fox, and manipulative. I don't know whether that's a good thing or a bad thing, although coming from Bernadette my guess is it's a bad thing.

She's hated me ever since Laura broke her arm in a wrestle. When we're all together my mum pretends to stick up for me. For example, today she said, 'I honestly don't think Gabriel would push Laura down the stairs.' And even when Bernadette told her she saw it with her own two eyes, my mum just smiled and went to get Laura some frozen peas for the bruising.

When Bernadette left the party, my mum dropped the smile. 'Tell me exactly what happened,' she said, which was really annoying because I'd already told her five times.

'Laura tripped over Mr Piddles, I didn't push her although I should tell you she kicks me all the time at school.'

'That's not what Bernadette saw.'

'Why do you always take her side?'

Dad looked at Mum when I said this. I guess he wanted to know too. Because in the family tree, I'm the strongest branch and Bernadette isn't even a twig.

Mentioning Mr Piddles was a big mistake though. When he gets me into trouble he's locked in the airing cupboard for days and comes out smelling of clean towels and not like himself at all. Seeing my mum reach for him I dived in first, grabbed him, protected him in a cuddle.

'Give him to me, Gabriel.'

'No.'

'I'll ask you again.'

'Answer's still the same.'

At this point my mum unlocked my arms and pulled him from me so hard his leg ripped. I watched the feathers of his stuffing drift down this way and that and land on the carpet.

'I hate you.'

Slap.

A slice on the leg. Red and stinging.

'Linda . . .' my dad said.

My mum held her hand out in front of her, staring, eyes big bowls of wonder. It shook like my gran's does when she drinks tea.

'Go to your room, Gabriel,' Dad said. My mum had lost her words.

I took Mr Piddles and ran away, feathers from his stuffing fluttering like we were in the middle of a snowstorm.

'It's his birthday, for God's sake. Why do you have to be so hard on him?'

'What, so we just do nothing and let him get away with it?' My mum had found her words again and threw them at my dad.

29

'Get away with what? You don't even know he did anything wrong. He's right, Bernadette is a witch. I don't know what it is she's got against him, but he can't do anything right in her eyes and why you listen to her is beyond me. He's a good kid, Linda.'

I was hoping my mum would say, 'I KNOW THAT,' really loudly, and then I could be sure she believed it. Instead she slammed a door so hard the tremors shook my bunk bed.

In my room, I inspected Mr Piddles. I wasn't sure this was the kind of injury anyone could fix, but I told him not to worry. 'People can do lots of things without a leg.' I'd seen a programme with soldiers who came back from the Falklands War with missing limbs and they seemed to manage just fine.

I'm so cold now the wind is chopping into my head. If my mum had bothered to kiss me goodnight she would know I'm not in bed, but she hasn't and there's no point carrying on with this game if I'm the only one playing. I want to be back under a warm duvet. I creep through the kitchen and past the living room door.

My dad isn't there. Just my mum. She has a wine glass in one hand and the other is holding the phone. Tears have given her a fat face. I wait for her to turn around because her eyes must know I'm here, but she doesn't. Maybe my wish has come true after all. It doesn't feel as good as I thought it would.

She is talking to Bernadette.

'I know I'm overreacting, but I can't stop worrying about him. And I can hardly tell Hugh now. You're the only one who knows.'

I go to bed wondering what is so worrying, and why my mum would keep a secret from my dad and hand it over to Bernadette, just like that.

# Tuesday

## *Jonathan Clancy*

'It's Jonathan Clancy from *The Times*.'
Even after twenty-five years at the newspaper, there are moments when Jonathan still gets a kick out of announcing himself.

This is one of them.

Given the choice, Jonathan knows that Curtis Loewe would never talk to him. Today. Any day. But he also knows he's a man driven by his public image. Can't pass up on an opportunity to make himself look good. It is this knowledge that provides him with his first shot of sunshine on an otherwise bleak morning. Gabriel Miller has been arrested on suspicion of murder. All the rumblings suggest he will be charged soon.

'How the devil are you?' Curtis asks, as if the men are old buddies.

*Keep your friends close.*

'I've been better.'

'Sorry to hear it. I assume this isn't a social call.'

'Correct. I wanted to talk to you about Gabriel Miller,' Clancy says.

'What can I say? I'm as shocked as anyone. I was introduced to him recently. Odd chap, if you ask me. A funny manner about him, but I wouldn't have thought he was capable of this.'

'Innocent until proven guilty.'

'Well, yes . . . but you know, it doesn't look good. You

never can tell what's going on behind the scenes. Poor Linda. It's a tragedy.'

'I didn't realise you were friends?' Jonathan asks.

'Friends is rather stretching the truth. We were acquainted way back when she was a newish Member of Parliament. I met her at a fundraiser. Would bore the hell out of you, those things. Linda was a breath of fresh air. There weren't many female MPs in those days. She was tasked with squeezing me for money.'

'She must have been good. How much have you given them now?' Jonathan asks.

'Millions. I've lost count. She was very persuasive, but I had little to do with her afterwards. Busy woman, climbing the ladder.'

'Until she was thrown off.'

'Resigned, Mr Clancy. You really should get your facts right. She resigned after her misconduct was exposed.'

'Of course she did. My mistake. Seen anything of her lately?'

'No call to really. From what I can gather, she shunned public life. I'm afraid to say these things happen. Some types bounce back from a scandal, others shrink away. Politics is a brutal beast from what I can tell. Mind you, she was bang to rights. Never knew what possessed the woman to do it. She didn't strike me as the greedy type.' He stops himself, as if he's realised he's laying it on too thick. 'Is it just a quote you are after?'

'Something like that.'

'Well . . . I always found her professional and persuasive and a great asset to the party. Will that suffice?'

'Just one thing . . .'

'Listen, I have a meeting in five minutes, I think I've given you enough time.'

'When did you say you met Gabriel Miller?'

'I didn't . . . It was a few months ago, after one of his shows. We were introduced. Can't remember much more than that.'

'Must be your age. It does that to the memory. If it comes back to you, do give me a call,' Clancy says and hangs up.

Clancy sits at his desk and stares at the squiggles of shorthand in front of him. He has no intention of deciphering them, he takes notes out of habit not necessity these days. Besides, the most important facts from the phone call are imprinted on his mind. Curtis met Gabriel. He'll be sure to follow that up, but first he needs to speak to Linda's friend Bernadette Mulligan.

'You're lucky, I've sent the rest packing,' Bernadette tells him as she ushers him inside her Clapham semi. 'What a bunch they are. But you're a friend of Linda's and that makes you a friend of mine too.'

There are really only a few questions Jonathan wants to ask Bernadette, but quickly he senses that she is not a woman to be rushed. Currently she's taking him on a detour through the years of her and Linda's friendship; from university to marriage and beyond. 'I thought she'd be with Hugh forever,' to the early years of motherhood, 'she doted on Gabriel.

'I still can't quite believe it. Poor Linda. But I will say there was something not right about that boy even from when he was a child. Linda could see no wrong in him but he was devious, you know, always up to tricks and lying. My goodness, the lies he told! I would say to her, Linda, you have to keep an eye on him. He had some temper on him too. Good God, the way he would spin out of control. All she could do was stand and watch. He needed a good hiding, if you ask me – not that I advocate violence, you understand.

'She wasn't well either and I put it down to him. I'm not talking physical illness, I mean up here, you know.' Bernadette taps her head. 'Depression, you'd call it now. You see, people think Gabriel is all smiles and jokes, because that's all they see on television, but there is another side to him.' She shakes her head and dabs her tears. 'We've been friends for more than forty years. Sure, she tried to cut herself off after that awful scandal – never knew what she was thinking, it was so unlike her; whiter than white, she was – but I wouldn't give up. I think she was embarrassed, ashamed to show her face, and you can't blame her, but we all make mistakes and you don't dump a friend when the going gets rough, do you? She'd ignored me for a good two years before I bumped into her at the shops. Jesus, the state of her – don't quote me on that now – she looked like she'd fallen out with the hairdresser. And to think she was always so particular. When I saw her, I said, Linda, I don't care whether you want my company or not but I'm visiting once a week. No arguments. Of course she put up a protest, but she needed someone because that boy of hers didn't come near. Imagine that, after all she'd done for him and he didn't so much as pick up a phone when she was in trouble. That sent her into a black hole. She had everything once and then nothing at all. Except the bottle. But I think the book helped focus her mind; when she started writing that, she seemed more like her old self again.'

Bernadette takes a sip of her tea and Jonathan seizes his chance to speak.

'She told you she was writing a book?' he says.

'Not a novel, if that's what you're thinking. Factual, she said. She always did like to be cryptic.'

'Did you tell anyone else about this book?'

'I don't make a habit of gossiping and Linda made it quite clear she didn't want anyone to know.'

Jonathan Clancy's eyes tighten as if he's trying to pull something into focus at the edge of his vision.

'Did she have any other visitors apart from you?'

'Well, she wasn't a total recluse. Gabriel started to visit again, sporadically, and she got some help around the house at my insistence. She was no domestic goddess, Linda.'

'Can you remember the name of her cleaner?'

'A housekeeper, she called her. Alice, I think. Or Anna. No, that's it. She was called Anna. Blonde hair, not natural but whose is these days? I only saw her once or twice. Can't say she made any difference, this Anna woman, not that I blame her. She was a cleaner, not a bloody magician. Linda had so much junk in that house. I warned her I was going to put her forward for that programme, *Obsessive Compulsive Hoarder*, if she didn't do something.'

'Going back to Anna,' Jonathan says, 'did you know her full name, anything else about her?'

'I'm afraid not. She was a relatively recent appointment. A bit shifty, I thought. I told Henry as much.'

'Henry?'

'Henry Sinclair. He's a friend of Linda's. A proper gentleman. She used to work with him. I bumped into him leaving her house one day. Can't imagine she made him very welcome, judging by the look on her face. She could be like that. I had to go back to my car to sort out the parking and got chatting to Henry. He was worried about her, weren't we all. Asked me to keep an eye on her.'

'And what did this keeping an eye on her involve?'

'Would you like a biscuit? Go on . . . Nothing much. We'd only chat now and again, he's a very busy man. I told him she had a publisher and she was spending all her time on her book.'

'I see. Did she tell you she had a publisher?'

'Linda? You're kidding, she wouldn't have told me the time of day. No, I arrived one afternoon to find him there. Michael, he was called. Scruffy-looking type. You get away with that in the media, don't you . . . Oh, I didn't mean you . . . you're very well put together . . . Anyway, Henry seemed happy that she was doing something productive with her time.'

Jonathan eased himself off the sofa, 'You've been very helpful but I'm afraid I must get going.'

'But you haven't even finished your tea.'

35

# December 1992

### *Gabriel, aged 8*

My mum likes to solve people's problems, which means everyone comes to her with them. Even when we're in Sainsbury's we can't get past the bananas without someone springing out to tell her the playing field in Balham is being sold off and what is she going to do, or that their son is disabled and he needs a lift in their house, could she please arrange it?

Often, they're quite rude but she wears her polite face and tells them, 'I'd love to hear more about it at surgery. Please make an appointment.'

I'd like to tell them to get lost and leave us alone and for goodness' sake let us choose our strawberries in peace, but that would be RUDE according to Mum.

I went to her surgery one Saturday and guess what, she isn't even a doctor! Her job is to listen to people moan all morning and write the moans down and take them to work on Monday and pass them on to important people who run the country. She's called a politician. 'But then you become the moaner,' I said.

'It's not moaning, it's helping people.'

Today she shouldn't be doing any helping. It's half-term. Elena has the day off and Mum says I get to pick what I want to do. I know exactly what my choice is and so would she if she ever got off the phone.

I draw a picture of a clock and a question mark. *How long?* She glances at it and pushes it away then shoos me off. I can't remember being this bored in my whole entire life.

I steal a custard cream from the cupboard and go upstairs. I'm not fond of them but beggars can't be choosers.

In my room, I play with Mr Piddles. We make a stage on the floor and I give my animals a role each. Then we start dancing around. Not the sissy sort of dancing, these are cool moves like Tommy and me do. I have all the animals jiggling about with me to the soundtrack of *The Bear Chronicles* and I'm so lost in it that I don't see my mum standing in the doorway.

'We're warming up for the film.'

'What film?'

'*The Bear Chronicles*, that's what I want to do today.' To strengthen my case, I do the bear dance along with a rendition of the song. Tommy and I have already learnt it off by heart.

At the very least I'm hoping for a smile or a round of applause, but my mum doesn't do a thing. It's like all the happiness has been scrubbed off her face and now it is just a blank. She can be weird like this sometimes. Her moods drop in and out like the signal on the car radio when we're travelling to Gran's house in the country.

'Mum?'

She walks over to the window and hooks her eyes on the tree outside. It is naked, stripped of leaves, but she must find it very interesting because she stands there with her back to me for an age.

'We could go to the soft play if you like,' she says.

*You've got to be kidding me.*

'Mum, I'm eight years old!' Soft play is for babies, everyone knows that. Sometimes I think it's a surprise to my mum that I'm getting older. As if she can't keep up with the years.

'What about the Science Museum?'

'Bor-Ring.'

'Or the zoo?'

'The penguins stink and it's raining.'

I look outside. The sky is mud. 'I want to go and see *The Bear Chronicles*.'

'It's not appropriate.'

'It's a PG!'

'I said no.'

'But you said I could choose. You said it in front of Dad and Elena. I have two witnesses. You can't break your promises.'

'Gabriel, I'm sorry but we're not . . .' She reaches out to touch my head, my curls. When we sit next to each other watching TV she likes to spool them around her finger. 'Get off!' I hit her hand away. Smack, it makes the sound of my anger. Satisfying. 'You're a liar, a liar.'

'Stop that right now.'

I can't. My anger has broken free, become its own person, like the Incredible Hulk, turning green and bursting out of me. My mum's shouts feed it and make it more powerful. It hits her. And again. And again. Serves her right. Keeps going. Can't stop. Won't stop.

Eventually she finds the strength to overcome it. She pushes me up against the wall and prises my arms apart. The Anger is still screaming at her, not words, they have melted into each other and become a long soundwave of fury. Tears rush down her cheeks and they make me cry as well.

Sometimes The Anger goes too far.

Later, she knocks on my bedroom door with a sandwich, a glass of milk and a biscuit. The biscuit lifts my mood because it's a Kit Kat, which is as good as an apology. 'Eat up and we'll go out.' Result! I wait until she leaves before I start humming *The Bear Chronicles* tune. I don't want her to think I'm rubbing her nose in my victory.

When we walk past the bus stop I get the first sign that all is not good. 'Are we walking all the way to the cinema?'

'I thought we could go to the park.'

She has to be joking. A trip to the park is about as unspecial a day as I can think of. I gulp down my tears but they set really hard like bullets in my stomach.

'But I thought we were going to the cinema.'

'I said no, didn't I?'

When we get to the park my mum finds a bench and I head to the swings, not because I like them but because they're as far away from her as I can get. I push my legs in the air and tip my head back and watch as the sky bursts like a water balloon and pours rain down. 'Let's go to the café,' my mum shouts, as if this is the most exciting thing and not some place I've been going to every week since I was a baby.

She buys me a hot chocolate with extra marshmallows and cream, which I presume is another peace offering because in normal circumstances she would deny me the toppings on account of them being too sugary. I am in no mood to make peace. I choose a seat at the window. They're steamed up and with my finger I write *The worst mum in the world*. When she sits down I add an arrow that points to her.

'Is that what you think?'

'Yes. I hate you.'

Tears now and they're not even mine. She turns away from me, looks out through the window, through the words I wrote, their own tears of condensation washing them away.

She pushed me into telling that lie. She always does this, makes me behave badly, leaves me with no choice. I don't hate her, I love her, but if I hadn't said yes, no was the only other option and that would make me look like a loser. She's not the worst mum by a long shot either. Shelley's mum waits outside the school gates in pink pyjamas. And Simon's mum doesn't allow him any TV. Not even *Inspector Gadget*.

Silence sits between us as thick and lumpy as school custard. She's edged away from me as if I might be contagious and twists her wedding ring one way and another. I want to break the quiet, say something nice, find words to mop up her tears, but nothing I can think of fits the shape of our argument. In the end, I give up. All I wanted to do was see *The Bear Chronicles*. What's her problem? The characters are animals and there isn't even any swearing. I shrink away from her and huddle as close to the wall as I can and we sit and wait until the rain runs out.

When we leave the café, I head into the tree house. It's not my best move because the rain has made it stink like a swamp, but I'm trying to make a point. I suppose I'm hoping that she'll come and find me here and we'll make up and sit and chat like Dad sometimes does with his knees hunched up to his chin. My dad is way too big for the tree house but it's nice that he squashes himself in just for me.

As it turns out, my mum doesn't do any squashing. After a while she shouts, 'We're going home, Gabriel.' I don't move because I'm still mad. I want her to say sorry or at least give me a hug like she does when she knows we've both gone too far and one of us needs to make the first move.

'Gabriel,' she shouts again and again.

It goes quiet. I peep out of the house through the branches. My mum is looking around, 'Gabriel,' she tries one more time but softer and slower, as if her batteries are dying. Then she walks out of the playground. It's the oldest parent game in the world and there's no way I'm falling for it. I watch her shrink into a dot before she disappears into nothing at all. I wait because I know she's coming back. There's no way she would leave me in the park alone.

I count the seconds and minutes on my watch. Two minutes then three then five and ten. Ten worries me. Double figures make it more serious. She must have known I was here, she watched me climb the ladders.

Should I move? Leave the park and try to find her? I give it a second's thought before deciding we could be lost to each other forever that way. I stay put, push back the tears. The light has misted. There's only one and a half people left in the park apart from me: a bored dad pushing his baby on the swing. When he goes, I force myself down the ladder. The dark is playing tricks on me. It's dressed the park for evening, turned it into a stranger. The trees laugh and the shadows try to eat me and the dogs have become wolves that snarl at me with foaming mouths and fang teeth.

The tears won't be held back any longer.

I run, pick up speed as I hear the traffic noise come closer and closer. I run and run and run until I'm spewed out at a massive roundabout. I don't know how to get across it so I wait but there's no gap in the cars just one after the other, never stopping. In the end I have to count ONE TWO THREE and step out on to the road. A horn yells at me, there's a screech of brakes. A man waves his arm and shouts. I retreat. I'm stuck in the park, cut off by a sea of cars and lorries and vans.

Back inside the park the night is so deep and thick I can't believe morning will ever fight its way out again. I don't care about *The Bear Chronicles* any more. I'm sorry I ever asked to see it. I'm sorry for being horrible. I just want to be back home with Mum and Dad and Mr Piddles and Pudding our cat. But I don't think that's going to happen because someone is sure to steal me out here and they won't even need a packet of sweets or the promise of a litter of puppies to lure me away from safety because I'm all alone.

I walk on a little and trip over something, grazing my chin on the ground, but that's the least of my worries. I look down to see a large stick, big enough to be a weapon but small enough for me to carry. I find a bench and sit waiting for something to happen, never letting go of the stick once.

*

I don't remember falling asleep, the night and the cold must have swept me up and carried me off. But I must be asleep now because someone is trying to wake me, pulling at my hair and wrestling the stick from my grasp.

'Get off me,' I try to scream but it comes out as a weak cry.

'Gabriel.'

He knows my name.

'Oh thank God, thank God.'

It's my dad.

He smells of fireworks and squeezes me really tight against his body.

*I'm safe.*

'Dad . . .'

'Yes, son,' he says into my shoulder.

'You're suffocating me.'

When my dad opens our front door my mum runs at me like I'm a rugby ball to be caught. Tears have bloodied her eyes. A moment of silence squashes in between us before she says, 'I'm sorry, I'm so sorry. I'm sorry,' over and over again until I begin to worry someone has stolen all her other words and she can't say anything else. My dad must be thinking the same thing because at the twentieth sorry he pulls her off and says I need a hot drink and a biscuit and some warm pyjamas, which I think is a polite way of telling her to do something useful.

Later, when he's tucking me into bed I tell him about the argument over *The Bear Chronicles* and the lame suggestions of soft play and the zoo. We share a disgust of the penguin smell and I'm pleased to see the mention of it wrinkles his nose.

'It was supposed to be my choice today,' I say and then in case he thinks I hid on purpose I add, 'I didn't mean to get lost. I thought she knew where I was.' I turn my voice down low as I can: 'I think she left me because she doesn't like me any more.'

My words unleash another bear hug and we lock together like two pieces of a puzzle. 'She loves you very very much,' he says, but there's something about the way his voice wobbles that makes me think he's not so sure himself.

'Will you sleep next to me tonight?' I ask.

'Budge up.'

My dad is six foot three inches and he has to coil up like a snake to fit in my bed but he doesn't once complain, he just strokes my forehead until I drift away.

Dad doesn't wake me up for school the next morning. When I find him in the kitchen I tell him I'll get a black mark in the register for being late.

'You're not going to school. We're going to the cinema. If anyone asks, you're ill.'

*The Bear Chronicles* is even better than I expected and because everyone's at school the cinema is empty, which means I get to sing along to the songs without anyone complaining.

'I didn't count a single swear word,' I tell my dad when it's finished. 'Why would Mum say it's inappropriate?'

He shrugs like he can't fathom it either. 'Who knows?'

It's only when I'm going to bed that I ask when Mum will be home.

'She needs a little bit of time, Gabriel.'

'Does she have a lot of work to do?'

'Not that kind of time. She needs some time to herself.'

I bite my lip. I was right, she doesn't want to be around me.

'Will she be here tomorrow?'

He shakes his head. 'Not tomorrow.'

'Then when?'

'A few weeks.'

*Weeks.*

'I promise I'll be better if she comes back.'

'Oh, Gabe. She hasn't gone away because of you. You must never think that.'

But what else am I supposed to think? She didn't even say goodbye.

I mark each day she's gone with a cross in my diary. It's four weeks and three days until she returns. I'm playing football in my room when I see her standing in the doorway.

'Hello, my darling,' she says, like she's just been out to the shops. I want to run to her and bury myself in her coat and cry and tell her I've missed her every single day, but the weird thing is I don't do anything. I can barely look at her because I'm frightened that if I get it wrong she'll disappear again.

We all have dinner together that night and I'm sure she's going to tell me where she's been or pull a present from her bag, ta–da! like she does when she's been away with work. Instead she moves the cottage pie around her plate and squashes peas with her fork and says the garden shed needs painting and my dad says no it doesn't at which point she sighs and asks me if I have any homework (no) and have I fed Pudding (yes) and would I like any more cabbage (as if).

'No thank you,' I say, and I draw a smile on my face like the one my mum has drawn on hers. Everyone gives up on talking after that, the only sound is of our knives and forks scraping against the plates. It's like our shapes have changed and we don't quite fit together any more and no one has noticed except me.

At bedtime, Mum kisses me goodnight. The kisses are wrong, they're skimming stones that do no more than brush the surface. She's here right next to me but I think it must be a magic trick for her to be this close and yet really far away.

On her way out she says, *Love you see you in the morning* and this makes me turn away and push my face into the cool of my pillow. How could she have forgotten? We don't say it like that. We say loveyouseeyouinthemorning as fast as we possibly can so it rolls into one big happy word that's all ours and ours alone.

# Wednesday

## Linda

My boy is front-page news.

FUNNY MAN ARRESTED ON SUSPICION OF MURDER, the headline screams, and written next to his photograph, a short description of where he was found. Yesterday morning in Kent. Hiding out in a holiday cottage.

*As if he's got something to hide.*

He tried to run when they came for him apparently, always was quick on his feet. Not quick enough this time.

I study his picture, taken out in the wild with no lighting or studio make-up to enhance him. The shot must have been snatched as the police were dragging him away, and I'm struck by the emptiness behind his eyes, the shadows that have formed under them. The man in the picture doesn't look like Gabriel. His exuberant curls lie flat on his head, weighed down by grease and dirt. By events. His nose is skew-whiff, broken in a scuffle perhaps? No sign of that bubbling, irrepressible spirit. All that is left is an empty husk.

And look at his cheeks, the ones I was so fond of kissing (if he allowed me close enough), sucked into his bones now. But his mouth, this I recognise, stretched around the same word he threw at me two days ago.

**Bitch.**

The weight of pain doubles me over and I retch as the bile collects in my throat, but nothing comes up.

★

Mariela isn't named. The victim is only referred to as a woman, and while it doesn't seem right – the least they could do is give her an identity – I am selfishly relieved not to see her face next to Gabriel's. I turn the page to find a photograph of another woman. Gabriel is not the only one who is unrecognisable. The old Linda Moscow was a woman who knew high office, whose fingertips leaked power and authority, who wore a stiff blow-dry and trouser suit. Her armour. In the newspaper, they refer to me as the former Home Secretary, former MP, a life in the past tense. Gabriel is *the disgraced politician's son*, and to frame his downfall, there's a précis of the scandal that ended my career. We're a bad lot says the subtext.

*The apple doesn't fall far from the tree.*

Upon seeing my own image stare back, my sadness and despair quicken into something more potent. It has a beating heart all of its own. It is rage and humiliation and a scorching sense of injustice. It is anger. White hot. And it is also fear that the choices I made in the past have both saved and damned him.

How will he ever get a fair hearing? Yes, he is tarnished not only by his reputation, but by mine too.

I'm in Scotland when I learn of his arrest, the Kyles of Bute in Argyll. Or the Secret Coast as it is otherwise known. This is where Naomi Parkes lives and tomorrow, with any luck, I will meet her. In the end, I agreed to make the journey from London however much my heart shouted at me to stay put. Anna was right, my meeting had been too long in the planning and there was too much to lose by throwing away this chance. Naomi Parkes is the victim of a crime and a cover-up. Without her story I can't expose the men who have never been made to pay. You'd recognise some of them; familiar faces, hidden crimes. And believe me, this is the reason, the only reason, that I fight the temptation to run back to Gabriel. Yes, I'm desperate to shrink the miles between us, speed up time and pull tomorrow closer, but to abandon my plan now would cost me the chance of nailing them once and for all.

I did however, as a condition of my travel, extract a promise from DS Huxtable to keep me informed of any developments. So far he's done a poor job, although in his defence, communication is proving challenging on two fronts; Anna forgot to pack my mobile phone. I can hardly blame her, given the circumstances surrounding our departure. Secondly, our temporary residence has made a virtue of being stuck in the twentieth century.

We hope you enjoy your time at Claremont Cottage and make the most of the opportunity to switch off from the distractions of the outside world.

Roughly translated this means there is no Wi-Fi, no television, no mobile reception, not even so much as a radio in the cottage.

'I guess that's what some people must want,' Anna said when she read it out to me.

*Not us.*

'I can't help thinking it's all my fault,' I tell her. We're at the kitchen table, eating the soup she bought from the local store.

'He's a grown man, Linda. I'm sure you did your best. You can't blame yourself for what he does.'

I grab her words like a lifeline. Maybe it was always going to end this way no matter how hard I tried. I sink into the armchair, defeated, struck by the crushing pointlessness of it all. The late nights, feeding Calpol to dampen fevers, the dressing of wounds, the endless encouragement, *you can do it*, the setting of boundaries, dispensing discipline, the unquestioning love. Was the outcome preordained? Had I uncovered parenthood's colossal con? Did any of it matter, the cajoling, the chiding, the bestowing of affection?

Perhaps it is as simple as this.

Nurture cannot outwit nature.

'I don't think he did it, you know, despite how it looks,' I say.

'Then I suppose he shouldn't worry. They'll work it out in the end.'

'You put a lot of faith in our justice system. Look,' I stab the newspaper with my finger, 'they might as well say he is guilty: *The dark side to the comedian, A sexual predator, His mother forced to resign in the cash for contracts scandal.* It's trial by media.'

'As the former Home Secretary, I thought you of all people would trust the system to uncover the truth.'

'Or maybe that's precisely why I don't.'

I wake from a nap mid-afternoon, and find a note on the table.

*Gone for bread and milk.*

I peer out of the window. The sky is a sheet of brilliant blue that dazzles and winks and asks me, what am I waiting for? Anna has been trying her best, tending to me, urging me to take it easy, rest, recuperate. 'Best to stay indoors until you're stronger,' she's advised. But I'm hardly an invalid. The swelling around my eye has subsided, assumed a yellow and brown tinge, the same colours as the leaves on the ground. I'm practically camouflaged, which is all to the good as I don't doubt my appearance has the potential to scare.

I crave the simple sensory pleasures the outdoors brings: exposure to sunlight, wind on my face, fresh air. The walls of the cottage are beginning to absorb me. I need to take my thoughts for a walk, break the endless loop – What is Gabriel doing now? What are they asking him? What is he telling them?

With no Anna to caution me otherwise, I wrap up and slip outside. The bright sky deceives. The air is sobering and sharp against my skin. Frost paints the path. I take it slowly, walking down the wooded bank towards the road. When I reach the end, it splits open to reveal the water, a sea channel, tinted gold and silver by the sun, packed full of treasure. Steep hills grow out of the shoreline, rich greens rusting at their peaks. I take a breath just as the beauty in front of me takes it away again.

Onwards, a slow but steady pace along the bank. I have no particular destination in mind, just to be out, alive, listening to the water rushing over the pebbles, birds overhead, a yacht striking through the water, is all that matters. Nature provides a perspective, soothes my mind but doesn't shrink my problems. Then again, I wasn't expecting miracles. I pass no one, not a single soul, and it strikes me as an odd world, so many people crushed up in a city like London, and this glorious place all but deserted.

Ahead, I spot a shop, perched precariously at the brow of the hill, as if a puff of wind might send it tumbling downwards. Hopes of a hot drink, a cake, power me on towards it but fade fast when I see the signage for a general store.

To my annoyance, the bell rings as I enter. I have no desire to announce my arrival, draw attention to myself, although these days I never get recognised. The air is laced with herbs and spices and meats. A woman replenishing a shelf with packet soups turns and says hello.

'Hello,' I say but my eyes are already drifting to the television mounted on the wall above the till.

She logs my interest.

'Same stories aw day. They run on a loop, don't they? Mind you, it's some business with that funny man, is it not?'

Gabriel's face on the screen elicits a pop of surprise from me. I don't know why; logic dictates they would be giving it blanket coverage. It's more that seeing it on the television news is another way of sealing it in reality.

'Have ye no heard?' the woman's voice breaks through my thoughts. 'It's all over the papers. They reckon he might have killed someone.' I detect a pride in her tone, as if she has solved the case herself. 'And te think a paid good money to see his show in Glasgow last year.'

I head for the fridge where I can escape her scrutiny and commentary but still retain a good view of the TV; Gabriel, a house and garden surrounded by fields where he was arrested. A clip of his stand-up, energy pulsing out of him, all smiles and laughter. A picture of my own house.

'You found what you're looking for?'

I reach for a bottle of water. Press it to my face. Cold against hot, and bring it to the till.

A picture of me. Another me from different age. A time when life was defined by my job and status, my family, the boy I kissed goodnight.

'Poor woman, I cannae say I agreed with her politics but she didnae deserve a son like that.'

*Did she?*

'I'm Emily, by the way. You on holiday here?'

'Yes,' I say.

The news moves on, a sea of ceramic poppies at the Tower of London commemorating the outbreak of the First World War.

Gabriel disappears.

And so do I.

Outside, clouds press down on the hills to muddy and shrink the light. The sky's smile has dropped. Darkness threatens, it falls quickly here. Fooled you, it says. I pick up speed, force myself forward, only for the wind to redouble its efforts and press against me. A drop of rain spits on to the path followed by another and another until they are snapping at my face. The waves, asleep and silent only an hour ago, have woken up and kick and jostle in the gathering storm. Their hungry jaws drive my fear into panic.

51

The determination that has fuelled this project deserts me. It is too much, an act of stupidity, of utter lunacy to come here. And for what? To right a wrong, to get justice, to expose the men whose power and influence has put them beyond the law. Tried that before. Once. Twice. And look what happened. They ruined my career, destroyed my reputation, turned my name into shorthand for political corruption.

I shouldn't be here, I should be hundreds of miles away in London, close to my son when he needs me. And the truth is I'm tired to my bones. Why not surrender to the storm, allow it to devour me?

Except.

I stop. Dead in my tracks. A single shaft of sunlight rips open the clouds and bounces on the water's dark surface to blind me.

This is about the men who abused their power and the girls who were told their stories didn't matter. But this is also about my son and me.

Why have I not seen this before?

The truth about us.

An impossible choice.

Life or death. Right or wrong.

The choice that has all but destroyed us.

I have to keep going otherwise we have no hope, Gabriel and me.

And my only source of comfort is knowing this; they have already taken everything I valued.

What else have I got to lose?

I muster all my strength to battle through the weather and get back to the cottage. When I spot the opening for the path, I almost cry with relief. Just a few more steps. I drag myself up the bank, the mud pulling my feet away from under me at every step.

The light from my bedroom spills on to the path. I must have left it on. Not my usual style, I'm a stickler for saving energy, but there's a first for everything, a sign perhaps that I'm not fully recovered. I'm still chastising myself when my foot hits something hard, the root of a tree disguised in the undergrowth. I manage to grab on to the window ledge and avert another fall in the nick of time. Pausing, I gather my breath, peer through the glass into my room as my heart slows and returns to its normal rhythm.

Anna.

The danger isn't immediately clear; it takes a few moments for the context to frame it.

It is my room, not hers. And she's sitting at my desk, my laptop open. My eyesight isn't what it was but never mind, I can still see the header at the top of the page.

## What Happened at Kelmore

She has opened the file containing my book. I can't think how she found my password, but fear overtakes my curiosity. She will know that it is not about female politicians of the twentieth century.

She will know I am a liar.

A connection trips, short-circuits, crackles and then goes dark. My body empties, no substance left, nothing to keep me upright. I fall down into freezing mud, sinking further and further. I should get up, shout for help, do something. I know, I know, but I can't. My reserves are empty, there's nothing left.

In the armchair, heat beating against my face. My toes still cold in defiance of the flames that lick out from the fire. Brandy sitting at my lips to coax me out of my stupor. 'Linda.'

I force my eyes open. Anna is crouched down, peering into my face. Her skin mottled and puffed. Distressed.

'You fell. You're heavier than you look.' She's peeled off my coat. I look down. It's cast in a puddle at my feet.

My throat is raw. 'Could I have some water please?'

'Here.' She holds it for me. Icy gulps shock me back to life. Then I remember.

'You were in my room,' I say.

She moves away from me, walking across to the window where I can't gauge her reaction, and stares out as the wind presses against the panes. 'You'd been gone a long time. I was worried. I thought you might have tried to meet your woman . . . Naomi. I was looking for a number,' she says.

She's testing me, I'm sure of it. I wish I could see her face.

'The meeting is tomorrow, Thursday,' I remind her. I consider saying sorry, giving her the full story, why I lied. *Didn't want to. I had to*, but my head is still woozy and the truth is too big to contemplate. I can't scale it right now.

Instead I say, 'I went for a walk, that's all. I fancied some fresh air. Not quite that fresh though. It blew all the stuffing out of me. I should have listened to you, taken it easy.'

'I'm not saying anything.' She tries to keep her tone light but there's a weight to her words.

'Anna, are you OK?'

'Me?' she turns around so I can see her. 'I'm fine.'

'You've been crying.'

She forces her lips into a smile. 'I found you outside, slumped against the house in the middle of a storm. You can excuse me a few tears.'

'I'm sorry.'

She bats the apology away with her hand, brings me a blanket, asks if she can get me anything. A hot drink, some soup? Am I warm enough? How am I feeling? Should she call a doctor? *She would but there's no bloody signal in this place.* I tell her to sit down, relax, I'm fine, I say. But my reassurances have little effect. A cloud of disruptive energy steams off her. I accept a cup of tea to make her feel better. It works, for five minutes, before she announces that she has to go out.

'In this weather?'

'I need to make a phone call. There's a spot on the main road where I can get some reception. I should get the number of a doctor in case.'

'I'm fine, honestly. Don't go out on my account.'

But it is too late, she has already opened the door and the wind that tears through the house casts my words back to me.

She returns a while later, thwarted and agitated. Streams of rain run off her hair and down her face. She removes her coat and the jumper underneath, hangs them over the chair where water pools on the floor. All that is left is a vest and jeans, a tattoo on her upper arm. An insect or a bird that seems to come alive as she shivers.

'That's pretty,' I say. 'Never thought I'd be complimenting a tattoo.' I'd warned Gabriel not to get any as a teen. *You'll regret it later.* At the last count, he had seven.

She ignores me. 'I'm starving,' she says. 'You should eat too.'

The smell of steaks cooking awakens my appetite. Anna serves them rare, blood oozing out on to a few green beans and a dollop of fried onions. She brings out a bottle, two glasses of wine.

'I'd better not,' I say.

The fire weights the air with a heavy, peaty scent that discourages interruption. We eat in silence, breaking it only to remark on the quality of the meat.

Afterwards, she throws another log on the fire and tops up her wine.

'Why did you go into politics?' she asks. This line of conversation isn't entirely unusual between Anna and me. She seems fascinated, in the way people often are, about my time in Government; did you meet the Prime Minister? (Yes.) Did you visit Number 10? What was it like? (Underwhelming.) Why did you leave? (It's a long story.) But tonight I'm alert, sensing the questioning has an undertow.

'The usual reasons,' I say. 'I wanted to make a difference.' The memory provokes a laugh in me. 'I was idealistic. You have to be, but the deeper you get into Government the harder it becomes. Sometimes you have to make tough decisions. It's not always a case of choosing what's right, but the lesser of two evils.' This is my stock response, one I trot out without thinking or believing. I cast my eyes over to Anna to see if she can smell the bullshit.

'That's nice,' she says, while making it clear it's nothing of the sort. 'Is that what you did?' She's pushing me into a corner.

'At times, yes.'

'Did you ever think about the people who were on the wrong side of your decisions?' A sting, right there.

'Every single day.'

'So why didn't you fight against them, those decisions that you didn't want to make?'

Good question. If only the answer was so easy. 'It was difficult. There were other considerations.'

*Cold, hard words.*

'Such as? Your career?'

'Oh, I couldn't have given a stuff about that in the end. Some choices are impossible, that's all.'

Anna stares at me, eyes sharp, digging beneath my flesh. She shakes her head, can't compute what I'm saying. She still sees the world in monochrome. Good people. Bad people. Right. Wrong.

*It can't be that hard to make the right choices, can it?*

*Trust me, it is.*

Now isn't the time to explain.

'I'm afraid the day has beaten me,' I say. And I make my escape and go to bed, willing tomorrow to come.

# Jonathan Clancy

'Do come through,' Valerie Sinclair says and leads Jonathan into a living room with grand views over the Thames. They're up on the top floor, penthouse apartment, the city scuttling about beneath them.

'Nice place.'

'You think? Henry's choice. I feel rather cut off up here, but some people like that. My husband is one of them.'

Jonathan considers Valerie. She carries the weary air of someone for whom wealth and status no longer matter. Life is full of surprises, he hadn't expected to warm to Henry Sinclair's wife.

'Such a terrible state of affairs, I'm sure Henry will be only too happy to talk to you,' she says.

'You didn't mention I was coming?' Jonathan called an hour ago, first thing in the morning, to speak to Henry about Gabriel Miller. It was Valerie who answered the phone and suggested he come round in person. An unexpected invitation, but not one he was going to decline.

'Do you know, I think it slipped my mind.' Valerie smiles. 'Henry!' she shouts. 'You have a visitor.'

Jonathan is examining the Sinclairs' art collection, one particular painting causing his face to pucker into a frown, when Henry appears.

'Caillebotte,' the man says, and Jonathan turns to find Henry standing before him. 'No one gets it right. But I assume you haven't come here to admire my art.' His voice has a clipped edge.

'Sadly not.'

'Take a seat.' Jonathan sits down, rubs his nose with the palm of his hand and plants it on the leather sofa. There's not much that can cheer him up today but seeing Henry's face ripen provides a small kick of warmth.

'How is it I can help you? If it's a quote you're after, I could have given you one over the phone. I don't know what Valerie was thinking. I have a very busy schedule today.'

'I knew you would want to carve a few moments out of your diary to speak about such a tragedy,' Valerie says.

'Of course.' He feeds her a look of loathing before clearing his throat. 'It's such a dreadful set of circumstances. I knew Gabriel as a boy; charming child he was. Full of beans, always up for a wrestle. But I haven't seen him for years, his professional work isn't my cup of tea.'

'Henry's tastes are a little more simple, aren't they, darling.' Valerie is pouring tea and offering biscuits.

'I'm sure Mr Clancy here is in as much of a rush as I am, Valerie.'

Jonathan accepts the cup of tea and helps himself to two biscuits, registering with some glee Henry's displeasure.

'What is it you want me to say?' Henry's tone turns brusque. 'He had a good upbringing. Linda was strict, not her way to spoil a child, you understand, but he had all the opportunities a boy could wish for. He was brought up to know right from wrong. Look at Linda. There's a woman who worked tirelessly for what she believed in, and many of the advances in child protection are a credit to her. She was a woman of the utmost integrity. OK . . . maybe not complete integrity. Her behaviour with the contracts was out of character. I'd say it was simply a case of bad judgement. It would be unfair for her whole career to be tarnished by one bad decision, wouldn't you agree?'

'If you say so.'

Jonathan allows the silence to sit between them and work up a heat until Henry can't bear it. 'Is that it?' he says.

'When was the last time you saw Linda?' Jonathan asks.

'About nine months ago.'

'Really, darling? You didn't mention it,' Valerie says.

'I wouldn't want to bore you with a full diary recital every morning now, would I?' He plasters a smile on his face, cracks it at his wife like a whip.

'Social call?' Clancy says.

'You could say that. As I told you, we go back years.'

'You were a regular visitor?'

'I wouldn't say regular.'

'So this particular house call was . . . out of the blue.'

'I didn't say that either . . . I was looking out for her. I got the sense she was lost, had been for a long time, lacked purpose after she resigned. And I heard Hugh had died. Thought I'd pay her a visit.'

Valerie's eyes narrow, fix on to her husband. 'Well, that would have cheered her up,' she says.

Her comment soaks up the last of Henry's patience. 'Look, what is it you want? I have very little time. I have to be at the airport in an hour.'

'You see . . .' In response to Henry's plea for haste, Jonathan keeps his diction slow. 'It's my belief she *had* a purpose. What would you know about that?'

Henry throws himself back in the chair, brings his hands down to slap his thighs.

'I assure you I wouldn't know anything about this purpose of Linda's that you refer to,' Henry says.

'But Bernadette Mulligan told you she was writing a book, did she not? Generous of you to look out for Linda like that, keep tabs on her. I'm sure she'd have been thrilled by your concern, if she had known, that is.'

Henry reaches for a biscuit, snaps it in two before turning to Jonathan with the full beam of his smile. 'Look, you know the woman, she could be difficult, tricksy even. She hasn't been accepting visitors for some time. It's hard to sustain a friendship when it's one-sided. But believe it or not, I'm fond of her, and yes, I was concerned for her wellbeing so I did what I could to watch out for her. Of course I offered her my support when the scandal first emerged, and I dare say I tried to limit the damage. But the truth was Linda brought it on herself. She was the one who awarded the contracts to her friend.'

'I wasn't aware the beneficiary of those contracts was Linda's friend?'

'Well, an acquaintance. They were acquainted. Our investigation found that the paper trail went back quite a few years.'

'But as I recall it didn't establish what Linda was getting out of the arrangement.'

'Come on, Clancy, it's not that hard to hide money if you want to.'

'I bow to your superior knowledge.'

'Look,' he says, trying to keep his voice even. 'We did as much as we could to support her throughout, but you can't carry someone forever. After her actions were uncovered, it's hardly surprising she didn't want to see her old political colleagues. She was embarrassed, let the side down. I suppose we reminded her of what she had thrown away. Now if you don't mind, I have a flight to catch.'

'Busy man. I won't take up any more of your time. Where was it you said you were going?'

'I didn't.'

'Business or pleasure?'

'A bit of both, you could say.' Henry stands to indicate Clancy's time is up.

'Thanks for accommodating me. I imagine you have got a lot on your mind right now.'

'I'll take the lift with you, Mr Clancy,' Valerie says. 'I find the air up here quite artificial.'

# October 1996

## *Gabriel, aged 11*

My mum reckons I need to think about what I'm saying before I speak. She tells me that before I open my mouth, I need to pause, look at the words from all angles and consider how they will feel when they land on people. This is no easy task. If I think about words too much they stick and come out in the wrong order and make me sound like I need help. The answer is to talk less, but that is easier said than done because when I don't talk the words pile up and throb in my head and make the room spin around me.

'All I'm asking you to do is be more considerate and think about what you are saying,' she tells me when I complain. 'You shouldn't have been rude to Mr Wallerman, for instance.'

Mr Wallerman is our next-door neighbour and hoses Pudding with cold water every time she sneaks into his garden. Granted, she's one thick cat to keep going back for more, but that is no excuse. She was sick last week and I'm convinced he's poisoned her.

'All I said was that I would get to the truth.' That threat will be the least of Mr Wallerman's worries. I have big plans for him.

Mum gives off a sigh like the iron does when Elena is doing Dad's shirts.

'Honestly, that mouth of yours will get you into trouble.'

Adults are weird. On the one hand they say you should always tell the truth, then the next minute they tell you not to say what's on your mind. And it's not as if my mum follows her own rules.

'Do you always think about what you say?' I ask her.

'I wouldn't survive in my job if I didn't.'

'So when you told Henry to fuck off out of our house last week, you really meant it?'

My dad's newspaper drops down to the table, reveals his face behind it. A smile lurks at the corners of his mouth.

'Gabriel! Don't use language like that.'

'I'm only repeating what you said.'

'About bloody time,' my dad says. 'If you ask me, the man's a—'

'Nobody is asking you.'

My mum was having a day at home. This is different to a day off work. All it means is she spreads her papers over the dining room table and talks loudly on the phone. Sometimes she has visitors, but not the kind who come round for a chat and a coffee like Bernadette. These people wear suits and carry brief-cases and spread *their* papers over what's left of the dining room table. It was Henry's turn today. He does this fake punching me in the stomach routine whenever he comes round, as if I'm four years old and he's Rocky Balboa. My dad drank loads of wine once and told him he was a prat. My dad is a very good judge of personality, let me tell you.

Anyway, Henry was here and I was off sick. Elena had popped to the shops, i.e. she wanted a cigarette. Their voices reached me from the dining room, firing off like gunfire and then falling silent, which is how I knew the rhythm of the conversation was all wrong. I crept closer to the door and peered through the keyhole. Sure enough, there was a charge in the air. If I'd poked my head around I swear I would have got an electric shock.

'What exactly is it you want me to do?' My mum's words

sounded strong and mean and wobbled a bit like she was trying hard not to shout them.

Normally I wouldn't have listened because the boredom would kill me, but I got the strong sense I should hang around because if Henry was in shit, I would have emptied my savings account to watch.

'Don't be naïve, Linda,' he said in a tone I knew my mum would call patronising. 'This is a case of people trying to make trouble, nothing more.'

'He's told you that, has he?'

'Of course he has. He has denied everything.'

'Well, if he hasn't done anything wrong, he has nothing to fear.'

Henry laughed even though my mum hadn't said anything funny.

'Linda, my dear, I would have thought you of all people would know how charming he is . . . how liberal with his affection he can be. But that is a very long way from what he is being accused of.'

My mum gave him this weird snaky smile, as if she'd just found out she was holding four aces. I'd never noticed it before but it was obvious now that she disliked Henry as much as me and Dad, she was just better at faking it.

I don't think Henry realised that my mum's smile was not a display of genuine affection because he seemed to take it as encouragement.

'One word from you, Linda, and the investigation is dropped. Nothing more. It will save time and money in the long run – after all, they're hardly going to get a conviction.'

A meaty silence fell over the room. My stomach tightened, clenched in a fist of nerves because there was my mum stroking her chin, looking like she was giving his request some serious consideration. If this was spectator sport, I'd have been screaming in her corner, stick it to him, don't back down. I didn't know what their argument was about but I knew I didn't want Henry to win it.

'Henry, do you know something . . .' She was still smiling. Maybe the smile was real after all. Maybe Henry knew her better than me because it looked like he was going to get what he wanted.

'You really do disgust me.'

Firecrackers and horns and victory trumpets went off inside my head.

She was good, my mum. Very very good.

'Careful, Linda, we all have our secrets.' Henry's face had gone the colour of my dad's vintage wine. He wiped his greasy brow of sweat. 'How is Gabriel, by the way?'

At the sound of my name I jumped, dived into the living room for cover, but not before I heard her say, 'Get the fuck out of my house.'

Sometimes my mum is the business.

It happens a few weeks later, on Halloween. We're at Tommy's house because his mum Kate is painting our faces. Kate isn't just any mum face-painter, she puts make-up on people for a living. I don't mean lipstick like my mum wears but proper stuff that turns men into lions and children into elves. She lathers our face in white and then red down our cheeks for blood. She even paints our eyelids white and tells us to keep them closed if we really want to scare people. When I itch my nose, Kate slaps my hand away. 'Stop fidgeting, you'll ruin it.' This transformation into a zombie is a serious business.

We're there for . . . like . . . hours. At least two. It's almost made me change my mind about wanting to be an actor, because this is way more boring than I'd imagined. 'I'm starving,' Tommy moans. So am I. The hunger is filling my head with bubbles and making me shake inside.

'Well, you can't eat now, you'll mess it all up. Why didn't you eat before?'

My mum says Kate's away with the fairies, which might explain why she forgets to feed us sometimes.

Tommy groans. 'Don't worry, more room for sweets,' Kate says.

This is another thing that makes Kate different to my mum. My mum would say no sweets without something proper in your stomach. Kate classes a Twix as a meal.

It's the first year that we're allowed to go out trick-or-treating alone, although my parents had to be reassured that Michael is accompanying us. Michael is Tommy's older brother.

'Don't think I'm going anywhere with you two losers,' he says, and gives Tommy a punch in the ribs.

'Oi, fuck off, would ya.'

'Thomas! Do not let me hear you use that language again in this house.'

'But you're fine to use it outside.'

'Do not encourage him, Michael,' Kate says. 'I need you to make sure they're OK.'

'They're never going to be OK, look at the state of them.'

'Just a few streets, Mikey. I promised Linda.'

Michael hasn't let Kate anywhere near his face. He has a Grim Reaper's mask that has pretend blood dripping all the way down it.

'Two streets and that's it.'

'Make sure you don't lose them,' Kate tells Michael as we jump out into the night.

'You two come straight back, do you hear me, no messing about. If anything happens, Linda will kill me.'

Michael takes us to a few houses on Tommy's street where we do our zombie song (words our own) and get a Mars Bar from one and a satsuma from another. Like who the hell hands out satsumas on Halloween? We try a few more houses but no one answers.

'Would ye feck off and leave us alone,' a man shouts from behind one door. Tommy's neighbourhood is only ten minutes away from mine but the big difference is you have to look behind you a lot when you walk around here.

'Time to go home, dickheads,' Michael says.

'We've only just come out. Mum said an hour.'

'As if I'm going to walk the streets with you two fuckwits for an hour. I'm going to the Common. Don't even think about following me.'

Michael's bark is worse than his bite, so we start trailing him anyway. 'Get lost,' he says and picks up speed, ducking under a tree before he loses us for good. Tommy and I are extra slow because our sleeves are tied together. We're not just zombies, we're zombie Siamese twins. It seemed like a good idea at the time.

I've eaten the Mars Bar but I'm still starving, the kind of hungry that sends waves of sickness rushing up from my stomach to my throat. The roadside is too bright; headlights pulse, streetlamps flash. The blare of the horns shudders through me and all the time I'm trying really hard not to spew all over myself and Tommy. Eventually he drags me into the Common where it's cool and dark. Relief. Fear too. 'We shouldn't,' I say. 'My mum'll go nuts.'

'Like she's going to know,' Tommy says. 'Let's hide behind that tree and see who we can spook.'

It's a shit idea but before I get the chance to voice my reservations he drags me behind the massive oak that borders the path.

I'm not hot or cold, I'm both at the same time which is all kinds of weird, let me tell you. The sensation is so odd I begin to believe that Kate is magic and has turned me into a real-life zombie. I slump down because the night has hoovered up all my energy and the urge to close my eyes and sleep to beat off the sickness overwhelms me, but Tommy has different ideas. 'Come on, Gabe, there's someone coming.'

Through the darkness I can just about make out two shadows inching towards us. As they get closer I can see they're holding hands, stopping to kiss . . . Correction: the boy keeps stopping her so he can chew her face off. Tommy looks at me and pulls a face and sticks his tongue out like he's going to barf. I know it's funny but I can't find any laughs inside me.

'Shall we?' he whispers. Those two words flutter down my ear canal, bounce into my eardrum and feed their vibrations through my whole body.

My head is way too heavy to shake and the word *no* has got lost somewhere. I can't reach it. The couple stop a few metres from where we're standing. Tommy digs me in the ribs, mouths, 'One, two, three,' and pulls me along.

'AHHHHHHHH!'

'What the fuck . . .' The girl shouts but stands her ground. The boy pegs it, his shoes dancing dots of neon that fade into black.

'You little shits!'

Tommy tries to duck but I'm too slow. The girl grabs us.

'It's OK, Marlon,' she shouts after her boyfriend, 'you can get your backside down here now. They ain't no ghosts, if that's what you're scared of.'

She starts to laugh; not at us. Her laugh is pointed at Marlon, who is trying to swagger back down the path, legs apart, like he has a massive penis and wasn't really scared of two eleven-year-old zombies.

Close up, Marlon's face is full of mean.

'I'm not scared of no one.'

'Well why did you go running off then? Leavin' me here alone.'

Marlon turns to us, sucks his teeth. 'You think that's funny, hmmm?'

I don't like the look that fills the girl's face; it knows Marlon too well, seems to predict what's coming next. Fears it. 'Leave them now, come on.' She pulls at his jacket. 'They're just kids.'

I want to go home.

'See if you think it's funny now.'

I'm not sure whose face Marlon's fist aims for. It doesn't matter. We're so close that one skull bounces off the other like Newton's cradles and dislodges something inside me that makes my head jelly and my body wobble and the ground around me melts until it's just liquid and I dissolve into it without making a single splash.

I'm trapped inside a dream. My mum and dad are here but I can't unravel their words. They criss-cross each other really fast, so I don't know who is saying what. It's better when I'm alone with one of them. Mum's hand is cold and soft and strokes me gently. I wish I could tell her how nice it is, just me and her and the stroking. I'd like to ask her to hold on to my hand forever and never let go. When she goes, I feel I'm slipping away. She talks to me about when I was a baby, how she had wanted a girl, didn't know how she would cope with a boy. This is news to me. She says sorry a lot, although I don't know what she's got to be sorry about because I was the one who went to the park and now look what's happened. What *has* happened? I can't tell. Sometimes my hand gets wet with her tears. I'd like to give her a hug but I can't move so I try my best to squeeze her fingers just so she knows that I can hear, that I love her.

My dad's hands are different, rough and clammy. They grip me, a bit too hard if I'm brutally honest, but I sense he's trying his best. His voice is filled with puddles. He reads stories I recognise from years ago about Narnia and the Twits, and James and the Giant Peach, and Faraway Tree. Maybe that's where I am. In the Land of Clouds, waiting to come back down the slippery slip.

# Thursday morning, 8.32 a.m.

## *Linda*

Today. Finally, it has arrived. I swing out of bed as fast as a child at Christmas and pull back the curtains. The sky is the shade of honey and the sunlight dances on my face. Relief, that is what today brings. We made it here, in spite of the odds. I see it as the beginning of another chapter; a step closer to bringing those men to justice. And of course, by tomorrow I will be in London, close to Gabriel once more.

Grabbing a jumper to stave off the cold, I walk into the hallway. Silence fills the house. I presume Anna must still be sleeping and decide to make coffee to take to her. Ten minutes later, carrying buttered toast and black coffee, one sugar, I knock on her door. She's been good to me, Anna. And with so many things to occupy my mind, it's been easy to take her kindness for granted. I resolve to be more considerate once we get back to London.

My knock goes unanswered.

'Anna, time to get up,' I say. I am reluctant to enter her room without permission, but when she doesn't reply I push her door ajar and peer inside.

She has gone.

I dump the tray on her dressing table, spilling coffee. What does it matter? All her belongings, her toiletries, everything has been cleared from the room.

The wardrobe has been stripped bare too. A swell of panic

rises in my throat. I can barely shout her name. 'ANNA.' She can't have gone without me. Can she?

Our arrangements were clear, nothing left to chance. Anna was to drive me to meet Naomi Parkes and afterwards we'd come back here, collect our things before heading for the late afternoon ferry to Largs. No need to book, hardly a rush on at the tail end of November. Nobody coming. Nobody leaving. Winter has everyone cornered.

Running to the window, I see she has taken the car. What am I to do if she doesn't come back? I don't even have my phone – not that I could put it to any use. I'd have to walk to the store and ask the woman there to call me a taxi, if she can track one down. I can't risk this whole trip amounting to nothing.

I shower quickly, pull on the black trousers and wool jumper I laid out last night, and throw my remaining items of clothing into the suitcase. These days my ablutions are limited to soap and water, a streak of deodorant. Anna packed a hairbrush for me and, taking the hint, I pull it through my hair to little effect. It has rebelled against years of being set into the right shape. Then I wheel my suitcase down the hallway and head to the kitchen in search of a coffee, something, anything, to drive away the simmering anxiety.

The morning is bright, a roll of blue sky unfolds as far as I can see and makes a mockery of last night's storm. The only evidence left is the splintered branch of a tree, the green bin displaced in the middle of the lawn, three empty bottles tossed out like the aftermath of a party without the party itself.

I pour my coffee, drink it too hot so it scorches my taste buds. Half an hour, forty-five minutes at the most, that's all I can give her.

Focus.

Make use of the time, I tell myself. I pull out my file, it is heavy with notes and printouts. I made contact with Naomi

Parkes through a website where survivors (not victims) have shared their stories. I approached the website founder, explained what I was doing and asked if anyone would speak to me anonymously. It's not been an easy task; the first woman I met went cold, refused to speak to me again, even threatened to call the police if I approached her. The website founder, who was all for going public, has not responded to my emails for months. Naomi Parkes' is the only testimony I have at the moment. On its own it's not enough, but it is a start. With one in the bag, I'm convinced others will follow.

I run through the questions I need to ask her.

At the top of the list is: when did it happen? But what I really want to ask is, after or before? The answer matters, to me, at least.

Time slips by. I glare at the clock. It's painted with an old family crest, hung on the wall next to a deer head that blinks in the sun. What are you waiting for, he seems to say.

On the map I search for the address of the farmhouse Naomi has given me. It looks remote but so does everything here. The distance should take us no more than half an hour to drive. Then again, factor in the roads, getting stuck behind a tractor, and it is anyone's guess.

I pull on my coat, fasten up against the cold; the bright sky won't trick me twice. My fingers tremble with anger. How could she do this? And why? I have to block these questions out for now. Nothing else for it but to walk to the general store where I hope Emily can twist some arms and get me a taxi fast.

I'm gathering my notes, feeding them into the file, when I hear wheels churn up the mud outside.

I turn around, see the red flash of the hire car in the drive.

Anna has come back.

'You look terrible,' I tell her. This is true, not meant to be unkind. Her eyes are bruised, lips chapped and red. Overnight, a cold sore has sprouted in the corner of her mouth.

'Thanks.'

'Where have you been?'

'I had to make a phone call.'

I want to know what could be so urgent to jeopardise the meeting, but I bite down the criticism. 'We should get going.'

She nods, eyes brimming up.

'Oh, Anna, are you OK?' My frustration melts into worry. She looks hollowed out, exhausted.

'I'm just tired, that's all. So much for the country air.'

I'm struck by guilt. Too focused on myself, on Gabriel, on securing this interview. Anna has been on the periphery of my thoughts. I *have* taken her for granted, not paid enough attention to her wellbeing.

'I'm sorry,' I say. 'This is all my fault.'

Anna is behind the wheel, my eye too swollen to be deemed safe. I don't want to criticise, her mood is fragile as it is, but her driving is something to behold. She corners bends at speed, crunches gears, teeters scandalously close to the edge of sheer drops. At this rate, we'll be lucky to make it to Naomi Parkes alive.

'Do you think you could slow down a little? I'm feeling rather nauseous.'

In response, she drops a gear but not her speed.

We should have twenty miles to cover but the road plays with the distance. Tries to make it last as long as thirty, forty miles. It entices us to slow down and appreciate the views. Acknowledge them at the very least. And when we don't, its patience grows thin, drags us up high, squeezes us down narrow tracks, shunts us into bushes. *Don't rush to your destination. The drive is the destination. Look at me! On the left a viewing point, perched*

*five hundred feet above the sea. A bench for you to sit. Take in the day.*
*Look at the pink lemonade light settling over the hills. The horizon that*
*melts into the water. Don't you want to know how the islands hover*
*above the sea and the tiny specks of fishing boats are stuck to the sky?*
*It's magic. That's what it is. Pure magic.*

We drive on. We see the magic beyond the window but don't let it touch us. The road loses patience. We are outsiders who won't play its game. It calls the clouds to shut out the light and within five minutes a coat of darkness dresses the sky. On the ground the shadows race us. *We'll beat you. Wherever you're going, we'll get there faster,* they say.

'Your book isn't about female politicians, is it?' Anna says out of the blue.

'I'm sorry?' I buy myself a second to formulate my excuse.

'Politicians – that's not what this is about.'

I exhale, the sound of a lie extinguished. 'No. It isn't. I take it that's what you were doing in my room last night?'

'Yes.'

'How much did you read?'

'Enough.'

'Then I hope you understand why I didn't want you involved in any way. Those men would do anything to keep this covered up.'

'How do you know that?'

'Let's just say this isn't the first time I've tried.'

The colour leaches from Anna's face. I've said too much and now she's scared. Has a right to be too.

'You can turn back if you want to. It was wrong of me to ask you here on false pretences. I'm sorry.'

She doesn't reply, keeps her eyes glued to the road, focused on the path ahead.

73

## Jonathan, 9.32 a.m.

Linda. Olympic drinker, debater, straight-talker, the woman with the filthiest laugh he knows. He always marvelled that people couldn't see what a hoot she was underneath the slick suits, the ferocious intellect. The first time they met, at a dull Westminster party, she force-fed him shots of flaming sambuca. 'For God's sake, we're facing certain death from boredom here, help me out.'

What he's never told her, carried around all these years of their friendship, is that he was in love with her once. Perhaps he still is. She was the woman he wanted to marry, and maybe he would have done if he hadn't been so bloody gauche. Wasn't he all set to divulge his feelings when he turned up at the pub late, thanks to a breaking story, to find his friend Hugh entwined in conversation with her? Hugh was slicker, faster, had the knack of making Linda know she was adored. Whereas he was a bumbling public schoolboy. No prizes for guessing who won her affection. Still, they remained good friends. He understands her better than anyone, knows what the woman has been through, the ghosts that follow her around.

How he wishes he could get hold of her, hit her with all the questions that are crashing about in his head. Damn the woman for leaving him like this. He tries her mobile. Pointless. Futile. He's tried it every day since Tuesday. But he can't help himself. All he wants is to hear her voice.

He's been out of touch for a while – hospital appointments, a battery of tests, not anything he'd want to share with Linda. She would only worry. He tries to recall their last conversation. Did she mention anything about Gabriel? Surely he would remember if she had. Her fractious relationship with him has long been a source of sadness. And while Jonathan adored his godson as a child, as an adult he could happily throttle him for treating Linda so callously. Gabriel has no concept of the sacrifices his mother has made for him. But then, why would he?

Yes, he was self-centred, inflated with the kind of ego fame too often bestows.

But a murderer?

Jonathan doesn't buy it. Not for a moment.

The police, on the other hand, seem to think they have their man.

Upon hearing news of Gabriel's arrest, the first people Jonathan wanted to talk to were Henry Sinclair and Curtis Loewe. He couldn't give a stuff about their quotes. It was instinct that drove him to them. And suspicion. He needed to hear the timbre of their voices, catch any irregular inflections, twitches half-hidden beneath their skin.

And he can't explain why he knows, but he does.

Just like everything else he has known for years but has never been able to prove.

Out of frustration he smacks his hand on the table, makes Sally the features editor jump. 'Lamppost day?'

*Some days you're the dog and others you're the lamppost* is Sally's favourite line.

He refuses to be the lamppost today. He owes it to Linda to become the dog.

*Think around the problem. If you can't take the direct route there are always other options*, Jonathan tells himself. And he does have another line of inquiry. He sent his first email twenty-four hours ago and another six since and yet she hasn't answered a single one.

'*I understand why you wouldn't want to talk to me, but I would ask you to put your misgivings aside*,' he wrote to the woman who set up the Kelmore survivors' website. He sounded like a pompous prick. No wonder she hadn't answered. Or maybe he's been sending his requests to an old email account. But then Linda mentioned she'd had trouble contacting her too. She posted her last blog on the website months ago. It could be she wanted to step back for a while. Or . . . something else. He searches for her name on an electoral database. Bingo! He gets up abruptly, and knocks a cup of tea over his desk.

'Going well then,' Sally says.

But Jonathan is already heading out, waving her comments away. He has found the woman's address. He'll pay her a visit, try the personal appeal since his virtual entreaties haven't worked.

'You'll be lucky.' A woman down the corridor has poked her head out of the door. 'Haven't seen her for ages.'

'Has she moved?'

'And you are . . . ?'

He walks over and holds out his hand. 'Jonathan Clancy.' He fishes out a card from his pocket, discreetly tries to remove the Tic Tac that is stuck to it.

'Saving that one, were you?'

'I work for *The Times*.'

'The *Radio Times* or the *TV Times*?'

'Just *The Times*.'

'I see,' she says, although it's clear she doesn't.

'Has she moved?'

'Not officially. Holiday, she said. Lucky her. Months and months she's been gone. Her things are still inside. Well, most of them. Someone came to collect a few boxes when she first left. A man. Scottish he was. Not particularly friendly, if I remember correctly.'

'How do you know what's inside?' Jonathan is looking at the slats of Venetian blinds. 'I can't see a thing.'

'I didn't say I looked through the window, did I? I have a key so I can keep an eye on things. She forgot to take it back. What did you say your name was?'

76

'Jonathan. Jonathan Clancy.'

'And what is it you're after, Mr Clancy?'

'I'm trying to find out where she is.'

'Is she in trouble?'

'I hope not.'

'Well, you seem like a genuine sort. I suppose it wouldn't do any harm.'

They emerge from the flat ten minutes later. Although the place isn't particularly homely – a few pieces of Ikea furniture, a sofa and a bed – it doesn't look like she was planning to leave long term. Her face creams and perfumes still sit on top of the chest of drawers. A few items of clothing in the wardrobe too.

'Her car's still in the car park,' says the woman, who has by now introduced herself as Marjorie, chair of the residents' association. 'I'll show you, come down here.' She points to the stairs. 'Everyone has to have a permit, you see, and it's my job to make sure they've all paid up. Charlie's hasn't moved for months. Mind you, if she's gone abroad she wouldn't want to be parking it at the airport. Can you imagine? She'd have to take out a mortgage to pay for it.'

Jonathan bobs his head in agreement. But he knows Charlie hasn't gone abroad. He's just seen her passport in her bedside drawer.

'Which one is it?'

'It's . . . well, that's strange, isn't it. It was here a few days ago, I swear.' Marjorie's face fills with confusion. 'I know I'm old but I'm not crackers.'

'I'm sure you're not,' Jonathan says. 'I don't suppose you know what kind of car it was?'

'I can do better than that. I have the registration number upstairs.'

★

When Jonathan has thanked Marjorie and said goodbye, he returns to his car and makes a phone call. It goes straight to voicemail. He tries again, and again. Five times until he gives it a rest. She won't want to speak to him, or any reporters for that matter, not while she's investigating the biggest case of her career. But she owes him a favour, and as far as Jonathan is concerned, there's never been a better time to call it in.

He makes one final call to Detective Inspector Victoria Rutter. 'Call me urgently,' he says. 'I might have something for you.'

# June 2001

## *Gabriel, aged 16*

A cute Liver Failure, or ALF as abbreviated by the doctors. I saw that written on my notes and ever since that's what I've called him. I needed a transplant, which means there's part of someone else in my body. It seemed a bit rude not to give him a name.

Alf saved my life and that should be a good thing, right? Wrong. My mum and dad argued about him a lot until it got so bad my dad fucked off. He lives three streets away now and we all pretend nothing has changed. Don't even get me started on that.

My mum doesn't like me so much now. That's not me over-reacting or being sensitive. It is a fact. Simple as. When I came out of hospital, nothing was the same. I mean, I was the same person. I was like, hello, it's me, Gabriel! But she acted like I was different. I used to moan that she watched me too much, now she can hardly bear to look at me. THE IRONY. It's as if I've done something wrong but no one will tell me what it is. And guess what? I miss her. I spend a lot of time in my room because it's less lonely than being around her. Fucked up, right?

My mum and dad told me they were splitting up over an ice cream after school one day. It was April. Sunny like June. They were both waiting for me at the gate. I should have known something was wrong.

I ordered a raspberry split with extra sprinkles and they had a coffee. I stopped trying to understand adults long ago.

'Gabriel,' my mum said. 'You know we both love you very much.' *Could have fooled me.*

'That is never going to change,' my dad said, but his body language was in no way convincing. To distract myself I focused on the raspberry veins that had spread around my vanilla ice cream, little inlets and streams of blood.

'The thing is, Mummy and Daddy think it's best that we don't live together any more.'

I hadn't called them Mummy and Daddy for years. I hoped this meant they were reading the script to the wrong audience.

'Do you understand what we are saying, Gabriel?' My mum stretched out her words like I was totally thick.

'They've put too much raspberry in my ice cream, I only asked for a dribble.'

Dad pulled the ice cream away from me. Impatient. 'It won't change things, not really. You can come and stay with me half of the time. You can choose your own bed and we'll still go to the game together.'

'I've gone off football, I told you.' We went to Highbury once last season and there were so many people Alf went crazy, screamed at me until I asked Dad to take me home.

'OK, not a football game. You get to decide. We can do whatever you want.'

'In that case, I'd like you both to stay together at home.'

'That's not possible.'

'So you lied?'

'What?'

'You said I could have anything I wanted and now you're saying I can't.'

'Please, Gabriel, don't make this any harder than it is.' My mum reached out for my hand.

*Holding hands is not going to make this better.*

'Is there anything you want to ask us?'

I gave this a moment's thought.

'Have you got another woman?'

'Gabriel!' Mum shouted, before compensating for her outburst with a whisper: 'There is no one else.'

*Not true.*

There is Alf. It is his fault.

I heard them last week, shouting at each other: 'There's part of him inside my son, how do you think that makes me feel?'

I didn't know how it made them feel, but I do now.

'I could get rid of him if it would help.'

'Get rid of who?' my dad asked.

'My liver. Alf.'

'Oh God, Gabriel, please . . .' My mum clasped her hand to her mouth. 'Please, never say that. It's not your fault.'

Dad always liked wine but before there was more of a point to it than just getting pissed. He talked about grapes and vineyards and vintages and bored all our guests senseless with his decanting and sniffing. Now it's about getting it down his neck as quick as possible. One bottle and he's my dad only a bit weirder and swearier. Two bottles and he's crying. He had two bottles tonight.

It's always about Mum. He talks about how he loves her and wants her back. I want to tell him that no one, certainly not my mum, is going to find him attractive in this state. He has rampant nose hair and his breath stinks. When he opens the third bottle, I know we're in deep shit. He starts talking about sex. Sweet Jesus! Could there be anything worse than my dad telling me about having sex with my mum. I get this image of the two of them sellotaped together naked, my dad on top, humping. I want to scrape it out of my brain and stamp on it until it smashes, but it is indestructible. My mum. My dad. My mum my dad my mum my dad.

'Every man wanted her and I was the only—'

'Dad, for fuck's sake, shut up!'

He stops and looks up at me. He's forgotten I'm here. He's talking to the bottle of wine. If I could turn myself into a bottle of claret, he'd love me more. This is the problem. I am surplus to requirements, at home, at my dad's house. My mum works late, our communication has been reduced to Post-it notes: *Lasagne, love you x*. She has time for me when I'm in trouble. Like the fire in Mr Wallerman's shed a few weeks ago. The old git called the police. Serves him right for putting broken glass in his flower beds to keep Pudding away. She's old now, and the sight of her in the vets having her feet stitched was horrendous. He's lucky I didn't kill him.

Not that I explained this rationale to my mum. She wouldn't get it. *You've got to make the right choices, Gabriel*, is her constant refrain. Anyway, the upshot of the 'shed incident' was that she shouted at me for an hour, *how stupid, what were you thinking?* and then dialled it down to give me a quiet bedside heart to heart. The attention warmer than the flames of any fire.

My dad is still staring through me as if I'm transparent and I get that sense, one I've had loads lately, that I might not exist, that I'm being sucked away through a black hole where no one can see me. To give my dad his due, he tries to stop me being sucked away by grabbing my arm and pulling me towards him. I smile and think he's going to say something nice like, Are you OK? But what he actually says is, 'Iwasn'ttheonlyonewasI? Youaretheproof.'

I know what this means but I can't know. I know. I don't. I pull free of his grip and dive back through the black hole where I don't have to face up to what he's just told me.

I can't remember making it to the door. I'm in his house and then I'm not. I run across the road to the Common. Alf is awake. He likes a bit of drama. 'Hide,' he says, 'they're coming for you.' Alf doesn't explain who 'they' are, but I do what he tells me to do. It's no good, crossing Alf. You don't want him as an enemy. I skirt the dark edges of the bushes where the streetlights can't reach. Alf is with me, shouting his directions: 'Three steps to the left. Go forward for ten paces. Watch out, bogey to the right. Duck down. Run.'

That's when I run straight into them.

A group of girls and boys. Older than me, bunched together. If I had been looking up I would have seen them, but my eyes were trained on the ground, counting steps, following instructions. I trip over a girl who turns out to be two people moulded together.

'Awww!'

'What do you think you are doing, man?'

He's up on his feet, coming towards me. I leg it. My path is blocked by another guy. I've run straight into the bogeys.

Alf's fault. 'Fuck you,' I say to Alf.

'What did you say?' A large guy has risen to his feet, chest puffed out at me.

Alf is still yelling, shrieking. My head is going to explode. 'SHUT UP. SHUT UP. SHUT THE FUCK UP.'

The big guy is killing himself laughing. 'Man, you need to be taught a lesson.'

He's right next to me, fingering my jacket. It's new. The one I saved up for with my birthday money. Nike. Swoosh on the lapel.

'Nice.'

'Thanks.'

'And the jeans too. Diesel, man. Take them off.'

It's not really a question because he starts to remove my top, but not before he relieves me of my rucksack and empties it out on to the grass.

'Little teddy, sweet.' He throws it to his mate and they throw it around. Mr Piddles is launched in the air. I go dizzy keeping track of where he's landing.

'Take your pants off. Now. Or else I'm gonna flatten you.'

'Off, off, off.' They're all chanting. 'Off, off, off.' Crowding too close, I'm surrounded, wind from their breath on me. They're going to eat me.

'OFF.'

I take my trousers off and then my pants.

'HA HA HA HA HA HA HA HA HA HA.'

'Now he's flashing, man. Your pants, not your boxers. Didn't want to see that.'

'Not much chance of seeing it,' a girl shouts, wiggles her pinkie in the air.

Wet trickles down my legs. A gap has opened up in the circle and I leap through it. Run run run run, Alf shouts. I sprint out the Common on to a side street. There's a woman coming up the road; I hide behind a car so she doesn't see me naked. A few more steps and she'll be gone. Wait. No! She's unlocking this fucking car, the one I'm hiding behind. She gets in. The headlights go on. I have to jump out otherwise she's going to run me over. I hope I'll be so fast she won't see me.

'FUCK. Oh my God!' she screams.

Lights flash. Locks fasten down.

I wave my arms in the air so she knows I am just on my way home and mean no harm but that's a lot of information to ask my hands to convey and judging by her face I don't think she's understood. I don't hang around to find out.

I'm cold and alone and I know there are bogeys everywhere but I can't run any more. The pavement has chafed my feet and the night air hurts my skin.

Turns out I don't have to walk much further because at the top of the road there's a car with flashing lights and two men jump out and push me inside.

I want my mum. My mum doesn't come. Evidently her first thought on learning I have been taken to the police station is not, there must be a terrible mistake but, how is this going to look? This is why she sends her emissary Camilla in her place. Camilla was my mum's SPAD when she was Home Secretary (yeah, I know, it stands for special advisor but still, there are some titles that really can't be excused). Camilla deals with it because her speciality is spinning a crisis into a triumph. Needless to say, she falls short on this occasion because she's good but not *that* good. The crisis is merely downgraded to an 'incident' and I am swept out of the back entrance into a waiting car dressed in clothes that aren't mine.

My mum is waiting for me when I get home, face a mask of displeasure. I need her arms to be open so I can fall into them but they're folded hard into her chest.

'I didn't do it,' I say, and she looks suspiciously at what I'm wearing as if to say, Did your *own* clothes just take a walk by themselves then?

'They've got it wrong.'

I want to explain about Dad being pissed and the black hole and the gang in the park and Alf shouting at me and the fact that I was hiding behind that woman's car *not* trying to expose myself but it all gets mushed up together.

'Sit down,' my mum says.

Camilla brings us tea and I expect her to go until I notice there are three mugs and she's sitting down with us with a notepad and pen. We need to thrash it out, apparently, carve out a more suitable story in case the press gets wind of it. This personal nadir is no longer my own, it's a political embarrassment to be managed.

Most of the ensuing exchange flies over my head but two things stick out.

1. My mum says, 'Christ, Camilla, how is this going to look?' before she asks how I am. Before she asks if I need anything or hugs me or even looks me straight in the eye.

(FYI, Camilla replies, 'It's OK, I'll kill the story,' like I'm vermin to be exterminated.)

2. She presumes I did it. And, yes, I know I don't give a very good account of myself, mainly because the sequence of the evening is all out of sync, but the main point is she had already accepted I was capable of such an act. My own mother.

Which begs the question, who the hell does she think I am?

It's a few weeks after the 'incident' when my mum corners me in my bedroom. The police gave me a caution. The woman I 'flashed at' is threatening to go to the press; though my mum hasn't told me, I overheard her talking to Camilla. I suspect the theme of this conversation will be, You can't put a foot out of line from now on, Gabriel.

'We need to talk,' she says.

Too right we do.

She sighs like I'm making her weary. 'You still haven't explained why you were walking around naked.'

'They took my clothes!'

'Who took your clothes?'

'The people in the park.'

I'm aware that my description of the people in the park isn't exactly *Crimewatch* standard but I wasn't in a position to commit all their distinguishing features to memory. They were young, maybe a bit older than me, there were a lot of them. They were taking the piss out of me. (*Language, Gabriel!*)

'Gabriel,' she says in a gentle tone that suggests she's ready to believe me. 'You can tell me the truth. Lying isn't going to do you any good.'

I hear a little hiss of air. It's coming from me. Her doubt is needle sharp, it punctures my skin.

I don't know why the look she wears produces the revelation. I've seen it before. But tonight my sensory receptors are wide awake, catch its meaning and send it high speed to my brain. It's not me. It's her. I've got the full technicolour picture for the first time. Deep down there's something that has stopped her loving, believing, trusting me. She searches for the worst because she can't shake the feeling that it is there somewhere, lurking beneath my skin, hidden in my core. A darkness. Didn't she always watched me like a hawk when I was little, ready to pounce when I did something wrong?

But here's the thing she doesn't get. If you look for something hard enough, chances are you'll find it.

School becomes a problem. The noise is too much for Alf and I can't concentrate in lessons with him screeching in my head. Mum doesn't understand. She makes me get out of bed, tells me to get dressed. She wears this face when she comes in my room that's like, '*Have you had a shower in the last week?*' The answer is no. I don't want to shower because I don't want to take my clothes off. I'm a little perv, scared of what I might do.

When she leaves for work I go back to bed. Or maybe I go to the kitchen and make a sandwich with ketchup, but I don't hang around. I can't leave my room for too long because Alf doesn't like it. He starts this weird cry, like the foxes shagging at night, half baby, half animal. If it's two minutes he's OK. But any longer, say 2.01, that's when he starts. When he cries I have to talk to him for hours and hours to calm him down. Alf likes me to play him songs and sing, and that is OK with me because I love singing. I don't necessarily share his choice of songs, mind you. He's a fan of Freddie Mercury. I spend a lot of my time singing 'Don't Stop Me Now' which is enough to finish anyone off, but sometimes when he's quiet I'll sneak in a few of my own.

One day I'm having a quiet moment, ALF is asleep, when the doorbell rings. It's a girl. A young woman. Shy.

'Is anyone home?'

'I am.' Not as smart as she looks then.

'Are you Gabriel?'

'I am.' This conversation is getting pretty repetitive. 'Are you from my mum's office?'

'Mind if I come in?'

I'm about to say I do but she's already in the hallway.

'Not at school?'

'Was sent home sick.' I don't want her telling my mum I've been skiving. 'Can I get you anything?' I'm relieved when she says no.

'Are you doing your GCSEs this year?'

'Yes.'

'Don't want to miss too much school then.'

'I'm going upstairs, to do some work.' I add for cover, 'My mum won't be home for a while.'

'Do you know a woman called Rose Waterford?'

'Nope.'

'You've met her though.'

'Have I?'

'A month ago, at night, she was . . .'

I know what she is going to say. I don't know who this woman is but I know who she isn't. I hear the words before she speaks them, IN. THE. CAR.

'And you were . . .'

NAKED.

'You said you worked for my mum.'

'No I didn't.'

'Well who are you?'

'I'm a reporter for the *Sunday Herald*. It would be good to hear your side of the story.'

I hear Alf stirring, he's not good when he wakes up. It never ends well. I try to whisper to him to stay calm, beg him not to inflame the situation but Alf isn't a great listener.

BOO! He runs at her. In her face. BOO! BOO! BOO!

The girl who doesn't work for my mum isn't smug now. All of a sudden my side of the story isn't so attractive. She legs it.

I want to tell her it was a mistake, I was attacked, robbed. I am the victim. But it's too late, Alf has scared her away.

'You freak,' she says.

That's me.

I don't want to be in the newspapers. I don't want to be in this house, to be in my life. I run upstairs, bury myself in the duvet, but I'm still here. It's no good. Alf calls me to go to the window and asks me to follow him out on to the flat roof. We're on the top floor, three storeys up. From my vantage point, life is toy people and buses and cars moving around the town's tracks. And I can see that no one ever gets anywhere, they just dart backwards and forwards, buses breathing them in, spewing them out so they can go home with their pasty office faces and do the exact same thing again tomorrow. This is life.

*Is that what you want?*

Time splits. Down there, on the tracks, is one continuum. We break off into another where it's safer and no one can touch us. Down there is a trap. It's questions and name calling and people in my face staring and pawing at my skin, telling me who I am. Bad. Rotten. Freak.

Colour drains from the sky. Streetlights shoot out acid strobes. Heat radiates through me. Sensors are packed into every single hair and pore on my body. My head soaks up the noises that rise up to us and pump them through me. I walk to the edge. The wind raises my arms skywards like it's showing me what to do. This is all completely natural. Any second the wind is going to lift me away from this. It's going to make me fly.

*This is it.*

Wait. Something is pulling at me. Time to go. But I'm pulled the wrong way, back from the sky, back, back, back.

'I can't do it. I can't.' I don't know what it is I can't do any more. My words make sense only to themselves.

'Gabriel . . .' My name is soft. I sink into it like a warm duvet. 'Gabriel.' I'm pressed into someone. The smell. My mum. She won't let me go. I don't want her to let me go.

'I can't do it.'

My head is shedding thoughts that flutter about the room and she's holding me tight so I don't break up too.

'Help me.' I'm crying because I can't work out what it is I am asking her to do, but it's OK, Gabriel, it's OK. My mum knows. I don't need to say anything more.

'Don't worry, I'll help you.'

The story doesn't appear. Not in the *Sunday Herald*. Not anywhere. No one mentions Rose Waterford again. 'What did you do?' I ask my mum.

'Nothing.' She's lying. My mum isn't any regular mum, she was the Home fucking Secretary (before they lost the election). She can make things happen.

And here's the thing, I'm glad she stopped it. But I wish she hadn't done it to duck the scandal and the shame and the fallout. I wish she had done it because she knew the story wasn't true.

Pity.

My mum is a powerful woman. She can do all kinds of things but she can't bring herself to believe me.

# Thursday 10.45 a.m.

## Linda

On we go. B roads give way to dirt tracks flanked by unruly brambles and hedges. The car throws us around, dipping into potholes and mounting verges, squeezing us down narrow lanes.

Nerves seize me. The exchange with Anna has given my doubt oxygen. *Those men would do anything to keep this covered up*, I told her. And this time I wasn't lying. The past is proof enough, the lengths they have gone to in order to silence me and my friend Jonathan Clancy. No one would believe us if we told them. I suppose that is the cruel beauty of their deceit.

I have been careful, as cautious as progress will allow, because I know they have eyes everywhere, ears to the ground. Only Jonathan is aware of what I am doing, and Michael, another old friend who I approached in the hope he may publish the book. I'd trust both with my life. As for Naomi Parkes, I have done as much due diligence on her as I can. A search on the electoral roll confirmed a woman of that name lives not far from here. I have pored over her posts on www.whathappenedatkelmore. com and, so far as I can tell, her story chimes with the others.

But.

Beyond that, this is a leap of faith.

A necessary one at that. Without any testimonies, the book is nothing more than the work of a woman with an axe to grind. It dies before it is born. And they win. Again. Again. Again.

★

'Are we going the right way?' I ask Anna. Sheep excluded, I haven't seen another sign of life for miles.

She hands me her phone to look at the satnav. 'These are the details you gave me. Check them.'

I do, against the address I have in my diary.

'We're on the right track, unfortunately,' I say. Her phone vibrates in my hand. 'You have a voicemail.'

I place the phone in the tray between our seats. She risks a look down, an ill-advised move that forces her to swerve in order to avoid a tree.

'I'm sure it can wait. It would be nice to come out of this alive,' I say.

The sudden movement makes my heart judder. I shift uncomfortably in my seat. Can't say I expected it to be this far out, so completely off the beaten track. Never understood why some people deliberately seek out solitude; life doles out enough of its own. Give me the buzz of a crowd, a coffee shop, the whir of traffic any day.

This isolation unsettles me. Thank goodness I'm not alone.

The car slows to a crawl. Ahead I can see the shape of a building frayed at the edges. It is desolate and unwelcoming and as we drive closer my mood slips into despair.

*Here?*

'Christ,' Anna says. 'I'm not sure about this.' She looks to me for reassurance but I have none to give.

'I suppose I should get out, check for signs of life,' I say. Anna nods. 'Are you coming with me?'

'I'll catch you up.' She cradles her phone. 'I need to check my messages first.'

It is an old farmhouse, Naomi was correct on that account, but it is far from the meeting place I had envisaged. For starters, the surrounding fields show no evidence of farming. Nettles fur the drive, bushes sway towards me. I plunge straight into a puddle, sending freezing water up my trouser leg. 'Shit!' There is no sign of a car. She could hardly have flown here. This can't be the place.

'Hello! HELLO.'

Nothing. Only the adrenal roar of my fear.

I look back for Anna, find her propped up by the car, phone stuck to her ear. Her presence reassures.

A little.

I inch closer to the house. Neglect has ulcered the paintwork, shrinks it from the door. Through the windows, cracked and cob-webbed, I find shades of darkness but no sign of life. I press the bell, a final flourish before surrender. Don't wait for an answer.

I circle the property. Everything I see and all that I don't builds up an inventory of dread. My muscles strain to leave, take flight, and yet I wait. To leave would be to abandon everything I have come for, the hope of justice. Five minutes. Ten. The slow clap of terror ringing in my ears. What is going on? Why has Naomi Parkes brought me out here for nothing?

Unless . . .

My breathing becomes thick and jagged and I grasp at the air for breath. I need a sign to tell me it is time to go.

Turning, I search the yard for Anna.

I find my sign.

She is running towards me, lightning fast, speed twisting her face into someone else.

And somehow I know.

'Linda.' Her scream pierces me, stabs the air. The pitch is all wrong. It is not Anna. The sky splits and shatters and crashes down around me.

'Get in the car.'

'Who are you?'

She answers with her hands, digging, pressing, pulling. 'Get in the fucking car.'

She's stronger than me. Younger, angrier. I'm dragged along with her.

I shout until my voice cracks but the emptiness buries my screams in silence.

Anna drags me towards the car, my feet kicking up against the gravel. The momentum is with her, my body is robbed of substance and my futile attempts to throw her off only tighten her grip.

'We have to get out of here.'

'Who are you?' I spit.

Everything I believed to be true, the conversations, the heart to hearts, the laughs that grew our working relationship into a friendship explode in my face.

Because I don't know how or why, but I know Anna is their eyes and ears. The sneaking into my room, reading my book, all the questions she's asked over the last nine months that I thought were driven by curiosity.

*Why?*

Why would she do it? Does she have the first idea what these men do? What they will do to me?

The thought turns my blood to ice.

'GET IN THE CAR.' Her voice is shrill. Fury bleaches her face. I push back, my last chance, scratch her with my nails.

Her hand slices my face and the white heat of pain radiates through me. But worse, much worse, is the pain of her betrayal and the evidence of my own stupidity.

'Just do as I say.' She throws me into the car, where I sit defeated, nothing left inside me to fight.

'Where are we going?' I ask while I still have the breath to speak.

No answer, she's too focused inserting the keys in the ignition.

There's a pulsing behind my eyes and in a vain attempt to block reality, I snap them shut.

'Shit!' Anna's scream curdles the air. My eyes flick open again. She pushes her body back into the seat, grips the steering wheel as if to steel herself against what is coming. A van is heading our way, spraying up stones and mud as it comes towards us.

The passenger door flies open before it has stopped.

The face. Out of context here. It takes a moment to process before the sweet relief feeds through.

DS Huxtable.

I haven't the first idea what he is doing here or how he knew to come.

But I know I'm safe.

# Eleven Months Before

### Gabriel, aged 29

If I had known it would be like this, I wouldn't have stood up that night and given the monster a pass to enter my life.

We were at the Comedy Club, an open mic night. My mate Bay had tickets. I was skint as usual, paying my way with moral support. It was going to be his big moment, the first step in his stand-up career.

Don't get me wrong, Bay is a funny guy, just not as funny as he thinks. He'd invited along some girls, Jax and Abbey, so they could witness his moment of discovery (his own words, I swear to God). One of the girls was supposed to be for me, but my attire – hoodie and ripped jeans, scruffy Vans – weren't the aphrodisiac she needed. She pretty much ignored me all night, directed her attention at Bay instead, until the vodka rendered him mute. That's the other thing you should know about Bay. He can't drink. I mean, he can, and he does, but it never ends well. Which is exactly what happened on the night in question.

It got to his slot and he was wasted. Head-on-the-table kind of ruined. Stand-up was out of the question. His legs wouldn't hold him.

The compere called out his name. Cue awkward silence. People started to boo and clap, they didn't like being made to wait. I'd had a few shots of tequila and before I knew it I was walking towards the stage. Moses parting the fucking sea. Everyone hushed and this fierce confidence shot through me. When I opened my mouth, I knew exactly what to say. The crowd laughed. We bounced off each other. The room was warm, like a massive cuddle surrounding me with electric love. I wasn't a disgraced politician's son (thanks, Mum) or a fuck-up serving PERi PERi with a side of corn on the cob at Nando's. I was Gabriel Miller. Funny man.

I hadn't had a knockout buzz like that since Tommy and I did our first bong when we were fourteen.

After I'd finished, a guy intercepted me at the bar. Slapped me on the back. 'Man,' he said, 'where did you come from?'

'Clapham.'

And he laughed like I'd cracked the funniest joke.

'What do you do?'

I told him about the PERi PERi.

'Fuck the chicken. I can make you big. I'm Palab, by the way.'

Palab Joshi turned out to be one of the best comedy agents around.

I could have fame or another week of shifts at Nando's.

That was six years ago and Palab was true to his word. I should be happy. And for a while I was. Ecstatic. All this adoration thrust my way. Love, or more specifically attention, now there's a thing. I didn't realise how starved I was of it until the love-bombing commenced. The women wanted me. Women with pneumatic tits and sprayed-on clothes and magazine-ready bodies. They reckoned I was the business in bed and you know what, they probably had a point. No one could get enough of me: the papers, talk shows, quiz shows . . .

So why am I moaning? Good question. Well, let me tell you, fame isn't what you imagine. It's not Emerald City. It's a baby monster that comes to live with you bearing gifts, a house, a car, guest lists, free clothes, new friends whose names don't stick. And love, yes, or a synthetic form of it.

Then the monster grows, it doesn't look so cute any more. It takes up too much room in your life. The house gets bigger and the car flashier. It throws more women at you than you really care to fuck, ones who'd never have spat in your direction before. I can't even have a shag without reading about my performance in the tabloids (FYI: pretty good). Women read these stories and before you know it they're multiplying, launching themselves at me. They all assume I want it dirty and they give me what I want because I'm Gabriel Miller. How they twist their bodies into those positions I have no idea. Yoga has a lot to answer for. And there's me, hankering after a bit of vanilla sex, a simple missionary now and again, maybe with the same woman so I can get past the games and get close to someone. But the monster won't let me. I have to give it what it wants.

The monster brings paps who snap their cameras in my face to get a rise out of me so they can make an extra few quid (always smile, especially when you want to punch them, Palab advises).

I want the monster to go but I need him to stay.

I worry that without the monster I'd go back to being Linda Moscow's disappointment of a son. It's taken years of therapy and medication to work through that. Mind you, who's she to talk? Got turfed out of her job a few years ago – cash for contracts. Yes, you heard correct, my mother who made a career out of bringing other people to book and lecturing me. The sheer fucking hypocrisy was staggering. The press was all over it. I had to stay clear. 'You've got your reputation to think of,' Palab said, but he agreed I could weave a few jokes about her into my stand-up routines. The audience lapped it up, a bit of self-deprecation goes far.

'It's not true,' my mum said. She expected me to believe her. *Shoe on the other foot now.*

It's not all bad, this fame thing. Take Thursday night. I'm on live at the Apollo and they're filming it for the BBC. I'm soaking up the congratulations backstage when Palab approaches me.

'There's someone who wants to meet you.'

'I don't want sex tonight.'

'Good, he doesn't want to have sex with you.'

I don't get a chance to argue because he's there in front of me, holding out his hand. Curtis Loewe.

'I'm a big fan of your work,' he says.

We chat briefly. He mentions a film he's working on, a big kids' animation. He's looking for voices, likes the pitch of mine.

'Let's talk more, some time soon,' he says. Palab is hovering over my shoulder, practically pissing his pants with excitement. I'm not saying being a talking car or plane or a pig – which happens to be the part he wants me to fill – is the summit of my ambition, but I have to admit, I'm flattered. The guy's a legend.

'*The Bear Chronicles* was my favourite film as a child,' I tell him.

Tonight I'm going to a party at his country house. The monster is in favour again. He's sent a car. There's a bottle of champagne in the back seat just for me. I've drained it by the time we arrive.

The house is comically large, reached by a grand driveway that's lit all the way from the main road. I can't help feeling like I'm about to crash the set of a costume drama. I've come smart but not this smart. As I approach the entrance, the door opens by magic. I turn around to see the car pulling away otherwise I'd run back and demand the driver takes me home. I've obviously been asked here for a laugh.

My coat is removed and I'm shown into a room, expensive soft furnishings in various shades of mud. Velvets wink in the light of the candles that line the mantelpiece. Champagne appears in my hand. Laughter bursts out of chatter only to fall back again.

'Gabriel!' the voice booms at me, accompanied by a back

slap. 'Glad you could make it. You know Alexander, don't you?'

At the sound of his name, Alexander joins us. He has a familiar face, though from where, I couldn't tell you.

I stick with him; not because there's any instant connection – the guy's a dick – but he's the only person in the room who's more pissed than me. Next to him, I'm a model of sobriety.

Oh, and at some point he offers me a line. 'Shall we?'

I shouldn't. I'm trying to cut it out. I don't want to be the car crash I'm threatening to become, but now isn't the time for abstention. I just need something to get me through the evening.

Alexander has been here before. He knows his way through the labyrinth of rooms upstairs and he knows where the drugs are. Turns out they're not his, they're freebies laid on by Curtis. I don't know why this makes it sleazier. I'm hardly averse to taking them. But not with this crowd. They should have learnt by now, some of them are touching sixty. Geriatric drug abuse, that's another level of wrong.

Back downstairs the party has loosened. Time has raced on. Hours lost. Men lounge on the sofas, tangled in girls. *Girls*. Too young for the men. They can't all have got lucky, judging by the state of some of them. Through the film of drugs I see the room properly. Everyone thinks drugs mess with your head, but the opposite is true. They bring everything into focus and what I'm seeing makes me sick to my stomach.

Curtis is next to me. 'I have something for you.' He motions for me to follow him and I do because I don't want to spend another minute looking at the men with those girls.

Only, it's worse upstairs. There are voices coming from rooms, muffled sounds I can't and don't want to decipher. I feel like I'm levitating across the hallway, wheeling after Curtis wherever he's taking me.

Finally, he stops, pushes open a door. 'I thought you'd like this room.' Then he's gone. It's just me and the girl.

*Could you?*

Everyone else here is doing it. It's obviously the point of the party. It strikes me how wrong becomes acceptable if enough people around you do it. Just look at the fucking Nazis.

*Could you?*

I assess her. She's out of it. Struggles to open her eyes, more wasted than me.

The question repulses me. I am not that person.

Is my public image so sleazy that Curtis believes I'm one of them? That I would sink this low?

'How old are you?' I ask the girl.

She shakes her head and peers past me as if searching the room for her answer. Her eyes can't grip on to anything. I'm far from sober myself but I try to follow her, scanning the back wall of the room to where her gaze leads me. It's easy to miss, sitting on a shelf: a tiny red eye. All-seeing.

'Bastard.'

I open the machine and remove the card.

'Now tell me how old you are.'

'Fifteen,' she pushes the word out and falls back on the bed and the room collapses around me.

The monster has tricked me again.

I run out of the room, out of the door. Down the drive. The country air bites into me, the road is pitch-dark, noises of the night chase me. I walk and walk until I'm capable of clear thought. I call a cab to take me home.

That weekend I wait until I've sobered up but I can't hold my disgust down. It's radioactive. I need to pass it on, to make all the things at that party stop. I call the police. An officer comes out to visit me. His name is DS Jay Huxtable.

I tell him about the pig role and the party. I don't like Huxtable. His face is a picture of disbelief. Curtis Loewe is a national institution, it says. You'd have better luck accusing the

Queen of joining ISIS. Fuck you, my face replies. I'm not letting this drop. The girls were underage. They should arrest him. It's clearly not the first time or the last. They have a duty of care.

Don't they?

Weeks later, after questioning Curtis Loewe, they turn on me: *What were you doing at the party, Mr Miller? We have eyewitnesses who say you were ejected for taking drugs. Do you take drugs, Mr Miller? What about this photograph showing you snorting cocaine off this woman's breasts? That's you, isn't it?*

It's not long before DS Huxtable calls to say there is insufficient evidence to proceed with an investigation. His tone is dismissive, weighted with a snigger. *Who would take your word over the legend that is Curtis Loewe?*

'Safe to say you won't be getting the talking pig part now,' he says.

I put the phone down. My hands are shaking and I'm not even hungover, but I will be tomorrow. I open a bottle of whisky and heave as it hits the back of my throat.

There is something sickeningly familiar about the feeling that floods my veins; the terror of telling the truth but having no one, not a single soul, believe me.

# Thursday, 10.55 a.m.

## *Linda*

A happy ending. Saved in the nick of time.
Not quite.

Spot the difference.

Anna gets out of the car. She's about to make a run for it, surely.

But.

She heads straight for DS Huxtable, and it is here, at this juncture, that the picture begins to warp.

They speak. There's an undeniable familiarity between them that causes my insides to shift, somersault. I can't hear the words they share; dread fills my head with its own sound.

Still locked inside the car, I bang on the window to attract the detective's attention.

*HELP!*

Neither of them take any notice.

They finish their conversation and Anna walks away from the car towards the van. She turns back once, a look that lingers.

*Why?*

It is left to DS Huxtable to extricate me. He saunters across the yard, in no hurry, not a scratch of concern on his face.

Help? The notion is fading. I root around, desperately, to get a handle on what has just happened, what is going to happen, but my vision is unsteady and the shapes are shifting in front of my eyes.

Huxtable reaches the passenger door, clicks the keys.

'DS Huxtable?' I say. A question now, not a greeting.

His face is a blank, scrubbed of emotion. 'If you say so,' he says. The ground that was solid only a few seconds ago tilts again. Relief vanishes as if it were an optical illusion.

'There's someone who wants to see you,' he says, pulling me out of the car. 'An old friend. I'm going to take you to meet him.'

*Henry Sinclair.*

Who else?

They win again.

Inside the van I shiver uncontrollably. My trousers, wet from the puddle, are now stiff with cold. Huxtable sits in the back with me, fleece, jacket, thick boots. He shouts to whoever is driving, 'Turn the heating on, I'm freezing back here.'

A glimpse of humanity blown away with his next breath: 'I should bring you up to date. Gabriel is about to be charged with murder.'

# Saturday, 15 November 2014

### *Gabriel, aged 30*

No matter how many women I fuck, I can't find what I'm looking for. In fact the inverse is true: the more I fuck, the less likely I am to find it. The 'it' is love. There, I've said it. I want to be loved. Pathetic, isn't it? A man of thirty craving the affection his mother never gave him. You wouldn't believe how much money I've paid for that insight and it doesn't change a thing. I'm no closer to discovering my holy grail.

The newspapers call me a womaniser, lothario or serial bonker (that last one courtesy of the *Star*), but what they don't know is that at the beginning of every liaison there's an honest to God, could-this-be-it? flare of hope. And yes, I am aware that the chances of finding someone special in a bar in Soho at one in the morning are slim to nonexistent, but the romantic (or the drunkard) in me ignores this probability and steams right in. The hope is always short-lived. At the most it lasts five minutes or so, sometimes less. On occasion, the first word a woman utters kills it dead, but on I march, my dick leading me forward.

Tonight her name is Mariela. We're in a sushi bar in Hampstead that's decked out like a boudoir. The few friends that accompanied me here are on their twentieth toilet trip of the evening, sniffing Colombia's finest from the porcelain loo seats. I'm aware of her picking me out of the crowd, her gaze burning into me, and by the time she throws me a smile, I'm a lost cause, a prisoner, felled by desire. She's got big glossy hair and a red dress that's scooped low at the back. I reach out as if to trace my finger down her spine.

*Please, let her be the one.*

Mariela is not the one. This I deduce when she tries to pull my trousers down in the street like I'm so hot she can't wait another second. I'm all for singing my own praises, but in my current state, ten hours into a session, I'd be hard pushed to elicit any kind of lust, let alone the sort that needs it right now. So I know Mariela is faking it but once I get past the disappointment there are consolations, like the way her hand is stroking my cock so expertly.

'Let's go to your house,' she says. As a rule, I use hotels but my dick makes the decision tonight. It says, whatever you want.

As predicted, Mariela is fiery, all nails and biting. She draws blood and smiles when she licks it from her lips. She wants it hard. She wants Gabriel Miller the sexual caricature and I've taken enough drugs to become him. I give her what she wants. Twice. Sometimes I wonder how I do it.

Afterwards, when her breathing goes sleep deep, I remember why I use hotel rooms. I can leave whenever I fancy, which is usually in the middle of the night. Sleep doesn't visit me much these days and there's nothing worse than lying listening to someone else's dreams when you have none of your own.

I wouldn't say the leaving thing is a strict policy, more of a habit. We both know this is about sex. I'm not breaking any hearts by bailing early.

I decide to take a walk on the Heath. Leave her to wake up alone so she gets the message. She could nick all my stuff, but honestly, if she wants to take a coffee machine or the Xbox, she's welcome. I want space in my head. I don't want to be reminded of who I've become.

As I leave, I shoot her a final glance. She looks peaceful.

I walk and walk to outrun the drugs that chase through my system and inflate my thoughts into terrors and catastrophes. I must go for miles. The first shoots of light infuse the sky as I head back towards home. Except, I don't go home, I go to Elsie's allotment. To her shed. It's quiet there, peaceful. Elsie is seventy-one and knows me simply as Gabriel. Her knowledge of popular culture is limited to *The Archers*. She gives me tomatoes and runner beans. I give her time and chat. She knows I come here when I can't sleep, that is the only place where I can close my eyes and find peace. And I know there's a spare key to her shed where she plants the marrows. She doesn't mind that I keep it stocked with red wine. I don't mind that she drinks more of it than me. Come to think of it, Elsie is probably the friend I value most.

As usual, I wrap myself in the blanket Elsie keeps in the shed, drink wine and drift off. Morning has scrubbed out the dark when I leave the allotment and return home. My house is empty, Mariela has gone. I change the sheets, shower and slip into bed. Sleep grabs me in fits.

I wake to bright light beating through the blinds. I pull on some clothes and decide to check on the allotment, make sure I didn't leave empty bottles and fag ends around.

I see Elsie in the distance but I don't get near. She is surrounded by police and an ambulance. A blanket shrouds her. Has she fallen? No, not Elsie. There's something else.

A tent has gone up in the furthest corner of her allotment. White, not the kind of tent to force-grow strawberries out of season. People in white suits pad around.

'A body,' someone says in the small crowd that has gathered.

All I can think of are Elsie's tomatoes, the juicy red flesh of them. Poor woman. Maybe she'll grow cabbages instead.

I catch a bit of sick and swallow it back down.

★

They knock at my door. Two uniformed officers. Routine, they say. 'Did you see or hear anything last night?'

'No.'

'Were you alone?'

'Yes.' This is true, partly. I was alone for a portion of the night.

'Do you ever use the allotments?'

'I know Elsie.'

'You do?'

'That's what I said. She's a friend. I help her out sometimes.'

'You're Gabriel Miller, right?'

'Correct.'

'And you help an elderly lady out with her allotment?'

Why is that so hard to believe?

'What's happened?'

'Your friend Elsie discovered the body of a young woman in her allotment this morning.'

'I see.'

'You see?'

'I mean, that's awful. Poor Elsie.'

'It's not too good for the victim either.'

I watch the news. Wish I hadn't.

There is a picture. She looks different, but not so different I can't recognise her. Mariela. Castell. We never got as far as her surname.

My mind cracks, wedges open, and all my thoughts are sliced into tiny pieces so nothing makes sense.

Was it me?

I close the blinds, get a pen and paper and write down what happened.

I brought her back here.

We fucked.

I left.

I walked on the Heath.

I went to Elsie's shed.

I scour the route for anything that might have slipped outside my conscious, a fragment of violence, her shadow following me. Back and forward, back and forward I go. Nothing. But even in this state, when the thoughts are cut up and skirting around the room, one keeps returning fully formed. You had sex with her and now she is dead. Dead in the allotment where you spent hours last night.

Afternoon. I open a bottle of wine to calm me. And another. It was always a long shot.

At some point the phone rings, a woman's voice. 'Mr Miller? This is DS Marek.' She signs off with the words, 'We'd like you to come in to Camden police station for questioning tomorrow at midday.'

It's only a matter of time. My cigarette butts will be in the shed, the wine bottle.

My semen inside her.

Hours fall away. Sleep is too distant a prospect to contemplate. If I sleep, I'm vulnerable. But I can't stay in the house. I call a cab. Without thinking, I tell the driver to take me to Clapham Common, where I walk briskly through the streets without any purpose, or so I think. I come to a halt outside a house.

It's her house.

This is the place.

Of course it is.

And the only thing that matters is that my mother believes me.

If I don't have that, what else is left?

# Thursday, 11.03 a.m.

## Linda

Huxtable pulls out a newspaper from a black rucksack on the seat next to him. 'It looks like Gabriel is going to be charged today.'

He hands me the copy. *The Times*. Written by Jonathan Clancy. The sight of his name sends a pang of longing through me.

But my thoughts race away from Jonathan as soon as I see the headline.

I read it once.

Twice.

Ten times.

But I still can't get the words to make sense.

### COMIC SUSPECTED OF HIS MOTHER'S MURDER

I turn to Huxtable. 'But . . .'

He passes on the chance to reassure me, shrugs and slides his eyes away from mine.

The air is sucked from my lungs. I am being buried alive, pushed down into an abyss.

*Someone is trying to frame me.*

That was what my son had said.

I didn't believe him, pinned it on his paranoia.

Because, even knowing all I do about them, I did not imagine, not for a moment, that they would go to such lengths to stop me.

Frame him to get to me.

And it *is* them. There is no one else it can be.

No one else who would plumb such depths.

I failed to understand the equation, didn't join the dots.

Their actions correlate with how much is at stake.

If they have everything to lose, they will do anything to win.

I stare at the newspaper, trace the outline of my son's face with my finger. Too far away from me now, out of my reach.

If he's charged, he will go on trial for my murder.

And me?

'Where are you taking me?' I ask.

'You?' Huxtable says. 'You don't even exist.'

# PART THREE

Good People. Bad Things.

# November 2014

## Anna

Anna is head girl. A teacher. A pair of court shoes. She's a neat bob. A little short on laughs, not the kind to stretch a night out beyond eleven o'clock, but she's dependable, trustworthy. Given the chance, you'd want her on your side.

My name is not Anna.

Anna is a creation designed to trick Linda Moscow, to allow me to get close to her, hear the beat of her heart. Make her pay.

You're thinking less of me now, admit it. It is there in your eyes. You've made a value judgement. Sure, Linda has her faults, but what could drive another woman to lure her into a trap? What scum would pull a trick like that?

It's complicated, let me tell you.

We are all a product of our environment, the choices we make, the ones others make that affect us.

I'm a good person at heart, but circumstances have driven me to this.

If you read my story you might understand why.

# 1992–94

I was thirteen when I arrived at Kelmore. Almost exactly a year after my mum died. My nan had been looking after me but without any real enthusiasm. She and Mum never got on and I think she blamed her for dying (of a tumour, FFS) and lumbering her with me. Considering she'd advised my mum to have me aborted, I guess this was adding insult to injury. Apparently, I ate too much food and played my music too loud and showed no respect. Our dislike was mutual. Her house in Watford stunk of fried fish – it was next to a fish-and-chip shop – and my nan's face was set in a permanent scowl. I made a habit of running away, dreaming of some kindly long-lost relative who'd appear in a puff of smoke and carry me off. My imaginary relative didn't materialise but a social worker did when I was caught shoplifting (two Mars Bars and a bottle of red nail varnish). My nan saw her chance and announced she'd had enough. That was how I ended up at Kelmore School for Girls.

I'd read Malory Towers so the prospect of relocating to a girls' school didn't terrify me. Wouldn't there be midnight feasts, ghost stories, secret trips to town? Besides, the school near Nan's was a total dump. This one looked like a stately home in comparison, an imposing grey-brick building buried in the countryside not far from town. Most importantly, there wasn't even the faintest whiff of fish in the air. It was a promising start.

My social worker, Jane, waited with me in reception until a woman emerged from her office pursing her lips together in what I presumed was supposed to be a smile. 'Welcome, Charlotte,' she said. She introduced herself as Mrs O'Dowd, the headmistress, all tartan and pearls with a fierce bob and glasses that teetered on the bridge of her nose. 'I'm sure you're going to fit right in. Rebecca here is going to take care of you.' I turned to find a girl had appeared behind me. 'Well, go on, Rebecca, at least say hello to Charlotte. You can tell her how much she's going to love it here.'

'Hello,' she said. Sullen.

'Off you go and show her the dorm.'

I carried my bag and made a lame attempt at chat. 'Why are you here?' I said. Wrong move. She stopped, spun round.

'You don't ask anyone that – got it?'

A few months later she told me her parents took drugs and her dad tried to sell her to one of his mates to pay for his fixes. We never spoke of it again but the fact she'd shared it with me meant a lot. I knew I had one true friend in Kelmore.

Bex (*don't dare call me Rebecca*) told me all I needed to know about the school. Mrs O'Dowd was a sadistic cow – I had to look sadistic up and then wished I hadn't. Never ever eat the meat stew. Stay away from Donna Cassidy unless you want your head kicked in. And the most important commandment of all: don't listen to the teachers when they tell you you'll never amount to anything.

Bex called it dream-crushing: 'They're into it big time here but it's just because they're all saddos themselves.'

Bex and I had big dreams. Our heads were fat with them but we learned to keep them hidden from the teachers so they couldn't be smashed.

We were going to be singers or dancers. Why not both? Bex said. If we were good, we were allowed to watch *Top of the Pops* as a treat. We'd commit the moves to memory and dance around the dorm afterwards as if we had fluffy duvets and new clothes and posters on our walls and kisses goodnight like every other teenage girl.

Sometimes at night Bex would interview me; using her hairbrush as a microphone she'd thrust it towards me. 'Charlie, congratulations on your Oscar. It's hard to believe what you've achieved when you had such a . . . well . . . a totally . . . like . . . shite childhood.'

'Yes, I can't argue, it was a miserable time but I never lost sight of what I wanted to do.'

'Do you have a message for your teachers?'

'Oh I do . . .' And I'd lean in towards the hairbrush, brandishing a can of hairspray as my Oscar. 'Mrs O'Dowd, if you're watching, who is the no-good bitch now?'

Even if I dredge my memories I can't recall a single nice thing Mrs O'Dowd did. The only kind person there was the drama teacher, Miss Reilly, who encouraged us and taught us some dance steps. She'd once auditioned for the Royal Ballet but said she was too fat and big-boned. I didn't think Miss Reilly was either. She was beautiful.

Now and again Mr Palatino would take drama. He wasn't a proper teacher. He came in for a few sessions a week. Some kind of drama therapy where he got girls to scream and sing and sing and scream as if that was going to solve all their problems. Rumour was that he was well connected. Knew film directors and TV people and the like. Once or twice he picked girls who showed promise for his stage plays. Whenever he came, me and Bex sucked up to him. It helped that he was pretty fucking gorgeous for an older bloke. He must have been in his early thirties.

One Friday a few years into my time at Kelmore, Mrs O'Dowd – who *was* fat and big boned – pulled Bex and me out of class and said, 'Lucky you, girls. Your talents . . .' (she said the word talent as if it was a bad fit for us) '. . . have been recognised.

Mr Palatino wants you to audition for a production of *Bugsy Malone* at the Watford Palace Theatre. You'll be allowed out of school this weekend.'

'I'm not happy about this,' Miss Reilly said when we told her. She and Mr Palatino didn't get on, although neither of us could fathom why. If they were in the same room teaching, her eyes would stick on him, watching, waiting for him to make a mistake or step out of line.

'Maybe she fancies him,' Bex said. I couldn't see it myself, didn't think he was her type.

'But, miss,' we chimed in unison, panicked at the thought she'd ruin our big break, 'it's thanks to your coaching that he's spotted us. Apparently, he thinks our dancing shows promise.'

'Does he now.'

'Please don't say anything to Mrs O'Dowd, please, miss. This is the best thing that's happened to us in like . . . forever.'

Saturday arrived and we were collected by taxi. The heat was stupid, one of those days that's not meant to happen in England. The driver had the windows right down but the breeze just circulated his BO. Bex stuck her fingers in her mouth like she was going to gag. I had to stuff my fist in mine to stop myself laughing. We had matching cut-off shorts on, spaghetti-strap sun tops. Sweat gathered between my legs, sticking them to the filthy nylon seats.

'Really, girls?' Miss Reilly had said when she saw us. 'I don't think your attire is appropriate.'

'It's like . . . two hundred degrees outside. We can't wear anything else. We won't be able to dance,' we said, and then the taxi arrived and we left her reservations behind.

'Girls, you've made it! We're very happy to have you here.' Mr Palatino came bouncing towards us.

'Hi, Mr Palatino.'

'Call me Greg, you're not in school now, rules don't apply. I'll take you upstairs and grab you some water. You can make yourselves comfortable until the others arrive and we're ready to start.' He walked off towards the lift. It was a red-brick building, gold and mirrors and flowers in vases and marble floors inside. Bex mouthed OH MY FUCKING GOD behind his back.

We had escaped, and neither of us could believe our luck.

Upstairs, he directed us to the dressing rooms. Bowls of grapes and melon and strawberries were laid out on the table. Croissants and bread too, none of the white sliced stuff they served at Kelmore.

'Help yourselves,' he said. Under normal circumstances we'd have been right in there troughing the lot but neither of us wanted him to think we were fat pigs. We passed.

A tall thin woman, who looked like a croissant had never come close to her lips, entered the room.

'This is Camille, she'll be putting you through your paces today,' Greg said. Camille wasn't the smiley sort. Her eyes stuck on our cut-offs.

'These are no good,' she said with an accent that was more exotic than Watford. 'I will bring you something else.' And with that she left.

'She's a darling really,' Greg said. 'Just don't get on the wrong side of her.'

When Camille left the room the reality slapped us between the eyes. Bex and I had no formal training. Correction, no training whatsoever. Why were we here? Five minutes with Camille and she'd be parcelling us back into the taxi to sniff BO all the way to Kelmore.

I tried to breathe through it like a social worker had once told me to do when I was angry or missing Mum. Think positive thoughts. Deep breaths, count, as long as it takes. I had made it to seventy-one when Camille came back, issued us with black leggings and told us to follow her.

'No . . . no . . . no . . . not that way, like dees,' she said, demonstrating the move so perfectly, so effortlessly, like water flowing across a pond, that we couldn't help but crave her praise.

'Dat's it, forget yourselves, listen to the music.' And I did. The music wrapped around me and carried me away to another place and when I stopped I couldn't tell you how long Greg had been watching us. Greg, and another older guy, suntanned, sunglasses on his head. Shirtsleeves rolled up.

It was only the sound of their applause that broke the spell.

Back in the dressing room, the suntanned man introduced himself as Curtis.

'Curtis is a film director,' Greg said. Me and Bex turned to each other at the same time and laughed. Mr Palatino did have connections after all.

Curtis poured himself a glass of wine. 'Girls?' he said, lifting the bottle. 'Greg won't say a word to your teacher.'

'Yes please,' Bex said, nudging me.

'OK then.' I didn't want to be the one to spoil the fun.

'Not bad for your first day,' Curtis said. 'Tell me, girls, do you want to be dancers?'

'More than anything,' Bex said.

'It takes a lot of hard work to make it.'

'Hard work doesn't scare us,' I said.

'Well, the show is to be *Bugsy Malone*, do you think you can make the grade?'

'Of course.'

'You have to learn to relax more. Let me show you,' Greg said and pulled me in front of the mirror. He stood behind me, hands pressing on my shoulders.

'Too much tension here, Charlie, you need to drop them.'

I ordered my muscles to relax.

'Perfect.' The word tingled down my neck.

'You'll come again then?'

Our faces answered for us. We'd landed the golden ticket. Entry to a glamorous world. An exclusive club.

'I'll send a car next week,' Greg said.

# Thursday, 11.45 a.m.

## Linda

We're tossed about as the van heaves up inclines and corners sharp bends. Conversation is one-sided: *Do you know what these men have done? How much are they paying you? You won't get away with this. You'll spend the rest of your life in jail.* Nothing pierces him, and I wonder if he can even hear me.

*You don't exist.*

What if he's right?

I study him, possessed by the urge to scrape away the mask, tear through the film of his skin and find out what lies beneath. But the set of his face doesn't reveal any expression at all, as if the circuit feeding his emotions has shorted, left him only a shell to inhabit.

And yet I cling to the notion that somewhere there is a pulse of humanity beating through him. It is my only sliver of hope. What I need to do is find the nerve and press it and bring it back to life.

'They'll kill me this time,' I say. 'They don't like getting their hands dirty, that's what you are for, so they can stay squeaky clean while you absorb all their filth.'

'Shut up.'

'I won't go quietly, you know. I'll scream until there's no breath left in me and when I'm long gone, weeks, years down the line you'll still hear my screams and you'll see my face last thing before you go to sleep, if you sleep at all, first thing in the morning.'

'I said shut up.'

I smell blood.

'They won't care about you. Not when they're staying in five-star hotels, yachts, hosting their parties, selecting their next victims. Sure, they'll let you think you can be part of their world but they'll never let you inside. At the first sign of trouble you'll be dropped, cast aside. And if you spend the rest of your life rotting in prison they won't so much as look back. You're nothing to them.'

He's up on his feet, launching himself at me. I'm thrust back against the side of the van, his hands around my neck. 'I told you to shut up, shut the fuck up.' I don't have a second to dwell on my miscalculation, how I should have kept quiet, all I can think is, *This is it. He's going to do it now.* I scratch at the air and catch my nails on his skin, draw them down his cheek.

His grip loosens.

'Bitch.'

His eyes lock with mine for no more than a second, but long enough for me to know that I was right, there is something beating under his skin after all. Yet, touching it, coming this close, glimpsing how black the darkness is, brings no hope, only despair.

I fold my arms into myself, to hold my shaking body still. My thoughts slide towards Gabriel, and threaten to tip over into hysteria. I don't know what they have done, how they framed him, but I don't doubt they are responsible. And the wicked irony of the situation chokes me; the devil's pact into which I entered years ago to save him could now be his ruin.

The van turns, revs up a hill before slowing to a stop. My heart, a bird thrashing in a cage. The door is opened by another man. I see with some relief that we are back at Claremont Cottage. 'Well, well, what do we have here,' the man says. His accent is Scottish, but not from these parts.

'I need to visit the bathroom.' This is true, although it is more about being alone.

'You'll have tae wait.'

'It's not advisable to argue with my bladder.' Bravado is a useful tool, I learnt that much in politics.

'For fuck's sake, on ye go then. Jay, keep the lady company, will ye.'

The cottage had never been to my taste, I'm not a fan of dead animals and tartan, but over the last few days we had reached a mutual respect. Now, it is stripped of its disguise. The dark wood cladding on the walls refuses to admit the thinnest thread of light. The animals' glassy eyes mock me. Draughts press along the corridor, pick at my skin.

'Do you want to watch?' I ask Huxtable. He has followed me to the toilet.

'I'm waiting here.' He removes the key from the lock.

I sit on the loo, trying to order my thoughts. The window in the bathroom is full length. Even if it were open, where would I go? They could move much faster than I. I stand up, pull at the handle. Locked.

'Are you done?'

'Just finishing up. Can't rush nature.'

I search the windowsill as I pull the chain. No key. I go to wash my hands, unsure if personal hygiene has ceased to matter in the circumstances. There is a mirrored cabinet above the sink. I open it and run my fingers along the shelves. Tucked in the corner, hidden by a jar of cotton wool balls, a tiny key. There's a thud thud through my body as I slip it into my pocket.

Huxtable shows me into my old room, only now it is empty and freezing cold. He leaves with the promise of a cup of tea and a sandwich. I ask for clean clothes, and to further my case, make a point of shivering in my wet ones, another appeal to his humanity.

'I'll get Anna to bring you some,' he tells me. 'I'm sure you'll have plenty to say to her.'

He leaves, locking me in. Outside, clouds fill a sullen sky, hunker over the hills and cast shadows in the room. From down the hallway noises puncture the quiet: a shout, a plate falling in the kitchen. Laughter. My body tightens a notch with every sound. There is nothing for me to do but wait for Henry to come.

I first met him in the late 1970s. He was the party chairman back then, and among newer MPs it was a common mistake to view him as a friendly fellow, albeit one prone to pomposity after a few glasses of Burgundy. He made considerable efforts to get to know incomers, spent time educating them in the arcane ways of the House, who to watch out for, whose favour to curry. He peppered conversations with indiscretions (*Valerie and I live separate lives . . . not separate enough for my liking, ha ha!*) and encouraged others, over long sessions in the Commons bar (*Oh, go on, have another, I insist!*) to do the same. Years after my own initiation, I would watch the new intake baring their souls, relaying whatever titbits of gossips they'd picked up like trained dogs, falling into his trap. This wasn't a kindness on Henry's part, though it was cleverly disguised as such. He was listening for the beat of their heart, noting how their eyes flamed at a child's name, a lover's, a pet cause, how their cheeks coloured at the mention of a secret, so he would know how to corner them if and when the time came. He was an animal stalking its prey.

I'd seen these indiscretions used against people many times. Everyone finds their way of surviving in politics; some bully or bribe, others brief against their enemies. Henry, using whatever information he had at his disposal, would present the errant MP with a 'choice'. I called it Henry's Choice because he'd engineer the situation in such a way, paint people into such a tight corner, that it seemed there was rarely a choice to make.

*

Noises reach me from outside. Anna's voice and Huxtable's too. A car door clicking shut, an engine coming to life. Spitting up stones as it clears the driveway.

After half an hour, the car returns, or so I think until an unmistakable tone pollutes the air. I spring up from the bed and my heart hammers as his footsteps march towards my door.

The key turns in the lock.

'Hello, Henry,' I say.

'I brought you some tea. And a sandwich. You should eat, Linda. We don't want you wasting away.'

I fight the urge to place my hands around the hot mug he has set down on the chest of drawers. My mouth is parched and I long for a drink of tea, but gratitude is the last emotion I want to betray.

I say, 'I suppose I should be flattered, given the lengths you've gone to. A simple invitation would have sufficed.'

A look of distaste passes across his face before he masks it with a grin.

If circumstances were different, the sight of Henry would bring me some light relief. He's wearing a Barbour, a cloth cap, and a tartan scarf that matches the throws in the cottage. Quite the Scottish laird. It slips into focus. Henry owns this place, that's why 'Naomi' persuaded me to book it. The knot tightens in my stomach. How many layers of deceit are there to unravel?

'Drink your tea before it gets cold,' he says. 'I wouldn't like to see my efforts wasted. Can't say it was a pleasant trip. I'm not in the best of moods myself. And now we find ourselves in this fix, what with you being dead and all.'

Henry is so close to me I can smell his breath. It's not pleasant – never was, if my memory serves me correctly; always the faint whiff of last night's whisky corroding his mouth, and something else deeper down, rotting inside him. I wince, push back into the wall to gain an inch of space. His hand comes to rest on my shoulder.

'I do wish you had listened when you still had the chance. All that nonsense you fed me about having nothing to lose. Changed your mind now? You never could see the full picture; always was your Achilles' heel. You obsess about what is in front of you, don't look beyond. These girls whose cause you're fighting, they were game. They didn't argue or say no. Nobody forced them to do anything they didn't want to do. But then you know that, don't you? This isn't about justice and you don't care about them any more than I do, you're using them to get to us. We are a reminder that you are not who you think you are, and you can't bear it. But the thing is, Linda, we're alike, you and I. Oh don't look at me like that, we *are* alike. We'd both do anything to protect ourselves. The only difference is I can live with who I am, whereas you can't stand who you've become.'

'The difference is I didn't do it to protect myself.'

'You think that makes you a better person? The decision was the same, Linda. That's what counts. If you really believe those women, ask yourself this: why did you decide your son mattered more than them?'

I recoil. It's too much, to be this close to him. I can't listen to his voice, watch his lips form the words, the same words with which I've been beating myself all these years. I try to unhook his fingers from my shoulder, but he digs in deeper. He knows my pressure points. He knows me. Knows the truth.

'It's time you faced up to who you are,' he says.

I boil over with hatred. Spit at him. It provokes a smile.

With one hand he holds my head tight against the wall and with the palm of the other, he wipes the spit away, then plants it on my face.

'Finally,' he says, 'we catch a glimpse of the real Linda Moscow.'

'This will be your undoing, Henry. You're going to be found out and they'll pull apart every rotten layer of your life and see what's hidden underneath the money and power. There are plenty of women out there ready to testify when they do.'

'Women like Jennifer Patcham, you mean?'

Her name hits me like a punch, a reaction that hands him an easy point. She was the first woman from the website who had agreed to meet me. Mum to a little boy called Trey. Being a mother had made her determined to speak out, she said. We met in a park, spent hours talking. She told me of the trips out of the care home, the entrance into a glamorous world, the preying on dreams and hopes.

'Changed her mind pretty sharpish, didn't she?' Henry says.

Now I know why. After the meeting, she didn't reply to my emails or phone calls and with few avenues left I followed her home from work one day. I wanted to reassure her, urge her to be brave and continue, but she spotted me first.

*Get away from me or I'll call the police.*

Henry lets the information hang in the air between us, waits for it to worm its way inside me, eager to witness the revulsion that will thrash around under my skin. It is the kind of reaction he feeds off. But this time I'm not giving anything away.

'What did you do to her?'

'Oh, Linda, you really are naïve. All she needed was a little nudge,' Henry says. 'We gave her a choice and like any good mother she chose her son. You of all people should understand that.'

He leans in, pushes a stray hair off my face. His finger runs down my cheek.

'Talking of sons, I hear he's not doing too well, that boy of yours. He's been put on suicide watch. I was always very fond of him. Anyway, I'll see you tomorrow. One last chance. And to think all this could have been avoided if only you'd listened last time I paid you a visit.'

# One Year Before

I was watching Gabriel's show on television when the doorbell rang. It would be Bernadette calling early, foisting another one of her fruit loaves on me. She had a key, *in case of emergencies*, but would never dream of using it to let herself in. I was already agitated when I opened the door and found Henry standing behind it. I'll admit to doing a double take, and as odd as it sounds I almost forgot how much I loathed him. It seemed my powers of facial recognition had sprinted ahead of my emotional response. Then he smiled, his upper lip hitched on his teeth, and it all came bounding back.

*What was the bastard doing here?*

'I heard about Hugh,' he said. 'Terribly sorry for your loss. I thought I'd see how you were doing.' He wielded a bunch of flowers and a bottle of wine, props to help him act the part.

'Hugh died eight months ago. We divorced last century.'

He ignored me. This was Henry all over, steamrolling his way through a conversation. 'I didn't want to intrude at the time. Lovely man.'

'The sentiment wasn't reciprocated. He thought you were a prat.'

'Glad to see you've lost none of your charm, Linda. Aren't you going to invite me in?'

'I hadn't intended to, no.'

'How kind. A cup of tea would be marvellous,' he said, and he pushed his way past me.

★

I found an old carton of milk curdling at the back of the fridge and tipped a generous amount into his tea. My lax approach to housekeeping had its benefits.

'Just like old times,' he said casting his eyes around and puckering his nose at whatever smell had caught him. 'Not much has changed around here, I see.'

It was true; the house mocked me. My career, my family, my life had altered beyond recognition and yet the house remained resolutely unchanged, right down to the duvet covers on the beds, the tea towels hanging from the oven door. Life had gushed like water through my home with a force that had seemed unstoppable at times. Too much. To think I had often dreamt of escaping for a day or two, *just a bit of peace and quiet, me time.* And now the supply of life and energy had been cut off. The only evidence left of a once busy household were a few memories pinned to the walls, moments where Gabriel had been stilled long enough for the camera to catch him.

'Of course *you* have changed, Linda, but age does that, doesn't it?' I pawed my face, hated the way he had made me feel self-conscious. I stood up, made a show of looking for biscuits. He took a gulp of tea, the milk hit the back of his throat, soothing my irritation. 'Good God!'

'If you'd warned me you were coming, I would have bought a fresh pint.'

He set the tea to one side as if it might do him serious harm.

'What is it you want, Henry?'

'I hear you're busy on a project.'

'You do?' My body tensed, as if I were facing a snake, unsure of which way he would try to squeeze the breath out of me.

'It is ill advised. You've been duped by hysteria again, and if the past has taught you anything, you should know you won't succeed.'

'We'll see shall we.'

'What on earth do you stand to gain?'

'That's where you and I differ. I don't have to gain personally to do something.'

'But you stand to lose a great deal. Surely I don't have to remind you.'

Laughter bubbled out of me. 'Do you honestly think I care about what happens to me? I have nothing left to lose. I suppose that's why I scare you.'

'Oh for goodness' sake, look at yourself. The only person you'd scare is the postman.'

The doorbell broke through my anger.

'Well, Henry,' I stood up, 'this has been entirely predictable. If you have nothing else to say, I really should be getting on.'

He sat for a moment, refusing to rise on my order. 'I can't say I've missed your company. What Curtis ever saw in you is beyond me. Mind you, even he didn't go back for seconds.'

'Get out.'

He walked through the hallway, 'Do you know, Linda, this is the second time you've thrown me out of your house.' He leaned in towards me, his gaze snagging on something on the wall behind me. 'He's doing rather well for himself, that boy of yours. Don't tell me you've got nothing to lose. There's always something. Always.'

I opened the door to find Bernadette. 'I've brought chocolate tiffins for a change. I have them in the car, wanted to check you were going to open the door first, just you wait till you taste them, my God, they're heavenly. Oh, hello, who would this be?'

I can't say I've ever been so pleased to see her.

# Thursday 12.25 p.m.

## *Detective Inspector Victoria Rutter*

'I have six missed calls and four texts. You'll tell me you're waiting outside the station next,' DI Rutter says.

'I'm just round the corner.'

'Jesus, I was joking. I have nothing for you, no updates, no new lines. We're still questioning him.'

'I'm not asking for information.'

'Then you're the only reporter in the country who isn't.' Gabriel Miller's detention was already a huge story, but when she confirmed to the press, late last night, that it was Linda Moscow, his own mother who he was suspected of murdering, it went nuclear. She's working inside a pressure cooker, whistling out steam with every move she makes. Victoria has headed investigations before but no other case has come close to attracting such intense scrutiny.

'I have something for *you*,' Jonathan says.

DI Rutter puts her decision to meet him in the park down to gratitude, the fact that in their short telephone conversation Jonathan didn't pump her for a quote or an off the record steer. She agrees to see him for five minutes, not a second more. Any other reporter and she wouldn't even contemplate speaking at this stage in the investigation, but Clancy is a decent sort. And she owes him a favour from a few months back when he ran a story about a young man who was killed in a homophobic attack. A key witness came forward after reading it and they charged a suspect as a result. Mainly though, she needs to get out of the station, craves a blast of icy air to shock her mind back to life. Right now, all she can see is what is in front of her face: the forensics that tell her Gabriel was at his mother's house, her blood on his clothes, in his car, under his nails. They don't have a body yet, but that doesn't mean he's not guilty. It is a credible motive or the lack of one that is bothering her. The theory that he killed Mariela Castell in some weird sex game then murdered his mother when she wouldn't cover for him is winning the popular vote among her colleagues. His muddy boots were found dumped in his neighbour's dustbin. But – and it is a big but – she has just taken receipt of the forensics from Mariela's body and they don't fit the story as perfectly as she might have hoped.

'I don't think Gabriel Miller killed his mother,' Jonathan says. A fine drizzle is falling, creating a wet fur on their coats. They have the park to themselves, give or take a lunchtime jogger or two.

'I'm fine, thanks for asking.'

'You've only given me five minutes, I haven't got time for pleasantries. Do you want to hear my theory?'

'I sense you're going to tell me anyway.'

'Henry Sinclair and Curtis Loewe – ever heard anything about them?'

DI Rutter knows Jonathan well enough to guess he's not asking for a biography or a list of their greatest achievements.

'Well, have you?' he asks again.

The answer is yes, although nothing concrete. A while ago a colleague told her there was a complaint made against Curtis Loewe years before. Nothing ever came of it. The investigating officer was signed off on the sick. Never came back, apparently. She's not ready to tell Jonathan this because she wants to know what he has first. She may trust him more than any other journalist but that's not saying a lot.

'Linda and I have been trying to expose them for years.'

'You and Linda Moscow?'

'We're friends, go way back. Girls, underage,' he continues. 'His theatre school charity provided him with a constant supply of them. We're talking vulnerable children here. He knew how to pick his victims. Linda has been trying to gather testimonies of women who were abused. I think they found out what she was up to. Speaking from experience, I can tell you that people who stand in their way have a habit of getting hurt.'

DI Rutter shakes her head so the nonsense Clancy is propounding doesn't settle. This is the most high-profile case she's ever landed, and the pressure, the unremitting appetite for updates and information and statements is cooking her brain. The top brass want results quickly too. She hasn't been home for three days, can barely remember her children's names. She missed a dance show last night in which her daughter Bella had the starring role. Frankly, she could be doing without the left-field conspiracy theories.

'Jesus, what have you been taking?'

And come to think of it, there are some images she'd rather not see tarnished. Certain people, figureheads, national treasures, who she needs to believe are wholesome and good because if they're not, the whole country has bought a lie. Curtis Loewe gives millions to charity, she watched his films as a kid, her own children have been brought up on them. She'd dismissed the earlier rumour about him as nasty gossip. Tall poppy syndrome.

'Tell me you're joking.'

'I don't think this is the time for jokes, do you?' Jonathan says. Victoria studies him and to her alarm, she realises that he actually believes Curtis Loewe could be behind Linda's disappearance. She's had enough of this, checks her watch, gets up to go.

'Wait!' There's a note of desperation in his plea that makes her stop. Hasn't he just said Linda was his friend? She should show some compassion, no matter what pressures are bearing down.

'I have something I want you to hear.' Jonathan reaches into his battered leather satchel and pulls out a Dictaphone, plugs earbuds into it.

'Listen to this. It's old, the sound quality isn't great.'

It's a recording of Jonathan talking to a woman. He's angry with her at first, venting his rage, but as she begins to speak he falls silent. The woman is Linda Moscow.

What DI Rutter hears, the account Linda Moscow gives, scorches images of happy family days gathered around watching a film, taints memories of her kids dancing in the kitchen to well-known soundtracks.

'Shit,' she says.

'Still think he's a good person?'

Clancy tells her about a website – www.whathappenedatkelmore. com – started by one of the victims. 'I went to her address yesterday, her neighbour told me she hasn't been seen for months, and now Linda disappears. You're probably going to tell me that's just a coincidence.'

'I don't like coincidences.'

Encouraged, he searches for the website on his iPad, 'So you know I'm not making this up.' But it isn't there, it has been taken down, a holding page in its place.

'It was there yesterday.'

'Really.'

'I have the screenshots to prove it. By the time you get back to the station they'll be in your inbox. You'll take a look at them, won't you?'

'I can't promise anything. Now I really have to go,' Victoria says. She leaves Jonathan in the park, wishing she could scrub everything she has just heard from her brain, turn the clock back an hour to when her biggest problem was finding a motive for Gabriel Miller to kill his mother. But that is impossible, Linda's words are imprinted in her mind and she cannot score them out.

# Summer 1994

## Charlie

'Bloody hell, have you seen the car?'

'No way is that for us.'

'Well, it's not Mrs O'Dowd's boyfriend, is it?' We both cracked up laughing. We'd spent days chewing over what had happened the weekend before, high on excitement. It felt like the load had lightened, as if our connection to the world outside made Kelmore bearable, or as close to bearable as humanly possible. We danced everywhere, to lessons, to the dinner hall. Danced in our sleep.

'Are you going to keep him waiting all day?' Mrs O'Dowd sidled up behind us like a ghost, appearing with no warning. 'Well, go on then. And girls . . .'

'Yes?'

'Don't disgrace yourselves.'

Two cans of Fanta orange welcomed us to the back seat. Next to them was a massive bag of Skittles that we wasted no time in opening. We were too busy throwing them into our mouths to notice we'd overshot the turning for the town centre and the theatre where we had rehearsed the previous weekend.

'We're being abducted!' Bex said. 'Help, help!' She stuck her hands to the window and pressed her face against it and snorted with laughter.

'You mad cow.'

There was a screen between us and the driver so he couldn't hear us when we asked him where we were going. Not that it mattered. If Kelmore was your life, you dreamt of being kidnapped.

We passed the time dancing, doing the arm actions to 'Vogue' when it came on the radio, bouffed our hair when Cher's 'If I Could Turn Back Time' came on, gyrated to Lil' Louis, 'French Kiss'.

By the time we hit the country lanes we were on the cusp of boredom. The Skittles were working their way back up. Bex had gone white. 'I get really travel sick,' she said.

'Now you tell me.'

The first view of the house silenced us. It was cartoon big, bursting out of the trees.

'Whoaaa!'

'Is that a hotel?' Bex shouted to the driver, who had dipped the music.

'No.'

'And I'm Annie at Daddy Warbucks,' I said.

'I wish we hadn't eaten all the Skittles,' Bex moaned.

'Energy,' I said. 'We'll burn them off.'

We did. We danced all day. Camille was there, still not chancing a smile. We joined a group of four girls. I say joined, more like hovered on the edge as they whispered to themselves and giggled when we messed up.

'Ignore them,' Bex said. 'Bitches don't want the competition.'

Now and again Greg poked his head around the door and watched a few routines, arms crossed, eyes pinched in concentration. He was very thorough in the way he studied us and how our bodies moved. I could tell he was looking after us, wanted us to do well. It felt good to have someone in our corner for a change. His attention forced me out of myself. The music lifted my body and pushed it in directions I didn't know it could go. Bex had come alive too. The thing about Bex was her eyes could often look dead, like she'd seen too much. Now they held diamonds in them, sparkling in the light. There was no limit to what we could do.

'Don't tell me you're worn out already?' Greg had found us in the hallway, propped up against the wall. My body sang with exhaustion. 'You've got a performance tonight.'

'A performance? Aren't we going back?'

'No, you get to stay here until tomorrow. You didn't know?'

We didn't. Mrs O'Dowd hadn't shared any details.

'There's food downstairs, go eat and then shower. Curtis has guests tonight, backers for the show, industry folk. You'll want to impress.'

'But we've only brought leggings.' Bex looked panicked. The thought of being shown up was too much.

'Don't worry,' he smiled. 'We've taken care of everything.'

We only knew one kind of make-up, the orange stuff that blanked out your face, but this was the real deal, done by a professional. She introduced herself as Anouk, spoke with an accent so thick it hurt my head trying to decipher it. I was mesmerised as she worked away at my face, inviting my cheekbones to pop out, magnifying my eyes with kohl and false lashes, turning my lips juicy red. My hair was combed in a side parting, tied back. If it hadn't been for the mascara I would have cried with happiness. I was someone else. I wanted her to take over and swap places with Charlie for good.

'Thank you,' I said to Anouk but she brushed me away and started on the next girl.

Bex was already in our room when I got back. She didn't look like Bex either.

'Well, heeellloo,' she said.

Camille had laid clothes out on the bed. Twenties silk dresses, one in red, one in black.

We made each other close our eyes for the big reveal.

'One. Two. Three. Open.'

'Oh my fucking God. Who knew we were so gorgeous,' Bex said.

This is what I remember from the first night: being seen; how the watching eyes electrified me. Kelmore taught us to make ourselves small, our bodies trained to apologise for their presence through stooped shoulders and bowed heads and eyes cast downwards. We had learnt to occupy the least space possible. No one wanted to hear or see us, why else would we be hidden away in a crumbling Victorian building miles from life?

Now our hands reached upwards and outwards and marvelled at the space they found. Our backs straightened, surprised that we could stand so tall. We faced the people gathered in front of us, drank in their smiles. We had been invited here. They wanted us. They liked what they saw. And the dancing, when our turn came, happened almost without thought or instruction. It was natural. This was who we were. Every molecule of air we touched thrilled us, every beat we hit made our smiles wider. Like our future had begun to flower in those ten minutes on stage, the past shaded away.

The applause. I remember that too. It ricocheted through me, brought every nerve ending to life. Bex's eyes found me, brighter than bright. The world had changed colour.

My first champagne, thrust into my hands. And another. And another. I drank them fast, like fizzy pop, as I was guided around the room by a man whose name I can't recall but was full of praise for my dancing. 'This is Charlie,' he said, and someone new would kiss my hand or cheek. Gentlemen, I remember thinking. The grown-up smells of aftershave, a woody cinnamon scent, cigarettes, champagne sweetening their breaths.

At some stage the room began to dart around me. The lights

dipped. I searched for Bex but my eyes couldn't pull anyone into focus and when I closed them trails of yellows and oranges and pinks danced on my eyelids.

'You were marvellous,' said a male voice from behind. I didn't recognise the voice but his arms on my waist suggested he knew me. His eyes travelled around the edges of my body. 'Look at you!' I tried to follow his suggestion and look down at myself but the movement pushed me off balance. I fell into him.

'Sorry,' I said.

'No need to apologise.'

The way he stared confused me. And then I remembered I was someone different tonight. Charlie Pedlingham from Kelmore was still in the bedroom hiding under an old hoodie and leggings. I was a woman, made up, dressed up. Borderline beautiful. A future star. The thought made me light. Light and free.

'I'm Curtis,' he said. By now I recognised him from the theatre and I wondered why of all the people in the room he had chosen to talk to me.

'You've got something,' he whispered.

I swelled at his praise, felt myself lifted on the curves of the music. 'I'd like to see more of you.'

What to say? A nervous laugh escaped and I tried to cobble together some words to form a sentence. 'Henry, my friend,' he called to a man passing us. 'Come here. Don't you think Charlie is wonderful?'

Henry stood in front of me. He looked like the kind of man who took a tie off to go casual. His face was ruddy with the heat. He kissed me on both cheeks.

'I couldn't agree more. Curtis here has impeccable taste. Stick with him and you'll go far.'

Outside the bathroom, Greg appeared. 'You were great before.'

I let the wall hold me up. 'I'm not used to drinking,' I said.

He laughed, traced a finger along my cheek. 'It's been a long day.' He produced his wallet and I thought he was going to give me money for a cab back to Kelmore. 'Here,' he said. 'To pick you up. Don't look so worried. It will straighten your head out.'

I stared at the pill as it danced in my hand. It looked just like a paracetamol.

'You sure?'

He held another in front of me before placing it on his tongue. 'Just promise not to tell Mrs O'Dowd.' His laughter caught me and made me laugh too, like it was the funniest thing I'd ever heard.

A hand pulled me along the hallway. It wasn't Greg's. Where was Greg? Did it matter? This hand belonged to someone else. My body was fluid, flowing like water through the crowd of people. Small glares of light pierced the darkness. Chatter rose and fell away from somewhere in the labyrinth of doors and rooms. What had Greg given me? Not paracetamol like Matron doled out for period cramps. I'd never felt like this in the sick bay. It was different to the champagne too; that had made me heavy, mixed up my words. This. This was light, stripped all the weight out of my body so I was a balloon being guided on a string. Soaring. Heat radiated through my bones, gushed into every part of my brain, waves of it pushing forward and slipping back. Turned my face into a smile. Nothing mattered but this moment. Nothing at all.

A door opened and the hand guided me inside. The air had dropped a degree or two. Cleaner, no one else breathing it, just me, the hand and its owner. The room was hung with a moody light. Being here meant something, I sensed it, but when I scratched my mind for an answer it revealed nothing. The effort of thinking was too much. I closed my eyes, fell back and landed where it was cold and soft beneath me. The hand moved over me, sent a tremor down my neck, a current of pleasure. And the answer flashed before me. This was grown up. I was entering an adult world where the edges were fuzzy and there was a new set of rules.

Something was swimming round in my veins. Flooding me. My body was soft, I could stretch it out in any way I wanted. I lifted my hand to my head, didn't quite make it. I held it out in front of me. My fingers cut shards of light out of the dark. I turned and found myself in a mirror. Not Charlie, the new version of her.

*Look at me, all grown up.*

I wanted to drift, stumble into sleep. Was I being helped to bed? Nice to be taken care of. The hands (two now) peeled my dress away, slipped off my underwear. No need, I wanted to say. I can sleep in my underwear and Mrs O'Dowd told us not to disgrace ourselves, but I didn't say anything at all. Too woozy.

The hands surprised me. Rougher now, they began to press me into a shape I didn't want to make. My legs split, arms raised above my head. I wriggled, tried to explain it wasn't comfortable, and please, I'm feeling very strange. But I couldn't speak because my mouth was covered with lips and there was a tongue inside. 'Shhh,' he said when he took the tongue out. 'Relax.'

*Relax. Like a grown-up. But surely it shouldn't hurt like this?* The weight on top of my body made me sink further down into the bed.

'It's OK,' he said.

*Is it? He knows the rules and I don't.*

*Play the game, learn the new rules.*

I tried. But the new rules stung my skin, burnt me inside.

'No,' I said. Not loud enough. I turned away. He pulled me back. 'Now, now. Don't be a tease.'

*A tease. Is that what I am?*

*All I want to do is sleep.*

*But I can't.*

*I've sold him a different version of me. Older. Grown up. He wants that one.*

*Too late to change my mind.*

'Too late,' he said. 'I'm inside.'

On the journey back there were no Skittles. I don't suppose we'd have had the stomach for them anyway. Bex and I stared outside as the country lanes turned into motorways and took us back where we had come from. We knew something had changed, could taste it in the air between us, but it wasn't what we had expected and we didn't mention it. Some emotions are too complicated to set to words.

'Lots of work to do today, girls,' Greg said. We were back at the theatre. The production was in six weeks, he told us, and we assumed this meant we had a part. His hand grazed Bex's shoulder, slipping down to the small of her back. Her reaction, I recognised that. Cheeks full of heat, jumpy. Pleasure and fear, equal in measure. What to do?

The day passed in a whir of music and dance. Bex and I were happy, that's the thing. Or at least we thought this was hapiness. We had caught a glimpse of a future, been pushed through a door of opportunity, and we didn't want to give up on it. Even the attention, kind sometimes, caring too, and the eyes that stripped us bare, better than eyes that turned away in disgust.

Evening came and with it trays of drinks and food. Bex slipped away. Greg had focused his attention on her. I imagined what she was doing, then tried to score it out of my mind. A stirring of jealousy in my stomach. I drained my glass. Hovered on the periphery of the girls' circle. Spinning round at the sound of his voice.

'There you are,' he said as his eyes picked me out of the group.

*Still special after all.*

He took me to another room.

'I want you to dance for me.' He pointed to the camera at the other end of the room. 'Give it a wave.' I obeyed. Didn't occur to me to say no.

I didn't dance for long, a few minutes or so, self-conscious at first, then warming to it as his eyes drunk me in. 'You'll go far,' he said, dangling bright lights and fame and freedom in front of me. 'If you want to. Do you want to?'

'I do,' I said. Then he came close. Closer. He pressed me down, unbuttoned his trousers, and pushed himself into my mouth.

I fixed my eyes shut, blocked it out. An explosion of light behind my eyes. There was something I wanted to say but the words were pushed back inside me, deeper and deeper down. *Can't breathe. It's not OK. Yes, it is. Relax. Once would have been a one-night stand, made me a slut. Twice means he really cares, makes it special, doesn't it? Doesn't it?*

'How is it going, girls?' Miss Reilly asked at netball. 'You look tired. Are they treating you well?' Bex and I exchanged a look. 'Girls, if there's anything you are not happy with, you can tell me, OK?'

'It's fine, miss.'

'Good, then you can get changed now.'

'I'm not feeling up to it,' Bex said. I'd seen the bruising on her thighs the night before. There was no way she could wear a netball skirt.

'Do you want to tell me what the problem is?' Bex shook her head. 'Then, Bex, I really need you to get changed. You have five minutes, otherwise I will take you to the sick bay.'

There was no way around it. Sick bay would mean a once-over from Matron, and she couldn't suffer that. Reluctantly, Bex dressed for games: gym top, socks, netball skirt last.

'You all right?' I said, pointlessly. It was obvious she wasn't.

'Ah, Bex, nice of you to join us,' Miss Reilly said when we made it out on to the court. A trickle of sweat ran down my back. The sun, when it cracked out from the clouds, was intense, but mainly it sulked behind them.

I was goalkeeper and our team was winning so I had plenty of time to watch Miss Reilly. The initial looks she cast across to Bex, running around in her position of wing attack, followed by the furtive ones, as if committing what she saw to memory.

After a few spits of rain she shouted, 'OK, girls, we'll call it a day.' No one could believe she'd surrendered so easily to the weather. 'Bex and Charlie, you can help me gather the bibs and balls.'

'Bex,' she said when we had finished our task. 'Can you tell me how you got those bruises?'

She looked to the ground, kicked up some gravel with the toe of her shoes. 'Dancing.'

'I've danced a lot, you know that, don't you, Bex? Practised for hours and hours. I've had bruises too . . . but not there.'

The sun had slipped out again, burnt on to Bex's face. She couldn't look at Miss Reilly without squinting. I watched a lone tear fall down her cheek like a drop of liquid silver.

'I don't know what you mean.'

The next day we saw Miss Reilly's blue Ford Fiesta swing out of the grounds for the last time. Bex said she looked back and waved. But I think she made that up. It was impossible to tell from the dormitory window.

The statue of the Virgin Mary watched over us as we sat outside Mrs O'Dowd's office. We'd been summoned an hour earlier, made to wait in the heat, sweat out our sins.

'She does this on purpose,' Bex said. 'I bet she's not even busy.'

Finally, the door swung open and Mrs O'Dowd's face filled the space.

'Gaarls,' she said. She was Irish, but insisted on talking like she was from Kensington. Her flat 'a's gave her away. She reached her arm out in a long expansive gesture. 'Do come in.'

Bex went first. I followed. We remained standing because woe betide you if you sat before you were invited.

'Take a seat . . . Do cross your legs, Charlie, you don't want to come across as one of those girls, do you?'

'No, Mrs O'Dowd.'

'Now, I want to talk to you about Curtis Loewe.'

His name lit a touchpaper in my head. I stared at the picture of Jesus on the cross above her head.

'Have you met him?'

I nodded.

'Do you know that you are extremely lucky to be chosen for his play? Two girls like you.'

Silence.

'Well, do you?'

'Yes, Mrs O'Dowd.'

'There are plenty of girls out there more talented than you two, I dare say, who'd jump at the chance. But he seems to see something in you.' Her stare tunnelled into me. My mouth filled with glue while my arse sweated in the plastic chair. I shifted to one side, made an unfortunate noise that sounded like a fart.

'Mr Loewe has been a very generous patron of the school. He has his own charity that raises money for unprivileged children. That's you, by the way. For instance, the trip you went on in the summer to Wales, that was thanks to Mr Loewe. He is very well respected. Do you understand what I am saying?'

'Yes, Mrs O'Dowd.'

'Good, I'm glad. I take it you have no reservations about continuing the rehearsals and appearing in the show?'

Time unspooled. It was a test. A moment presented to us. One way or the other.

*Legs apart. Hands eating me. Weight driving through my body. Stealing my breath. Slut. Slut. Slut.*

*Do you want it?*

'Rebecca?'

'Of course, Mrs O'Dowd.'

'That leaves you, Charlie. Or would you rather be doing jobs here on a Saturday?'

'Yes, Mrs O'Dowd.'

'Yes what?'

'Yes. I'd like to continue.'

That summer lasted years. Me and Bex, taken out every weekend, pulled into a different existence. New rules were drawn, secret ones that we weren't to speak of, *they're just different, it doesn't make them wrong, but not everyone would understand.*

I was wanted in a way that was complex and confusing. But being wanted was more than I'd had for a long time. We saw the sights, ate crisps and sweets and cakes, champagne, pills that fuzzed my edges and melted my body. Different men, who laughed and chatted and asked me questions but didn't wait for answers and did what they wanted anyway. Sometimes it hurt, but it was an adult hurt, not a bad hurt. A love hurt, I told myself. So long as we made them happy we could stay happy.

This was happiness, wasn't it?

Except. We began to shrink. Couldn't tell at first, but slowly Bex's body curled into itself, her eyes deadened again. We became smaller and smaller to make ourselves fit their shape.

*This is the adult world. Our escape.*

*So why is it closing in?*

I showered, religiously, obsessively, scrubbed manically, but the handprints didn't wash away. Indelible marks all over my body. I could have traced around them. Everything hurt, every bone, every wish we made, even our dreams hurt.

*But shhh.*

*Keep quiet. Don't tell a soul.*

*You're going to be a star.*

The show ran for two weekends at the Watford Palace Theatre with none of the West End glamour we'd hoped for. We were crammed into a dressing room with twenty other dancers, all fighting for a slice of the mirror. When the time came for us to perform we were shoved at the back, beneath layers of proper dancers. We didn't have enough room to move our arms or kick our legs out so we quit trying. We were paralysed by our own stupidity.

After the final performance there were drinks and a few sausage rolls and crisps backstage. Cheap, warm wine in plastic cups. Greg stood up and thanked the cast and I knew Bex wanted his eyes to fall on hers, but they didn't, so she found him instead.

She waited next to him while he spoke to the leading man. Waited and waited. I wanted to pull her away. He could see her and still strung out the conversation. When he finished, she touched his arm.

'Bex,' he said in a new voice that was loud and cold. 'Thanks for the hard work. You were a bit out of step tonight, but not bad for a beginner. I'll see you get home.'

I could read her thoughts because the same ones were clicking through my mind. *He's acting like nothing happened. Like she's nothing to him.*

'Gre-eg,' she said. Desperation thickened her voice.

'I have a lot of people to see, Rebecca.' She hated Rebecca. She reached out to touch his shoulder but he moved away too quickly and she upended a tray of drinks that a passing waitress was carrying.

Still, she wouldn't give up, pushed through the crowd. I followed, desperate to rein her back.

'Greg.'

'Don't, please don't . . .'

She didn't listen. She tracked him all the way down the corridor to a dressing room. He was inside, pushing the door closed to get rid of her, so she stuck her foot in it.

'What the hell do you think you're doing?' His scream shrunk her.

Curtis was there, drinking a glass of wine. He wasn't alone. I would have said she was younger than me but who knows, it was hard to tell. Fresher, at least. That was it. A fresh body to touch. Not grubby like me, stained by his hands.

'Get them out of here,' he said to Greg.

His tone winded me. My stomach curdled with shame. And jealousy. I wanted to be that girl. I would have scratched her eyes out to swap places. I would let him do whatever he wanted if it meant he didn't throw me away.

Greg pushed us out of the door.

'Get your things, there's a taxi waiting outside.'

Inside the taxi it was cold. The night air goosebumped our bare arms. We watched the lights of the town stream by. Not a single word passed between us.

# Thursday 1.05 p.m.

## Linda

The effects of Henry's visit sit in my bloodstream like poison long after he has gone. Anger scorches me, enflames my cheeks, disturbs my vision.

*One. Last. Chance.*

I know Henry. He'll push me into a corner until I can't see, can't breathe, until there is only one choice left to make. That is what he does. I should know, having been there before.

If there is a means of escape, I can't see it. The yawning isolation of this place compounds my despair. No one would think to look for me here, not even Jonathan. He's been out of contact for weeks with no warning or explanation. The man can be infuriatingly vague and elusive at times. That's not to say he won't have his suspicions. Instinct will tell him my demise is too convenient for Curtis and Henry, but proving their involvement is another matter. And time is not my friend. *Tomorrow*, Henry said. I may have less than twenty-four hours left.

Fear circles me like a predator. In an attempt to escape it, I tell myself it is probably for the best that Jonathan doesn't know where I am. I wouldn't put it past the fool to come up here alone, follow me into their trap. And since it was me who dragged him into this mess years ago, I wouldn't want to be responsible for his death as well as mine.

And yet the thought of not seeing him again punctures me. I love Jonathan. There, I've said it. No point in hiding away from the truth now. If I'm going to die, I might as well be honest with myself. It is hardly a revelation after all. I think I loved him from the very first time we met and sank a bottle of sambuca and argued about the welfare system until our words turned to syrup and we were the only ones left at the party. We walked out into the throbbing London night and fell into each other at a bus stop. And we kissed. I thought it was the start of something, but when we met again he seemed awkward and disinterested. Not that I let it put me off, this was the late seventies after all, women didn't have to wait to be seduced. So I steamed in one night with a kiss, but the look on his face as he reeled back, the humiliation it produced in me, warned me off for good. I settled for friendship instead. Jonathan was a man I could rely on, whom I trusted with everything, so when Henry tried to push me into a corner, he seemed like the obvious person to turn to.

# October 1996

## Linda

Henry's visit was unannounced, all the better to wrong-foot people. He opened with a few inquiries about Hugh and Gabriel – *Such a charming boy, how is he?* – before moving on to the real purpose of his house call.

Curtis Loewe. Film director, philanthropist, generous party donor: 'All thanks to you, Linda. Squeezed him for millions! I knew you were going too far when you worked your magic on him. You remember that night, don't you?'

'I do.'

'Anyway, we have a spot of bother. Girls. Curtis gave them a stab at stardom. You know he helps hundreds of children every year through those theatre schools of his. Most of them have been in some kind of trouble, and they haven't got a thread of acting talent between them, but he gives them a shot. Doesn't promise any more than that. These particular girls didn't make the grade. And bingo, they're crying wolf, trying to exact their revenge.'

'Crying wolf?'

'They're alleging something untoward happened. What a shame their acting doesn't match their imagination.'

My blood was on simmer, hand gripping the edge of my chair.

*Maintain your composure. Henry doesn't get to look at what is underneath.*

'I'm afraid you're going to have to be more specific.' I watched him squirm. A small victory. Not much in the grand scheme.

'Rape. For goodness' sake, Linda, I didn't think I'd have to spell it out. Curtis and another man – the drama teacher, of all people – they're accusing them of rape.'

The word crawled over my skin. I waited, needing time to take it in, process the allegation before I asked, 'What exactly is it that you want me to do?'

'Don't be naïve, Linda.' He wasn't expecting resistance. Henry could make or break people. Those who argued with him came off worse. 'This is a case of people trying to make trouble, nothing more.'

'He's told you that, has he?'

'Of course he has. He has denied everything.'

'Well, if he hasn't done anything wrong, he has nothing to fear.'

Henry paused, raised his nose in the air, caught the scent of blood. His laughter drilled through me.

'Linda, my dear, I'd have thought you of all people would know how charming he is . . . and how liberal with his affection he can be. But that is a very long way from what he is being accused of.'

I forced my face into a smile. Played the good girl. Obedient. Hands on chin, like I was giving his request some consideration. He took the bait – surprising how easy he was to fool. Desperation does that, I thought.

'One word from you, Linda, and the investigation is dropped. Nothing more. It will save time and money in the long run – after all, they're hardly going to get a conviction.'

'Henry, do you know something . . .' I said, smile still intact. Not for long. I couldn't wait any longer, the words pushed up, burned my throat. 'You really do disgust me.'

He darkened, turned puce, like I had set off a flare underneath his skin. 'Careful, Linda, we all have our secrets. How is Gabriel, by the way?'

'Get the fuck out of my house!'

Henry was not one to give up easily. Ever. The following week he hand-delivered a letter, insisted on me opening it in his presence. It was addressed to Chief Superintendent Bill Joplin of the Metropolitan Police, urging him to drop the investigation.

My eyes fixed on a few choice phrases: *'witch-hunt'*, *'national security'*, *'spurious claims with no foundation in fact'*. It was from the Home Secretary, Linda Moscow.

Me.

'All it needs is your signature,' he said.

'Please leave,' I told him.

I waited until evening, when I was at home, and called Jonathan.

'I have something for you. Can you come round?'

'Curtis Lowe, what do you know about him?'

'Film director of some repute, moneyed. Important donor to your lot.'

'Anything else?'

'I wouldn't have thought it was in your best interests to dig. He's not a donor you'd want to lose.'

My silence encouraged him. 'There *was* something, a few years back. It went away almost as soon as it was discussed. No evidence . . .'

'Go on.'

'A girl, at one of his infamous parties in the Cotswolds. She was underage, she came forward to make a complaint. I got a tip-off but then she disappeared.'

'Vanished?'

'She withdrew the complaint, apparently. That's as much as I know. Don't tell me, he's at it again?'

'They want me to bury it.'

'Government's a dirty business.'

'There are two women, identical complaints. They were at

Kelmore School for Girls, plucked for stardom and taken to one of his charity's theatre groups, but the only dancing they saw was at his parties. Sound familiar?'

'Almost word for word. You know they'll end your career for this if they find out you've told me.'

'That man deserves all he has coming. Besides, Jonathan, I trust you.'

I leaked the document outlining the case to Jonathan. It was a breach of confidentiality, without question, but I repeated Henry's old line to myself: *Sometimes you have to make decisions for the greater good.* Jonathan was my security. Even if Henry succeeded in having the investigation binned, Jonathan was a dog with a bone. Nothing would persuade him to drop it.

Sure enough, he called me a few weeks later. He'd found the girls and they were willing to talk to him. I didn't ask how, I didn't want to know, but I slept well that night, knowing I'd done the right thing.

# Eleven Months Before

## *Henry Sinclair*

Linda. Linda. Linda. It can't be. The woman is as good as dead. A recluse trapped inside her own home. The photographs he has seen over the past few years show a degree of decrepitude that startles him. He almost feels a tug of sympathy, it's like life has staged a practical joke on his old colleague, bestowing her with success and recognition only to whip it away. He knows she's fond of a drink too – wasn't she always – and he likes to think she spends her time indoors pickling herself, shrivelling like a grape to a raisin.

This is why he is not ready to believe Curtis when he calls to tell him Linda is causing problems again.

'I'll be damned if it's not her. I've found the website. I was tipped off . . . Yes, there is a website . . . swarms of them moaning about injustice. What next? Look it up yourself. Have you a pen? It's www.whathappenedatkelmore.com – not the most original name, eh? If you read the threads you'll see a former politician has asked to talk to the women so she can expose the scandal, as she calls it. It's got to be her. Who else can it be?'

Henry gives the question some thought. 'Any number of people.'

'Then we're in even more shit. I want Linda ruled out first off. And fast.'

He hangs up. Curtis is not one for unnecessary pleasantries.

★

You don't get to have a career as long as Henry's without mastering some of the darker arts. He knows people. People who can find numbers and tap phones. They're not figures with whom Henry would ever admit to being associated. They're discreet. Do what they have to do. Leave no trace.

One such man slipped into Linda's house and stole her relic of a laptop. Today he has presented Henry not with the computer itself – it wouldn't do to have the physical thing in his possession – but with the email activity from her account. And what do you know, Linda and her old accomplice Jonathan Clancy are plotting once again.

Sent: Friday, 13 September 2013, 13.07 p.m.
To: LindaJmoscow@btinternet.com
From: jonathanclancy@thetimes.co.uk

Dear Linda,
You opened it!
That's a start. I'm not going to ask you how you are because I know you will be much poorer having not had the pleasure of my company for these last few years. This can be remedied, of course, but that is not why I write.
I write because I came across a website this week, www.whathappenedatkelmore.com. I will assume you haven't read it, although I know the name of the establishment will ring a bell. Having gone through it and ingested the information I wonder if this gives us another chance to expose them. I know you are still licking your wounds, yet surrender is what they want. On that basis alone we should never give up.
I will do what I can to bring this to light although, given my previous association, I can't imagine the women would agree to talk to me. You, on the other hand, might have more luck.

Get in touch. You still owe me lunch.
It's never too late.
Yours, in hope,
Jonathan


Sent: Saturday, 14 September 2013, 4.57 p.m.
To: jonathanclancy@thetimes.co.uk
From: LindaJmoscow@btinternet.com


Dear Jonathan,
I've read the website, the blogs. I've read it all. I don't think
I could despise myself more.
What to do?
Yours,
Linda


Sent: Saturday, 14 September 2013, 5.07 p.m.
To: LindaJmoscow@btinternet.com
From: jonathanclancy@thetimes.co.uk


My Dearest Linda,
With the greatest respect, you don't have the monopoly
on self-loathing. Jan divorced me two years ago. Apparently,
I had never made her feel loved. She took the dog, and has
shacked up with our old neighbour Vanessa. I bet you didn't
see that coming! I'm ageing and lonely and on a bad day, I
dare say I stink – at least that's the inference I draw from
the looks they shoot me at work.
But let us put our self-pity aside. The past is the past. It
can't be redrawn. You did something bad for the best of
reasons. So did I.
Stop navel-gazing and say you'll do something to help.
Yours, in admiration,
Jonathan

PS You didn't mention lunch.
PPS I miss you.

Sent: Saturday, 14 September 2013, 5.48 p.m.
To: jonathanclancy@thetimes.co.uk
From: LindaJmoscow@btinternet.com

Dear Jonathan,
I will help. There, I said it. I take it you want me to contact
the woman who runs the website and start gathering
stories? I can't imagine it will be easy to persuade her.
Understandably she distrusts authority – or former
authority, in my case. I only have myself to blame.
We must be careful to keep this quiet until we have
everything we need.
As for lunch, I'd invite you here but then you'd see how
slovenly I have become. There's a café-cum-deli nearby.
Shall we meet there next Tuesday for lunch? They do sweet
potato brownies, but don't let that put you off.
Yours, in hope,
Linda
PS I'm sorry to hear about Jan. But you shouldn't blame
yourself, I always suspected she had a thing for Vanessa.
PPS I miss you too. No one brings me good wine any
more.

The emails sit in Henry's gut like last night's Stilton. He pours
himself a malt, gulps it down. He takes this resurgence as a
personal affront. Never would he have predicted Linda would
become such a monumental pain in the derrière. When he
first clapped eyes on her at a hustings in Croydon in 1978
she was a plain Jane with unfortunate glasses and hair in need
of attention. In fact, he questioned whether she had got the
wrong party, surely she was one of James Callaghan's lot? But

no, it was his party she had chosen; well, not his exactly, but theirs. Later, when she became an MP and began climbing the ladder, he put the dress and the glasses and the haircut down to a deliberate plan to make people focus on her politics and intellect rather than her looks. It hadn't done Hillary Clinton any harm, had it?

What he hadn't foreseen was the ambition contained in that slender body of hers. When she accosted him in the House he could smell the ambition on her breath. No lunch, no break. 'What about this?' she would ask. 'And are we going to do anything about that?' He really did need to take her under his wing. Not to break her spirit exactly – didn't he pride himself on mentoring new MPs? He knew that by and large they all went into politics to effect change. His role was not to disabuse them of their fancies. Experience itself would do that. No, his job was simply to point out that politics and the business of government involved hard choices. 'It's not Utopia,' he was partial to telling them. 'We live in the real world. The decisions we take are based on the general good, not what is best for one or two constituents.'

It was during a drink in the Commons bar that he glimpsed another side to her. With each glass of wine the whiff of worthiness evaporated. Her clothes had improved, her hair had been brought into line. He'd be damned, but in a certain light the woman looked almost attractive. If she hadn't he wouldn't have considered inviting her to the fundraising ball.

She turned up alone. Waved at him across the room. He had to look twice. Was it her? The transformation! He waved back then wrenched his eyes away. Didn't want to make it too obvious. She was quite the vision, wearing an off-the-shoulder full-length dress in a distinctive emerald green that caught the light and shone like a jewel. Her hair, customarily tied back in a knot, was left down and snaked to the middle of her back where it settled between her shoulder blades. But it was the self-consciousness more than anything else, the sense that she was as surprised by her beauty as anyone, that did it for him.

He was formulating a plan for the evening, a slow, cool seduction, when he heard the question.

'Who is that?'

His heart dipped. Curtis Loewe. He'd recognise that predatory tone anywhere. And now he would have to concede, find another Jane or Jemima to see him through the night. Second best. Curtis had dangled a considerable donation to the party in front of him. Tonight was all about sealing the deal. It wouldn't do to thwart him in his conquest.

*Politics is about the greater good, old boy.*

'Linda Moscow,' he told Curtis. 'One of our new intake.'

'And there I was thinking tonight would be a bore. What do you say, Henry – an introduction?'

'I'll do my best.'

Linda, it appeared, was grateful for the company. Her husband was elsewhere she said with a hint of annoyance. More fool him, Henry thought. 'Another drink?' She asked for a martini. He told the barman to make it a double.

'There's someone I'd like you to meet. We're hoping for rather a large sum of money from him tonight, boost the party coffers.'

Linda turned to him and smiled. 'And you want me to charm him, I suppose.'

'I can't see how you'd fail.'

Later, they stumbled out into the night, the four of them: Henry, Linda, Curtis and one of the secretaries from central office whose laugh didn't wait for the jokes. It was a warm evening. A light wind rolled off the Thames, catching Linda's dress. She wore a shawl around her shoulders that slipped periodically to reveal her back.

162

'Everybody back to mine,' Curtis said. They hailed a cab and Henry, who knew the drill, toyed with ignoring the protocol just this once.

'I'm afraid I can't,' he said, just as they pulled up outside Curtis' Mayfair flat. 'I have an early meeting. I'll take you home, Sharon.'

'Sarah, it's Sarah.'

'You go on, Linda. I wouldn't want Curtis to think we are all spurning his hospitality.'

On Sunday, Curtis rang him at home to offer the money they had hoped for and then some.

'It must have been a good night,' Henry said.

'Night?' he said. 'She's only just left.'

Henry swallowed his coffee, surprised at how he could be simultaneously thrilled and disgusted.

After reading the emails, Henry decides it is time to pay Linda a visit, warn her off the little project upon which she is embarking. It's hardly worth the effort, he'll tell her, what with her political reputation in tatters. Who would believe anything she says?

The meeting does not go according to plan. Linda throws him out of her house (again), but not before she attempts to poison him by slipping putrid milk in his tea.

'The lady's not for turning,' Henry reports to Curtis. 'I tried, but you know what she's like; gentle persuasion doesn't work with Linda.'

'This is all very inconvenient,' Curtis says.

'She's meeting one of those women from the website next week.'

'Is she indeed? I trust you'll arrange for someone to keep her company.'

'Already done, but it's not the women who concern me.

They can be dealt with. It's Linda. We need to present her with a more convincing case.'

'Do you have one in mind?'

'As a matter of fact, I do. There's only one thing left she cares about.'

'Go on.'

'Gabriel. Her son. We already know she'll do anything for him.'

'That was years ago and he was only a child. I don't think you can compare the two situations.'

'A mother's love doesn't wither with age, I'm told.'

'If you say so. But how exactly do you suggest we use Gabriel as leverage?'

'Well, we know he likes a party; what do you say we extend an invitation to him?'

Curtis pushes back into his chair and closes his eyes. For a moment Henry worries he is going soft, has found a scrap of sentimentality at last and will veto his plan. His fears are allayed when Curtis sits bolt upright and shouts to his PA. 'Deirdre! Get me Gabriel Miller's manager.'

It doesn't take long. In the entertainment industry Curtis Loewe is not a man you keep hanging on the phone.

'Palab, how are you, good sir?'

Henry hears a babble at the other end, imagines Palab rubbing his hands when Curtis says, 'That comic of yours, Gabriel Miller, his voice is the exact thing I'm after for my new animation. I happen to be coming along to his show on Thursday. I'd love to meet him.'

'It went well,' Curtis reports a few days later. 'I told him I was interested in using him for the part of the pig in my new film.'

'And what did he say?'

'He said he was a huge fan of my work. Apparently, *The Bear Chronicles* was his favourite film as a child.'

On Sunday Gabriel turns up in the papers. Henry pores over the pictures of him snorting cocaine off a woman's breasts. Kimberly, aged twenty-one, says he was something else. *He stayed up all night. He was so passionate. On fire. We drank champagne and then he poured it all over my body before licking it off.* The story cements Henry's plan. There is no way a man like Gabriel will turn down what's on offer. He adds Gabriel's name to the guest list for Curtis' next party and pours himself a whisky in celebration.

Nothing is left to chance. Henry sends a car to collect their special guest and bring him to the party. He even puts a bottle of chilled champagne in the back so Gabriel will show up loose and inebriated. There's a lot riding on his performance tonight. Before Gabriel arrives, Henry pulls Alexander aside and tells him to stick by him. Alexander is a DJ, once a household name though no one can quite place him now he's on Southern FM. Years of partying have frayed his edges, and he's teetering on the precipice. A single push, a sex scandal per se, would ease him over the edge. He'll do what he's told tonight or else.

'Don't fuck it up. We need him,' he tells Alexander.

'I hear you.'

Henry gives the waitresses instructions to steer clear of Alexander on their refill rounds but by the time Gabriel arrives his words are slurry. Either that or he's doing a good impression of a sober person trying to act drunk. Damn fool, if he messes it up they're all buggered. He gives Gabriel a wide berth himself, thinks it wise. Knowing Linda, she would have blamed him for the scandal that forced her exit from public life and he doesn't want anything to upset him tonight. Instead he leaves it to Curtis to play the generous host and show him what is on offer.

They both remain uncharacteristically sober, Henry and Curtis. Tonight is not about their personal enjoyment, tempting though it is. Tonight is about survival. It's about getting Gabriel to sign up to their club. See how Linda feels about her exposé once she realises her son has enjoyed the best of Curtis' hospitality, that he is one of their gang.

'I showed him to his room,' Curtis tells him. 'You should have seen the look on Gabriel's face! Almost better than the sex itself,' he laughs.

That Gabriel can't be found in the morning doesn't bother either of them unduly. They've held enough parties over the years to know everyone jumps off the ride at a different time. Some favour goodbyes, others the sharp, unannounced exit. He'll suggest Curtis gives it a few days before he contacts him to ask if he had a good time, and if he would like to come again. What he wants more than anything is to watch the recording from the camera they set up in Gabriel's room. He wants to see him with the girl. Once he has that, he's certain Linda can be persuaded to drop her crusade. Her morals fade away when it comes to her protecting her son, the past has told him that much.

Except . . . there is no recording. He checks it over. This was the room Curtis brought Gabriel to, no mistake. And yet there is nothing. No card inside the machine. It can't be. Is he going mad? He paces the room, lashed by sweat as a wave of pain breaks behind his temples. The worst hangover without the indulgence. It must be here. He personally saw to it, went so far as to test it out. There can only be one explanation.

He calls Curtis, tells him about the card, the lack of it. Curtis is silent. The loud silence of his anger.

'I'll call him,' he says finally.

And he does. Once. Twice. Three times.

'He's probably out having sex with a prostitute right now, snorting a bag of white powder off her backside. He's the type, if ever I saw one. Give it a few days, he'll be in touch, begging for more,' Henry says, but his statement carries no weight, it is void of belief.

Plan A has failed.

Worse than failed.

Five days later, Curtis is visited by a police officer investigating an allegation of underage sex at his party.

The officer introduces himself as Detective Sergeant Jay Huxtable.

# Eleven Months Before

## *Jay Huxtable*

Detective Sergeant Jay Huxtable is used to wiping his feet when he leaves people's houses, showering when he gets home to scrub the shit of the day off his skin. This house isn't like those other ones though, not by a long shot. It's clean, for a start. No doubt the guy has staff, doesn't look the domesticated type himself. Jay wouldn't be afraid to accept a cup of tea – if one were offered, that is. In fact, the only thing that bothers him when he sits down on the leather sofa is thinking of how many women Gabriel might have had here.

And my God, girls must love this house, the sheer luxury of it. The way Gabriel walks around clicking his fingers for lights to come on and music to play. He presses another button and the blinds lower. Just like that. No wonder he pulls all those women with a house like this. It's been a while since Jay had any action himself. Not since Stacey left. She wanted more than Jay could give her, apparently. Something bigger, better. That still hurts. He can't get over her. Bet she wouldn't have left him if he owned this place.

Turns out she already had a bloke lined up. Toby works in the City and drives a Beamer. He lives in Maida Vale. Course he does. Not Harlesden or Willesden Green. Maida Vale. Jesus, why did he have to think of Toby? Now he can't get him out of his head. Him and Stacey and that peculiar little moan of hers that he thought was reserved especially for him. How could he have read it so wrong? He thought she was the one. She *was*

168

the one for him. He had it all planned out: wedding, two kids, a boy and a girl. Today is their anniversary. Would have been. Five years together.

'Aren't you going to ask me anything?' Gabriel Miller is still standing, which makes Jay's decision to sit a little awkward.

'Errr . . . yes. The details of the night. I need to go over them.'

'Again?'

'Again.'

'Curtis Loewe invited me to his house. He said it was a party. I knew it was never going to be my scene. I mean come on, the guy's north of sixty, but my manager was gagging for me to go. I should have said, he wanted me in one of his films, an animation . . . he wanted my voice to play the role of a pig . . . don't look at me like that, you never heard Jack Black in *Kung Fu Panda*? Anyway, I went along. I like to keep people happy. Only, it wasn't a party like I'd ever been to before, it was some kind of weird sex thing with girls. And I mean girls. They weren't women. They were off their faces too.'

Jay shifts in the seat. He didn't have breakfast, yet whatever contents his stomach contains are reacting to Gabriel's allegations. He hates this kind of talk. It disgusts him. If it is true. But Curtis Loewe? He can't quite believe it. The man's a legend.

'Are you saying they were drugged?'

'You don't get like that from drinking orange squash.'

'Did you get any of their names?'

'Yeah, they'd drunk a bottle of vodka and taken God knows what and gave me all their details.'

'Without any victims, it's hard to prove a crime.'

'Do you think I'm making this up? Listen, that wasn't his first party. No way. It won't be the last. I don't want to tell you how to do your job, but seriously, how hard can it be?'

Jay feels his bile rising again. He wants to like Gabriel, take him seriously. He totally rates his shows and Christ, he's been

169

watching enough TV these last few months, but the guy isn't doing himself any favours. He's a patronising knob, used to clicking his fingers and watching people jump. Jay isn't going to jump. He did enough jumping for Stacey, and look where that got him.

'Don't tell me it's OK to fuck young girls now.'

'What I'm saying is, we only have your word that they were underage and . . . you know . . .'

'And you know what? Whatever you're thinking, I do have standards.'

'We'll be speaking to Mr Loewe in due course,' he says, and then as an afterthought, adds, 'I reckon you can kiss your dog role in his film goodbye though.'

'It was a pig. He wanted me to be a pig.'

DS Huxtable is called into The Boss' office before he pays a visit to Curtis Loewe. 'Low key, do you hear me?' DCI Patel says. 'The press can't get wind of this. I want it done properly. It's not a circus, got it? If I see any of this in the press I'm going to personally boil your head. This man has friends everywhere, and we all know if you put the accuser in the witness box they'd tear him and his sex life to shreds. So we go easy. Got it? Go on then, what are you waiting for? Go and see how the other half live. And Jay . . . ?'

'Yes, sir?'

'Remember your manners.'

Curtis Loewe's flat is in Mayfair. Where else? Jay's not sure you call them flats in Mayfair. His nan lives in a flat in Peckham. This doesn't look anything like his nan's home.

There is something to be said for the estates his job takes him to and the filthy carpets and drug-addled inhabitants. By comparison he knows he's achieved something with his life. He's going places (all right, mainly he's going back to the station canteen for a bacon butty, but he has a purpose nevertheless). Mayfair shrinks him and his achievements. His perception shifts, he looks at himself through the eyes of antique dealers and Russian oligarchs and BAFTA-winning film directors and he doesn't like what he sees. By the time he buzzes the number for Curtis Loewe's flat he wishes he was dealing with a breach of the peace on the Mozart Estate instead.

'Do come in. Huxtable, did you say?'

Jay lets himself into the lobby at the sound of the buzzer. Makes his way to the top floor in the lift. When he emerges, he finds the man himself waiting for him in the entrance, dressed in jeans and a navy jumper, all understated except for the red suede slip-ons, no socks, that encase his feet.

He looks like a well-preserved version of his younger self. Trapped between middle age and old age. His face shines like silk, as if he's been buffing it all morning in anticipation of Jay's arrival.

'DS Jay Huxtable.'

Curtis shakes his hand. 'Good to meet you. Come inside. Let me get you a drink.'

He's pleased to see some celebrities have manners.

Jay sinks back on the leather sofa, his knees coming up to his chin, wishes he'd opted for the armchair where Curtis is sitting upright.

'Now do tell me what brings you here.'

At the sound of Gabriel Miller's name, Curtis claps his hands and slumps back into the chair laughing. 'Good God, I've heard it all now.' He chuckles away for a good minute before pulling himself upright again to face Jay. 'We discussed a part. He has this manager, Palab, a very successful man, but he's a pushy little fellow. He's been trying to get Gabriel in one of my animations for a while. We discussed the role of the Elliot the pig . . . I know what you're thinking, a part made for that man, but his

171

voice is just too high. And between you and me, I need people I can rely on.' He puts his index finger to his nose and sniffs. 'I hear his reputation is well earned.'

'Did he attend a party at your house?'

'Attend as in he turned up, drunk as a fish, then proceeded to powder his nose in the bedroom. How the man could have ascertained the age of anyone there is beyond me. The last time I spoke to him that night he couldn't have told me his own age. Look, I'll be straight with you. I throw a party every now and then. I like to let my hair down. I invite my friends, they bring their girlfriends . . . beautiful women, let me tell you . . .' He leans a bit closer so Jay catches his aftershave, feels like he's taking him into his confidence. 'Not always their wives, yeah . . . People stay the night. I have fifteen bedrooms in that damn place. I'm sure some of them have sex, yes . . . I know, some people have sex. It's not a crime. Do you want to lock people up for having sex?'

Jay wishes he hadn't mentioned sex. His mind is whirling again. Stacey is undressing in front of him, pushing him down on to the bed, covering his face with her tits.

'Were you aware of anyone there being underage?'

'Of course not. It's not a crèche. It's a party for adults. I know who I invited and I'll happily provide you with the names. I can't vouch for who they brought along. It's bloody hard these days. The seventeen-year-olds look like they're twenty-five and vice versa. But the idea that it was some kind of planned mass underage orgy is preposterous. It was very laid-back. Champagne, cocktails, music, dancing. I'm sure you know the thing.'

Jay does not know the thing but he's flattered Curtis thinks he might.

Curtis stands and walks over to a mahogany sideboard and withdraws a small leather box. 'Cigar?'

Jay shakes his head.

'They're very good.' The smoke clouds his features so all Jay can see for a moment is two glassy eyes and the orange glow of his cigar.

'The only problem I have out there is security, but I'm afraid your lot don't seem at all bothered by break-ins any more. I'm having to sort it out myself. You seem like a man who looks after himself, am I right?' Jay smiles. He likes the gym, glad someone notices. His muscles ripple in reply.

'I like to keep myself fit.'

'Good man. Kids, wife?'

'Neither.'

'Ah, best way. Haven't found the right woman yet. Well, when this is all cleared up, as I have no doubt it will be, get in touch if you fancy some extra work. Always good to have someone sensible on board with security.'

He passes Jay a card. Chadwick Security. 'The firm I use.'

'Thanks. I'll keep it in mind.'

'Please do. Was there anything else?'

'I don't think so for the moment.'

As predicted, the investigation reaches a dead end. No witnesses, no victims, Gabriel Miller's word against Curtis Loewe's. He enjoys telling Gabriel there is insufficient evidence to proceed, likes the way the silence between them crackles with anger.

And when he informs Curtis Loewe that he has nothing to worry about, he puts the phone down assuming that will be the last he will see or hear of the man, in person at least.

But he is wrong, because the next month Jay finds himself in a spot of trouble.

He's spent the day with his mates at the match (Chelsea lost) and having sunk ten pints of Stella Artois, he is wandering home when he realises he is not far from the flat Stacey shares with Toby. Before he knows it, he's standing outside looking up to the second floor where he sees a low, moody light escape from the living room. They're probably having a takeaway or a shag on the sofa, Jay thinks, at which point the kebab he's just eaten turns violent in his stomach. When he spots Toby's red BMW sitting outside, he knows exactly what he is going to do. Jay was never a grade-A art student but every boy grows up knowing how to draw a knob and, pleased to find his skills have not deserted him, he carves one out on the bodywork. His only regret is the size of it. It's too big. Toby definitely has a small cock.

Unfortunately, Toby also lives on a busy street with CCTV cameras. Jay should have thought about this. Should have thought, full stop, but the ten pints didn't leave any room for thinking. So you could say he wasn't covering all his bases in the normal sense. Satisfaction, that was what he was after. To teach the guy a lesson. In the end they didn't need the CCTV because Toby (and now Stacey's) neighbour filmed him doing it. Again, that might not have been such a big deal (you couldn't see his face) were it not for the fact he was wearing his football training jacket with *Huxtable* emblazoned on the back.

'Who's the knob now?' DCI Patel asks. Huxtable, in possession of his faculties once again, deduces this is a non-rhetorical question. He says nothing. 'Your stupidity might cost you your job.'

He suspends him, pending investigations. 'I should tell you it's not looking good,' he says in the understatement of the year. 'It's a shame, because you could have had a good career. But if you want to blame anyone, look no further than yourself.'

Jay doesn't fancy looking at himself. It is the last thing he wants to do. His job is a barrier between him and the estate people. Makes him better than the next scrote. Now DCI Patel is stripping it away and he doesn't like it one bit.

He goes to the pub. Stella got him into this situation, Stella can console him now. He fishes in his pocket for change and finds a card instead. Chadwick Security. Curtis fucking Loewe.

Jay drains his pint and orders another. He will call the number tomorrow when his head is clear.

After the police force, it doesn't feel like a job. It doesn't have a description other than security and he doesn't have a rank. He's just Jay, the man who drives a Beamer (Up yours, Toby) and works for Curtis at his house which is really a mansion in the Cotswolds. After a month, he gets invited to a party. 'You'll have to do a bit of work, but I like to keep my staff happy. There'll be time for fun too,' Curtis says. Jay is transformed, has barely thought of Stacey once.

He looks different too. The Burton suits are out. It's amazing what money can do for a man. Bought himself some designer gear, a suit that fits like it was made for him. Christ, he feels good.

At the party, he's introduced to John, a Scottish guy who shows him the ropes. He's to take the guests' keys and park their cars around the back. Some of the faces he recognises, some he doesn't. But he knows enough to sense they're rich. The air is thick with the smell of money. He's mainlining it, can't help smiling as it rushes through his bloodstream.

By midnight John says their work is done. 'Time for a drink.' John finds them a beer, although Jay had fancied a champagne, just because. He's got a bit of catching up to do by the looks of things, everyone is well into the evening, but the strangest thing is he doesn't feel out of place. Not even when the most fucking gorgeous woman sidles up to him. 'I'm Mariela,' she says, and her breath hits every sex-starved nerve ending. She's wearing a dress that defies gravity, sliced to the bone of her sternum and scooped out all the way down to her arse. Is she for real?

Her presence spins him out. She gets more drinks, talks to him like he's the most important man in the room. He's grown five inches in her company. She whispers in his ear, 'Follow me.'

Who is he to argue?

It happens quickly, although given the choice Jay would like to stretch out every moment until it's ready to snap. Mariela is kneeling. Not his idea. He didn't even ask. But here she is. Just the thought of it makes him want to come. Steady, he tells himself. Her tongue is on him. Stacey is smashed out of the water. Obliterated. He holds on and holds on until he's ready to explode. He comes like it's his first time, his last time. All the other times rolled into one.

They drink some more. He gives it a while, not long. Then it's his turn. Mariela likes it hard. He wants to consume her. She couldn't be more perfect.

Life is good. Great in fact. Sometimes his face hurts because he smiles so much. They used to call him Happy in the station to be ironic, but when John calls him Sunshine, he knows it is because he's pumping out the megawatts. DCI Patel hasn't been in touch with the date of his hearing but as far as he's concerned he can stick his job where the sun doesn't shine. *Who's the knob now?*

Curtis likes him too. Sometimes, at the house in the Cotswolds, they share a beer. 'Got to stay on your toes in this game, always someone plotting your downfall.' Jay had no idea film-making was so cut-throat. 'Not the film-making. The politics, the charity. I do a lot of public work. My head is above the parapet, so to speak. And in this country, no one likes a success. I'm telling you, I should have gone to the States years ago.'

The latest person who wants to cut him down is a woman called Linda Moscow who happens to be Gabriel Miller's mother. It all makes sense now. 'She must have put him up to lodging the complaint against me,' Curtis says. 'She's a one-hundred-carat bitch, that woman. And she knows I have something on her. She's out to destroy me.'

Jay is not a particularly emotional man ('It's like having a conversation with a wall' – Stacey) but he can see Curtis is upset and he doesn't like it. Curtis is the man who has given him money and a Beamer and the suit he's wearing (he tried DKNY, today's number is Paul Smith), not to mention Mariela, but he can't think of her right now because he'll go hard and that's not a good look in front of his boss. In the simple equation Jay makes, Curtis = success and sex and feeling happy for the first time in months. Anyone who is going to subtract from that total is no friend of his.

'Now that Gabriel's mudslinging hasn't stuck, she's trying a different tack.' He reaches for his iPad on the table. 'See this website? My charity helped many of these women when they were girls. So they didn't make it in theatre or TV, that's not my fault. This is what I mean. You try to help people and they throw it back in your face. They want to squeeze me for money, blackmail me. And Linda is encouraging them. Take a look.'

Jay takes the iPad from Curtis. Makes a note of the website: www.whathappenedatkelmore.com.

'This woman who set the site up, I want you to find her and find out what they're up to. I want to know what they are planning.'

'How am I going to do that?' he asks.

'Be creative. What do you think I pay you for?'

# Autumn 1996

## *Charlie*

Bex and I made it to London. Not the London of dreams and riches or the Cool Britannia of the nineties; our London was a scummy little sideshow. A studio above a kebab shop barely bigger than the bed we shared. We took to walking through the West End, inhaling the black cab fumes, soaking up the sound of hawkers selling their wares, posing next to the theatre billboards, the musicals, *Cats*, *Phantom of the Opera*, *Mousetrap*. 'One day it'll be us!' I said, but when I saw the look in Bex's eyes I wished I'd kept my mouth shut. Who wants to be reminded of what they're not going to be?

The closest Bex got was a job interview at the Cambridge Theatre on Earlham Street, but two days later they told her that her application hadn't been successful. 'They didn't think I had the right kind of experience,' she said. 'Like, what kind of experience do you need to sell ice creams during the interval?' She lit the letter with a match and watched it burn until the flame licked her hand and she threw it in the sink.

'You were too good for it anyway.'

'Obviously not.'

'There will be others.'

'How would you know?' She opened a bottle of wine and filled her mug to the brim, slurped it like cola. By the third mug she started to cry. At the end of the fourth she threw up.

\*

On the other hand my CV was a riot of indiscriminate postings, random shifts at frozen food factories in far-flung corners of the North Circular, catering in an old people's home, a summer job on a hot-dog stall, and finally 'floor manager' in Stratos' Café, where the only people I managed were myself and the cleaner. Stratos, a Greek man in his fifties, was fat and balding and had, as far as I could see, an outrageous approach to food hygiene. His business only survived because it was in Soho. An endless supply of tourists meant he didn't have to rely on repeat custom.

I was about to say what Bex did all day was a mystery, but this isn't strictly true. She made drinking her hobby; secretly at first, so I would get a waft of vodka through Polo mints and wonder whether it was my imagination or was she really a bit pissed.

Sometimes she wouldn't come home. She'd turn up the next day having lost hours. Her nails filthy, her skin the colour of Stratos' jacket potatoes. On a bad day there would be bruises; mostly on her arms, her legs, but occasionally they crept on to her face. 'A fall,' she'd say, if my eyes asked any questions. But the worst times were when she came back with money, because Bex didn't have a job and the thought of her earning that cash broke me in such a way I threw it back at her, told her where to stick it.

I should have done more to help. Every time I caught sight of Bex's disappearing frame and the spots on her face and the way the light never entered her eyes any more, I knew I should do something. But what? We were floundering in our own distinct ways: Bex drinking to anaesthetise herself and me auto-piloting to work every day, losing myself in coronation chicken and tuna and cheese toasties. Was this it? Was this all there was? We had empty lives and no idea how to fill them.

There was one weekend when I locked the doors and refused to let her out.

'It's an intervention,' I said. Too much American TV to

thank for that. She was sweet at first, lucid. 'I know, you're right . . .' Full of sorrys and tears and snot. 'We can get through this together,' I said, and made us spag bol and a cup of tea. But after she pushed a few twirls of pasta around her plate the air changed, her need polluted it. The remorse ebbed away, along with her willpower. Promises evaporated. 'Let me out,' she said.

*Bitch.*

At ten o'clock she pushed past me and when I came after her she punched me. The blood burst from my lip. It tasted like the end. But it wasn't. That had still to come.

It was September, around six o'clock. My legs were heavy and I prayed the woman nursing her cup of tea would bugger off so I could close up. My heart dived when I heard the bell above the door tinkle. Another customer. It began to race when I saw who it was.

'Charlie, is that you?'

I toyed with saying no, pretending I was her doppelganger.

'Miss Reilly.'

'How *are* you?'

She was kind enough not to wait for an answer. 'Lovely to see you. What time do you finish?'

'Depends on how long she stays.' I nodded to the woman with the tea.

'Don't worry, I'm going,' she said. 'I was only trying to avoid the rain. The sandwich was disgusting by the way.'

She wasn't Miss Reilly any more. 'Why don't you call me Gabby.' I wasn't sure I could, or wanted to. It was over-familiar, twisted our relationship into something it wasn't.

'Let me buy you a coffee . . . dinner. I've often wondered . . .' She let the ellipsis hang.

As soon as I sat down and the waiter issued us with menus I

knew it was a mistake. I had left Kelmore behind. And though she was one (the only one) of the nice teachers, I didn't want the conversation to drag me back there.

Besides, I wasn't hungry.

I brought her up to date, skirted over the Bex situation. 'She's fine, picking up work here and there.' By the time we had ordered our food, I had exhausted the chat.

'I'm sorry,' she said.

'What for?'

She stared at me, her eyes all-knowing, and it sat between us for a moment as she considered how to pierce it and pin it down and say its name out loud.

'I reported it to the police, you know. They said unless I had evidence they couldn't take it further. They accused me of being an embittered former employee, said I had been sacked because I had touched a girl . . . made it out like it was me in the wrong . . . I didn't, you know. I would never ever do anything like that.'

'I know,' I told her.

'Thank you. It wasn't your fault.'

'I . . . I . . .' Words drifted away from me. She saw everything. She saw everything I wasn't. Not the young woman who was making her way in the world, who wore lipstick and didn't look too bad, who smiled on cue. She knew they were fake. What she wanted was to talk to me, the real me beneath them, pick me apart so she could lessen her guilt.

Suddenly I was properly angry. What made this woman with the neat hair and the soft voice and the baby-pink sweater think that her concern mattered, amounted to anything, could make a difference to us? What gave her the right to probe and push and ask questions in the search for answers she had no business knowing?

'Shall I tell you something? We chose it.' The force of the words winded me. I hadn't spoken them before, hadn't admitted them to myself, but here it was, out in the open, the truth that ate away at me, at Bex. *We let it happen.* Miss Reilly or Gabby or whoever she was tried to dive in but I wouldn't let her, not now the admission was out there. There was no stopping me.

'We wanted to go. Do you hear what I'm saying? We would have done anything to get out of Kelmore. And we were gutted when it stopped. Does that fit your picture? Didn't think so. So what does that make us? You think you understand. You drove out of Kelmore every day and went home to your nice life and you shut the door. You only ever dipped a toe in. But it was all we had. That awful building with its smell of decay and damp and the shit food and the teachers who made us so small we almost disappeared. So when they came along and offered us something else, we took it. It was our choice. We could have stopped it and we chose not to.'

I took a breath and doubled over, gripped by a pain that made the room tilt and spin and the picture in front of my eyes fizz with interference. It was as if the confession had torn into me, ripped out a malignant growth, a tumour that had been polluting and poisoning. And now it was laid out before us I couldn't decide whether it was all for the best to speak the truth, or whether I should have kept it hidden.

She waited a moment before she gripped my hand with an anger so hot it chased the pain away.

'Don't you dare. Don't you fucking dare!' *Fucking*. Now there was a shock. Hadn't expected that from Miss Reilly, or those eyes of hers to stab me with such fury. 'It was their fault. They knew exactly what they were doing. They knew you were vulnerable. That's what they want you to think. If you believe that, they win. Do you want them to win?'

That night after I left Miss Reilly, the heavens opened, sheets of rain came down creating rivers in the backstreets and lanes.

'You should go to the police, report it,' she said, and gave me her number. In return I gave her a warning to mind her own. We didn't need her meddling, we were fine, just fine.

Bex wasn't at home when I arrived sodden and freezing but that was fine too, wasn't it, because she would be OK wherever she was. Me, the master of self-delusion, stick your head in the sand, turn the other way, avoid the truth until you can't avoid it any longer.

It was gone ten o'clock when the moment came, announced by the buzzer. I went downstairs and found Bex slumped in the doorway, the stench of vomit thick on her clothes, eyes semi-open, lolling to the back of her head. I couldn't move her, not by myself, not upstairs, and there was no one else to ask so I put her in the recovery position, tried to rouse her, called her name, and when she didn't wake I rang 999.

'She's lucky to be here,' the doctor said. *Lucky.* Not a word I would have used.

'If she carries on like this, she won't be much longer.'

I used my last tenner to bring her home in a taxi, watched her sleep. How thin she had become, her jaw sharp, the downy hairs that feathered her emaciated arms. My beautiful friend. She believed she was worthless and the effort of heaving her worthless body around day after day was too much. She drank to disappear. Soon she'd be gone altogether.

It wasn't her fault.

Mine neither.

We had to report it to the police. Not for Miss Reilly or the girls before or after us. We had to do it because we needed to hear it wasn't OK. To know we were worth something. To survive.

I called Miss Reilly the next day, used Stratos' phone when he was out having a fag.

'You've made the right decision,' she said.

★

We dressed plain for the police station. Neither of us said it, but we didn't want to look like sluts. No make-up. No hairspray.

*No blame.*

We were seen by a male officer at first until Gabby Reilly, who'd come with us, insisted we saw a woman. That was another hour to wait. The police station smelled of Kelmore, of stagnant air and decay. Bex shuffled and tutted a lot. I prayed for them to get a move on and see us before she took flight.

DS Priya Sulliman shook our hands and smiled a lot, which I thought was a bit inappropriate given the subject matter.

She smiled when she said, 'How old were you when it started?'

'Fifteen.'

'Where were you taken?'

'Lots of places. Apartments in London. A house in the countryside. The theatre, the studio.'

*We'd do it anywhere.*

We gave her the names of the men we were introduced to and she smiled.

We said Curtis Loewe's name. That made her smile disappear.

'This stopped two years ago. Why haven't you said anything before now?'

'Because they were scared, for goodness' sake!' Gabby said. I was glad she was there. I didn't have an answer.

'Did you drink at these parties?'

'Yes.'

'Were you drunk?'

'Probably.'

'Did you take drugs?'

'Yes.'

'And you didn't tell anyone at Kelmore?'

Another sigh from Gabby. 'They were the ones facilitating it.'

We told her everything, laid ourselves bare, stared at the discoloured posters on the walls as we described the men, the rooms, the drugs and drink, the force. *Don't be a tease, relax. I can make you a star, legs wide open. Remember to smile for the camera.*

'What happens now?' I said.

'Are you going to arrest them?' Bex asked.

'We will fully investigate the allegations.'

'Just let it go. I told you nothing would happen.'

It had been two months and we hadn't heard a thing from the police. 'No one cares. Why is that so hard to understand? It's just us, me and you, they don't give a stuff.'

'They have to,' I said. We were dealing with the situation in our different ways. Anger had taken root inside me, grew stronger every day. It made me tall, pushed me through crowds on the Tube, on the street. It made me sharper and brighter, switched me on. The flip side was the world stung more than it used to; seeing kids out in the park playing with their families, watching couples hooking hands, owning their happiness. But I wouldn't have traded it. I held on to my anger. I sensed it could be the making of me.

Bex, on the other hand, had started drinking again.

'Can you no concentrate?' Stratos said. 'This eez tuna and this eez egg mayonnaise. Yes?'

'Sorry.'

'What eez the matter with Charlie, eh?' Stratos held his arms open wide for a hug. ''As someone upset you?'

I ducked out of the way. Despite his shortcomings in the food hygiene department, I had grown fond of Stratos but physical contact was a step too far.

It was the letter that had shot my concentration. I couldn't turn my mind to anything else. I found it the previous night while changing Bex's sheets after another vomiting episode. It was tucked down the side of her bed in an envelope addressed to both of us. The seal had been broken. Bex had hidden it from me.

> *Dear Ms Pedlingham and Ms Alderly,*
>
> *I hope you forgive the direct approach but I understand that you are former residents of Kelmore School for Girls and have recently made a complaint to the police about the abuse you suffered during your time there.*
>
> *The documents detailing the claims have been passed to me – leaked, if you will – by someone who feels your case deserves to be fully investigated. I'm sure you know some powerful figures are involved. It is my understanding that they are applying pressure to have these allegations buried.*
>
> *Sometimes it falls to the press to expose injustices and wrongs, and I believe yours is one such case. If you are willing, I would like to talk to you in private. I can assure you that your identities will be protected.*
>
> *I'd be grateful if you could contact me on 0171 467 4098.*
> *Kind regards,*
> *Jonathan Clancy,*
> *The Times*

Laughably, he had suggested coming to our flat. Only a man with no previous experience of bedsits would suggest that.

'So we can all sit on the bed together and have a nice chat? Tell him to fuck off,' Bex said. She'd accused me of going behind her back by calling him.

'You hid it from me in the first place,' I countered.

'Because I knew this would happen. I knew you'd suck up to him and get me involved. And I'm right, aren't I?'

'He's taking us to a steak restaurant,' I said. 'I told him he couldn't come here.'

'I'm a vegetarian.'

'Since when?'

'Since now.'

'Let's practise,' I said. I was attempting to force some toast and a coffee down Bex before we set off. 'It would be good to run through what we need to tell him.'

She pushed the toast away. 'You think?'

'It might make it easier.'

Her hair was shower-wet, skin scrubbed red and blotched. Eyes robbed of sleep. 'How about this then,' she drew a breath. 'There were men. Lots of them, and we let them fuck us every which way for a can of Fanta and a bag of crisps. Sometimes it wasn't just Fanta. It was vodka or whisky. It was even champagne the first time, but that was just to impress us. They weren't all bad. The thing is they were much nicer than the teachers at Kelmore who didn't actually fuck us. And they did nice things like show us the sights of London. We saw the Tower of London, Big Ben, surely that's worth a man of fifty slamming into you three hours later? A fair exchange. Of course we could have stopped it; we were asked if we wanted to go back and we said yes. We were desperate, you see, and they could smell the stench of desperation rolling off us. They said it was a really special secret, so special that even if we had told anyone – which we didn't – they wouldn't have believed us. No one would have believed us then and no one believes us now.

'What you need to understand is that we thought there were two choices: go with those men or stay at Kelmore. No one ever offered us anything else, nothing pure like love or attention or praise, without taking more from us than they gave. The worst thing was the trick of it, making me feel like I wanted it, that it was happiness – that's what shames me most. It has left this thing inside me, this deep, throbbing mass that gives off noises and throws out colour and distorts the day. Every day. It doesn't have a name. I don't know what it is, but it's so fucking heavy I can barely carry myself around. It's just there,' she punched her stomach, 'and it will always be there.' Bex let out a groan, a noise that came from somewhere hidden away, deep and visceral.

'Bex . . .' I said. I reached for her and we fell into each other, my pain touching hers, burning away inside us.

Jonathan's voice could have cut glass. I wished it was a Brummie accent or Welsh. Not the Queen's English. At least he didn't have the smart suit like Curtis Loewe. A stain sat proudly on the lapel of his jacket. His shirt-tail hung out of his trousers, buttons fastened unevenly.

His appearance gave me a crumb of hope.

He had nabbed a booth at the back of the restaurant. The menu was expensive, six different kinds of steak to choose from. A photograph of the cow they killed to make it.

Flank, rump, fillet. I thought of all the corresponding parts of my body, parcelled up in much the same way.

Jonathan seemed like a pleasant bloke, a bit wet, not the kind to fill me with confidence. His hair fell over his face and he'd take the errant piece and place it back where it came from, only for it to fall again.

Bex chose steak and chips and a Diet Coke. Jonathan told the waiter he wanted his bloody, almost blue. I didn't have to look at Bex to know she was screwing up her face. I went for steak, well done. 'Scorched,' I told the waiter, noting his disapproval.

Bex ate her chips with the enthusiasm of someone who hadn't been fed for months, as if she'd forgotten why we were here. Jonathan cut his steak in small, precise squares and chewed it at the front of his mouth so he reminded me of a rodent. In between mouthfuls he attempted small talk. 'What do you do?'

'This and that,' Bex said.

'I work in hospitality,' I said. Bex sniggered. I immediately hated myself for trying to impress him.

'Why were you sent to Kelmore?'

'Because we were bad girls.'

'My mum died. I went off the rails after that,' I said.

He finished the last piece of beef, loaded a chip and the remaining bit of broccoli on to his fork, driving away the gravy.

He chewed it thoroughly and when he was finished he placed a small Dictaphone on the table between us and said: 'When did it start?'

We stripped ourselves naked in words, splayed our legs again. We gave everything away. We told it fast, without stopping or looking at him, because we were scared we might find blame and disbelief in his eyes, or the words, *You brought it all on yourself* written on his face. We gave him names – Alex, Curtis, Greg, Henry. Described locations as best we could remember. I focused on his Dictaphone, imagined it sucking all our words, reconfiguring them later to build the case against the men.

'I'm going to do all I can to expose this. It will take time. Don't expect quick results. I'm sure they'll try to block it, but I'm not the kind of person who takes kindly to being pressurised, do you understand me? It makes me want to get them all the more. You have my number. Call me if you need to talk, otherwise I'll be in touch and let you know how it's going, OK?'

'OK.'

He paid the bill. 'Don't hang around for me, I have a few calls to make.'

We said goodbye and as we turned to go he said, 'By the way, it's them, not you. Always remember that.'

I tucked his words away for safekeeping and walked out into the bright afternoon with Bex. We held hands all the way to the number 37 bus stop.

A few weeks after meeting Jonathan Clancy, the police called and we were summoned to meet. DS Priya Sulliman, straight-faced this time.

'I'm afraid . . .' she said.

*Not for you to be afraid. That's our job.*

'. . . there is insufficient evidence to continue with the investigation.'

I waited for the smile, the joke, the punchline. Instead, a flush to her cheeks, teeth clamped down on her lips. Contagious, this shame.

I turned to Bex. Eyes full of hate towards the DS, Gabby Reilly. Myself.

Jonathan, our last hope. A meeting in Hyde Park. Bex was resistant, 'You want this, not me.'

I worked on her all morning. Begging, pleading, bribing. Eventually she caved when I threw in a Big Mac and milk-shake.

He was circling the bench when we arrived, too much energy to sit on it and more dishevelled than before. He knew about the police, I'd called him straight after, didn't sound surprised but was still upbeat, confident. Less so now.

'I'm sorry,' he said.

*Don't want to hear that word.*

'For what?'

'I can't take it any further. I . . .'

*I can't be arsed.*

*I don't believe you.*

*I've been warned off.*

A lightning strike to my head, my whole body charged with pain. I salvaged two words from the rubble. 'You promised.'

'I'm so sorry. I didn't want this.'

Bex spun out, paced backwards and forwards. 'Why did

you ask us to tell you all that? Did you get a kick from it? Is that it?'

'Please . . .'

'You shouldn't fuck with people.' Rage steamed off her. 'Why us? You came to us, remember. Why didn't you just leave us alone?'

'Because I wanted to do this, I do want to. I will. I just can't now.'

'You said you couldn't be pressurised.'

'It's not what you think, I promise. It's complicated. Very complicated.'

'Why did you do this?' She wasn't screaming at him now, was aiming for me. 'I told you, didn't I. Why wouldn't you listen?' She pushed me, some force in that tiny body.

'Bex, please,' Jonathan intervened, tried to hold her back. 'It's not Charlie's fault. It's mine. I'm sorry. I won't let this pass. I will get to them, somehow, but right now I can't.'

'Get off me.' Her scream travelled down to the Serpentine, across the water to the swings, the sandpit, drowned out shrieks from children and laughter and the whispers of kissing couples.

And the thing was, nobody stopped to say, Are you OK? Do you need help? Can we do anything for you?

Everybody walked on by.

No matter how much noise she made.

No one could see her.

Bex ran away, out of the park, sucked up by the London throng. No point in following her, I thought. She needed space, time to calm down, and my presence would only make her worse. I stayed back, with the one question I had to ask Jonathan.

'If it isn't them, what is stopping you?'

He said the person who leaked the information to him was a friend and had been put in an impossible situation.

'She's not a bad person,' he said. 'She wants to get to the truth as much as I do.'

'Then what could be so important for her to sacrifice it?'

He couldn't answer that.

Bex didn't come home. I searched pubs and bars, scoured parks at night and during the day. Walked the streets listening for her voice, watching for her shadow. I called the police. Unsurprisingly, they showed little interest in finding her.

I waited days, weeks, months for her to return, for a letter, a note, a telepathic message just to say she was OK.

My anger at the police, at Jonathan, at his source, set into hatred. To them, we were collateral damage, pawns in their game.

And now Bex had gone.

Easy to disappear when you are invisible in the first place.

# Thursday 2.51 p.m.

## Linda

'Henry thought ye might like some reading material, tae pass the time so tae speak.' It isn't Huxtable. It's the Scot, dumping a pile of newspapers on the chest of drawers. 'He's some character, that boy of yours.' His presence flushes the air with a disturbing energy. I try not to think what those shovel-like hands might have done, what those dead eyes have seen.

He leaves me with a wink. 'Laters.'

I ignore them for as long as my willpower allows. My logic is this: Henry wants me to read them, therefore I shouldn't. But the temptation is too strong and the afternoon too empty of distraction. After ten minutes I spread them out on the carpet and allow the full horror of the stories to assault me.

### Sleazy Secrets of TV Comic

### The Dark Side of the Funnyman

### A Sexual Predator

These are just a few of the choice headlines. Every woman who's so much as looked at Gabriel in the past five years has offered her two penn'orth: 'There was another side to him that scared me,' said Laetitia from Surrey. (Scared her so much she went back for more the following week.)

Legally, they aren't allowed to call Gabriel a murderer. Innocent until proven guilty. But the papers only pay lip service to the law. His guilt protrudes from every word and sentence. Even his professional photographs have been made to look sinister: *What is he hiding behind the smile?*

I scour the columns for Mariela's name. Has he been accused of my murder and hers too? One killing away from becoming a serial killer. The only information I can find are a few paragraphs on page two of the *Telegraph* saying police are still investigating the murder of another woman close to Gabriel's house. Nothing else.

Our mother/son relationship is held aloft for forensic scrutiny. Had life in the public eye affected the young Gabriel? Had I been too soft/too hard on him? Too absent? In one, there is a feature under the banner, NO, WOMEN CAN'T HAVE IT ALL, a neat photo of me as Home Secretary to illustrate how a woman's decision to pursue a career can have deadly consequences.

Then there is the army of psychologists wheeled out to waffle on for eight hundred words about our relationship. *Did Gabriel always feel inferior?*

Every possible line of examination and discussion is wrung dry. It is an editor's dream, after all – ex Home Secretary's son held for her murder. What hubris!

But what tops off all the acres of utter nonsense are the quotes from my friends.

*Bernadette Mulligan, a close friend of the family, said she was numbed by the news, 'I'm absolutely devastated. Linda was my best friend for more than forty years,' but she added, 'I've known Gabriel since he was a baby and he was always trouble. Linda could never see the wrong in him.'*

*'Words cannot express my sadness,' said Mrs Moscow's former colleague Henry Sinclair. 'Linda was a great friend and inspiration. She worked tirelessly for what she believed in, and*

*many of the advances in child protection are a credit to her. It's particularly sad because Linda was a wonderful mother who would have done anything for her son.'*

Each word of Henry's sends a dart of pain shooting through me. He has no shame, nothing sticks to him, no dirt, no suspicion. I stand by the window, look out at the darkness circling, sucking the light from the day. These men are untouchable. Unassailable. And unless I find a means of escape, they will remain so.

I go to the door, hammer on it with my fist. I summon my voice, force it out. 'Someone come . . . please!' I regret the 'please' but politeness is a hard habit to kick. I listen for a reaction but hear only snippets of chat rolling up from the living room. 'Help me!' I scream.

Nothing.

Then.

Footfall.

Keys twisting in the lock, the sound judders through me. The door is pushed open. Anna stands there with her finger to her lips.

*Shhhh.*

So much to say, to squeeze into a moment. Questions thrash at my skull. *Why why why?* But not now. We exchange a look, packed with too much meaning to decipher.

'I'm desperate for the loo,' I say. Back to the script.

She turns to check the hallway behind her before standing aside. 'Be quick.' Her voice is a comfort, it is Anna again. But I tell myself not to be fooled.

The bathroom is next to my bedroom. Quietly, I slip inside, close the door, trying not to invite creaks or groans, any noise at all.

The small window key. I pull it out of my pocket. A ribbon of sunlight gleams on the metal, all that is left of my hope. But first, I fill a cup with water, pour a little down the loo for Anna's benefit, should she be listening.

Jittery fingers guide the key into the lock. It turns, first time.

*Don't say it's too easy.*

I press the pane of glass and the window creaks open with a child's whine. I peer out. The drop is about five foot, nothing more. I climb on to the loo, then on to the ledge.

*How did it come to this?*

*Shut up and jump.*

I land on my shoulder, the grass damp and cold against my cheek. Pain trickles down my back but I drive it away with an order: *Get to the road. Get help.*

I start to run – as good as – hunkering as low as possible, hiding in the uneven tufts of grass.

I'm covering ground, moving at pace. I steal a look behind me. Anna's face a smudge of white at the open window.

'Linda.' She is barely audible.

Then. 'LINDA!' She shouts this time.

Shouts but doesn't move. Not an inch.

She's not coming to get me.

I turn eyes back towards the path ahead, fix them on moving forward. *Run run as fast as you can. Ignore the roar of your lungs, the acid streaming through your legs. Concentrate on the rhythm of your motion. All you have to do is seal this moment off so they can't breach it. Stretch it out for as long as it takes to get help.*

But.

A tumble leaves me sprawled in the mud. I scramble to recover. I can't give up, not when I'm this close to the path, the road, the sound of the water, to saving Gabriel.

More shouts inject the air, pack it full of surprise and panic. They're not Anna's this time, they belong to the Scot, to Huxtable, and they're chasing me down, an army of feet gaining ground. The road, the road, I try to draw it closer. I can see the opening now, a car passes by.

Help! I'd shout, if I had any breath left.

The ground begins to shake, the thunder of their footsteps. They are near, running at twice my speed. They are hunters. I am their prey.

The first contact sends me hurtling forward.

A crack. The sound of bone against rock. Pain consumes me. Obliterates everything else.

I count four boots and two trainers. The toe of one boot digs into my skull. 'Ye need tae be a bit faster next time.' The Scot yanks me up. My wrist dangles from my arm as if attached by a thread.

'I think Anna here needs tae teach ye a lesson. You could've got her intae a lot of trouble running away like that. Isn't that right, Anna?'

Her face is leached of colour.

'I said, isn't that right?'

'That's right,' she says.

'I for one,' said the Scot, 'am very upset that Linda decided tae spurn our hospitality. Tae think Henry has gone tae all this trouble. Perhaps she wasn't comfortable enough. Maybe we can do better.'

His fist clenches and my body tightens, readies for the impact.

'Oh, you've no need tae worry about me. I'd never hit a woman . . . Well, maybe not never, but I don't make a habit of it. See her . . .' he points to Anna. 'She can hit a woman because she *is* a woman.' He is pleased with himself, as if he is the only person who could have made such an observation.

Anna's eyes flit between the Scot and Huxtable.

'What are you waiting for, an invitation?'

'I'll take her back to the cottage,' Anna says.

'Or maybe ye don't want tae, is that it?' The Scot is an extraordinarily ugly man with deep lines and ridges slicing up his face. Huxtable hovers behind, eyes to the ground, silent.

Even in my current state, I know Anna is out of her depth, so pale and thin I imagine putting a finger through her and seeing it come out the other side. She's trapped like a fly behind glass. The Scot watches her every move, goads her into action.

'Anna,' he says, harsher this time.

And then she obeys.

Slaps me with such force that I fall back into a tree. It creates a cleft in my body, adds new layers of pain.

I steady myself on the tree trunk as Anna moves closer again, her back towards the Scot and Huxtable. She mouths a word that sits in the silence between us.

*Sorry.*

'A bit feisty that one, eh?' the Scot says, his smile packed with pride. 'I'll take ye back, shall I?' he says to me. 'Make sure you're safe.'

And he does, all the way back to my room, locking the door behind me.

I sit and wait as the night draws close and smothers me in darkness. Tomorrow is on its way and Henry and Curtis have me cornered, just as they did before.

# November 1996

## *Linda*

**B**ad mother. I didn't see it coming. The nausea, sleepiness, stomach pains were all clues, if I had been looking close enough, but I was busy, too busy and I thought he was putting it on, trying to carve a few extra days off school. *Always think the worst before anything else.* I hadn't noticed how much he'd changed, how all the words that used to run out of him in a stream of consciousness had dried up and hardened into silence.

It was the night of Halloween when he collapsed, hit on the head by some delinquent he'd scared, according to Tommy. Kate, Tommy's mother, was beside herself: 'It's all my fault, they weren't supposed to go that far.' It wasn't of course and I didn't blame her for a minute, but Kate's guilt was the least of my worries.

I took fright when I saw him, his pallor, the deathliest of whites, and his lips so red. A gash down his cheek too. I wasn't fully in charge of myself because it took the paramedic to remind me it was Halloween and his face was painted white to look like a ghoul. Kate had done quite a number on him. But even once I was in possession of the facts, I couldn't shake the sense that someone had spirited Gabriel away and left behind only his shadow.

My memory of the following days is foggy. We were thrown into a world of tubes and bleeps and a clinical starkness that chilled me. We were dealing not with a virus or a bug that the days and weeks would make better, but acute liver failure. Every time I ventured out to the loo, or for a gasp of fresh air, I sucked in the colours and the smells, reached out to touch the life that whizzed by on the streets in the hope I could feed it back to Gabriel. I'd known trauma before, tough times, but nothing prepared me for this. It was a new level of grief. My son, my beautiful boy, holding on to life, as thin as a thread.

For many couples, a child's illness brings them closer together. Not us. Hugh tried, at least at first. He was a gentle man and our love had always been the calm, supportive type, without any of the high drama or heated arguments some couples endure. Often, I'd retreat from Gabriel's bedside to grab a cup of tea or some air and on my return I'd stand behind the door watching Hugh stroke his hand, catch whispers of him reading from *The Twits* or *The Lion, the Witch and the Wardrobe* and the scale of his love for the boy winded me. It was total, complete, irrepressible. And yet, having overheard the doctors speak, I knew Gabriel wasn't responding to treatment and he might need a transplant. I could see what was coming like a tsunami gathering force on the horizon.

The consultant wanted to talk to us about the possibility of a familial donor.

'The odds of a mother or a father being a match are thirty per cent. If neither of you is a match, we'll start looking through the register. What helps us in these cases is to know the ethnic origin of the child from the father's side; it gives us a start, if you like, points us in the right direction and can speed up the process,' Dr Zaskias told us. 'We can arrange for testing immediately, if that's what you wish.'

'No reason to wait,' Hugh said. And I rested my hand on his, the last time he would allow such affection.

'I can't let you do it,' I said.

Hugh's brows knotted together in disbelief. 'What are you

talking about?' But I could tell the question wasn't fully formed before the truth hit him.

'I wanted to believe he was yours,' I said, immediately regretting my choice of words. Now wasn't the time for weak excuses. 'I'm sorry. I'm so sorry.'

He looked at me as he might a stranger who was trying to broach an intimate subject and then said in the calmest voice, 'I don't want to know who he is, but if you aren't a match you are going to find him and beg him to do one thing for our son. *Our* son, not his. My son.'

He picked up his polystyrene cup and left the room before I could tell him I didn't know if that was possible. I wasn't sure I had it in me.

I was not a match. God must be evil, if he existed at all. To punish me and punish my son. No other explanation for it.

'There are no suitable donors on the register at the moment,' Dr Zaskias said quietly, so as not to hurt us with his words.

Hugh led me from Dr Zaskias' room to see Gabriel. 'Look at him. Look at our boy.' The tears he'd held back spilled out and collected into sobs. My husband, breaking. 'I would do anything to be able to save him, but I can't. I can't do a thing. Even if there's the smallest chance that it might work, you have to do it.' But I already knew I would. Nothing mattered more than saving Gabriel.

I called ahead and spoke to his secretary, couldn't risk turning up and missing him. I didn't trust myself to go back again.

'Will he know what it's concerning?' she asked.

'I have no idea.'

She asked me to hold the line, came back a few minutes later. 'That shouldn't be a problem.'

★

Affluent Mayfair, red-brick buildings, Land Rovers and Porsches, antique shops, discreet boutiques – I couldn't stand the place. His house loomed up before me. I trawled my mind for alternative options, another way to make my son better. There were none, and Gabriel was all that mattered. I had to overcome the past to give my son a future. I was here because I wanted him to live.

I told my security detail to stay outside and rang the bell. He made me wait, unlike the last time when I was swept inside, a drink pushed into my hand and then another. What had I been doing all those years ago? The answer slapped me. I'd been playing a game. Flirting; I wasn't beyond it, knew that it could be a useful tool in politics. It was after a fundraiser. We wanted money from him and it seemed churlish to reject his invitation. I was thinking of my career and advancement. If I could get him to say yes to the sum we needed, it would get me noticed, give me a push on the career path. The sad thing was, it worked. In that respect, at least, I got exactly what I wanted.

This time he made me wait. It was never going to be any other way. Eventually, he opened the door.

'Linda,' he said. 'To what do I owe the pleasure?'

'Hello, Curtis.'

I followed him upstairs, the walls decked with awards – best director, best screenplay. Posters to promote his films, *The Bear Chronicles*, I, II and III. I never did manage to persuade Gabriel they were overrated.

Inside the drawing room, he offered me tea. 'Or a gin and tonic – wasn't that always your tipple, Linda?' Hadn't been able to drink the stuff since.

'I'm fine.'

'Oh now, don't be rude. It's been so long, and I've made a space in my diary for you. I insist you have tea, and lunch.'

'Tea will suffice.'

He signalled for me to sit on an old slouchy sofa. I chose the leather armchair. Better support.

'Haven't you done well for yourself, Linda. Always did know how to network, maximise your assets.' He emitted a booming laugh.

'I need your help,' I said. Couldn't stand another moment of his talk.

'You do?'

'Gabriel, my son. He's ill. Seriously ill.'

'I'm sorry to hear that, but I fail to see what that's got to do with me.'

'He's yours too,' I told him. 'Gabriel is your son.'

Standing at the window overlooking the square, I recounted the whole story. From this position, I didn't have to watch his reaction. I'm certain he would have feigned surprise if I'd given him an audience, but it was my strong suspicion that they (Curtis and Henry) already knew. *How is Gabriel?* Henry had inquired directly after asking me to cover up the abuse allegations. Besides, it was a lie. Curtis was no more Gabriel's father than the driver who delivered me to his door. It was Hugh who had taken him to the park, taught him how to throw a ball, cheered as he scored a goal. It was into Hugh's arms he snuggled when he wanted five more minutes before bed.

But emotions were swept aside for now. I had to plug away. No one is good or bad, I reminded myself. What I needed to do was dig deep, uncover the tiny fossil of kindness that must have existed inside Curtis.

'He's only twelve,' I said. Had his birthday a few days ago. It couldn't be his last. 'He loves rugby and he's very very funny.' *Don't cry. Do not cry.* I thought about showing him a picture of Gabriel, then decided against it. I didn't want his eyes to steal any part of him. 'There are no available donors. He doesn't have long. He'll die if we don't find anyone. I know it's a lot to ask, but there is no other way. I wouldn't be here otherwise.'

He didn't speak, seconds suspended in the air above us. I

focused on the patterns on the antique rug at my feet. Wished it was magic, that it could fly me away from here. Because I knew this was all for nothing, Curtis was never going to help. Altruism was not a concept with which he was acquainted.

'That's quite a case you've put forward, Linda.' He rose from his seat, moved towards me. 'I was always rather upset it was only that one weekend. We had a good time, didn't we.'

I was straining against my reflexes to fight back, to run, to tell him I didn't want anything from him, never would. And yet I couldn't. He held all the cards. 'Well, didn't we, Linda? It does wonders for a man's ego to be reminded.'

'We . . . we did.' I forced the lie out and a tide of self-loathing engulfed me. Impossible to sink any further.

'I never wanted children myself. But I'm glad I could give you what Hugh couldn't.'

He walked over to stand beside me. His finger brushed my hair back from my face. I stepped back. 'I . . .'

'Oh, for goodness' sake.' His laugh, like swirls of acrid smoke, smothering me. 'Don't worry. You're not exactly to my taste these days. I think you ought to let me consider this for the afternoon at least. It is a big undertaking.'

Hope surged within me. I studied him properly for the first time since I'd arrived and I swore I saw it rising to the surface, a scratch of light glimmering in the black of his eyes.

'Thank you,' I said.

The very next day he came back with an offer to be tested.

No one is good or evil, I thought, not even Curtis.

Curtis was a match for Gabriel. I knew he would be. There was something inevitable about an ending I both wanted and dreaded.

The day after we received the results, Curtis summoned me to his office. I had spent the morning with Gabriel, held his hand and saw his eyes flicker as if he was summoning the strength to push them open. If only love alone could help him.

I wore my best smile, my smartest suit, a touch of gloss on my lips. Whatever it takes, I told myself.

'Take a seat, Linda,' he said. I tried to read the answer on his face. 'This is a lot to ask.' He sat back in his chair, let his statement linger. Curtis knew all about timing, how to use it to create drama. 'There would be huge risks on my part, as I'm sure you are aware. There is also the chance you could wait and a suitable donor would be found.'

He's slipping away. *Doesn't have . . .*

'Time. It all comes down to timing, doesn't it? I understand and, as you say, he is my son even if I've never set eyes on the boy.' He inserted another silence to torment me. 'But I am willing to do it – save the boy's life.'

The relief rushed through me, exploded into hope. With this, Curtis fed me oxygen, let me fill my lungs, before he threatened to cut off the supply once more.

A letter. Pushed across the desk.

It was from me, Home Secretary Linda Moscow, to Chief Superintendent Bill Joplin. The same one Henry had shown me.

*I would ask you to consider the sensible use of police resources in this matter. Would they be better directed at tackling the spike in violent crime we saw last year or engaging in a witch hunt that will only serve to embarrass the force?*

*Yours sincerely,*
*Linda Moscow*
*The Rt Honourable Linda Moscow MP*
*Home Secretary*

My signature. All that was missing.

Curtis handed me a pen.

My boy, the softness of his skin, the smile on his face, eyes set ablaze when the sunlight caught them, I thought of this. Also, the tubes and monitors, bones jutting out from his skin, the grip of his hand on mine, holding on, not wanting to let go, but slipping all the same.

Could I?

Would I?

Live with myself.

Damned if I do.

And if I don't. Damned too.

I signed the letter.

No one is good or bad.

We are all of us capable of both.

# 1996–2013

## Charlie

I stayed in London for two years after Bex left until one day, I finally cracked. The moment came as I was ladling chilli con carne on to a jacket potato at Stratos'. Outside, the sun danced on the street, but all I saw were the dirty marks on the glass, handprints that hadn't been wiped clean, the scuffed paintwork, the sign on the window with a missing S and T, so it read R ATOS CAFÉ. I served the woman her potato and said, no, *thank you*, when she forgot her manners, and then I removed my apron. I told Stratos I was sick.

'You look fine to me,' he said.

I shook my head. 'God's honest truth.'

I had waited long enough for Bex. I couldn't wait any longer.

I cobbled together something that vaguely resembled a CV. I fancied somewhere exotic. Bex and I had come to London for opportunity and riches and the city had trampled on us, brushed us to its margins. It welcomed people from all over the world into its restaurants, theatres, designer shops but it wouldn't even give us a seat on the Tube, never mind a big break. No money, no prospects, no entry. We were on the outside looking in.

I got ahead of myself, imagined a job in the Bahamas or Europe at the very least, a Greek island, the Balearics. But it seemed Greece and Spain had enough waitresses of their own. The only job I was offered was in Loch Lomond.

The Murray was a four-star hotel on the banks of the loch,

owned by the Murray family for four generations. It had a spa and a swimming pool and a laconium (me neither; it's a dry sweat room). I worked nightshift on reception, having majored on the customer services area of expertise during my telephone interview. After a few months, Mhairi, one of the daytime receptionists, said that with a little attention I'd be a shoo-in for the daytime role: 'Carys is leaving – not that anyone'd notice the difference, lazy cow that she is.' We were in her room sharing a bottle of cheap wine. I caught her staring at me.

'What?'

'When was the last time you had your hair cut? Auch, don't look at me like that. I'm only this upfront with people I like.'

'I'm honoured.'

'A month, six, a year maybe?'

'I can't remember.'

'Aye, that'd make sense. And the eyebrows?'

'What about my eyebrows?'

'When was the last time you had them plucked? C'mon, don't tell me you haven't, like, ever?'

I ran a finger over my brow.

'Fuck me, tweezers are your friend, Charlie. Did you not know that?' She marched to the bathroom, returned wielding a pair. 'I'm not going to lie, it'll hurt like a bastard first time.' She topped up my wine. 'Have another drink and we'll get started.'

Halfway through the second bottle Mhairi told me she was a hairdresser too, although she wouldn't be drawn on the specifics of her employment (here and there). 'Honest to God, I can work magic on your hair. You won't recognise yourself.'

The fake-tan application at midnight wasn't my wisest move, but Mhairi insisted, 'You're too peely-wally' (pale and sickly). But she was right about two things: I didn't recognise myself in the morning and I got the job.

★

Unlike London, Loch Lomond greeted me with a smile every morning. In the summer, I'd rise early and go for a run along the banks of the loch, sit with a coffee afterwards and marvel at how the light painted the sky with a different palette each day. I dragged Mhairi up hills with picnics ('Yer fucking joking me, aren't ye?') and pressed my fingertips against the clouds. I watched sunsets spill on to the water, set it on fire. The vastness of the space, its rugged beauty soaked through me, rinsing me clean of London's smog and grime.

Mhairi, who subsequently admitted to having no hairdressing experience whatsoever, had a baby a few years after I arrived. A daughter, Iona, who became my godchild. 'You have to say yes, all my other friends are headbangers.' The baby's father was an Australian barman called Lachlan, who was only supposed to be staying for the summer. They were still together when I left years later.

I worked hard, saved money. I was promoted to deputy manager, then manager. 'And to think you had a face like a smacked arse when you came here,' Mhairi said when I told her. 'It was the eyebrows that did it, I'm telling you.'

I didn't live like a nun exactly, but I was careful not to make any lasting connections. The closest I came was with a Spanish guy called Jorge who arrived in the summer of 2006 to run a youth hostel. He taught me some basic Spanish – 'Me llamo Charlie' – and I showed him the best walks. We had sex halfway up a Munro in the rain. 'If we wait till it stops, it doesn't happen,' Jorge said in broken English.

Jorge wanted more intimacy. 'Tell me about yourself. You are a mystery, Charlie.' I couldn't work out the exchange, what he was supposed to give me and I was supposed to give him. Mainly, I think, he wanted to make me come. And when he started on the performance analytics – 'Eez this good? You like dis?' – I conceded defeat and faked it. I'd always been a good faker.

Eventually, Jorge moved on. His mum was ill, he needed to go back to Spain, would I come with him? (No.) I think he was relieved. A mystery loses its appeal if it can't be solved.

Still, I was happy. I had my job, my friends, my gorgeous goddaughter. I couldn't imagine leaving Loch Lomond – until the news came, twelve years after I arrived, that brought my old life crashing into my new one.

Bex.

A body had been found in a flat in Brighton, having lain there undiscovered for a few days. A search of her bedroom revealed a passport. Did I know a Rebecca Alderly, they asked. She had put me down as her emergency contact.

I don't know why that choked me so much. That after all those years she still cared enough to write my name on an application form, that I was as close as she ever got to having a family.

I arranged a few days off work, packed a bag and caught the train to Brighton the following morning. Hours passed as I scored through the miles that had separated us, thoughts of Bex cramming my mind. I arrived to the smell of the sea and the gulls squawking and swooping, and a line of blue where the sky met the ocean at the bottom of the road. Then I took a taxi straight to the hospital where I finally found her.

Afterwards, the police told me she was known to them, an addict, a sometime streetworker, *one of those women who don't count*. I took all this information about her life, bagged it up and cast it out to sea. This wasn't Bex. It was simply what life had done to her. Once she had had a bright future, fierce ambition crammed into that tiny frame of hers, and they'd taken it and stamped on it and destroyed her. And despite what she'd said all those years ago in Hyde Park, the insults she'd screamed at me, I knew she had wanted to be heard just as much as I had. Bex needed to know that we counted, that our experience mattered. It was the rejection she couldn't take. The same rejection she faced every day and month and year that passed with no investigation, no arrests, no trial, no justice, no voice.

There were six people at her funeral. Me, the priest and a few assorted friends who had shared late chaotic hours with her. She was thirty-one years old. Not even a friend for every year.

The priest said dying so young was a terrible shame and that God would look after her now. Ironic, because he hadn't given a shit about her when she was alive. Which got me thinking, why had I chosen a church in the first place? We'd stopped going as soon as we left Kelmore. And now here we were, sending Bex off listening to the drone of the priest's voice surrounded by the Virgin Mary, Jesus on the cross, the candles, the statues, the gold, sitting on wooden pews as hard and unforgiving as life itself. Why did we need to ask to be absolved of our sins?

We had done nothing wrong.

They didn't play a final hymn. Instead I had asked for 'Fame' (*I'm gonna live forever, I'm gonna learn how to fly*). The priest had protested, it wasn't very appropriate, but I was glad I had insisted.

It was the only thing I got right.

Outside, the day took me by surprise. Spring had snuck up. The blue sky dazzled, a gentle warmth loaded the air and scented it with grass and tulips and new life. I found a bench to rest on and watched as a bird, a tiny fragile little thing, landed in front of me before lifting off on a gust of wind. The afternoon was glorious, blissful, and yet its beauty tainted; every colour and smell and sound, the sharpness and clarity of the picture laid out in front of my eyes, made me ache for my friend. This was all out of Bex's reach now. No second chances, no dreams, nothing. I sank down to the ground, not caring who saw me, what they thought, and I cried ugly tears of rage.

I returned to Loch Lomond, but the moment I stepped out of the taxi I knew I couldn't do it any more. Couldn't find happiness in pretending it was all OK, in faking a life. My anger had a burn to it, an acid taste. All the strength I thought I'd built up crumbled in front of my eyes. My fury seeped into the loch, created a bottomless sea of black, dulled the sky, blunted the hills.

'Fucking hell,' Mhairi said when she saw me. 'You look like utter shite!' I would have laughed if I could. Instead I fell into her and cried and cried like a baby while she drew the truth out of me, line by line, until there was nothing left to say.

Mhairi found me Agnes, a therapist, because, she said, 'This kind of shit needs professional help and I might be a convincing hairdresser but I'm no shrink.'

I went to visit Agnes once a week. A woman with a kind face and blonde hair that sprung out in curls and bounced with her when she walked.

'We're going to give this a name,' she said during my first session. 'It is rape. Abuse, yes, that too, but the bottom line is, this is rape. Rape is never OK, under any circumstances. Remember that. Always remember that.'

Mainly, Agnes would listen but she wasn't averse to making suggestions.

'You do whatever you have to do to make this better. You take control. If you think no one is prepared to write your story or print it, then why not do it yourself?'

By evening, her words had taken seed and flowered.

I started writing a blog.

If you've found this site, there's probably a reason. One you haven't told many people, or anyone. A secret that is grafted to your skin, become who you are. My own secrets have a pulse that beats through me day and night, runs at a different tempo, against my tide. They beat me down when

I want to stand up, silence me when I want to scream.

Firstly, I should say I'm not here to give you comfort. This is about me and my story and finding a place to write it down because, when I speak, no one listens. I could reel off a list of people I've talked to: teachers, the police, a reporter who promised to out the truth. You didn't read that story, did you? Neither did I. It wasn't printed. There was a reason he had to drop it, but he never did explain what that reason was.

It's hard not to be heard, but the toughest part is being heard and not believed.

So here I am.

I don't know where this is going to take me or where it will end.

The chances are a few people will read it. People like me, searching for the pieces of themselves that were stolen years ago.

This isn't about justice either. I believe in justice in the same way I do Santa Claus. Justice is for the rich and successful, the people who did this to me. The faces you might recognise from television, public life, voices that bring back memories from your childhood. Some old, some younger. They're good people, they'd tell you. They smile and raise money for charitable causes. But most of all they are untouchable people. I might describe them or give their initials but I won't name them. I can't afford to be taken to court, to fight the power of their money. Their words are mine to the power of ten.

I called it www.whathappenedatkelmore.com.

★

After my first blog, I posted another three in as many days. It was a small step, but the process of organising my thoughts into a story and making sense of the jumble of emotions was helpful. I'm not going to say it was cathartic. It wasn't. You can't scrub your mind clean with a few pages of writing. It was more of a housekeeping exercise, tidying up and labelling my emotions to clear some head space.

At the end of the week I logged on to find my first comment.

Thank you so much for writing this. I too was abused and my abusers were never brought to justice. I was at a care home not far from Kelmore and the set-up you describe is very similar. How can people get away with this?

The following week another appeared:

I was at Kelmore four years before you. I think the teachers knew, at least some of them did. That's the worst thing. I think they knew what they were sending us out to do.

This was strange and new and something else that I couldn't put my finger on. *There were others?* Of course there were. It was blindingly obvious when I thought about it. The other girls at the parties. Boys, too, on occasions. But the cruel genius of abuse made me think Bex and I were the only ones with our dirty secrets. Safer that way. For them, not us.

With the exception of the police and the interview with the reporter, this had always been an internal conversation. Bex and I never spoke about it. Why would we? In our own clumsy way, we were trying to move on, thought we could leave it behind and re-form ourselves. What we didn't know was that it was as much a part of us as a leg or an arm. It was attached to our bodies, had taken seed within us. What had been done could never be undone.

When the comments on my blog began to multiply, and slowly those first few echoes grew into a chatter which turned into a chorus, I knew something was happening. It came one day, a year or so in, when I looked through the comments and saw a sea of people just like me. My secret had made me an outsider, cut me off. Now I had found my tribe.

Inevitably, with the power of a crowd behind us, the subject of justice came up. Was it enough to share our experiences and support each other? For some it was. But what if it was still happening, others asked. Wasn't it time these men paid for their crimes? I knew what I wanted; I wouldn't rest until these men were unmasked. It was then I made my decision to leave Loch Lomond and move back to London, for the very same reason I had left.

The city had beaten me, but this time, with the wind behind me, I would win.

Six months later, I was settled in London and exploring ways of getting our case wider coverage, when one particular email landed in my inbox.

It was from Linda Moscow. She had read the blog and wanted to help.

Now, I wasn't completely stupid. I did my homework because I still carried a deep mistrust of anyone related to the establishment. I knew Linda Moscow was once the Home Secretary and later quit politics in the middle of a scandal where she was accused of awarding Government contracts to her mates.

But, and this was a big factor, she had spent much of her career campaigning for tougher child protection laws. She would be well connected, influential. Where was the harm in replying?

From: CharlieP1979@hotmail.com
To: LindaJmoscow@btinternet.com

Dear Linda,
Thank you for your email and your offer of support. However, many of the women feel let down by the establishment, justifiably so. Trust is a big issue and you haven't explained why it is you want to get involved.

From: LindaJmoscow@btinternet.com
To: CharlieP1979@hotmail.com

You are absolutely right to ask these questions.
I do know some of the men you accuse. I won't deny it. But please be assured they are not my friends. I haven't seen any of them for years.
If you have searched for me, as I'm sure you have, you will have seen that I campaigned for more rigorous child protection laws. Learning that this abuse could have taken place during my tenure in the Home Office shames me. While I can't change the past, I am determined to push for justice for you and your associates.

From: CharlieP1979@hotmail.com
To: LindaJmoscow@btinternet.com

Between us we have spoken to the police, the press, we have told social services. Nobody seems to care. Nobody has ever taken it further. They think we're prostitutes and alcoholics. They think we did it willingly and therefore that makes it OK. Nobody believes our testimonies would stand up in court. Why do you think you can succeed where everyone else has failed?

I understand you must feel let down by a system that was supposed to protect you. I can only apologise. But surely that doesn't mean we should all just give up and let them win? I'm not saying it is going to be easy. I'm not making any promises. But I give you my word, I will try to expose them. I can't do it alone. I can't do it without speaking to people who they preyed on and hearing what happened. That is what I want from you. I want to hear your stories – not just yours, but as many as I can. Because while they might be able to ignore one or two, it is much harder to ignore ten or twenty or fifty.

I would ask you to pass on my contact details to anyone who wants to speak to me. As you know, there are many people who would like to keep this covered up. I am taking sensible precautions to keep what I am doing under wraps until such times as I have gathered enough evidence.

With best wishes,

Linda


*www.whathappenedatkelmore.com*


*Community board*


*Please read the rules on the top right hand of the screen before posting. Remember, we're all here to support each other!*


*Posted by Charlie Pedlingham*


*We've been contacted by a woman who formerly held a senior position in the Government during the 1990s. She wants to write a book uncovering the abuse that has taken place and exposing those involved. I have checked her out as far as I can and she seems to be genuine. She would like some of you to share your stories with her for research. She has promised to protect your identities. If you want to speak to her, please message me first and I will put you in touch.*

*It's a leap of faith, but if we want justice, maybe it's one we have to take.*

*Charlie*

The first woman to contact me was Jennifer Patcham, who agreed to meet Linda the following week.

It was the last I heard of Jennifer.

# Thursday, 3.36 p.m.

## *Detective Inspector Victoria Rutter*

In DI Rutter's opinion, it is hard to disappear comprehensively these days. God knows, there are times when she's fancied doing it herself for a day or two, for some peace and quiet, no one shouting ma'am or mum at her. But there is always some form of communication stream flowing – social media, texts, mobile phone calls – that prevents escape. Charlie Pedlingham seems to have achieved the impossible: she's closed them all down and slipped out of her life without making a single splash.

Victoria has already had two officers search her flat; following a chat with her neighbour, Marjorie, they've reported back with the same story Jonathan recounted. A call to her former boss at the Langdale Hotel revealed Charlie left abruptly eight months ago. Her mobile phone contract elapsed in June but no calls had been made on it since March.

They have her passport and the registration number of her now missing car. If it's in use, it will appear on the ANPR database. At the very least, that should throw up some clues as to her whereabouts.

A few other findings have piqued DI Rutter's interest. There was a break-in at Linda Moscow's house last October, yet the only item she reported missing was a six-year-old laptop. After reading the file, she has noted that Gabriel's allegation of abuse against Curtis Loewe seemed to have been shelved quickly – prematurely, in her view. This has caused a stirring of unease. Gabriel Miller would not have made a credible witness, that much is true, but does she also detect a streak of institutional reluctance to believe a man of such standing could do any wrong? DS Huxtable was the investigating officer; she makes a note of his name, will have a discreet chat with him today.

She has read some but not all of the website posts Jonathan Clancy sent her; www.whathappenedatkelmore.com was not a figment of his imagination, she is satisfied of that much. With each new story of abuse she found, her indignation grew and a queasiness settled in her stomach. Now Victoria senses she is peering into a pit and she can't see the bottom. Gabriel has been in custody since yesterday. Even with another extension, she doesn't have long left. The question she has to ask is, will any of this bring her closer to solving the case?

She stares out of the window at life racing by on London's streets. The answer is this: she could spend weeks and months chasing Clancy's theories and in all probability she would emerge looking like a first-class eejit. Never before has she had so many eyes trained on her, voices clamouring for a quick result, bosses eager to put an end to the hysteria around the Linda Moscow Affair that a ravenous press is stoking. Not only that, she has to make the decision whether to formally link Mariela Castell's murder with Linda Moscow's. They have Gabriel Miller's DNA on her body, but he's admitted they had sex. What is complicating matters is that they've found traces of another man's DNA too, and a footprint. All of which may yet come to nothing.

Basically, there's too much to do to get sidetracked.

Still, one last phone call wouldn't hurt anyone, would it?

'Jonathan.'

'At your service.'

'You said Linda was trying to gather the survivors' testimonies. Who has she spoken to so far?'

'Not much luck on that front, I'm afraid. She was supposed to be talking to Charlie Pedlingham before she went quiet. And there was another woman . . . Let me check my emails, she sent me the details . . . Here it is . . . Jennifer Patcham. According to Linda, they met and she was eager to speak out. The strange thing was she went cold after that initial meeting, ignored her calls and emails. When Linda approached her, she threatened to call the police if she contacted her again.'

'I wonder what made her change her mind,' DI Rutter says, aware of the tingle on her skin, a magnetic draw that is pulling her down another path.

She puts the phone down and asks her sergeant, DS Clyde, to find out where Jennifer Patcham works. She will pay her a visit this afternoon. But first she asks for Gabriel Miller to be brought back to the interview room.

'Did you kill your mother?'

'No.'

'Did you hurt her?'

'Yes.' Gabriel's solicitor coughs. Until now his client has answered most questions with 'no comment'.

'How did you hurt her?'

'I was running out of the house and I pushed her out of the way.'

'You pushed her.'

'That's what I said.'

'Was she injured?'

'She hurt her head, it was bleeding. I got her something for it. A towel. I remember pressing a towel to her head.'

*All heart.*

'And then you left her?'

'I had to get out.'

'Why?'

He presses his fingers to his temples, as if the answer he has found is causing him flashes of pain.

'Why did you leave her?'

'She didn't believe me.'

The solicitor's stare is burning into Gabriel but he seems oblivious.

'What didn't she believe?'

'That I hadn't killed Mariela Castell.'

'Your mother thought you were capable of murder?'

'No . . . I mean, I don't know. It's difficult to explain. I didn't kill Mariela. We had sex, that's all, but I didn't do anything to hurt her. I told my mum someone was trying to set me up.'

'Why would you say that?'

'Because I didn't do it but it looks like I did, just like I didn't kill my mum.'

'Is there anyone who would have access to your mother's house, apart from you and her friend Bernadette? There was no sign of forced entry.'

'There was a woman who came to the house to help.'

'Help?'

'Clean and stuff. Anna, that was her name.'

'Do you have any contact details for her?'

'I only met her once, nearly killed me with a vacuum cleaner.'

'What did she look like?'

'She was British. Medium height, short blonde hair.'

'Has your mother ever mentioned the name Curtis Loewe to you?'

'Why would she talk about him?' he spits. A darkness clouds his eyes.

'What's your relationship with him?'

'We were introduced about a year ago. December. He called my agent, Palab, invited me to his house – massive place in the Cotswolds. I left early. Made me sick. Lots of young girls there. There was even a camera in the room, they had set it up to record me, but I wouldn't do that, not with a girl. I'm not that person,' he says. 'I reported him to your lot but no one was interested. What's he got to do with this?'

# Nine Months Before

## *Jay Huxtable*

Jay Huxtable sits on the sofa in his flat. It is directly outside his bedroom. The guy in the furniture store said it was regular size but it doesn't fit the space. There's an overhang from the breakfast bar, deadly really. He's cracked his head on it more than a few times. To think there were queues of people to buy these flats, a band playing, free croissants and coffee. The brochure said they were bijou. Jay thought that meant modern. Didn't realise it meant they were built for fucking dwarves.

He's been trawling www.whathappenedatkelmore.com all evening but he has to register in order to read the posts on the message board. Nobody uses their real names. There's *jennypenny*, *southlondonmama*, *voiceofthenorth*, *ladybythesea*, so he'll be fine making one up. He's racking his brains, trying to think of something appropriate or feminine when John calls.

'All right, sunshine.' He's shouting over the background music, which Jay recognises as one of his favourite old school tunes. 'We're needed at Curtis' house at 9 a.m. tomorrow.'

'No problems.'

Jay smiles, returns to the website and registers NorthernSoul as his new alter ego.

Christ these women can talk. And moan. There's a lot of moaning going on. He's got to admit it, some of their lies are convincing. When he read Charlie's blog, it clouded his mind. He doesn't want to get involved in any wrongdoing, certainly not that kind of shit. It disgusts him. But Curtis – he doesn't have him down as one of those types. Mind you, he should ask him, just to make sure. He considers how to broach the subject, delicately; doesn't want to upset the man, after all. 'Is any of it true?' No, that wouldn't do. He's hardly going to admit it, even if it is. Thankfully, Curtis spares him the bother.

'You've read it all, I suppose,' he asks him the next day.

'I have.'

'It's good, isn't it? Tell me you weren't a little sucked in by their stories.'

'I . . . I . . .'

'It's fine.' He raises his hands in the air. 'I won't hold it against you. Ever been lied to by a woman?'

*Stacey. Every time we had sex.*

'Uh huh.'

'Course you have. They're good at it. They lie so well you don't know what's real any more. These women are down on their luck. They want someone to blame. So they blame me because my charity offered them a chance and they thought they were halfway to Hollywood. Let me tell you, most of them wouldn't get through an audition in the Dog and Duck, but you know, we're a charity so we take pity and give them a chance. Then when it doesn't work out they think it's my fault and they go about twisting what happened to bend it out of shape and make it ugly. You've been to my parties – see anything wrong?'

'No,' he says without hesitation.

'See anyone forced to do something they don't want to do?' Huxtable shakes his head. 'Exactly. They're leeches. Now, what have you got for me?'

'One of them is meeting up with Linda next week.'

'Find out where. I want to know who she is, where she lives. I want to know where she works, what time of day she has a crap.'

★

Direct message, NorthernSoul to jennypenny: Hey there lady. Are you sure about meeting up with this woman by yourself?

Jennypenny to NorthernSoul: I think so. Anything to help. I'll let you know what she's like.

NorthernSoul to jennypenny: Where are you meeting her? Somewhere public I hope. You can't be too safe!

Jennypenny to NorthernSoul: Next to the cafe in Bishops Park on Wednesday. I can nip out from work on my lunch break. You can't get much more public than that.

Jay's exchange with jennypenny had conjured up a certain picture in his mind. She was blonde, smallish. Cheeky smile. She'd wear skinny jeans and those pointless little ballet shoes that Stacey used to wear. Leopard print. With a pink bow.

Jennypenny is sitting next to the woman he knows to be Linda Moscow (Christ, what happened to her?) and she is not wearing skinnies. He's not sure they'd sell skinnies in her size. Black work trousers that look like they're hiding two small children in each leg. Her hair's the fine flyaway stuff that parts to reveal too much scalp.

He positions himself across from them and for the first time in his life he wishes he had a child or a book. Neither has ever appealed, but at this moment either one would make his appearance less conspicuous. Thank fuck for his phone. He pretends to be talking to someone. 'I know what she said, but she's a liar,' he says to no one at all. He's getting the hang of this creativity lark. 'Yeah, I hear you . . . OK . . . I'll see you later. Seven o'clock for dinner.' This is no lie. He's meeting Mariela later on. Taking her out. Her choice. The restaurant looks expensive, serves food he can't pronounce and doesn't like the sound of. But if Mariela is his dessert, he'd eat his own shit.

He takes pictures of Linda and Jenny when he ends his 'conversation'. The pair of them, as thick as thieves. A boy of two or three with a snot trail running down to his lips keeps kicking sand his way from the sandpit. Where the hell's his mother? He scans the park for her but finds only a selection of bored-looking women and a few men staring into their phones. What hope is there for the kids of today?

Jennypenny works for an estate agent's round the corner from the park. She leaves work at 3.45 p.m. and gets a bus to Parson's Green where she collects a boy, presumably her son, from Boundary Road Primary School. When they emerge from the crowds and stand at the crossing, he manages to get a decent photo of the pair of them. Curtis wants info coming out of his arse and Jay isn't going to let any opportunity pass. They go to the park before walking the remaining mile or so home. Jenny lives in a first-floor flat (definitely not an apartment) with her son, who is called Tray or Trey (who knows?). He waits for the rest of the evening and is on to his fourth bag of crisps before he decides no one is coming home to Jenny. Given the hair and the legs, it's no surprise to him she's single. *I mean, you wouldn't, would you?*

The following day when he calls round to Curtis' house with the information, he's ordered to pass all the details and the photographs to John.

'He'll deal with this from now on,' Curtis says, without elaborating on what exactly it is John intends to do. 'Don't look so put out. You're going to have your hands full. I want you to meet Charlie Pedlingham, the one behind the website.'

'In what capacity?'

Curtis laughs and it's disconcerting because his face doesn't move, it remains a smooth mask, no smile or crease to intrude on its perfection.

'This woman believes Linda Moscow is out to help her. Your job is to convince her otherwise.'

Jay is beginning to understand that working for Curtis is a game, like *The Krypton Factor*, and he was no fan of that show. Pass one task and the next becomes tougher.

Curtis walks across his office and studies the rows of box files in front of him before selecting one. 'This should do the trick.' He pulls a document from the box and hands it to Jay. It's dated November 1996. It is from Linda Moscow to a Chief Superintendent Bill Joplin of the Metropolitan Police.

'Charlie Pedlingham has been trying to stir this up for years and Linda knows it's all bollocks. She knew it then and she knows it now. But she's using them to get to me. If she believed any of it, why would she have written to the police ordering them to drop the investigation?'

Jay stares at the letter, his eyes catching on a few choice phrases: *'witch hunt'*, *'national security'*, *'spurious claims with no foundation in fact'*.

'Linda Moscow is an opportunist with a grudge. She fell on her own sword years back – cash for contracts scandal, you may recall it.' Curtis assesses Jay and shakes his head. 'Anyway, doesn't matter if you can or can't, the point is she accused Henry and me of tipping off the *News of the World* and exposing her. I mean, who knows how they get these stories, but it wasn't our fault they found out that she had awarded several contracts to . . . Are you following?'

Jay nods. The last thing he wants is for Curtis to start the story over again.

'Good . . . well, the whole episode caused an outcry and Henry was forced to establish the Warren Inquiry, which investigated standards in public life. Let me tell you, that was the end of it for Linda. The woman was corrupt. To think she used to be our Home Secretary and spent years pontificating to others.'

'So what is it you want me to do?' Jay shifts uncomfortably under the pin of Curtis' stare. His boss wears a look of disbelief, as if the stupidity of others never ceases to amaze him.

'I was rather hoping that was clear. You arrange to meet this Charlie woman. You show her the letter so she can see for herself that Linda isn't on her side.'

'But—'

'No, for God's sake, man, you don't tell her you're working for me. A few strategic lies never hurt anyone. I want to know what Linda is up to and Charlie might be the very person who can tell us. Got it? Let me spell it out for you. You're Detective Sergeant Huxtable, investigating Linda Moscow and the men Charlie accuses – that's me and Henry and God knows how many others. You get an in with Charlie so we stay one step ahead of them. Don't look at me like that, it's not difficult. You're still technically a police officer, aren't you?'

'I'm suspended.'

'Exactly.'

'They took my warrant card.'

'And now you have another.' From the drawer of his desk he produces an envelope.

'I'm reinstating you.'

It is indeed a warrant card.

He is Detective Sergeant Jay Huxtable once again.

John calls him a few weeks later while he's sitting in front of the TV eating a takeaway chicken chow mein. 'You need tae go on to the message board and explain why jennypenny is taking a break,' he says.

'She is?'

'A long break. She won't be talking any more.'

'What did you do?' The words are out before Jay edits them.

'I'm a very persuasive man when I want to be.'

'You met her?'

'Not exactly. Her son. Nice wee lad. Tray. Imagine calling a kid Tray, for fuck's sake. I took him for a ride after school. Bought him an ice cream, so I did. Sent her some photos. Told her to keep her mouth shut if she wanted to see him again. She didn't even thank me. The manners of some people,' he laughs.

Jay pushes his plate away. His appetite has deserted him.

'You'll do it tonight, yeah, before those women start asking questions . . . Jay, are you there, man?'

'Understood.'

Jay sits back on the sofa. He wanted this, didn't he? To be in Curtis' inner circle. Except he hadn't expected it to be so dark. Dark like he's never known. He searches around but can't find even the smallest spit of light.

# Nine Months Before

## *Charlie*

Linda warned me that bringing the men to justice wouldn't be quick or easy. 'As you have discovered, they have friends everywhere,' she wrote in one email. 'Far better to gather as much evidence, as many testimonies as possible, so you become impossible to ignore.'

I assured her that time wasn't an issue. 'I've waited half my life already. I've got as long as it takes to see them punished, and the people who covered for them too,' I told her. 'In my eyes, they're as guilty as the men themselves.'

After her meeting with Jennifer Patcham, Linda suggested that it would be good for us to talk face to face. Eager to push ahead, I agreed, but she postponed the day before our first date. She'd been struck down with a stomach bug, would I mind delaying until the following week, she asked. We settled on a date two weeks from then. I didn't turn up because by that time I had found out what kind of woman Linda Moscow really was.

It was evening, dark smudging out the last of the day, when I first saw him. I was almost home, jaded and feet throbbing from a shift at the Langdale Hotel where I'd been working for the past year. As I approached the block of flats where I lived, he emerged from a BMW. He was smart like his car, wore a casual shirt, jeans, a Barbour jacket. I thought he might be Marjorie's son. Marjorie was my neighbour. 'Very bright, my Ryan is. He's a businessman, you know,' she was fond of telling me.

'Charlie?'

I stopped. Felt the key in my pocket, ran my finger over the sharp end of it. Just in case.

'Who are you?'

He raised his hands in surrender. 'I didn't mean to scare you. I'm Detective Sergeant Jay Huxtable,' he said, and held his warrant card out to prove his point.

I studied it. *Detective Sergeant Jay Huxtable, Metropolitan Police.* 'I promise you, it's me,' he laughed. 'Do you know a woman called Jennifer Patcham?'

*Jennypenny.*

'Is she OK?'

'She's fine, but there are a couple of questions I need to ask you . . .'

It was near closing time in the café around the corner, but to my relief a few stragglers remained. The waitress shot us a dirty look when we took a seat.

*Been there.*

'What's happened to Jennifer?' The air was fat with the stench of fried food.

'She's a bit shaken up, but she'll survive.'

'Shaken up?'

'You run the website, don't you? That's why I'm here. I understand she met a woman called Linda Moscow a few weeks ago?'

'She did.'

'You helped set up the meeting?'

'Well . . .'

'No one is blaming you, Ms Pedlingham.'

'I put them in touch with each other, if that's what you mean.'

'Jennifer's son Trey was picked up from school a few days after they met . . . by a man who said he was a friend of Jennifer's. He wasn't.'

232

'Oh my God . . .'

'He's fine. Returned safe and well. But Jennifer was beside herself, as you can imagine.'

'Thank goodness.' I paused for a beat, let the information roll around my brain. 'I don't understand what this has to do with her meeting Linda.'

DS Huxtable handed me a look full of pity. A band of sickness wrapped around me.

'This is confidential, do you understand?' I didn't want to know what was coming next.

'I am part of an investigation looking into allegations that a sex ring, operated by influential people, took children from residential homes and abused them . . . It's all right, you don't have to say anything. I know you were at Kelmore and I can confirm that is one of the establishments we are focusing on. The nature of the investigation, given those involved, is highly sensitive. Very few people within the force even know it exists. Do you understand what I'm saying?'

*Do you?*

His words ricocheted through me. And I wanted them to be true, no question. This was everything I was working towards.

And yet.

Not here. This wasn't how I had imagined it. I was exposed, caught off guard. All the work with the website, with fellow survivors, had put me in control. I was driving our case forward. To be told the police were one step ahead unsettled me, shunted me to the back seat again.

DS Huxtable paused for encouragement, continued when I gave him none.

'Our inquiries have led us to Linda Moscow. We're confident she never met any of the children. She didn't abuse them herself, but—'

I raised my hand to stop his flow. 'Linda is helping us.'

'We have evidence to suggest that she was part of a cover-up. We believe Linda Moscow abused her power to put a stop to an investigation that could have exposed these men years ago.'

I shook my head to dislodge his accusations.

*No. No. No.*

'The allegations were brought to her attention in 1996 when she was Home Secretary.'

1996. Insufficient evidence, they said. It's not *her* fault, the reporter had told us.

*Her.*

'Are you familiar with a man called Henry Sinclair?'

His name passed between us like a vibration.

'Unfortunately.'

'Do you know Linda's connection to him?'

'They worked together. She doesn't have anything to do with these people now.'

'This was taken two months ago.'

He handed me a photograph. All I could see was the back of a man's head entering a house. A dishevelled woman, surely not her, standing in the doorway.

'That doesn't tell me a thing.'

'Let me show you this one then.'

Another photograph of the same man, leaving this time, face in full view.

Henry Sinclair.

'Do you know how much money Curtis Loewe gave to the Conservative Party in the 1990s? Millions. Guess who was instrumental in tapping him up for that money: Linda Moscow. We think he threatened to cut off the flow of funds if she didn't step in to stop the investigation.'

His words became white noise. A relentless drone. Heat trampled over my body, bubbled up, gathered in a lake in the small of my back.

'Are you OK?'

The lull in conversation fanned me like a cool breeze. But it wasn't enough. The heat marched on, spreading up to my head, my brains, gushing down to the tips of my toes.

'Why should I believe you?'

*I don't want to believe you. Can't believe you.*

'It's a lot to take in, I understand. Perhaps this will persuade you I am telling the truth.'

He produced a letter, what looked like a copy of the original. The paper was the same shade as the coronation chicken sweating under the counter lights.

It was from Linda Moscow to Chief Superintendent Bill Joplin.

November 1996. A few months after Bex and I made our complaint.

> *Dear Chief Superintendent Joplin,*
>
> *I'm writing to you about a delicate matter that has been brought to my attention. I understand your force is investigating two allegations of abuse made against Curtis Loewe and relating to incidents at his home in the Cotswolds and various other locations. Mr Loewe has given me his word these spurious claims have no foundation in fact. For my part, having spoken to him and reviewed the evidence, I am satisfied of his innocence.*
>
> *You will be aware that Mr Loewe contributes a considerable amount of money to various children's charities. A public investigation of the nature you are undertaking would not only be fruitless but harmful to the prospects of hundreds of children who continue to benefit from his generosity.*
>
> *I would ask you to consider the sensible use of police resources in this matter. Would they be better directed at tackling the spike in violent crime we saw last year or engaging in a witch hunt that will only serve to embarrass the force?*
>
> *Yours sincerely,*
> *Linda Moscow*

I opened my mouth to say, I don't understand, but the words disappeared in DS Huxtable's steam.

'You think it's a coincidence that after Jennifer met Linda her son was taken? Jennifer showed Linda a picture of her son. She told her where he went to school. She trusted Linda. These people will go to any lengths to protect themselves.'

'Why are you telling me all this?'

The look of concentration on his face gave way to something softer, relief maybe, as if he'd been digging away and had finally struck gold.

'We want you to help us, Charlie.'

*Linda.*

The information left me clutching at the air for breath. Incontrovertible proof that she choked off the investigation. And Bex. My mind was alight with images of my friend, lost, desperate to be found, for someone to listen. It was Linda who silenced her, who pulled the investigation, who put pressure on Jonathan Clancy to spike his story. Suddenly, I was back in Hyde Park planted in that pivotal moment where all Bex needed to hear was, *I believe you, I will help you*, and she could have walked down a different path, had a brighter future. But the police and Jonathan Clancy said, *No, I don't believe you, I won't help you*. Together they pushed her down the route that led to her death. And for what? Power. Money. Ambition. To keep the millions flowing into the party coffers.

The force of my hatred stunned me.

'I'll help you,' I told DS Huxtable.

Because the only thing that mattered now was making them pay.

★

Linda lived at 14 Ruthermore Road, Clapham, in a house that stood out like a beacon of protest against the street's gentrification. No bay trees guarding the door. No neat path lit by downlighters. Heavy curtains instead of shutters. Untamed bushes blocked the ground-floor windows, as if the garden was trying to swallow the house. In this neighbourhood, it was tantamount to a crime to resist gentrification so blatantly.

The woman herself cut a pathetic figure, unrecognisable from her politics days. I had expected the business hair, maybe not a suit but slacks, a wool cardigan, a few pearls. An air of refinement at the very least. Not so. On colder days, she wore a man's old ski jacket, way too big for her scrawny frame, and a hat, trainers of no decipherable make. She ventured out very little. You could have drawn a two-hundred-metre radius around her house and she wouldn't have stepped out of it. Few visitors were admitted to her home. I saw her son once. There was also a woman around Linda's age, who stood outside and knocked (and knocked) and shouted, 'I know you're in there. I've brought a fruit loaf,' until Linda answered the door and let her in.

I'd been watching her ever since DS Huxtable had told me what she had done. It wasn't hard to find an address if you were committed. And committed I was. Oh, the times I'd considered bumping into her as she waited to cross a road, pushing her towards an oncoming bus, letting fate work its magic. I had an image of her flattened by the number 94, a crowd gathered around gawping at her trainers sticking out from beneath the wheels. On the other hand, I figured it would have been a shame to throw everything away on such a tawdry death. The revenge had to fit the crime. Ordinary wouldn't do. I wanted to get close to her, hear the beat of her heart. I wanted to know what she loved, so I could destroy it.

*

Obviously, I didn't tell DS Huxtable what I was up to. It was unlikely he would approve. Besides, I wasn't altogether sure what my stalking was going to achieve. I considered it to be a reconnaissance mission, one that involved a certain reorganising of my day job at the Langdale. Thankfully, no one expressed surprise when I volunteered to take on the role of duty night manager. It wasn't exactly a sought-after position. For me though, it was perfect. My shifts finished at two in the morning, which gave me enough time to sleep, and watch Linda all day.

One particular morning, I woke up with a stinking cold. My bones, lead-weighted, begged me to stay in bed. *It can't hurt to miss one day, can it?* I made a deal: if it was raining, I'd stay indoors; sunny, I would go. I whipped back the curtains. The sunshine stung. I dragged myself out of bed and started my journey from my flat in Hammersmith to Clapham.

At eleven o'clock Linda emerged in the usual state. I should point out, I wasn't hanging around outside her house inviting arrest. There was a café on the corner of her street and if I muscled in on the right seat, which I always did, I could see her front door. With a laptop in front of me I looked like your average freelancer eking out a latte and clogging up table space. Once, I even ordered a vegan sweet potato brownie to help my cover. But they're not the kind of things you order twice.

She headed down the street and I gathered my things to follow her at a safe distance. She was on her way to the supermarket, where else. Once inside, she selected her goods and took them to the till. There she spoke to the cashier, whose name I knew to be Pauline, courtesy of her name badge. Linda handed her a small card. Whatever it was, Pauline didn't look impressed. 'You sure . . .' was about all I could pick up because there was a kid in the shop screaming for chocolate buttons and his mum was making a big show of refusing him. She was dressed in slim black trousers and an olive padded jacket with a ring of luxurious fur around the collar. Stiff leather tote bag on the crook of her arm. 'That kind of behaviour gets you nothing, Bertie, how many times have I told you?' She threw her blonde hair back in defiance. I glanced in her basket to make a final assessment: olives, Parma ham, ciabatta, your everyday working lunch.

'Anna, my goodness, this can't be your baby.' Another woman, almost identical save for the brunette hair (glossy and smooth like mine never was), stood in front of the screaming Bertie proclaiming what an absolute poppet he was. 'You want chocolate buttons? Oh, let me treat him, won't you?'

The sideshow almost cost me the sight of Linda – who had by now collected her groceries and packed them into her bag – exiting the shop. As she left, Pauline inserted Linda's card into the window alongside the offers of French tuition and window cleaning.

I fought the urge to leave immediately, counted to fifty and considered who would pay the astonishing price of blueberries (people like Anna, who'd force-feed them to Bertie – no wonder he howled for chocolate) before I skipped outside to read the advert.

## HOUSEKEEPER WANTED

I had to stifle a laugh. She lived in a semi! But my mirth was quickly displaced by a surge of excitement.

An hour later, having practised my spiel, and come up with a name, I called the number on the card.

'I saw your advert in the supermarket.'

'You did? My, you're quick off the mark, you must have been following me.'

'I . . . no, I was in there just now, buying bananas.'

'Bananas, I see, can't stand the things personally. The devil's fruit, bung me up something awful. Why don't you tell me a little bit about yourself.'

I kept it vague but persuasive, upbeat, like I was the kind of cheery personality you'd welcome into your home.

'Well, why don't you come along tomorrow and we can chat. My address is 14 Ruthermore Road.'

'That would be great,' I said. 'But I should tell you I don't have an up-to-date CV. It's on my to-do list. I can give you references though.'

'I wouldn't read it if you did. I don't need a piece of paper to tell me a person's right or not. I'll see you at one o'clock then, Anna.'

That night I invented Anna's backstory. She'd spent several years in Australia, although specific time frames were to be avoided in case I tripped myself up. She had recently broken up with her boyfriend (or would Anna say partner?). Infidelity, if Linda asked. But most importantly she was efficient, organised, focused. When she set her mind to something she saw it through.

I set off the next day a few hours ahead of our meeting in case a stray leaf on the overground line screwed my chances of getting there in time. As it transpired, the journey didn't last nearly long enough. I arrived too early, took myself to the café and ordered a coffee. It was more than enough time for doubts to take root. I was about to meet her, this monster, hear her speak, enter her house, look her in the eye.

*How. Can. You?*

My head was hot, burning. It was the cold, still flushing around my system, I told myself. I needed to go home.

Can't do this.

I stood up, too fast, bumped the table, knocked the coffee over, attempted to soak it up with a few serviettes to no effect. I was out of the café, pushing past a father with a pram when I saw her. A girl. Thin, dark hair, the gait identical to hers. And suddenly the past was erased as if it had never happened. I started to run after her. 'Bex,' I shouted. 'Come back.' But the girl didn't turn around.

She wasn't Bex.

Bex had gone.

And her death was the reason I was here.

'You must be Anna. Bang on time. Punctuality is a dying art, I fear.'

She extended her hand and it slid into mine. Cold, bony, liver-spotted.

*Linda.*

I forced my eyes in her direction.

'Do come in, you'll perish out there.'

All the words I'd prepared ran away, leaving nothing in my artillery but a smile. I followed her through the hallway, down into the bowels of the house. It was more disorganised than I expected but she made no attempt to apologise for the clutter. Posh people are allowed to have crap everywhere and get labelled eccentric. On an estate, this would have been called a dump.

Bookshelves filled every inch of space through the hall, as if they were the structure that was holding up the house. In the kitchen, copper pans hung from hooks and the worktops were populated by mismatched jars, half-drunk wine bottles with their corks stuffed back in. A pan sat on the hob with what I presumed were leftovers. My nose wrinkled in protest.

She sat me down at the dining room table next to a teetering pile of magazines and letters.

'Now, Anna, tell me a bit more about yourself.'

I searched for my pre-prepared stories but my mind had jumbled them up and they didn't make sense any more. Thankfully, she mistook my panic for nerves, quickly adding,

'Would you listen to me, I've completely forgotten my manners. Can I get you a cup of tea?'

I didn't drink tea but the diversion was welcome. It was one question I could answer, 'Milk, one sugar please.'

She pottered about, taking cups from the sink, rinsing them, giving the milk a cursory sniff before pouring it into my tea. 'The perils of living alone,' she said.

I'd been working abroad for a time. Australia, I told her. I sensed my curt answers were harming my prospects. I wouldn't win any prizes for this act, needed to crank it up a gear. 'The weather is a shock, let me tell you.'

'And what brings you back here?'

I hesitated, the emotion threatened to overwhelm me. 'A relationship that didn't work out. It was the right thing to do . . . to leave.'

'Life can be a bugger,' she said. 'I'm sure you've made the right decision.'

'Why have you decided to enlist a housekeeper now?' I asked, pleased that I was beginning to warm to the role. Enlist was definitely an Anna word.

'Well, as you can see, I can't look after the house myself. I've let it go. A sensible person would sell it, but it was our family home, my son grew up here. I couldn't bear to get rid of it. But now I've got an extra workload I've decided I need to draft in some help.'

'You're working?'

'Of a fashion. I'm writing a book.'

'I've never met an author before.'

'Well, I'm not one yet.'

'What is it about?'

She paused, ran a finger round the rim of her mug. 'Oh . . . it's about female politicians in the twentieth century.'

It was a blatant lie, given away by the flush of her cheeks. I smiled, made a glib comment that it wasn't my typical reading material.

'Don't worry, I won't make you read it. Now . . .' she said, 'I suppose this is the point where I ask what you can do. Can you cook?'

My turn to lie. 'I love cooking.'

'Are you organised?'

'I'm afraid so.'

'And why would you like the job?'

I should have known this answer by rote, but it slipped away. My head grew light while my limbs went heavy as if they were a mismatch. I tried to work out what was wrong, what was knocking me out of kilter. I stared at Linda in search of my answer and she beamed a big smile of encouragement to fill the silence.

She was a disappointment, that was it! I wanted her to be a monster. I wanted her to make my skin crawl. But she was just a woman like any I walked past in the street, sat next to on the bus or the Tube; nothing out of the ordinary.

'I'm desperate,' I said. *Didn't rehearse that word.* To my disgust I started to cry.

'Please don't upset yourself, dear.' Her hand brushed my shoulder to soothe me. Tears stole my energy and rage. My eyes raked over her, hoping to snag on something to reignite my fire.

'What do you say we have a trial period? Three weeks? If your cooking doesn't kill me and you can instil some order into this place and we seem to rub along together, then the job is yours.'

The heat. Too much now. Around my neck, melting my bones. I had to go while I could still stand.

'You'll think about it, won't you?' she said.

I told her, yes. I would think about nothing else.

★

I was coming down with something. A bug, a virus, flu. It swept through me. I couldn't hold my head up. Couldn't stop crying, not even on the train home. Passengers gave me a wide berth in case I was contagious. Nobody wanted what I had. I didn't want it either. *Never asked for it, did I?*

I made it back to my flat. Lost days to sleep. When I came to, I found a voicemail from DS Huxtable. I'd seen him a few times since our first meeting, in parks and cafés, me furnishing him with the scraps of information I'd gleaned from email exchanges with Linda. This time he suggested a location out of town. Surrey, next week. He was working down that way and it would make life easier for him.

There were two more messages, both from Linda, pushing me for an answer.

Did I want the job?

*Did I?*

# Eight Months Before

## *Jay Huxtable*

Jay Huxtable wouldn't go so far as to say he likes Charlie, but she's not as objectionable as he'd expected. It would be easier if she was. They've met a few times and spoken over the phone for updates, and as far as he can tell she is in full possession of her marbles. If he didn't know the people involved, he'd say her story sounds believable. Maybe it's about perception. Charlie perceived she was abused and therefore she had been. Curtis, on the other hand, read the situation differently. Whoa! This is way too deep for nine o'clock on a Thursday morning. He hasn't even had a cup of tea or an egg McMuffin yet.

Unfortunately, John has been keeping tabs on Charlie and has spotted her lurking outside Linda's house. 'Has she no sense of boundaries?' John asked when he imparted the information. 'She's a liability, that's what she is,' John said, stringing out the syllables like liability was five words not one. 'She'll have tae go.'

Jay's eyes rolled over him, searched for clues in the lines of his face. They were too deep, formed over years of casual cruelty. He could have asked him outright where it was exactly that Charlie had to go, but he decided against it. John liked to play with him and he didn't fancy being his toy.

Jay is seeing Charlie today. Normally he'd look forward to these meetings. Charlie's 'information' is so piss poor it's laughable, but her ignorance is sweet. He finds her . . . endearing. Now that's not a word he'd often use.

Today, however, is different. He's dreading it. Watching the clock. If only he could stop time. They're meeting out in the wilds of Surrey. John's suggestion. That's enough to make him worry. That and the fact John will be following in his car, 'to keep you company, so tae speak'. There's a purpose about the day that scares him. The air is light and quick with momentum and he is caught in its jet stream. He looks up to the clock. The second hand races around. Another minute passes. Jay doesn't know how to stop it.

'Christ,' Charlie says. 'What's wrong with Regent's Park?'

It's not quite the middle of nowhere but the edge of it. Off a B road, by a stream. Picturesque, on another day maybe. He can't appreciate the scenery. Just sees the two of them standing in the fog of their own breath, and beyond them . . .

Charlie stamps her feet against the hard frost. 'You've chosen a place without a café on a freezing cold day. I've only just got over the flu. Have I done something wrong?'

Has she done something wrong? She *has* done something wrong or else John wouldn't be two hundred metres away, his car disguised by the bushes. Or maybe she hasn't. Maybe Charlie never did anything, but they're going to make her pay all the same.

'Are you all right? You look like you're crying.'

'It's the cold,' he says.

They sit in his car, just like John suggested. Charlie talks and Jay tries to grab the words but they run away from him. He stares out of the window, listening for footsteps. His heart is so heavy it is dragging him down. He worries he might be pulled down to the ground, buried alive.

'Have you heard a word I've said?'

'I'm listening.'

'Go on then, what did I say?'

He holds his hands up. 'You win.'

'I've got a new job,' she says.

'I see.' But he doesn't see. Doesn't see the point in her telling him. She won't start the job. She won't get promoted. She'll never make it there.

'You mean congratulations.'

'Congratulations.'

'Don't you want to ask me about it?'

'I'm all ears.'

'I'm going to be a housekeeper.'

'I thought you liked working in a hotel.'

'This job is more interesting. Ask me who it's for.'

'An oligarch in Belgravia?'

'No, Clapham actually.'

'Right.'

'Ruthermore Road. It just sort of happened.'

Finally, it hits him. No wonder she's looking so pleased with herself.

She extends her hand to him. 'I'm Anna, by the way. I start working for Linda next week.'

He's out of the car before he knows what he's doing. Calling John. 'Just wait, don't do a thing.'

'I have my orders.'

'I'm going to speak to Curtis now.'

'You have five minutes,' the Scot says.

For once Curtis answers the phone. It's a sign. A fucking sign.

'She's got a job with Linda . . . much more use to us there, inside her house than . . .' he trails off, knows not to say too much over the phone.

The silence spreads out, gobbles up his time. Five minutes, that's all he has before John moves in.

'Curtis?'

'I'm thinking . . . give me a chance . . . OK. On this occasion, I think you are right. I'll call John now.'

He waits, can't be too sure. An engine fires up, wheels grind along the gravel track until the sound fades.

He has gone.

Jay runs back to Charlie, a buoyancy fills his body, he could be flying. The sun cracks through the clouds, pours a milky haze on to the windscreen.

He sits down, gathers his breath, turns to her and his face breaks out into a smile.

'So tell me about yourself, Anna.'

# Thursday, 4.38 p.m.

## *Detective Inspector Victoria Rutter*

Jennifer Patcham greets DI Rutter with the enthusiasm of an estate agent eyeing a prospective buyer. The smile is so genuine Victoria feels a pang of guilt as she slides her warrant card across the desk and imparts the real reason for her visit.

'Is there somewhere we can talk discreetly?' she asks.

Thankfully the office is quiet and Jennifer guides Victoria into a small kitchen at the back.

'Is it Trey? The childminder was collecting him today. Tell me he's OK.' Victoria is alarmed to see the tears bubbling in her eyes.

Trey is Jennifer's five-year-old son and Victoria does her best to assure her that his welfare is not why she is here.

'I understand you met Linda Moscow some months ago.'

At the mention of Linda's name, Jennifer winces. 'We only met the once,' she says, using the tips of her fingers to drive away her tears.

'Can I ask why. Didn't she want to speak to you again?'

Jennifer's gaze swims around the room as if the answer might be hidden behind the fridge, through the window, amongst the box files.

'It is important you tell me. I understand Linda Moscow was working on a book that would expose historical sex abuse and you agreed to share your experiences. I need to know if it was a personal choice not to continue, or if any pressure was applied to help you reach your decision.'

More tears, hysterical this time, as if they've been building up for months and Victoria Rutter's question has burst the skin, prompted them to come flooding out.

'I thought that was why you were here,' she says, her hand covering her mouth as she relives the trauma of the day when a man took her son, the day she feared she might never see her boy again.

Back at the station, Victoria mulls over what Jennifer told her, not just about her son, but also her years in care and the horror of what she was subjected to. *Believe no one, trust no one, challenge everything*, these are the starting points in any investigation, but why, Victoria asks herself, would Jennifer and the legion of other women with almost identical stories feel the need to lie? The suggestion that they are suffering from some kind of collective fever does not hold water.

Jonathan Clancy's theory is appearing less fantastical by the hour.

She needs food, her body is running on empty. Too many strands to pull together, like handling spaghetti. The salad her husband Doug made her, lovingly, as per instructions, is sitting in a Tupperware container on the table. It's not calling out to her. She's on the 5:2 diet and today is a restricted day which means a few slices of cucumber, a handful of olives, shredded carrot and some sorry lettuce leaves. Sod it! She can't think straight on salad. She'll save the starvation for tomorrow.

DS Clyde intercepts her as she's heading for the canteen. 'Chewing gum,' he says.

'No thanks, I'm after a sausage sandwich.'

'I'm talking about the chewing gum found on the bottom of Gabriel Miller's boots. We've just got the results from the lab.'

'Yes?' Her hunger gives way to a surge of excitement.

'The profile matches a man with a colourful criminal record.

The bins are emptied on a Friday, which would place him around Gabriel Miller's house between then and Sunday.'

She turns, walks away from the canteen. Never does get her hands on that sausage sandwich.

# March–October 2014

## *Charlie*

'If you want your cover to work, you've got to do this properly,' Jay said. 'No shortcuts.' He advised stepping away from my own life and creating a new, temporary one that belonged to Anna. The thing was, I didn't have much of a life in London to step away from in the first place, and the idea that Anna not Charlie would go to work for Linda appealed. I figured the distinction would make it easier to stomach.

Jay found me a flat in an anonymous block in Putney close to the river. My old place still had ten months left to run on the lease. I wrote to Marjorie saying I was going away for a while and that sadly I wouldn't be able to look after her cat. Jay said he'd post the letter through her door when he went back to collect my things. I had requested a few items of clothing, and a box with the possessions that had survived my years in care. It wasn't much: a photograph of me and Mum, a dress she used to wear, and a book, part one of *The Wonderland Trilogy*. We read it together every night for six months before she died. On the inside she'd written, *To my gorgeous Charlotte, may your life be a fairy tale.*

The book didn't make it back to me. I thought I must have left it under my pillow and Jay had missed it. Sometimes I'd leave it there in the hope her voice would flood my dreams.

Email communication with Linda had to stop too. This came as a relief. There were only so many times I could claim an emergency dental appointment or a burst pipe to call off a meeting. My withdrawal from the website was more of an issue.

'Trust me,' Jay said. 'You keep it simple on jobs like this. You don't over-complicate things or give yourself an opportunity to slip up. And it's not forever.'

I agreed, reluctantly. Truth is, I would have done almost anything he asked. The last thing I wanted to do was mess up.

Anna was a useful disguise. Anna was allowed to smile at Linda and make her lunch without spitting in it. She was a chameleon, could turn herself into whatever Linda wanted her to be – organiser, planner, chef, cleaner. She was also a relief. I walked lighter when I stepped into her shoes, cast off Charlie's baggage for a few hours a day.

Halfway through the second week, Linda, who had until then been holed up in her study, invited me to join her for lunch. 'I feel we've been skirting around each other. Quite rude of me.'

I ladled the minestrone soup I had made (from scratch) into a bowl and sat opposite her at the table. 'Gabriel was going to be an Anna, you know,' she said. 'Oh, listen to me! Gabriel is my son. You might recognise him. He tells jokes for a living. He was always a funny little boy.' She gave a mirthless laugh.

'It's Gabriel Miller, isn't it? I saw a photograph of him in the living room. You must be proud.'

'Yes, I am.'

'Is he your only child?'

'Yes.' She stared into the soup bowl as if she had found something not to her liking. 'He was a surprise. Hugh and I, we tried for years.'

'Hugh is your husband?'

'Was. He's dead now. We separated years ago, when Gabriel was a teenager. Divorce is hard for children. The poor boy had a tricky time of it. Are your parents around, Anna?'

'My mum died when I was twelve. I didn't know my dad.'
I paused, heat flushed through me. Wrong story. Charlie's not Anna's.

'Oh, you poor thing. I'm sorry.'

'She would have loved it here, all these books. She was always trying to get me to read more.'

'Sensible woman. Do you have a favourite?'

The answer was a reflex, came out unchecked. '*The Wonderland Trilogy*. I know they're kids' books, but we used to read them together. Well, Part One, anyway. She was going to buy me the others.' I stopped. Why was I telling her this? Didn't want her pity. 'Anyway, I went to live with my aunt when she died. She wasn't into books.'

'Well, that's something at least, that you had family to step in. Putting a child in care often doesn't result well. I should know. I've dealt with a lot through work. I'm afraid to say the system lets them down.'

A thread of pasta lodged itself in my throat. She'd opened the door to me, too tempting not to follow with a question.

'That was your area of work, wasn't it?' I blushed. 'Sorry, after you mentioned you were in politics, I looked you up. That makes me sound like a stalker.'

'Not at all, you want to know who you are dealing with, it's only natural. It *was* my area, as you say, but I can't claim to have made a huge difference. Politics can be brutal.'

'Is that why you quit?'

'I didn't quit. I was pushed out. Framed, if you like. Not that anyone believed me. But that's a story for another time.'

Months passed and my initial eagerness to find out what she was up to, sifting through letters while she worked in her study, taking screenshots of paperwork, trying to find the password to her laptop, settled into something more relaxed. Now and then this stirred up a current of panic, a fear that my anger was ebbing.

Linda was perfectly pleasant in the flesh, caring even – 'Oh, go home early, the washing can wait,' she'd say. When I arrived with a cold one day, she ordered me to sit down, put my feet up, before foisting a Lemsip on me. For lunch, she made a vindaloo. 'Trust me,' she said, 'it'll do wonders for your sinuses.'

Was there a danger she could suck me in?

*As if.*

I'd lost none of my determination, I told myself. It was simply impossible to maintain that level of tension on a daily basis.

Gabriel's visit in June set off the first major alarm bell. Linda had abandoned her study, spent the morning in the kitchen, apron on, preparing homemade hamburgers. 'He still thinks they're the best.'

There was a marked change in her appearance. I wouldn't say her hair was presentable but she'd certainly made an effort at taming it. A comb had been involved. She was dressed in pale blue cotton trousers and a shirt. No jeans. The trainers were banished. I could have sworn there was a trace of lipstick gracing her lips.

One thirty came round and no sign of Gabriel. I found Linda staring at the kitchen clock. 'The traffic is terrible these days, isn't it,' she said when her eyes caught mine.

'I'd have thought he'd take a taxi. You fly through in those lanes,' I replied. Her shoulders sagged a little more, the weight of expectation pressing down.

I'd hit the mark. I should have been elated, a small victory, but I derived no pleasure from it.

A complicated emotion, hate.

The bell rang. 'I'll get it,' Linda called, and shot off to answer the door.

'Gabriel . . .' She sang his name but his greeting didn't match hers.

'Come in . . . you look tired . . .'

'You always say that.'

'Do I?'

'No, I'm making it up.'

'Oh . . . cup of tea, coffee?'

'Coffee, thanks.'

Their footsteps took them into the kitchen and I moved to the hallway where I could eavesdrop.

'Where's the machine that I bought you?'

'Oh, that thing. I couldn't get on with it,' Linda said.

Cupboards opened and slammed shut as Linda searched for the missing coffee machine.

'Have you given it away to charity?' Gabriel asked.

'No, I have not. There's nothing wrong with this coffee anyway.'

'If you say so.'

I'd heard that comedians were often a disappointment in real life, a pale intimation of their public personae, moody and cantankerous. While I wouldn't claim ten minutes of an overheard conversation was enough to make a judgement, I can vouch that Gabriel's presence brought a cool draught to the house.

'It's really no way to behave, if you ask me,' Linda said a little later. Her voice had grown shrill.

'I didn't ask you.'

'I despair, really I do. Bernadette said she'd seen you in the newspaper the other day.'

'You can hardly talk. Anyway, I don't need Bernadette's seal of approval, she of the virgin conception.'

'Gabriel!'

'If ever a woman could be doing with a bit more fun in her life, it's her. Though I can't say I blame Pat for not going near her.'

'Gabriel Miller! Do not talk about my friend in that way.'

'You don't even like her.'

'That's not true.'

'Or is it just her fruitcake you despise?'

Linda let out a laugh, despite herself. 'That woman's fruitcake is still lying in my stomach from last week. The worst part is, she thinks I like it.'

'You see, she's trying to kill you with her baking.'

Linda's tone softens. 'I worry, Gabriel. It's all too much. Your health will suffer.'

'How many times do I have to tell you? I'm fine. Jesus, I had kale and spinach juice this morning, what more do you want me to do?'

'Nice?'

'Disgusting.'

'I've made hamburgers for lunch.'

'I can't stop. I have a meeting in town.'

'But they're your favourite.'

'I'm not twelve, Mum.'

Precisely thirty-two minutes after he arrived, Gabriel left. Spying an opportunity to meet him, I decided it would be the perfect moment to vacuum the hall.

He didn't see me, walked straight into it, tripped.

'Fuck!'

'Are you OK?'

'I've survived worse,' he said, cheeks ferocious red. 'And you are . . . ?'

'This is Anna,' Linda said. 'She works for me.'

'Just watch she doesn't kill you.' He stabbed me with a withering look. His face had a waxy appearance, tiredness darkened his eyes. Nothing like the TV Gabriel Miller. He needed more than kale juice to sort him out.

'I'll call you in a few days,' Linda said, before diving in for a hug.

And then he was gone.

★

Linda didn't move from the hallway. The arms that embraced her son were suspended mid-air, as if they hadn't registered his departure. When she finally moved, it was to pivot around, regard a photograph of Gabriel on the wall. At a guess, he must have been thirteen, his boyish face still fresh, smiling. She wore a puzzled look, couldn't quite equate the man who had breezed in and out with the boy captured in the frame. Finally, she shook her head, vigorously, as if to dislodge a trapped thought, and headed to the kitchen where she took the hamburgers from the oven and threw them straight in the bin.

I watched all this, fighting the urge to go and give her a hug.

After a few months Linda let the female politicians of the twentieth century lie slide, and began to refer to her work simply as The Book. For my part, I'd uncovered precious little of use to anyone. Doubt had gained a voice, and it grew louder by the day. What if Jay Huxtable had made a mistake? Who was to say Linda had written that letter? Politics is brutal, that's what she'd told me. I took endless routes around unlikely scenarios that would explain away her involvement until I was hit by the truth: I didn't want it to be her. As hard as I tried, I couldn't reconcile the creature of my nightmares with the woman who, come Friday, would force me to down tools and insist I share a jug of her special summer punch.

It was always a Friday, *because we damn well deserve it*, *Anna*, she'd say. We'd sit in the back garden, under a gazebo if it rained (*I refuse to give in to the vagaries of British summertime*). In contrast to the front of the house, the back garden was remarkably well kept. It wasn't big, few London gardens are, but Linda had packed it with flowers, sprays of pink roses, daisies that bent in the wind. There was a water feature too and the afternoon's drinking was set to the gentle sound of a flowing stream. Sweet peas climbed the trellis, scenting the air. Linda turned her face to the sun. 'It's a little paradise, is it not? Ready for another? Of course you are.'

I was on my third glass before I realised that the punch was special on account of its effects. I was completely bladdered.

One particular Friday, an afternoon lazy with heat, we were cowering in the shade of the magnolia tree. A bee droned above my head. I was on my second glass when Linda jumped to her feet.

'I nearly forgot, I have something for you.'

She returned carrying a brown parcel that she laid out on the trestle table.

'They arrived today. Not in print any more, but I managed to find some first editions.'

Linda set both books out in front of me. Parts two and three of *The Wonderland Trilogy*. I ran my finger over them, feeling the shape of each embossed letter. Memories flooded my head. My mum's voice weaving through the air to find me.

I turned to Linda's expectant face. She didn't say anything, just placed a hand on top of mine and held it firm.

'I don't know what to say.'

She heaved the jug up from the ground. 'Say you'll have another.'

I stumbled through to the end of summer, fell into September. The lie had grown too big to carry around, suffocated me. I didn't know who Linda was but I knew I couldn't be Anna any more. By October, my speech was rehearsed – a job opportunity in Jamaica – I had practised my responses – *I know! I've never been either, but it's too good an opportunity to pass on.*

I made the mistake of mentioning my plans to Jay.

'You can't,' he said. 'It's just about to get exciting.'

★

'We want you to go to Scotland with Linda,' Jay said. We were in my flat. I'd made him a coffee, black no sugar. It was easier meeting here than in parks and cafés.

'Scotland?'

'It's a country in the UK.'

'Thanks for enlightening me. I told you, I've had enough. The lying is killing me.'

Jay shot me a look, half frustration, half panic. Colour smacked his cheeks, gave his face a hot sheen.

'You like her, don't you?'

'I'm not doing it, Jay.'

'Christ, you're going soft. She's good, I have to hand it to her.'

'She is who she is. I just don't know whether she would have done that. She . . .'

'Doesn't seem like the type?' His laugh was like gravel. He raked his next words out of it. 'Oh Anna, stop being so naïve. She's a politician. She has many faces. That's what makes these people so dangerous. We're close, this close.' He pressed his thumb and index finger together. His eyes were bright with alarm. 'Just one more thing and we're done.'

'You called me Anna.'

'Did I? Well you should be Anna.' His shoulders sank, the pressure hissing out of him. 'It suits you better. Have you got any beers? I could murder a drink.'

Unusually, he stayed longer than half an hour, ordered a curry, his shout.

'It'll take more than a Balti to persuade me,' I said.

'She's meeting Henry Sinclair up there, that's what we think. You won't be alone, but we need you on the inside otherwise we could miss her.'

'Why would she go all the way to Scotland when she could meet him here?'

'Privacy. Away from prying eyes. I don't know. Sinclair has a place up there.'

'She hasn't mentioned anything about Scotland. Do you ever consider that you might be wrong about her? Who's to say someone didn't fake that letter you showed me? It's not like the police to make a mistake.'

He took a swig of beer. Slowly placed it back on its coaster before he turned his body towards me. 'You know, it's sweet to see how loyalty has bloomed out of hatred.'

'Don't take the piss.'

'I'm not. You're one of the good ones.' He said it like it was a shame, like he wished I wasn't.

'Turns out I'm not such a hard-nosed bitch after all.'

'Listen, she'll ask you to go to Scotland with her, you wait and see. She'll spin you a line about it being a research trip or some other crap. And even if you still doubt me, ask yourself this: what's the harm in going with her and finding out who is the liar once and for all?'

Huxtable was right in one respect. At the end of October Linda sat me down and asked of me 'a rather large favour'.

Would I consider accompanying her on a trip to Scotland?

# One Month Before

## *Henry Sinclair*

'I spoke to Linda's friend Bernadette yesterday. She mentioned that Linda has been talking to a publisher,' Henry says.

They're in the dining room at the Charter Club. It's an Indian summer, though you wouldn't find any signs of it inside the mahogany walls of the dining room. The air-con is the only concession to the heat. Jackets remain on. Shirts buttoned up. Sweat slides down Henry's back. The heavy Burgundy was a bad choice. Curtis spits out a chunk of steak into his napkin, loosens his top button and drains his water.

'Are you OK?' Henry asks.

The look he passes Henry holds a lot of history, blame too. Curtis had wanted something more definitive for Linda last time round. It's not enough to disgrace her, he'd said, she knows too much. He'd mooted an accident or a suicide even, but Henry had limits and persuaded him that publicly shaming her would be enough to neuter the threat.

He was trying to be kind, show his humane side, but now his generosity has come back to haunt him and he hates her all the more.

'The steak is tough. Waitress, this steak is rotten. I know a bad steak when I smell one.' There's a murmur on the table next to him and the man turns to remonstrate before he sees who it is that's speaking.

'I'm terribly sorry. I'll get the chef to make you another.'

'I don't want steak. Get me a Caesar salad.'

Henry looks alarmed. He should be. The choice of food tells Henry everything he needs to know. Curtis is not a salad man.

Henry eats his coq au vin. Sweat pebbles his forehead. He gulps water, fills his glass then downs another. 'Such a filthy thirst,' he says, but he's playing for time and Curtis knows it. Trying to come up with a solution to the Linda problem to justify the money Curtis funnels into his offshore account every year. 'Christ,' Henry says, 'the air-con is as good as useless in here.'

The waitress brings the Caesar salad. Curtis takes a mouthful of lettuce before admitting defeat. 'Who eats this crap?'

Henry places his knife and fork on the plate with a clatter. His face has ruddied and not just because of the wine. It is an idea that has fired him up.

'Gabriel,' he says.

'Is that the best you can do?' Curtis says. 'Look what happened after the party.'

'It was too open-ended last time. This time I'll make sure we do it properly.'

They sit in the park, tucked under the shade of the trees. Kids wheel and shriek. Above them, the whir of a police helicopter chasing a car thief, or an armed robber no doubt. A plane's contrail slices a brilliant sky. Jackets are off. Sleeves rolled up.

'The thing is, Curtis, we can't just go in and deal with Linda. It's too risky, what with that moron from *The Times* sniffing around. We have to be creative.' Henry knows Curtis likes a bit of creativity. 'We got it wrong last time. But we know Gabriel can't refuse a woman. A proper woman. Tabloid circulation would collapse if it weren't for his sex life. We set him up with . . . Mariela. Yes, that's who. Mariela disappears after their rendezvous. Gabriel is in the frame.'

'And what do you propose doing with Linda?'

'Linda will be with me. My cottage in Scotland is lovely at this time of year.'

'And how do you plan on getting her to Scotland? She'll hardly agree to be your house guest.'

Henry laughs at his own audacity. 'No, she won't. But what if one of the women from the website lived up there and happened to offer her an interview?'

Curtis snaps his eyes shut. Henry knows he's trying to decide whether this is the most ridiculous plan he has ever suggested, or if it is quite brilliant. He's hoping for the latter.

'Linda travels to Scotland where our fictitious victim lives. Meanwhile, Gabriel will be under investigation for Mariela's disappearance. Her choice will be simple: save her son and stop digging or—'

'Or?' Curtis interrupts.

'Gabriel faces the music and we deal with Linda.'

'She'll check the woman out. You won't be able to fool her with some fictitious name. She's not stupid, unfortunately.'

Henry considers this, refuses to accept his plan is flawed. All it needs is a little refinement.

'What say I give her the name of a real woman, one of the cleaners in the cottages. I'll find someone who is around the same age. They'll be none the wiser, and Linda will be satisfied.'

Curtis whacks Henry on the back with such force he almost falls off the bench. 'I knew there was a reason we were friends. Just one thing . . .'

'Yes?'

'Make sure that woman who runs the website accompanies Linda. I wouldn't want to miss an opportunity to get rid of her when no one's looking. Two for the price of one.'

264

# Thursday 4.20 p.m.

## *Linda*

Knock knock. Who's there? Someone is at the front door. A persistent type, whoever they are. Thank God for perseverance. My spirits soar. *I'm here. Back here. Help!* Footsteps circle the cottage, squelching against the mud and the mulch. My face is pasted to the window, fist pummelling the glass. Whoever it is is moving closer, not far from my window now. I try to reel this visitor towards me by sheer force of will.

'Can I help?' It is Anna's voice asking, a pitch too high, laced with nerves. The footsteps stop their march, turn and walk in the opposite direction, towards the entrance.

'I brought you . . .' Words snatched away by the wind. '. . . brown trout. Freshly caught . . .'

I move to the bedroom door, press my ear to it, desperate to hear the conversation. A sing-song lilt I recognise. Emily, the woman from the general store. Why would she have come? And when had Anna expressed a liking for brown trout?

'Thanks.'

Emily dispenses advice on how to cook it, six minutes in the pan, a pinch of salt, a knob of butter. I feel a stab of pain, nostalgia for a time when recipes and cooking mattered.

'Oh, wait a second,' Anna says. 'I'll get you that shopping list.'

'Shopping list . . . oh aye. Visitors, have you?'

'Just a few. Here you go.'

'Right. Well, it won't be ready until tomorrow evening. I'm rushed off ma feet right now.'

She walks across the driveway, slams the car door and my last sliver of hope drives away with her.

In the mirror, I consider my injuries. I take a towel, wet it in the sink and scrape it across my bloodied face. Then I press it to the back of my head, where the tree has cut an incision two or three centimetres long. My body sings in agony, but the pain itself is an irrelevance now. What is worse is the knowledge that Anna did this to me.

I see her face again, white with fear as the Scot's voice insisted she hurt me. 'What are you waiting for?' he'd asked, like a bully in a playground forcing the weaker child to collude in his game.

And she had obeyed.

*Sorry.* Did she really say that? Or was it simply what I wanted to hear? The fact is I don't trust myself any more. How can I, when Anna turned out to be a stranger.

I employed her after Bernadette insisted I get some help around the house, 'because it's clear you're not up to it yourself' was her constant refrain. Usually, while I was still drinking, her words would run off me like water, but now in sobriety and with a purpose, the book, the website, the renewed zeal of getting to Curtis and Henry, I saw my house through her eyes. The old newspapers stacked high, books tumbling out of shelves, piled by doors, the grime. Christ almighty, I had let it go. It was to Bernadette's credit that she hadn't admitted defeat and persevered with her visits through the years; my home was enough to end the most hardy of friendships.

Anna was hired on the basis she didn't flee the house at first sight, and yes, there was something about her I immediately liked. I sensed she was fragile, bore damage from the past which I attributed to the death of her mother, but during our time together she relaxed, opened up, gave me glimpses of a warmth, a kindness at her core.

At least, this was what I believed.

Now it transpires she was simply a very good actor.

Except, I'm not ready to believe she is rotten. Call me a fool, but I'm convinced there is something that eludes me, a catalyst for her actions that has set her on such a destructive path.

And until I work it out, I cannot find it in myself to hate her.


Time drifts. At some stage a knock on the door stirs me from my stupor. It is Huxtable with a hot drink, another sandwich. He bends down to place it on the floor and for a moment, I am above him, his head close to my foot. I consider kicking it, snatching the key from him, but these are precious seconds I waste to thought because before I know it, he is upright again, closing the door behind him, turning the key in the lock. Another chance gone.

I am too slow, too old, too tired for this game.

Picked myself up too many times. Lost again and again.

Perhaps I should have learnt my lesson the last time they tried to stop me.

# 2000–2008

## Linda

It came as a relief to leave the Home Office. I wasn't fit to be in the post and limped through to the election safe in the knowledge an annihilation was on the cards. It seemed like a fitting end to be buried under the opposition's landslide.

Unlike many colleagues who lost their seats, I won mine by a narrow margin. Without a Government post, I found myself with more time on my hands. I could have thrown myself into being a good Member of Parliament, railed from the backbenches against factory closures, the sale of playing fields or the high cost of rents. Or I could have turned to my son, acknowledged that he was struggling, couldn't cope, that he needed me. I could have held him and listened and maybe we could have worked through his problems together. Instead I went through the motions, shook him awake in the morning, insisted he washed and went to school, kept him fed and watered. Arranged for him to see a therapist, and when she recommended a hospital stay, I agreed to that too. I doled out his medication when he was discharged, encouraged him to retake his exams, and all the time he slipped further and further away because what he needed wasn't a timetable or a menu or expensive counselling, a mother on autopilot. He needed love and attention, but my mind was elsewhere.

The girls the girls the girls.

How to right a wrong?

I couldn't think of anything else.

By 2001 Jonathan had persuaded his news editor to run a story about Curtis Loewe and Henry Sinclair and the dubious behaviour at their Cotswolds parties. There was no outright accusation of sexual abuse, the lawyer wouldn't countenance it, but it was written in such a way as to suggest they had serious questions to answer. It wouldn't have landed a killer blow, but we hoped it would persuade more victims to come forward with their stories. Jonathan had tried to trace the original two girls who'd made the police complaint but they had disappeared, slipped between the cracks of life.

The night before the story was due to run, Jonathan got a call from his friend on the newsdesk. The editor had personally intervened to spike it.

'The fuckers must have found out,' Jonathan said in the pub that night. He was already a bottle of wine down. 'They've got friends everywhere.' He was distraught. 'No one wants to believe it, that's their trump card.'

We stayed at the pub until last orders, when I called a cab. Against my advice, Jonathan refused my offer of a lift. He needed to walk off the rage, he said, otherwise he'd never sleep. He made it halfway home before he was attacked, punched and kicked in the face. Two ribs broken. He woke up in hospital three days later.

Jonathan was stubborn, always has been, and he refused to connect the attack with his attempt to unmask Curtis and Henry. I suspected this was for my benefit; he wouldn't have wanted me to blame myself. 'For God's sake, Linda, it was probably your run-of-the-mill homophobic attack.'

'But you're not gay.'

'How were they to know that, late at night?'

'They almost killed you.'

'Don't be so dramatic. We live in London. It was bound to happen at some time. And by the way, you can stop bringing me those stews now. You have many attributes, but cooking is not one of them.'

I decided to try a different tack and devoted my time to campaigning for better laws to protect children, tougher safeguards against abuse and checks on those who worked with children. No question, I was a hypocrite, but better this than nothing at all. When I was asked to chair a report into historical abuse in children's homes, I thought my time had finally come, a golden opportunity to root Curtis and Henry and their ilk out once and for all.

I should have known they would never allow me to get too close.

It was late Saturday afternoon, not long into the role, when a call came in from the *News of the World*. They were running a story the next day, front page, and would I like to comment?

They'd seen documents relating to my time in office that allegedly proved I had offered companies Government contracts in return for sizeable donations to the party. Not only that, but there was the accusation that I had siphoned off a portion of the money for my own personal benefit.

Henry had done a number on me. It couldn't have been anyone else. He had encouraged me to fundraise in those days and I was only too happy to oblige. I had no idea he was offering sweeteners on the side. And if the amount going into the party account was less than the donations, it would have been Henry taking his cut. If anything, I was guilty of naivety. I had trusted Henry back then, but even when I thought he was on my side, he'd been incriminating me to cover his own back.

My name was filth, I resigned before I was sacked from the abuse inquiry. Hounded by the press, I retreated, locked myself away, refused to answer the door for fear a reporter or photographer would spring from the bushes. I hit the bottle for comfort – such a bloody cliché – watched television for company.

Gabriel didn't come near, muttered something about his reputation when I questioned his absence on the phone. But he had been thinking of me. When I tuned in to watch his stand-up routine at the Apollo, I was the butt of his jokes.

He got some laughs, at least.

Worth it, I supposed.

# Saturday, 15 November 2014

## *Jay Huxtable*

His knee is twitching. He places his hand there to still it but it has no obvious effect. For once he's grateful that John is playing techno. Jay can't stand it, hates the way the beats crash against his skull, but tonight at least, it's doing him a favour, disguising his unfortunate nervous tic.

They're in the van together, parked opposite a Japanese restaurant in Hampstead. It is Saturday night and the streets are bulging with people rich enough to burn money on raw fish and order wine from way down the list. Jay has pressed his nose up against the glass of that world but it's not his, never will be. Take tonight, for instance. Even if Jay liked sushi (he doesn't), he won't be eating it. He'll be lucky if he scores a bag of crisps. They're here on a job, the scope of which no one has fully explained. 'Surveillance,' John unhelpfully informed him. 'Should be right up your street, Sunshine.'

Mariela is meeting Gabriel Miller for a date. Yes, you heard it right: Mar-i-fucking-ela. Of all the women whose talents could have been enlisted to ensnare Gabriel Miller, they had to choose the one he has fucked. Not just fucked – that makes it sound cheap. Jay made love to that woman, coaxed screams of pleasure from her. And there's no way Gabriel Miller, for all his millions and his tedious crowd-pleasing jokes, will ever get her to come like he did.

That said, he's angry with her. Correction, he is fucking furious. Hasn't had so much as a text since the night he spent three hundred quid taking her to dinner. What a bitch. But my God, look at her! He feels a warmth spreading between his thighs at the sight of her outline sashaying into the restaurant, a dress sprayed on to her body. He's thinking of her face, and that gyrating thing she did that was just so . . . Don't think of that. Don't fucking go there.

Gabriel Miller is already inside the restaurant. He and his crew of friends arrived half an hour ago. John has told him that everything tonight rests on Miller falling for Mariela's seduction, but seriously, is there a man in London who wouldn't?

'You have tae wonder, are there any women left he hasn't shagged?'

'He hasn't shagged her yet.'

'No, but he will.' John starts to laugh. 'Oh Jesus, I forgot, she treated you tae a night, didn't she? Did you think you were special?'

'Fuck off.'

'Hey man, chill. I'm just having you on. Here, have some of this, it'll perk you up.'

John hands him a plastic bullet packed with cocaine. Jay considers abstaining but the prospect of spending a sober night with John coked up to the eyeballs is too much even for his willpower.

'Thanks. Don't mind if I do.'

He sits back and closes his eyes while he waits for the drug to burst into his bloodstream. When it does, a few seconds later, the chemical whoosh, like a slice of lightning, makes him smile for the first time tonight. The taste of burnt plastic dripping down the back of his throat is less pleasing, but hey, you can't have everything, can you?

'Look, he's over at her table now,' John says. His jaws are chewing gum, fast and furiously, like it's an Olympic sport. 'Next stop, Gabriel Miller's house.'

'How do you know he's going to invite her back?'

John eyes him up as if he's some kind of alien life form. 'Ah like you, man, but if they were handing out medals for sheer fucking stupidity, you'd be right up there on the podium.'

They follow the cab through Hampstead to Gabriel Miller's house. Jay recognises it from his previous visit and once again it makes him itch with jealousy. It doesn't seem fair, how one bloke can have everything he wants and all Jay gets to do is peer in at his beautiful life. He used to be funny himself, all his mates at school said so, even the lads in the station would have agreed, but that was before Stacey went and took all the fun out of him.

Jay wonders if Gabriel has said something to make Mariela laugh, because they're giggling like a pair of schoolkids as they fall out of the taxi and into each other. Gabriel takes her hand and leads her down the path. At the door, he stops, his hand goes up her dress, and Jay can feel it, soft and wet, as if he's touching her himself.

'Now what?'

'Give them a bit of time tae settle and we'll take a look.'

A look! Jesus Christ, this is his personal fucking nadir, have some mercy, please.

'Hello . . . Hello . . . anyone there?' John taps him on the forehead. 'Ah thought ah'd lost you for a moment. Here, have another toot, get sparky.' John hands him the bullet again. He takes it without thinking this time. He needs something to help him. One nostril, then the other, and the first one again for good measure. It kicks into his head.

'Better?'

BOOM. BOOM. It's like someone's fixed an amplifier to his heart. The noise is crazy, drowns out everything else. He shouldn't have topped himself up, but this flare of self-awareness comes way too late, the drugs have already whizzed him past the

274

tipping point, one layer of agitation sits on another and another, like he's a human lasagne shot through with anxiety.

Gabriel's garden backs on to allotments, which means they can get a bird's-eye view. Everything is conspiring against him tonight. At John's insistence, they go along the outer perimeter, 'so we leave no trace,' he says, but the instruction doesn't reach Jay and he falls into a plot.

'Watch where you're going,' John hisses. 'Ah said leave no trace. What's the matter with you?'

A question flies through Jay's mind, *Why no trace?* But it's stolen away before he has the chance to say it out loud.

'Oh aye . . . !' John has scaled a fence. He's now crouched down in a hedge at the far end of Gabriel's garden.

'Take a look at this . . .' He hands Jay the binoculars.

Look. Don't. Look. Look. Don't look. Fuck, fuck. Is she really doing that? He thought that was just for him. The ecstasy painted on her face, that can't be right. Only Jay could make her come like that. She said so herself. But no, she's doing it now. It's in her repertoire, one of her many acts for sad saps like him and Gabriel. They have something in common after all. Now she's sinking down and her mouth . . . fuck that mouth and those lips . . . fat juicy lips . . .

'Give us the fucking binoculars, you perv! Come on, let's get back tae the van.'

John makes a call on the way back to check nothing has changed. Jay doesn't know what might have changed and what the original plan was, so he keeps shtum, the word *bitch* melting into his bloodstream to run alongside the drugs.

He remains in this chemical holding place for hours. Time liquefies, goes gooey in his hands. Now and again he does a reality check and remembers he's sitting in a van with a guy who repulses him, having just stood in an allotment, watching through binoculars as the woman of his dreams fucks another man (a famous man). Fuck, there's a lot to be said for the police force.

Jay won't be going back to the force.

The force is elsewhere tonight. It's flown away. It's on the Mozart Estate sticking shoes to carpets. There's no Jedi left in him. It's the dark side that's gripping him, squeezing, pulsing, strangling. He can't make it stop.

Gabriel leaves the house first. Strange, Jay can't understand: why would you leave a woman like Mariela in bed alone? But there you go. The street is still dressed in black when she emerges. It's gone three in the morning and she pulls on a coat, as if stung by the cold, and goes over on her ankle. She curses in a language he doesn't understand, but he recognises a curse when he hears one. Casting around, her eyes happen on the van and she walks hesitantly towards them. John steps out and opens the back door for her but before this, he turns to Jay: 'I'm relying on you, pal. Just do as ah say.'

John tells Jay to sit in the back with her. 'Hey, it's you,' she says, as if he didn't know. He can't even raise a smile. Can't look at her. Her face is red with Gabriel's stubble, smudged mascara. He thinks of that look he believed was all his until she gave it to Gabriel. He hates her, a viscous drug-fuelled hatred that's shouting at him, needling him, demanding an answer.

As the engine starts, Mariela hands Jay a pair of men's boots. 'Gabriel's shoes. Just like I was told.' She eyes them expectantly, waiting for some kind of acknowledgement: *Didn't I do well?*

The van stops, could only have gone round the corner.

'What now?' Mariela says as John climbs into the back. 'Are you taking me home?'

'Not exactly.'

Her eyes flit between the pair of them. John and Jay. Jay and John. 'Hey, c'mon, what's happening?' She's smiling at first but fear quickly floods the smile. 'I did everything you told me to do,' she says. Jay senses her terror and it pleases him. He can feel her heart boom-booming in the van. That's the style, his anger says, she deserves to be shaken up a little.

'Hey, darlink,' she says in her accent. Spanish? Italian? He can't quite remember. 'It's me, come on. We had fun, didn't we?' She changes tack, reaches her hand out to him. It touches his face and he can smell it on her fingers, her breath.

'You fucking bitch!' His hand flies out in front of him, connects with her face. She falls back, on to a bag. It's only a bag, for fuck's sake. Why is there blood? Too much blood. Jay moves her. She groans, a different groan this time, not one he wants to hear. 'Mariela, Mariela. Fucking hell. Do something, John.' John isn't doing anything, it's like he's faded from the picture. Jay edges Mariela off the bag, slowly, gently. He's practised in first aid. There's something in there that's hard, something else sharp that she has fallen on. He unzips it to find a knife, a hammer, handcuffs.

John's voice leaks into the air.

'Welcome to the dark side, son.'

Jay is having one of those nightmares where he's done something irreversibly bad and he's waiting to wake up. Wake up. He can't. This is it. However much he hates Mariela, it doesn't add up to her listless body.

John, on the other hand, is in full swing. Like Mariela is all in a day's work. He's done it before. Course he's fucking done it before. This knowledge sends a momentary flare of hope through Jay. John has done this before and he can still breathe and drink a pint and smile. Jay looks again at his face. Has he seen him smile? A proper smile. He hasn't. The hope is ash. He doesn't want to be John. He wants to be Jay. The old Jay. DS Huxtable. Not going anywhere fast. Speed is overrated. It costs. Why did nobody tell him this before?

John is wearing latex gloves. Jesus Christ. Jay has found himself on the wrong side. He solves crimes, doesn't perpetrate them. John rips Mariela's dress and for a second Jay thinks he might be trying to help her.

His perception is quickly undone. John opens the door. They're right next to the allotments.

'The third plot on the left,' he tells Jay. 'Saw some woman with her grandson there today. Looks tidy, like she goes there a lot. We want her to be found as soon as possible.' He hands Jay a pair of gloves before telling him to put Gabriel's shoes on. 'You'll have tae carry her the rest of the way.'

Jay can see the plan as clear as day now. He's finally listening to the lines of unspoken conversation. It's where he's been going wrong. The truth, he realises, is packed in between the words where the gaps and silences sit.

He does what he's told – what choice does he have? With some difficulty, he carries Mariela's body (because she's dead now and even if she isn't, she will be soon) to the edge of the allotment and leaves her there. But before he walks away he pulls her dress down to make her decent and scratches himself as he finds a few branches to cover her. It is cold, the temperature hovering below zero, and he doesn't like the idea of her freezing out here. He gives her one last look and decides to close her eyes. Who knows, she could just be sleeping. With any luck, she might wake up from this nightmare. And so will he.

One last stop before they return home. Jay removes Gabriel's boots and notices one of his socks is caked with mud. He can't explain why; did the boot fall off in the allotment? An alarm goes off in his head but it's drowned out by John hissing at him to hand over the boots. He does as he's told and John walks up to a house two doors down from Gabriel's and places the shoes in the wheelie bin.

★

Alone, back in his flat, Jay sits on his sofa. Who knows what he does in the hours that follow – watches TV, makes a cup of tea, drinks a beer . . . He really couldn't say. The only thing he can be sure of is that he's sitting at the edge of a black hole with a mouth so big it's only a matter of time before it swallows him.

When the phone rings and he hears Anna's voice, he can't work out how many hours or days have passed.

But he surprises himself when he says the words: 'I'll be there in half an hour.'

# Monday, 17 November 2014

## *Charlie*

Monday, the Scotland trip, not too late to drop out.
And yet.

It was. I had to go, to put the lie to bed, to find out who Linda was and find my way again.

I arrived to a silent house, toyed with the notion Linda might have taken off without me. Why else wouldn't she be crashing about, readying herself for the journey, packing a cool box with sandwiches and the toffees she promised me in return for driving.

'I can't stand motorways myself,' she'd said.

'Linda?'

Nothing.

'Linda!'

I heard her voice, thin and broken as if her signal was running out. I raced up the stairs, two at a time, found her propped up against the wall, circled by a pool of blood.

I swallowed my scream. Hysterics wouldn't help.

'It looks worse than it is,' she said.

'Jesus, Linda, are you OK?'

My immediate thought was intruders. She'd mentioned having a laptop stolen the year before. In any other circumstances, I would have called 999, but I remembered who I was, who I wasn't. Questions – didn't fancy answering them, giving my name and details as a witness. *Very few people within the force even know this investigation exists*, Jay had said. I needed to call him first before I called anyone else.

I crouched down to inspect the cut on her head, eased the blood-soaked towel out of her hand.

'Just a fall,' she said.

'Come on then,' I said, keeping it light. 'You can't sit there all day. Let's clean you up, and after that you can tell me what the hell happened.'

I took her into the bedroom, brought a fresh towel for her head, an extra blanket to keep her warm, worked my way around the cut with tepid water and cotton wool. She started to cry, not in pain but because her travel plans were ruined. Tougher than she looked, Linda. I suggested emailing the interviewee, Naomi Parkes, and asking if we could postpone the meeting. Linda muttered her agreement but didn't appear reassured.

It was only when I headed back downstairs to make some tea that I saw the state of the living room: the upturned table, coffee cup spilt, plant pot upended. Bloody handprints on the hallway wall. A noise in my head fired like a siren. This wasn't a fall. Someone had been here. I switched on to autopilot, brought her tea and biscuits, settled down into the armchair next to her bed and said, 'Are you going to tell me what happened?'

She repeated the lie about having fallen. Blamed it on a dizzy spell. 'Nice try.' I described the mess downstairs, the handprints and footprints painted in blood.

'I should call the police.' *Don't want to, but I should.*

'Please don't,' she said, with a force that surprised us both.

'Who did this?'

'Gabriel,' she said. 'It was an accident.'

Linda told me about a woman called Mariela and a body and Gabriel being the last person to see her alive as if she was relaying a fantastical story she didn't quite believe herself.

I questioned whether the injury had knocked the sense out of her.

'I'm not making this up,' she said when she caught my disbelief. 'I wish I was. He came here because he wanted me to help him. He thought I was calling the police, you see. He wanted to get out, pushed past me, that's all.'

'And he hit you when you refused?' She wiped her eyes, winced at the pain. She was diminished, ashamed even. But then, who wouldn't be, if your only son had done this to you? I felt a swell of hatred towards him.

'Why aren't they here then?'

'Oh, Anna,' she said, 'he's my son. I was calling a friend first. I wanted his advice, but the damn fool never switches on his phone. Not that I would cover for Gabriel if he had really done something wrong, but I just don't believe it. This isn't him.' She pointed at her face. 'He's not a monster. You won't call the police, will you? Not right now, anyway. I'm not asking you to lie, it's just . . .'

'You should get some rest,' I told her when her words started to run slow. She closed her eyes and was gone within seconds.

I crept downstairs and called Jay from my mobile. He picked up the phone, spoke his name in a voice that suggested he'd just woken up from a long, deep sleep. I tried to explain the situation, that the trip was off, what should we do?

'I'll be there in half an hour,' he said, and hung up before I could warn him I had promised Linda I wouldn't call the police.

Jay arrived not long afterwards with a colleague he introduced as John. I told them Linda was sleeping, and could they come back later. Jay shook his head; no, that wouldn't be possible. He looked like shit, blamed it on flu, the worst bout, he said.

'Aren't they always, where men are concerned.' He didn't laugh and before I could say anything else, John was inside, prowling round Linda's house, telling me not to touch anything; 'It's a potential crime scene, so it is.'

Later, after he'd questioned Linda, he took me aside; 'You have to persuade her to go to Scotland. It's only a cut.' He'd already suggested she should leave the house for her own safety, but Linda, being Linda, was having none of it.

'The woman's just had a shock, you can't expect her to drive hundreds of miles.'

'Come on, this has been months in the planning, I don't want to mess it up now.' A whiff of desperation rolled off him, stress had formed shadows under his eyes. 'Besides,' he said, softer this time, 'it's you who'll be doing the driving. All she has to do is sit there.'

'It's too late, I've already emailed the woman she's meeting to see if she'll postpone.'

He shot me a look full of frustration. 'I'm going outside for air,' he said.

In the end, it was Naomi Parkes' reply that convinced Linda to go. She said she couldn't delay the meeting and had been having second thoughts anyway. It was now or never. That settled it. Jay arranged a hire car, since Gabriel had relieved Linda of hers, and promised to keep us up to date with any developments. It was late into the night when we left London.

The morning beat us to Largs, where we were to catch the ferry. The sky, an intense blue, teased by wisps of cloud. A syrupy glaze settled over the water. Scotland. It was good to be back here, have the canvas stretch out for miles beyond me and soothe my eyes. In London, the buildings were bold and greedy and tussled for space, but here I could catch the horizon and hold it in my gaze.

When we reached Claremont Cottage, a couple of things hit me. It was remote. Not some quaint village with a pub kind of remote. The road from Dunoon had twirled us round and round until I wondered whether the satnav was playing me for a fool. Our nearest town, Tighnabruiach, was three miles away.

The second thing I discovered when I tried to call Jay was that there was no reception anywhere in the cottage. No television either.

Thirdly, a search through the house manual for the Wi-Fi code informed me there wasn't one:

> We hope you enjoy your time at Claremont Cottage, and make the most of the opportunity to switch off from the distractions of the outside world.
>
> From the team at Isle Escapes.

The woman at the general store rose from her chair behind the counter to peer at me like a novelty. Not many new faces around here in mid-November, I guessed.

'I'm visiting for a few days, staying just down the road,' I said, pre-empting her inquiry. 'Holiday.'

'You're brave. Don't be fooled by that.' She pointed to the window and the blue sky beyond. 'It can change in a minute. Whereabouts are ye?'

'Claremont Cottage, just down the road.'

'Oh aye, I know the one. Big place, if yer on yer own.'

'I'm with a friend.'

'First time here?'

I nodded. 'I worked in Loch Lomond for years but never made it this far.'

'You and the rest of the population,' she laughed. 'We like tae keep it secret. I'm Emily Lune, by the way. Lune as in French for moon. Now what can ah get ye?'

The woman could talk, and listening to her served as a form of relaxation. She insisted I take some salmon, 'fished by my own Tom. At least he's good for something. A knob of butter, four minutes on either side, no more or you'll ruin it. Ah'll have some trout for ye later this week, if yer interested.'

'You're on,' I said.

'Some business this, isn't it?' She tapped her finger at a newspaper on the counter. 'That funny man. Murder, they reckon. Just goes to show, ye cannae trust anyone.'

Emily turned the newspaper around to let me read it. Gabriel Miller was plastered over the front page.

### Comic Arrested on Suspicion of Murder

He looked bashed up, unlike himself. Linda's smiling teenage boy nowhere to be found.

'Can I buy a copy?'

'Ah used to stock them, but no bugger bought them around here. Ye can have this one. Ah've read it cover tae cover.'

Outside, I sat by the water and read every word written about Gabriel, about Linda, even the short biography. *Gabriel Horatio Miller was born in 1984* . . .

And then I found a pocket of signal and phoned Jay.

'They found him yesterday. He's being questioned now. I'll be in touch as soon as he's released or charged.' He suggested hiding the news from Linda in case she decided to come home. 'And keep her inside. We don't want anyone to know she's up there. The last thing we need is for her to be frightened off before the meeting.'

'I'm not her jailer,' I was surprised at how callous he could be.

'No, but if she leaves, you've had a wasted trip.'

Over the next few days, time fell into a maddening slumber. I took long walks, willed myself to appreciate the lush green hills, the sound of water quickening over rocks, the shriek of a bird, the clouds rushing through a blue sky. Anything to

*285*

capture my imagination and push time onwards. But my anxiety won every time.

Waiting for the meeting, being with Linda in such close quarters, removed from the noise and distractions of London, sharpened my dilemma and its edges cut deep in to my skin. Was she the eccentric, generous woman I had come to know over the past eight months, or was she the Linda who had schemed with our abusers to stamp all over the truth?

Was it possible she was both?

The afternoon before the interview with Naomi Parkes, I arrived back from a walk to an empty house. Until now, Linda had heeded my warnings to rest, recuperate and stay indoors, but I had sensed she was growing restless. It came as no surprise to find her gone. I wasn't particularly worried; without being cruel, she looked nothing like her old self. The chances of her being recognised were slim.

I spied her laptop sitting on the desk in her room. It was open, she must have been working before she left. I'd tried to get into it many times back in London, when she was sleeping, when she'd popped out to the shops. I'd racked my brains for her password, variants on Gabriel, Linda's date of birth, zinnia, her favourite flower, all to no success.

This time I sat down and without thinking I typed Horatio1984.

I was in.

As predicted, her tome on female politicians of the twentieth century was nowhere to be found. The most recent file, last opened a few hours ago, was entitled **Whathappenedat** . . . This one had the shape of a book, with chapters, headings, and a foreword that I started to read:

*These girls weren't drunks or prostitutes, they didn't willingly go*

*along with it, as was the received wisdom at the time. They were*
*groomed. They were shown love and affection and then fed*
*alcohol and sometimes drugs so men of power and influence could*
*have sex with them at parties. Men who always got what they*
*wanted and whose money and influence has bought them out of*
*trouble. No thought was given to their victims, nor to the effect*
*the abuse would have on their lives.*

*For my part, I could have done more. I should have done*
*more. I am culpable too. I can't undo the wrongs of the past or*
*heal the damage, but I can say this to the survivors: you matter,*
*you deserve justice. You have the right to be heard.*

The moment collapsed. My anger and mistrust of Linda,
once so tightly packed, unfurled. She had been on my side all
along. And Jay? He had got it wrong. The police had made a
mistake, turned me in the wrong direction. I gripped the table,
something solid to grasp in a spinning world. *What have I done?*
*You've betrayed the woman who was trying to help you.* Tears of rage
blurred my vision. The words on the screen rushed in and out
of focus:

*You deserve justice.*

*You matter.*

*You have the right to be heard.*

I don't know how long I sat there, but it was late and darkness
had fallen when I turned and saw Linda, her face a white moon,
peering through the rain-lashed window.

And then it was gone.

I ran out through the cottage to open the door.

'Linda!'

I found her, unconscious, sodden and lying in a pool of
mud.

Drenched and beaten by the storm, I managed to drag her
back to the cottage and into the armchair closest to the fire,

where I removed her sodden clothes. 'Linda!' I patted her cheek. 'Linda, wake up!'

Was she dead? *Don't let her be dead.* Terror thudded through me. I felt her wrist. A pulse pressed through her veins. Thank fuck. I waited, held water to her lips and when that didn't work found some brandy because I'd seen someone do it on TV once. Slowly, her pallor changed, a trace of colour painted her cheeks, the blue of her lips turned to pink. Eyes fluttered open and closed.

'Wake up, Linda. You fell. You're heavier than you look.'

She licked her lips, tried to find the moisture to wet her words. 'Could I have some water please?'

'Here.'

'You were in my room.'

'You'd been gone a long time, I was worried,' I lied, turning away so she couldn't see my tears.

I let an hour pass, long enough to settle her. 'Are you OK? Can I get you anything?'

'Low blood pressure,' she said. 'It's a bugger, but I'm fine really. For God's sake, stop fussing.'

'I need to go out. Not for long.'

'In this weather?'

'I need to make a phone call. There's a spot on the main road where I get a signal. I should get the number of a doctor in case.'

She shouted something but I was already on my way out, the wind tearing her words away from me.

Jay. I had to speak to him, tell him what I had found. This was all wrong. Linda couldn't be meeting Henry. Why would she, when she was trying to expose what he and Curtis and their cronies had done? What a monumental cock-up. How had he got it so wrong?

The wind shook the car as I drove along the shoreline. The water was black and agitated and the lips of the waves danced in the storm. After a few minutes, I pulled over and checked my phone. Two bars. I called Jay. Voicemail. I started to speak, fast, my words running out before I lost reception. I tried again. Voicemail full. I raised my head to the sky as the rain pelted down, and screamed, deep and visceral, a scream loud enough to travel for miles. Anywhere but here. The wind caught it and spat it back at me.

Despair seized me. I told myself I'd try again in the morning, that losing my sanity wouldn't help anyone. I got into the car, ready to drive back when a nugget of information rose to the surface of my mind, glinting and gleaming like a diamond in the dark. DS Huxtable worked at West End police station. Secret investigation or not, I needed to contact him.

I dialled 101, the non-emergency police number, because it wasn't a life-or-death situation, was it?

'I need to speak to DS Jay Huxtable at West End police station, please.'

'Just a second. Caller, can you give me your name? It's a bad line, I can't hear you very well.'

'Anna Robertson. I've got a poor signal. My number is 07440 818 355, if I get cut off. It's important that I speak to him. He's given me a mobile number, but it's unobtainable.'

'What is it concerning?'

'An investigation he's working on. I can't say much more.'

'I'll do my best . . .'

I hoped she meant it, because the line went dead.

The storm had turned the road hostile. Rain lashed the windscreen and shrunk my vision. The wipers, manically toing and froing, were as good as useless. I wanted to go home. To my home. Not Anna's. God no. I would shed her like a skin as soon as we returned to London. To think I had been making progress, getting there, wherever there was in life, until Jay had come along and derailed me.

Snap. Something hit the car. I swerved out into the middle of the road, my body as tight as a spring. I looked for the culprit, saw the trees bent over in the wind, their branches reaching out on to the road. Nothing to worry about. I was nearly back at the cottage.

The fuzz of oncoming headlights surprised me. I hadn't seen another soul so far but here was someone else as stupid as me, battling the weather. I dipped my full beam but theirs streamed towards me, burnt everything else out as if the road belonged to them and them alone. I beeped my horn. Bad idea. The driver, startled, veered his car towards mine. A finger's distance before he righted it. I caught his eye as I passed. A nanosecond, nothing more. Long enough to feed him my anger.

Long enough to see who was at the wheel.

A face I'd recognise anywhere, even after all these years.

It was Henry Sinclair.

# Thursday

## Jay Huxtable

Events have thrown Jay off piste. This isn't how it was supposed to play out. He's a good guy, walks on the right side of life. Until last Saturday, his criminal highlights were nicking a Toffee Crisp from Sainsbury's aged eleven and drawing the knob on Toby's BMW. Fuck, if only he'd known what that simple act of vandalism would do for him, he wouldn't be here, wondering why he doesn't recognise himself any more.

'I don't like this. I want out,' he told John when they left Linda's house on Monday. He'd seen a flash of inspiration, the thrill of an opportunity, in the Scot's eyes when they arrived and surveyed the chaos. *Don't touch a thing*, he'd told Linda and Anna. *It's a crime scene*. What did he know? That was Jay's territory.

'Too late, sunshine,' John told him, 'you've already signed up for the ride. No getting off now.'

But he *had* tried to get off again, before they headed to Scotland. Hadn't answered John's calls, locked himself inside his flat, spent the whole day reading through the posts on that website, www.whathappenedatkelmore.com. The women's accusations stuck to his mind like sludge this time. On the balance of probabilities, he knew they were telling the truth, and he asked himself how the fuck he had missed all the signs. The answer stung: the dazzle of fame and glamour and money had blinded him. And now he had killed Mariela and her face, the listless face he last saw in the allotment, stalked him. He was

291

not that man – a murderer, a thug, the kind of scum who would hurt a woman and dump her body for an elderly lady to find the next morning.

Was he?

The evidence suggested otherwise.

Jay couldn't bring her back to life, but he could have gone to the police, turned himself in, paid for his crime. He considered being questioned by his old colleagues, the same ones who only a few weeks ago were admiring his new gear, the suits, the car.

*Done well for yourself, mate.*

And he contemplated going to prison, getting beaten up and worse . . . for being a copper.

He picked up the phone, dialled the number, repeated the confession, *I killed a woman, I killed a woman, I killed a woman.* Let it ring. Listened to the operator answer and the silence expand between them.

And then he hung up and wept like no man ever should.

He needed to get out, buy some food to make him feel human again. He was thankful for London, the way its streets swallowed him up and hid his crimes, made him insignificant. In the Indian takeaway, no one cared what he had done, as long as he paid for his Jalfrezi, and in the off licence the assistant smiled as if he was just a normal bloke buying a six-pack of beers.

Maybe, he thought, if no one knows, you can bury the truth from yourself.

But when he returned to his flat the truth was waiting for him.

'You seem to have forgotten your manners. When ah call, you pick up, right?' John said.

Jay would have nodded his head if he could've moved it, but John had him up against the wall, his jaws clamped between the Scot's hands.

'Aren't ye going tae invite me inside? I'd love a beer, and

that curry smells the business,' he said when he released him. 'I've something tae show ye.'

Four photographs, taken at night. Or last Sunday morning, to be precise. They showed Jay lifting Mariela's body through the allotments – *You'll have to carry her the rest of the way*, Jay remembered John saying that. *Why me?* he'd thought, but didn't ask. Now it was clear why.

Leverage.

'Let's just say ah'm holding on tae these in case ye have any second thoughts. Ye had better pray tae God they charge Gabriel Miller, because if they don't they'll start looking for another suspect. Do you hear what I'm saying?'

*Loud and clear.*

When he reaches the farmhouse in Scotland, it is not the real Jay Huxtable who talks to Anna or Charlie (he's not the only person who's taken on an alter ego), it is someone else, pretending to go along with John's plan. He sees Anna in the car and before the van has even stopped, he is out, sprinting to get to her first. He knows something John doesn't. The short clip of her on his voicemail last night. No more than a few words before she was cut off, but enough to convey her panic, her outrage that he had got it wrong. Linda was trying to help, not obstruct them.

Now he needs her to calm down before John picks up on her vibes.

'Just play along for now,' he says, hopes she understands, prays his face is conveying the danger she is in. He can already hear John's boots stamping towards them. Tension stretches the moment so tight he fears it is going to snap. 'Don't say a word to him. I'll do what I can.'

You see, despite everything, Jay has not given up on being the good guy just yet.

★

The day runs on and he's desperate to carve out an opportunity, but he can't find one anywhere. When he hears Anna letting Linda out of her room, his heart jumps with hope, and when he sees her streaking through the grass he doesn't move. Only when John screams at him – 'What the fuck . . . Are ye asleep, man? She's out there now!' – does he make a show of running after her.

Later, when the woman from the general store delivers a trout (a trout!), he allows Anna to answer the door and write the shopping list.

He reads it before she hands it over, his eyes running down the page. Once, twice. He's about to say something when he realises what she has done. As chances go, it is Rizla thin.

But he lets her take it anyway.

# Thursday 5.05 p.m.

## *Detective Inspector Victoria Rutter*

'Nice man,' Victoria Rutter remarks as DS Clyde runs her through a list of John McKee's greatest hits. GBH, ABH, possession of an offensive weapon, to name a few. He works for an outfit called Chadwick Security, and the company's website, although too discreet to go into detail, claims to organise security for high-profile clients in the banking, media and film industries. What Victoria wants to know is what was John McKee doing chewing gum outside Gabriel Miller's house on the weekend Mariela Castell was killed?

The news of DS Huxtable's departure has also unsettled her. Victoria had envisaged chatting to him on the quiet about his investigation (if you can call it that) into Curtis Loewe. But Jay Huxtable was kicked out of the force in January after painting a knob on his love rival's BMW. She's heard it all now. With regard to his current employment, his former colleagues informed her that he is wearing better suits and smiling, *because he was a miserable bastard before*, but they couldn't be more specific about his new role, other than telling her he worked in security.

*Security.*

She's in the middle of having a word with herself, issuing a warning not to leap to hasty conclusions, when DC Rita Halton informs her she has located Charlie Pedlingham's car.

The white Volkswagen Polo was found abandoned on the coast in East Sussex three days ago.

'I've checked it out and a few personal effects were

recovered,' Rita says. 'An old wallet and a kids' book, no note. That's something, I suppose, but it doesn't look good.'

'Clancy, I need your help.'

Victoria brings him up to date with the news about Charlie's car. 'The sea has been rough all week. It was parked by the roadside, fifty metres or so from the edge of the cliff. We didn't find much inside – a book, no note. Although suicide has to be one line of inquiry.'

'Maybe that's what they want you to think.'

'I'm pulling together a press release. It's one missing woman, not the kind of story your lot would normally deem worthy of more than a couple of inches. I'll give you all I've got. A picture of her, her car, her possessions. Any chance you can twist a few of your fellow hacks' arms and get it as much coverage as possible?'

'That's the advantage of being an old git, I've been around long enough to have some favours owing.'

'One more thing . . .'

'Go on.'

'I'm thinking of charging Gabriel Miller.'

'What?'

'If you were to suggest as much in your newspaper tomorrow, I'd obviously have to deny we ever had this conversation.'

'You've lost me.'

'If Sinclair and Loewe *are* behind this, it wouldn't do any harm to let them think their plan has worked. After all, it would be a terrible shame if they got careless.'

'I always knew there was a reason why I liked you,' Jonathan says.

'The time is 5.32 p.m. on the twentieth of November 2014 . . .'

DI Rutter assesses Gabriel Miller. Experience tells her he is close to the edge, the precipice reached by some suspects where sleep deprivation and endless questions and the filth that's built up on their skin, the stench of three-day-old breath, their unwashed bodies, leaves them beaten, open to suggestion, inclined to say whatever the hell it is they have to say to make it stop.

DI Rutter doesn't want Gabriel Miller to fall over the edge. In many respects, the man is odious. What kind of son would hurt his mother and leave her bleeding, in pain, alone? But, she doesn't believe he killed her. A hunch? Not quite. It is a theory born out of the evidence amassing to the contrary.

The set of his jaw, the way he holds his body ready for impact, tells her he is braced for another onslaught, a barrage of accusations and questions, so much so, that when she passes him a photograph of a man, and asks him, gently and quietly, if he has ever seen him before, Gabriel's face is filled with such relief, she thinks he might cry.

'No,' he says in a soft tone that mirrors her own. 'I would remember that face if I'd seen it.'

'Did your mother ever mention that she was planning on going away anywhere?'

Gabriel begins to shake his head, then hesitates, screws his eyes up as if he is mentally scrolling back to Monday morning.

'The car. She said I couldn't have it because she was going to Scotland. And there was a suitcase in her room.'

'Do you know where she was going, or why?'

'No. I didn't bother to ask her.'

DI Rutter lets a silence fall between them as the information settles. It is broken by the sound of Gabriel crying.

'Please,' he begs her, 'find my mother.'

# Thursday

## Charlie

After my encounter with Henry on the road, I knew sleep would elude me. My mind chattered and churned throughout the night. What was he doing here? Was Linda really meeting him, and if so, why? By early morning, exhausted and defeated, I got up, dressed and left the cottage in the hope of reaching Jay.

Outside, an eerie calm had replaced the storm, the water winking in apology for the previous night's antics. I walked up and down the roadside, phone aloft, willing a few bars to rise up on my phone.

Nothing. It was as if the storm had blown it away and severed my last connection to the outside world.

Linda was waiting in the hallway when I got back. Suitcases packed.

'You look terrible.'

'Thanks.'

'Where have you been?'

'I had to make a phone call.'

'We should get going . . . Oh, Anna, are you OK?'

Tears burst out. *Get a grip.* 'I'm just tired, that's all. So much for the country air.'

Linda's face was etched with worry. 'I'm sorry,' she said. 'This is all my fault.'

I fought the temptation to tell her I was leaving, right now, to catch the first ferry. But curiosity and doubt encouraged me

298

to see it through. If I left now, I'd never know for sure what Linda was up to.

'Let's get on the road . . .' I pointed to the deer's head on the wall '. . . and then we can kiss him goodbye forever.'

The route pulled us further and further away from civilisation. Roads narrowed to single lanes, carried us up heights and revealed sheer drops to the water below. Ripe clouds, fat with rain, closed in behind us. We were at the edge of everything. Isolated, cut off, removed. Normal rules of engagement were chased away.

My anxiety swelled to bursting point. 'Your book isn't about female politicians, is it?' I said. The accusation charged the air between us.

'I'm sorry?'

'Politicians . . . that's not what this is about.'

She sighed, caught out. 'No. It isn't. I take it that's what you were doing in my room last night.'

'Yes.'

'How much did you read?'

'Enough,' I said.

'Then I hope you understand why I didn't want you involved in any way. Those men would do anything to keep this covered up.'

'How do you know?'

'Let's just say this isn't the first time I've tried.'

I glanced at her, looking for a sign that would dilute my worry. Instead, I found fear fixed in her eyes. 'You can turn back if you want to. It was wrong of me to ask you here on false pretences. I'm sorry.'

Questions smashed against my skull, but I held them down. The further I probed, the greater the danger that the truth about my deception would leak out. I had to hold my nerve and my counsel. For now.

I drove on in silence, concentrating on the road ahead,

299

burning everything else from my mind. There were only the next few hours to get through, and then it would be over.

'You have a voicemail,' Linda said. She'd been using my phone to check directions and planted it in the tray between us.

Jay. It must have been him returning my calls. My heart stuttered. I needed to know what he said, what I was to do. I chanced a look down to the phone. Linda screamed. A tree reared up in front of us.

'I'm sure it can wait,' she said. 'It would be nice to come out of this alive.'

The meeting place was a crumbling wreck, cracked paintwork, moss sprouting on the windowsills, roof tiles missing. A few panes of glass were smashed. It didn't seem right. Every bone in my body screamed that something was wrong.

*Why?*

The question burned through my body.

Why were we here?

The lack of any logical explanation unnerved me. What if Linda had tricked me? Fear set inside me like concrete. Clouds swept across the hills and shaded them black. The stench of stagnant water threaded the air.

Linda headed off to investigate and I told her I would follow, but first I needed to retrieve the message from my phone.

Reception. Here of all places. My hands shook as I played it. One eye on Linda, stalking the place, shaking her head in confusion. If she was a liar, she was a class act, no mistaking.

*This is DS Clyde. I understand you had an inquiry about DS Huxtable. I'm afraid to say we can't direct you to him because he is no longer employed by the Metropolitan Police. You mentioned an investigation when you called. I'm assuming this must be a historical one because DS Huxtable was suspended in January and has not returned. I'd be grateful if you would call me urgently on 0207 302302 to discuss the matter.*

The sky cracked, split right down the middle.

*Jay.*

He had lied, set us up, lured us out here where no one would hear us. I'd been looking in the wrong direction all the time. It wasn't Linda who was out to get me. It was him, and whoever he was working for.

Curtis. Henry. The men who stood to gain by making us disappear.

'Linda!' I screamed. It wasn't my voice. Panic strangled me, blood flooded my head. We had to get out. Now. She turned to look at me but didn't move. I ran towards her. 'Linda, get in the car.'

Fear. That's what I saw. Something had changed. She was frightened of me.

'Who *are* you?' she whispered. Her voice was thin and frail.

What glorious, terrifying irony! The first time my intentions were honest, Linda chose her moment to uncover me.

'Get in the fucking car.'

I grabbed her, dragged her towards the car. 'We have to get out of here.'

'Who are you?' she asks again.

What to say? The explanation went back years, one lie layered on top of another and another. Hurt and pain. The loss of a friend.

Too much to squeeze into a second. Words would slow us down.

'Just do as I say.'

She didn't. Not Linda. I always knew she was stubborn.

She kicked and clawed and scratched, and when she refused to get in the car I slapped her hard. A reflex, a survival instinct, a moment where all that mattered was getting away from the farmhouse.

*

301

In the car, doors locked, Linda shrieking, fists thudding against the window.

The key was in the ignition and we were there, almost there, an extra minute, thirty seconds. That is all we needed.

Time we didn't have.

The van swung off the lane into the drive, sent up plumes of dust. It was them, couldn't have been anyone else. No point driving away, a car chase on those roads would send us over a sheer drop. An accident, they'd say. Convenient. There was nowhere to go.

Linda exhaled relief, she thought they'd come to save her, and in those ticking seconds I made a calculation: should I tell her who they were? Or should I say nothing, play along as if I was still on their side in the hope that I could find a way to save us?

Jay reached me first. 'Just play along for now,' he mouthed, barely audible.

I wanted to scream and kick and bite and scratch his eyes out for everything he had done, but where would that have got us?

'Don't say a word to him. I'll do what I can.'

*Him*.

John, heading towards us. 'I promise I'll try to find a way . . .' Jay let his sentence hang, unfinished.

Did I believe him? Did it matter?

He was the only hope I had.

Later he let me go to Linda, pretended not to notice me slipping out of the living room. And when she jumped out of the bathroom window, streaked towards the road, if he saw her making a run for it, he didn't react. I watched, gripped by elation and hope as she ran, then by fear as exertion slowed her pace. Only when John spotted her and screamed, 'What the fuck . . . Are ye asleep, man? She's out there now!' did Jay move and follow John out to chase her down. John was fast. It was an unfair match. He pounded the ground, arms like pistons, closing in on her. Our chances of escape shrinking to nothing. When he pushed her, I turned away before I saw the inevitable fall. Couldn't look at her face. I had enough tears of my own.

Then he made me hit her.

A test I had to pass.

The appearance of Emily Lune from the general store provided another flash of hope. She called round with an unsolicited trout. 'Ah brought ye one just like ah promised.' Had she? I couldn't remember. Not that it was relevant. She was there, standing in front of me, a friendly face. A link to the outside world.

'Thanks. How do I cook it?' *A knob of butter, pinch of salt, not too long in the pan.* I knew already, was only playing for time, trying to convey with my eyes what I couldn't with my speech. Emily stared back blankly.

My hand twitched, desperate to reach out and beg for her help. But I could hear John in the kitchen. One stray word and my act would shatter. Besides, Emily was alone. She wouldn't have been able to save us, and she would have come off worse for trying.

'Well, I'll be going then,' she said.

'Wait a second, I'll get you that shopping list.'

'Shopping list? Oh aye, visitors have you?'

'Just a few.'

I nipped into the living room, grabbed a pen, a piece of paper from the sideboard and wrote in a scrawl.

| | |
|---|---|
| *Ham* | *Milk* |
| *Eggs* | *Eggs* |
| *Lobster* | |
| *Potatoes* | |

Jay studied the list, eyes running up and down it. Did he see? Did he care? Was he allowing me one last chance of escape?

'Righto,' Emily said when she took it. One eyebrow raised at the presence of lobster. It was a pitiful effort, sure to fail, but it was the best I could think of in the circumstances.

# Friday

## Linda

The house is resting. Quiet. I suspect it is playing games to fool me.

Silent.

Before the storm.

Cortisol flushes through me, urging, pressing, begging me to do something, but the windows are shut, the doors are locked, my body is defeated. It is this combination of circumstances that produces a unique form of torture.

*Run run run.*

*But where?*

*There's nowhere to go.*

The thought that I might never touch my son's skin again, hold him, hear his laugh, watch him walk through my door, is too much to bear. Worse still, he will be locked up for a crime he didn't commit. My boy, rotting in jail, crying out his innocence, but having no one listen. I let out a wail, a mewling sound, that is pathetic and weak and mocks the intensity of my anguish.

I pull my knees into my chest, curl myself into a ball in an effort to staunch the pain that slices through me from every angle. My life has been reduced to one desire, one single wish: to see my son again, to tell him I am sorry, for not believing him, believing in him.

It was never his fault.

It was all mine.

I had longed for a baby. Hugh did too, but he never felt the lack as keenly as I did. The months racked up disappointments. We went for tests. Nothing wrong, they said, just unlucky. It might happen. *It might not.* I should get over it. And I tried, I really did. I threw myself into my career. But there was always this emptiness, this aching hole I could never fill. And then Curtis happened.

A cruel miracle.

I prayed for a girl, thought it would be easier somehow, and when Gabriel was born I wondered if I could do it, this motherhood thing, but his face and his skin and his touch told me I could. He was perfect, but still I watched for the imperfections, ready to stamp them out as quickly as they appeared. Didn't want to see a glimmer of Curtis in him.

My love was tarnished by what I imagined lay under the surface. I shaped my son with my doubt, the fear that nature would outwit nurture. Where was the trust? I never believed him when he was in trouble. I helped him, I was good at that. Easier to get him out of a fix than give him the very thing he needed most: my belief. I judged him against the past, a father he never knew, and I hoped he would be good, but the truth, the ugly, wretched truth, was that I expected him to be bad.

Then the transplant happened.

And it changed him, so I thought.

His furtive looks, stealing glances at Hugh and I, only for his eyes to dart away when he was spotted. Why did he lurk at the fringes of conversation as if he was no longer able to understand us? He would bury himself in his room, immune to our entreaties to go for a walk, enjoy the sunshine, do something. Anything.

We'd stand outside his bedroom and listen to him talking. Not to his friend on the phone, not to anyone real. He was talking to the other person inside him.

I looked it up, did some research. A third of all transplant patients believe they take on the characteristics of the donor.

Curtis had given me my son and stolen him away. And I was scared to look at Gabriel, fearful of what I might find.

And now, when it is too late, when I have little chance of seeing him again, the lucidity that has eluded me all his life comes raining down like a firestorm. My ignorance floors me. It was me who had changed. Hugh as well. Not Gabriel. After the transplant, he came home to a different house, to a mother whose lie had been exposed, and a father who loved him deeply, absolutely, but was heartbroken himself. We could barely exchange a civil word. No wonder the poor boy slunk away. And the worst part? He blamed himself. *I could get rid of him if it would help*, that is what he said when we told him we were splitting up. Why hadn't I recognised that we were destroying him? He was lost, and we didn't come to find him.

The transplant had created a perfect storm. I was relieved, yes, beyond measure, but I was also disgusted at myself for what I had done, what it had cost. I expected Gabriel to achieve the impossible; to be irreproachable, faultless, to prove that I was right to sacrifice justice in order to save him.

What teenager can meet those expectations?

I had set my son up to fail.

The evening he was picked up by the police, running through the streets naked, I believed the police, the woman to whom he'd exposed himself. Not my son, not for a second. This is it, I thought, his transformation into his father, complete. Too blind to see I was forming him in the image of my nightmares.

'I'm telling you the truth,' he said. 'There was a gang on the common and they made me strip. I didn't mean to scare that woman. I was hiding so she wouldn't see me.' His eyes begged me: *Say you believe me, just say it.*

If his mother didn't believe him, what did he have left?

But I didn't listen. I let the past come up and break us like a wave.

And weeks later, when I found him on the roof's edge, faltering in the wind, contemplating the drop, I held him and told him I loved him, but I didn't say, 'You are my son and I know you wouldn't do this.' I tucked him into bed and lay with him until his breaths grew deep with sleep. Then I went to my study and found the woman to whom he'd allegedly exposed himself, the one who was threatening to go to the press. I called her the next day. One thousand pounds for her silence.

I thought it was cheap at the time.

In truth, it cost a lot more.

As I lie in the darkness, the minutes racing towards the end, I weep tears of frustration, knowing that everything I was missing had been there all along.

## Emily Lune

A cup of tea and a wee sit down is exactly what Emily Lune needs. It's been a long day, what with all the deliveries, and she's not done yet. Not by any stretch. She still has tomorrow's orders to get ready. People think all she does is sit in the shop and read the newspapers all day. As if! An hour's break, that's all, and then she'll get motoring again. She grabs a caramel wafer and makes herself comfortable in the armchair beside the fire. She's behind on her shows. All the crime dramas. Can't get enough of them. 'Should I be worried?' Tom routinely asks her. 'You're not looking for ways to do me in, are you?'

'No need tae. I've already thought of plenty.'

It's not that she likes the violence. No, she likes to see the bad guys getting their just deserts. And she's become a dab hand at guessing the whodunnits way before they're revealed. So much so, Tom refuses to watch them with her any more. 'Easy,

DI Lune, some of us are just here for the ride,' he says when she propounds her theories mid–programme.

With the TV dramas she gets to step into another world, walk outside of Tighnabruiach where the worst thing to happen was when Billy Carrigan ran off with the Christmas Club money and spent it taking his fancy woman on a Hawaiian cruise.

When her hour is up, Emily gets back to work. The shop is off her living room and her commute involves walking four short steps. The deliveries are mainly for the elderly folk who can't make it out. A visit from Emily is sometimes the highlight of their day, God love them. She fetches Peggy's order. Five malt loaves again. She must be anticipating a worldwide Soreen famine, the way she stockpiles them. Creamed rice, a packet of chocolate fingers.

'Are ye not having anything proper?' she routinely asks Peggy, but Peggy just smiles. 'I've had a lifetime of eating broccoli. I'm eighty–seven now. If I want to live on chocolate fingers and mini rolls, I bloody well will!' Emily makes a mental note to bring her some soup tomorrow.

Anna's list is next. That's a strange one. 'What's wrong with ye legs?' she wanted to say when Anna handed it to her. She would have made a joke about her laziness, but she didn't know the woman that well. And she didn't appear the full shilling today; she'd looked at the parcel Emily delivered like it was piece of moon rock, not a sea trout.

And her eyes were awful strange too, as if she'd started a staring competition without telling Emily.

| | |
|---|---|
| Ham | Milk |
| Eggs | Eggs |
| Lobster | |
| Potatoes | |

She's asked for eggs twice, Emily notes. Is that a mistake, or does she really want twelve eggs? If she wanted two boxes of eggs, surely she'd have put eggs x 2 like a normal person. Maybe it was an oversight; after all, it wasn't just the two of them anymore. Anna had guests. Emily had clocked the men standing behind her in the hallway. And she'd seen an extra car parked at the back of the drive.

Emily stares at the list again. She likes her customers to have a balanced diet. At a glance, she'd say this was a bit protein heavy.

And then she sees something else that makes her heart thud.

'Tom,' she calls into the house. 'Come and take a look at this, would you.'

Tom emerges from behind the curtain that divides the shop from their living room. 'What am Ah supposed to be looking at?'

'See that?'

'Ah can. It's a shopping list.'

'What does that spell?'

'Ham.'

'Not that, ye numptie. Look down the list: HELP ME. It spells, help me.'

'So it does.'

'What if she's asking me to do something?'

'You know what, I think yer on tae something, DI Lune. She *is* asking ye for something. She's asking ye tae help deliver her shopping.' He chuckles to himself and gives her a kiss on the cheek. 'I'm off tae the Kames Hotel for a pint.'

It's gone eight o'clock when Tom returns and she's in bed with a hot chocolate, reading the remnants of the day's newspapers. Emily refuses to let them be thrown into the fire until she's read every last story, or every headline at least, except for the sport and the business. And if she has to read about another no-sugar diet, she'll caramelise her own head.

Tom has a different approach to bed. He gets in and he falls asleep in an instant. His descent into sleep is accompanied by a strange sucking noise, like he's storing air up for the whole night in a few frantic breaths.

She hears the first one of these breaths as she reads the final story on page nineteen.

## FEARS GROW FOR MISSING WOMAN

She shakes him. 'Wake up.'

'Wha . . . Jesus Christ, is a man no' allowed some peace?'

'Look at this, that's her.'

'Who . . . what are ye talking about?'

'This picture here – that's the woman at Claremont Cottage. Anna.'

Tom sits up and snatches the paper. 'It says here she's called Charlie Pedlingham. It can't be.'

'For the love of God!' She grabs it back. 'Thank goodness our lives don't depend on ye being a criminal mastermind. Ah'm going tae phone the police.'

## *Linda*

'Darling . . .' Henry has the charm of a snake. 'I'm back. I get to see you twice in as many days. A man really can be spoilt, can't he? Do come and sit down. We have a lot to discuss, Linda.'

He taps the bed for me to join him. He is dressed in a thick coat rimmed with fur, sturdy boots. A tartan scarf.

'Well, hurry up – time isn't on your side.'

I move to the end of the bed, as far away from him as possible. 'Oh well, suit yourself,' he says. 'Now, you know me, Linda, I'm fair. I always like to offer a person a second chance. Admittedly, you've already had a second chance and I really did think I made myself plain back then, but maybe age is mushing your brain. Why you even contemplated resurrecting this is a mystery.'

'I never planned on giving up.'

'The thing is, I am prepared to give you another option . . . Don't look so overwhelmed. It goes without saying that I don't *have* to. It would make my life a lot easier if I didn't. But we go back a bit, don't we? And I was always fond of the boy, although I dare say he's turned into something of a let-down, morally speaking.'

His voice scratches my brain, like someone is drawing a knife along its surface. 'Are you going to tell me what it is you want?'

'Patience, Linda, I'm getting there. The thing is, everyone out there . . .' he stabs the air with his finger '. . . everyone thinks you're dead. You have your friend to thank for that. Bernadette, lovely woman.'

'Bernadette has nothing to do with this.'

'That's where you're wrong. You see, she turned up the morning after you left with Anna. Let herself in when you didn't answer. The blood, that shocked her, I can tell you. She called the police straight away. When they came, it all looked a bit gruesome, that scene. If only you'd cleaned up a bit, you might have saved yourself. Anyway, one of your neighbours saw Gabriel driving away in your car and he missed his appointment at the police station. It wasn't looking good for him even before they found him in a T-shirt covered in your blood. Blood in your car too. They assumed he'd done away with you. And, as you know, you don't need a body to convict a man of murder. It wasn't even our original plan – that involved Gabriel and another woman – but when Bernadette got involved and the police headed down one path, it seemed too good an opportunity to pass on.'

'Mariela. You killed her to frame Gabriel?'

'Me? Don't be daft! Wouldn't harm a fly.'

'You've overstretched yourself. Didn't you always advise people to keep it simple?'

'Linda, they're already bought it. Look here,' he pulls a newspaper from his jacket, lays it out on the bed, 'they've already charged him with your murder. But it must be a comfort to know people have been saying very kind things about you, myself included. Death really can be the making of a person.'

'I'm not dead, Henry.'

'You always were perceptive, Linda. It's one of the reasons I liked you. You are still technically alive and so you can remain, if you choose to.'

'I'll drop the story, drop the book, whatever. I'll stop digging.' I would say anything to get out of here.

He nods his approval, rises to his feet and marches a few steps to the window. The rain smashes against it. 'God, it's bleak out there, isn't it. A whole different level of dark. And the water – I passed it on my way here, looked like a giant black hole. Quite beautiful in its own way. Now, about this offer of yours, the trouble is you have promised as much in the past and it turns out that you lied. It's all about trust, Linda, you should know that. I'm afraid once it's gone, it is hard to restore.'

'There's nothing else I can offer.'

'Oh, have some imagination. There is much more you can give. I would suggest some warm clothing. A waterproof, if you have one.'

'Where are we going?'

'Were you not listening when I said the water was lovely at this time of night?'

Slicks of black oily water lap against the boat. 'Quite a sight, don't you think? And so quiet,' Henry says. 'Listen . . .' He cocks his head to one side. 'Not a soul around.'

I imagine my body slipping beneath the surface, my limbs shocked by the cold, the water closing in around me. A splash and then no trace on the smooth glass of its surface, every last particle of heat sucked from me until there is nothing left.

'Seen enough?' I don't answer. 'I'll take that as a yes. Let's go inside. The cold is brutal.'

I assume the boat is Henry's, or it belongs to a friend who is willing to lend it out and ask no questions. It wouldn't have been a rental one – not Henry's style. Too messy.

'You have it all planned out,' I say.

'Don't sound so surprised. I'm not one for leaving anything to chance. Which brings me to you and our little problem.'

We sit down, him across the table from me, a bottle of wine, a Rioja, from which he pours two glasses. For a second I allow myself the small indulgence of believing this is a meeting of two old friends, sharing a drink and gossip, but the illusion shatters almost before it is formed.

'I want to talk about Anna. Her name's not really Anna, but I suppose you already know she's not who you thought she was.'

I feed him a thin smile and consider the wine, what I should do with it. Drinking seems too risky; I need to keep a clear head, and throwing it in his face would be too inflammatory. I push it to one side.

'But the interesting thing is, you *are* acquainted. Well, virtually, at any rate. Does the name Charlie Pedlingham mean anything to you?'

*No.*

'It's true,' he says.

Charlie. The cabin tilts. The whoosh of a fever rushes through me.

Anna is Charlie. Charlie is Anna.

It doesn't make sense.

'Why . . .' I say. The words choke me. 'Why would she work for you?'

Henry takes a slug of wine, expels an *ahhh*. 'Maybe she doesn't know she *is* working for me. Maybe she thinks *you* are

314

trying to deceive her, get close to her so you can cover it up again. After all, you did it once before. Poor Charlie was most upset when she read the letter you wrote asking that the police investigation be dropped.'

He stretches his arms out wide. The pleasure he derives from punishing me sets my head alight, turns it white-hot.

'I'm sorry to be the one to remind you, Linda, but your hands are as dirty as mine.'

She has known all along. Every day she has come into my house and put on an act when she despised the very bones of me.

'I had a reason . . .' I say.

'Everyone has a reason, Linda. Yours doesn't make you special. We are the sum total of our actions.'

Suddenly, the freezing waters appeal, the heat inside me too fierce, all consuming. Breathing the same air as Henry is scorching my lungs. I would run on to the deck and jump, end it all.

But.

Gabriel.

If I die, there's no hope for him.

'What are you going to do with Charlie?' There is no vestige of anger left towards her. I understand, completely, utterly why she would hate me. I don't blame her for anything. After all, who am I to apportion blame, given what I have done? But I know she presents as much of a threat to Henry and Curtis as I do. It is no coincidence she is here.

'Funny you should say that, Linda, because I was about to ask you exactly the same question.'

Henry's Choice. Not the sort you experience every day – the salad or the beef? Walking or taking the bus? Henry has me mapped out, the locations of my pressure points, the secrets I hide under my skin, what and who I value. He has drawn on this knowledge to present me with a question.

How far would I go to save my son?

It is not enough for me to drop the exposé. I'm a fool to think Henry would ever accept such a crude offer. Not when he has something far more sophisticated in mind.

'It seems poor Charlie has been having a rough time. She couldn't cope with the pressure of running the website. No one has heard from her in months, no chat on the threads – that is the correct term, isn't it? – no updates on her crusade for justice. She's been missing from her flat too . . . And now this.'

From a stack of magazines, he lifts a newspaper and pushes it across the table towards me.

'You'll have to search through it. Charlie has none of the front-page appeal of Gabriel. To tell you the truth, I'm surprised her disappearance even made the papers.'

He watches as I turn the leaves of the paper, scan the columns of political tittle-tattle and royal gossip and the birth of a baby panda, until I find it.

A small square of news, hidden away where no one cares to read.

## FEARS GROW FOR MISSING WOMAN

The owner of a car abandoned on the Sussex coast has been identified as Charlie Pedlingham, a hotel manager from Hammersmith in London. Miss Pedlingham's white Volkswagen Polo was found at Rottingdean near Brighton a few days ago. Detective Inspector Victoria Rutter said police were growing increasingly concerned for her safety.

'Charlie Pedlingham told neighbours she was going on holiday some months ago. She has not been seen since. On Monday, her car was found in a secluded spot near Rottingdean on the East Sussex coast.'

DI Rutter said the car contained several items thought

to belong to Miss Pedlingham, including a copy of the children's book *Wonderland* inscribed with her name.

The missing woman recently worked at the Langdale Hotel in Kensington, although she had previously lived and worked in Loch Lomond in Scotland.

'I want your help, Linda. I'd like to see you get more involved. Don't look at me like that. She was going to kill *you*. You could almost justify it as self-defence.'

'There is no way—'

'Don't be too hasty. If you do it, you are free to go and so is Gabriel.'

'And Mariela's murder?'

'We can clear that up too. Let me show you these photographs. I should warn you, they're quite upsetting.'

I look down to see three images of a man carrying a body. They're grainy, appear to have been digitally magnified, but they're good enough to reveal the woman's mane of dark hair and the man's face.

Huxtable's.

It is not a promise Henry wants from me, it is blood on my hands. Anna's blood. Charlie's. He could do it himself, sure he could, but it wouldn't be the same. This way he holds the axe over my head. I would be bound to him for the rest of my life, if he let me live.

The boat tilts and tips and when, seconds later, I hear footsteps on the gangway, panic crushes my internal organs.

Charlie is on board.

## Anna

'Where are we going?' I ask.

'You'll see.'

'I'd like to know before I see.'

'It's a surprise,' John says. We are in the driveway, the two porch lights throwing geometric shapes on to the ground.

'In you get,' he says, opening the back of the van.

'Not before you tell me where I'm going . . . Jay?' I reach out to touch him but he ducks past me into the passenger seat as if I'm not here.

'See, no one's listening.' John forces me inside.

It is dark. The cold snaps at my body. They don't feel the need to fool me any more, the pretence has shattered. I hadn't realised how reassuring it was until it was gone.


A breeze rises from the water, sneaks through my coat and down my back, where it settles like a promise. It chips at my face, draws tears from my eyes. Above, a smattering of stars are nailed to the black velvet sky. A sound rings in my ears, the slow haunting rhythm of the water slapping the boat.

'She's in here, since you're so keen to see her,' John says, tugging at my arm.

It is the tang in the air that hits me the moment I enter the cabin. A woody scent, cinnamon or something close.

Henry Sinclair is standing in front of me.

'Anna! Come and join us. We were just talking about you,' Henry says.

Linda is hunched at the table. She shifts her gaze in my direction. Her skin is pale like she is half dead. Blue and red veins knit together under her eyes.

'My name is Charlie,' I tell him.

'Then you have my sympathies.' He thrusts a newspaper in front of me.

## FEARS GROW FOR MISSING WOMAN

The owner of a car abandoned on the Sussex coast has

been identified as Charlie Pedlingham, a hotel manager from Hammersmith in London . . .

DI Rutter said the car contained several items which were believed to belong to Miss Pedlingham, including a copy of the children's book *Wonderland* inscribed with her name.

The book. My book. They must have taken it when they went to my flat, the plan already laid. Close me down. Erase my life. I'd made it so easy for them, agreeing to move home, to stop posting on the website. I had shrunk my world until I ceased to exist.

The wine glass, the nearest thing to me. I grab it and run at Henry. Don't care what happens to me, all that matters is to gouge him, make my mark on his skin like he had on mine.

'Get the bitch off me!' he screams. John moves quickest; the man is a spring, hands impatient for action. I kick him, spit, tear at his eyes.

'Help me out here, for fuck's sake,' John says.

Jay pulls me back and John's fist swings in, punches my face. The cabin spins and whirls around me. And then it goes black.

## Emily Lune

Emily calls the Crimestoppers number in the newspaper and speaks to a man who sounds sleepier than Tom, so it comes as something of a surprise when, fifteen minutes later, her phone rings and a proper police officer announces herself as Detective Inspector Victoria Rutter. Emily repeats the story because she is not confident the man from Crimestoppers would have registered all the details.

'I'm sure it's her. Her hair is different – short, like a man's,' she tells DI Rutter and, seeing the way Tom rolls his eyes, wonders whether that's classed as un-PC. 'And she didn't say her name was Charlie. She said it was Anna . . .' Emily is beginning to lose faith in her own story. Now that she's saying it out loud to a proper officer of the law, she can see it sits on the wrong side of outlandish. 'Oh yes, Ah can tell ye where she's staying: Claremont Cottage. It's a rental place owned by an English fella. Well, he says he's Scottish, but ye know the sort . . . his great Aunt Aggie once had a cup of tea in Gretna Green . . . Tom, what's the fella's name? Ah can't remember.' Tom is sitting up in bed now and takes the phone from Emily. 'Henry Sinclair, that's who owns the place. Some big cheese in Government a while back, and my God does he let you know it. He's here at the moment. Ah've just seen him get on his boat down by the moorings at the Kames.'

She recognises a pulse of excitement in Tom's voice, his words run breathless into each other. 'Yes, he was with someone. Ah couldn't tell ye who, though.'

When he's finished talking, he takes a few gasps to make up for the lost breaths and holds the phone out in front of him as if it's some kind of wonder.

'What is it? What did she say?' Emily is annoyed that Tom stole the phone and is now in possession of more information than she is.

'She said they're going tae send a team.'

'A team?'

'That's what she said.' He swings his legs out of bed and pulls on his jeans.

'Where are ye going?'

'Well, if he is up tae no good, he'll have got away with it before their team make it past Glasgow.'

The man has taken leave of his senses. 'Ye can't go out alone.'

'Who said anything about being alone?' He shoots her a wink and picks up the phone. 'Danny, how are ye, man?' She trails her husband downstairs. 'We might have a wee spot of bother. A late-night trip down the West Kyle, what d'ye say? Good man. As quick as ye can.'

By the time he leaves, he has made five phone calls. 'We have a wee posse, so we have.'

'And what if it's nothing?' she says. 'Dragging them out of their beds tae chase a boat through the night.' There's a twist of annoyance in her voice. For someone who's always mocked her own sleuthing, he's remarkably keen to get stuck in. And more to the point, where does he think he's going without her?

'Then,' he says as he walks out the door, 'they'll never let me live it down.'

She grips his jacket and pulls him back. 'Oh no ye don't. If ye think yer leaving without me, ye've got another think coming.'

## Linda

The impact of the Scot's punch fells Charlie. She slumps to the floor. I spring up from the table to offer comfort, a kind word, whatever it is I have left to give, but Henry holds me back.

'Hardly worth it, I'd say. It's time to go up on to the deck.'

The Scot carries Charlie up the narrow steps. Her eyes are closed but the rise and fall of her chest tells me she is still alive. For now, at least.

The air smells of fire and frost. In the sky, a few stars burn through a ceiling of black. And the waves, the rhythm of their call, a slow clap against the boat, tell me this must be the end.

Huxtable holds Charlie up while the Scot drags me forward, but it is Henry's voice that speaks.

'You can both go. Or Charlie can go. And you save yourself and your son.

'That is your choice.'

I rest my hand on Charlie's shoulder, feel the cut of her bones through her clothes. I press my eyes shut, pray to God I can be spirited away.

And maybe this once, my prayers have been answered. A bright blinding light dazzles and soaks through my lids.

I open my eyes to see her slipping away from me.

Falling into the water.

Charlie.

Then another splash.

I look around to find there are only three of us left.

Huxtable has jumped in after her.

## Emily Lune

They meet at Tighnabruiach pier. Six of them who make up the small flotilla of fishing boats. The night is black save for a few wisps of grey cloud and a small scattering of stars. Tom checks the navigation system. There aren't many boats out at night in the middle of November. Henry Sinclair has made the job of finding him very easy indeed.

Half an hour or so down the West Kyle, Sinclair's boat comes into view. Tom knows the one, it's a cruiser, expensive. It has stopped in the middle of the channel, an arm of land on either side, agitated by the nighttime breeze. Tom speaks to the others on the radio. The lights go off – against the rules, but they don't want to announce their presence, do they? They use the radar and instinct earned over years sailing these waters to guide them instead.

When the last boat has sailed into place, the final link in the chain that surrounds Henry's craft, Tom gives the signal and they turn on their lights.

In an instant the black glassy waters are washed luminous green.

## Anna

The bite of the air lifts my stupor. My head is dull with pain. A slow, cool terror trails round my body.

John props me against the side. I say nothing. No words or screams will help me now. We are in the middle of the sea channel, cloaked by hills either side. Only the beams from the cabin scratch the water with light. Otherwise, the darkness is complete.

They are all present: Jay, Henry, John, not a flicker of heat from any of them.

Henry talks of a choice.

*Both.*

*Or me.*

It is Linda's choice, not mine. To push me overboard into the jaws of the waves. To become one of them in order to save herself and her son.

Seconds pass and the water grows impatient, hungry for an answer. It smacks the boat, rocks us from side to side. Linda's hand grips my shoulder, her fingers press into the bony nubs.

Pushing me backwards.

She has no intention of pushing me to my death. She is going to jump first.

The realisation hits me in a spray of light.

Someone is out there. And I throw myself towards the water, send out a scream that rips through the sky as I fall.


## Emily Lune

'There!' Emily shouts. A head crowns the surface before sinking again. Emily grabs the torch and waves it across the water. 'Tom,' she screams, 'over here. There's someone in the water.' Emily waits, counting seconds in her head to measure how long they have been in the freezing waters, how long they have left

323

before the cold draws the life out of them. When she sees a head smash through the surface once more, she takes her chance and casts the lifebelt out towards her. She waits. Time rushes on. And then there is a hand on top of the belt and she pulls and pulls until there is no water left between the woman and their boat. Tom hauls her up. Her eyes are closed, lips frosted blue. He whips off his jumper, his coat, finds a blanket and they swaddle her in it.

Anna.

Charlie.

Just as Emily knew it would be.

There is someone else in the water too. Another figure jumped from Henry's boat. Tom's crew circle the spot where he fell and call out. Emily has swaddled Charlie in blankets, pushed her into the cabin, and now she is scanning the waters for signs of life.

She finds none.

They wait and before long the judder of a helicopter shakes the air. It hovers above, showering light on to Henry's boat. It tries to move. But Tom's men have him surrounded.

He has nowhere left to go.

# PART FOUR
Second Chances

# April 2017

## *Linda*

There was one photograph that summed up the effect that night had on Tighnabruiach. It appeared a few days after we were rescued, an image of twenty or so television satellite vans parked along the shoreline, their dishes raised up to the sky, transmitting the details of our story to various far-flung parts of the world.

Unlike most news stories, this one gathered steam rather than expended it. Every day, sometimes by the hour, came a new development. John McKee was charged with Mariela Castell's murder. He denied it, but was convicted by a jury at the Old Bailey. Jay Huxtable's body was never recovered. Charlie lodged her complaint against Curtis afresh; he tried, almost comically, to distance himself from Henry and claim they were barely acquainted. For a while, it looked like he might wriggle out of it again. He was all bluster and threats. How could anyone accuse *him* of such a thing? Ten million pounds raised for charity, thousands of children given once-in-a-lifetime opportunities by his theatre trust . . . The same old lines trotted out in his defence. His creations – Otis the Bear in *The Bear Chronicles*, a case in point – had been the childhood friends of millions. The sound-tracks to his films were the music of early years. His work was a canvas of innocence and happiness and smiley faces, where the goodies prevailed and the evil witches were vanquished. This couldn't be right. It was blasphemy.

So cemented in the national psyche was his reputation for

do-goodery, it required a paradigm shift to persuade people otherwise. But slowly commentators began to grasp that this was precisely what made him so dangerous. The cloak of fame had allowed him to carry on doing as he wished in plain sight.

It was information from the unlikeliest quarter that sealed his fate. Henry's wife Valerie had uncovered her husband's offshore bank account to which Curtis made generous payments every month. He struggled to explain that away.

News of the charges against Curtis Loewe proved a watershed. Within weeks, police were dealing with another fifty allegations of abuse. Henry, already on remand for attempted murder, was charged with ten counts of child abuse going back to the 1980s. Gradually, years after it began, the full picture began to emerge: a network of abusers allowed to flourish, thanks to an industrial-scale cover-up. The dissenting voices, those who suggested the girls might have lied about their age (*They were fifteen, almost legal*), the same types who defended the groping of women in workplaces as a bit of fun (*It was just what people did back then*) fell silent. Their noise replaced by the clamour of survivors' stories. At long last, people were listening.

I submitted my own statement to police. I told them what I had done, the letter to Chief Superintendent Bill Joplin that Henry Sinclair had drafted, and why I agreed to sign it. But I knew nothing could excuse what I did. It was an abuse of power. The Crown Prosecution Service investigated and decided not to press charges. I couldn't decide whether I was relieved or disappointed. I should have paid for what I put those women through. Selfishly, I'd hoped a spell in jail might cauterise the shame I had carried around for so long.

Charlie set up her own charity to help survivors of abuse. She invited me to be a trustee, an offer I gave much consideration before accepting. 'I don't expect you to forgive me,' I told her.

'There is nothing left to forgive,' she said.

I can't be so sure.

Frequently, the spool of images from that night plays out in my dreams. My hand on Charlie's shoulder and then she is gone, disappearing below the black surface.

The shock has thinned my memory, only the outline of events remains, little of the substance.

What I'm trying to say is that I only have Charlie's word for what happened that night.

## Charlie

This is what I've learnt:

Being listened to doesn't take the pain away, it just changes its composition.

I have let go of the shame, but regret has taken its place. I am still angry about what was taken from us and how it has changed the texture of our lives.

I wish Bex was still here but, wherever she is, I hope she knows her story has been told. That it matters. That it always did.

Right and wrong aren't diametrically opposed. Choices are complicated. We do what we have to do to survive. And protect.

I'm stronger than I thought.

You have to be strong to forgive.

I will never forgive Henry or Curtis or all those other faces who stole from us and have yet to show remorse.

But there are others who I have forgiven.

Here I am, sitting in Linda's garden on my third glass of special summer punch. We are friends, Linda and I, a wildly unlikely pairing. We are each other's reminders that good people can do bad things.

She gave a speech at my wedding last year, read a passage from *Wonderland* and said my fairytale had been delayed but was now unfolding. She said she had no right to be proud but she was nevertheless, and wasn't she blessed that I came into her life. And no, she didn't hold it against me that I had once wanted to kill her. All's well that ends well . . . she said.

The magnolia drapes overhead. Its blooms are cups of pink and cream where bees settle, lazy on pollen. The day's residual heat lingers. My head is fuzzy with Linda's lethal concoction.

Beside us, my son is dozing in his pram. His fat baby cheeks are pillow soft, arms splayed in surrender to sleep.

'Will you tell me?' Linda says.

And so I launch into the story I've told her countless times before. One day, I think, the repetition will remove all doubt.

'I felt your hands on my shoulder, right in between the nubs,' I say. 'The wind was biting at my cheeks. You pulled me back and I knew you were going to launch yourself in. I stood a much better chance of surviving the cold water than you. No offence, but age was on my side.'

She makes the pfft noise she always does.

'I jumped,' I say.

She looks down at my son, brushing her finger gently across his cheek. 'He's beautiful.'

'Takes after his mother.'

I would do anything to protect that boy. Anything.

I understand Linda's decisions, the fierce protective love that trumps everything.

But Linda didn't push me that night. I jumped to save us both.

## Linda

So what of my son, the boy who is at the beginning and end of all of this?

I made it down from Scotland in time for his release from prison. A private moment set to the flashes of a thousand cameras. The press had rejoiced in the nightmare, now they wanted the happy ending. They're nothing if not fickle.

'Give your mother a hug,' the photographers shouted, desperate for the money shot.

And Gabriel, dazed by the lights, not quite himself (not for a long time after), did as he was asked. I remember that embrace, the warmth of his arms folding around me, the purity of the moment I had longed for. 'I'm sorry,' I said and kissed his cheeks. A new start, I thought.

Not quite.

My boy was sick. The life that had showered him with celebrity and wealth had turned on him quick as a flash. It was a brutal lesson in fame's ephemerality. It wasn't, as Gabriel had allowed himself to believe, a permanent structure, but nothing more than a shimmer that the gust of a storm could destroy in an instant.

Our rapprochement didn't last long. No more than a few days before I had to explain that Hugh was not his real father, that Curtis Loewe, the most vilified man in the country, was the secret I had kept hidden. It shattered him. Our whole foundation rested on a lie, he said.

'No,' I told him. 'It is built on my love for you.'

But they were just words, with no power to reach him.

I suppose this is my penance.

My relationship with Gabriel resists repair.

It survives in some form because Jonathan is too stubborn to let it die. Gabriel moved in with him shortly after his release. It was a temporary arrangement, born one evening when he broke down halfway through Jonathan's beef en croute.

'Who the hell am I?' he cried.

'Trust my cooking to provoke an existential crisis,' Jonathan said. He made him a bed in the spare room and insisted he stayed. It was Jonathan who coaxed his emotions out and ultimately persuaded Gabriel to seek the help he needed.

He tricks Gabriel into meeting me, lunches where he omits to mention I am coming. He breezes through awkward silences. Leaves us alone to talk. Even locked us in his house on one occasion – 'quite by accident' of course.

To this day, it is the only time we allowed the past to spill out. And Gabriel spoke honestly about the memories that have jagged his mind all these years: the day in the park when he was all alone.

'You left me, didn't you?'

'I did.'

Depression, I told him. That's what you would call it. Everything has a name now. Back then I could have been diagnosed if I'd insisted. Instead I tried to push through. And most days I succeeded, maintained a relatively even keel. Work kept me afloat, the desire to do good. Other days were inescapably black, like when I found my boy acting out Curtis' film, telling me he hated me. In those moments, my mind twisted out of shape.

I left the park that day because I couldn't be around Gabriel. I couldn't be around myself. He was right. I walked away and left an eight-year-old on his own.

Some mother.

'I always felt I had to be perfect for you to love me. It makes sense now, I suppose. I had to be perfect otherwise I might be like . . .' He didn't finish. No need, we both knew who he was referring to.

We talked and talked, exhausted ourselves going round in circles. Whatever answers I offered did nothing to make sense of his confusion. And we left empty, both of us. We wasted hours but made no progress.

Perhaps this was the way it would always be.

'The healing powers of truth are vastly exaggerated,' I told Jonathan over a drink that evening.

'That's because you haven't told him the truth,' he said. 'I wish you would . . .'

'You promised not to say a word.'

'As long as I live,' he said.

# May 2017

## Gabriel

It's Jonathan's birthday and the old bastard is up to his tricks again. We've been waiting half an hour, Mum and I. Only the wisened black olives are left and we've hoovered up the bread. I'm in danger of being spectacularly pissed before we've even ordered the starters if he doesn't hurry up.

Mum and I have given polite conversation our best effort, but we're running seriously low. If I tell you we've just finished a discussion about the relative merits of the Swedish education system over our native one, you'll get my point. I've never been to Sweden and neither has Mum but we have nothing else to talk about – or maybe we have too much. I can never tell.

It's not that we don't speak. We're perfectly civil. I visit her from time to time . . . Christmas, her birthday. I like to think we've reached an understanding; there are certain things we can't get past no matter how much we talk. I can't forgive her lack of taste in Curtis. I hate what it did to Dad, although I can't dwell on it too much otherwise I get swallowed by a cloud of existential confusion. After all, I wouldn't exist if she hadn't. Now there's a concept to fuck with your head.

Jonathan takes it as a personal affront that we've resisted his efforts at reconciliation, and honestly, I wish it were possible, if only to please him. The guy is a legend, admittedly a curmudgeonly cynical semi-alcoholic one, but still, I wouldn't have survived without him. He was there in the car waiting for Mum and me when I got out of prison, shouting at the paps to bugger orf now they had their shot. On day two, I found him in my back garden, having shimmied over the wall to avoid the photographers outside.

'Haven't you got a job to go to?' I said.

'The advantage of doing so little is that no one notices when you're not there. Now go and have a shower and a shave, you're too young to smell like that,' he told me.

When I emerged from the shower, dressed in clean clothes, he had taken command of my mobile phone. 'All press inquiries are to go through me,' he announced. 'They're slippery little fuckers, the lot of them. I should know.'

'Why are you friends with her?' I asked him one night while battling through a slab of beef Wellington he'd brutally incinerated.

'Your mother is a fine woman, always was. You can't see it at the moment, but you will.'

'She's not perfect.'

'Neither are you.'

'So why don't you leave me alone?'

'Because I'm a stubborn git and I won't give up until you realise you're a better man than you think you are. Besides,' he said, watching as I cleared my plate, 'you're the only person who is willing to fake admiration for my cooking.'

I order a second bottle of wine and there's still no sign of Jonathan. 'I'll call him,' I say, for all the use it will do. He's never understood the concept of the mobile phone. As predicted, he doesn't answer. I catch the waiter's attention to ask for more bread.

I wish he'd hurry up because I'm fucking starving.

Jonathan doesn't come. Mum and I have a short discussion about whether to eat then go to find him, but we agree this is bad form, seeing as it's his birthday we're supposed to be celebrating. Instead, we pay for the wine and the olives and bread, extract the cake I (hand) made from the kitchen and hail a cab.

Jonathan lives in a surprisingly spacious 1970s house in Battersea. I ring the bell even though I have a key. I finally moved out eight months ago, but I still spend at least a quarter of my time here. It's peaceful and calm and he's always well stocked with good biscuits and wine.

When he doesn't answer, I decide to let myself in. The place has the cold, settled air of an empty house. 'Jonathan,' my mum sings like he's four years old and not in his eighth decade.

We turn into the living room from the hallway and see him sitting in his armchair. He's all dressed up, shirt and tie with its customary stain. His shoes are by his feet but not on them. He's staring ahead towards the TV, which would be fine, if the TV was actually switched on.

'I've made you a cake,' I say. 'It'll probably kill you.' But even before the words are out I can see they are in bad taste.

My cake isn't going to kill Jonathan.

He is already dead.

Jonathan had cancer. We learnt he was diagnosed early in 2014. 'I blamed his absences on holidays,' my mum said, her face heavy with guilt. He went into remission but it had returned this year. He wrote us each a note. I don't know what my mother's said, but this was mine:

> You are probably annoyed that I didn't tell you, but the truth is I couldn't be bothered with the conversations around death. Much better this way, to go without any fanfare.
>
> A few final words. Your mother loves you, always has. You're a fool if you can't see it. But I die knowing I have failed in my mission to reconcile you.

*My wine collection is yours in return for clearing my house. I hope you will continue to think of me fondly, regardless of whatever you may find.*

*Yours with love and hope,*
*Jonathan*

It is the day before his funeral and I'm supposed to be writing a eulogy. It's not going well. Not a single word I've written in the past twenty-four hours has survived a read-through. How can you condense a life into sentences and paragraphs? I'm lost. Lost without him.

When I reach his house, it is late. For a while I wander around, sinking deep breaths of air. The smell of his home, its unique olfactory key, is one I associate with comfort and safety. This was my sanctuary when my mind was breaking up, where I found slivers of sun to score the black. And his nagging, cajoling, cynical presence cut through all the bullshit that had surrounded me for so long.

I sit down in his armchair and remember the day Palab came to the door.

'Palab Joshi, Gabriel's manager.' I imagined Palab had thrust his hand out in his usual business-like manner.

'I'm pleased you called,' Jonathan said, 'because there's something I've been desperate to tell you.'

'Oh yes, what's that?' Palab asked.

'Fuck off!' And Jonathan had slammed the door in his face.

There are boxes in his bedroom, black bin-bags of rubbish. He's been preparing for death in the same way most people do a house move. I rifle through a few on the floor, reminding myself that this is the task he has set me and it is therefore OK to read whatever notes and paperwork and personal correspondence I find. They contain reporter notebooks written in a gibberish I assume to be shorthand. I turn my attention to the crate on the bed to see if there's anything more interesting. That's when I find a shoebox with my name written on it. I open it to discover a Dictaphone and a small tape labelled *Linda Moscow 1996*.

There's also a handwritten note from Jonathan.

*Dear Gabriel,*
    *I promised your mother I wouldn't tell you as long as I lived.*
    *I hope you understand.*

    *Jonathan x*

It is a version of my mum's voice, the younger, more strained one from her politics days. She's having an argument with Jonathan about a story he wants to run.

'I'm sorry,' she says. 'You have to drop it.'

'Sorry? I can't do that. I've already spoken to these girls. They trust me. They opened up to me. I made them a promise. I'm about to file the story next week. I can't let them down. Have you any idea what they've been through?'

The crackle of silence.

'Well . . . ?'

'I was older,' she says. 'Should have known better. It was only supposed to be a drink after a fundraiser. He'd raised the prospect of a large donation but was playing hard to get, dangling his wallet out of reach. We were walking along the Embankment, Henry, another woman, Curtis and me, trying to hail a cab. Curtis suggested drinks at his place. Henry agreed at first, but once we were in the taxi he said he needed to go home. "You go on, Linda, I wouldn't want Curtis to think we are all spurning his hospitality." I knew he wanted me to schmooze him, so I went ahead. I thought I could handle him.

'He made us gin and tonics – lethal bloody things. My head started to spin and I excused myself to visit the loo, throw some water on my face. He followed and I felt his arms behind me, pushing me towards another door. "You can use mine," he said. He was there waiting for me when I came out, started kissing me. The stupid bloody thing is that I was embarrassed. I'd been flirting with him, teasing him. And now I was wondering how the hell I was going to get out of it without hurting his ego. I made a joke of it, told him I was flattered but I was a married woman. He pushed me towards the wall and opened my legs with his knee.

'I told him I had to go and he laughed. "We both know you're not going anywhere." Then he forced me on to the bed.

'It didn't occur to me to scream. Isn't that odd? I always thought I would have screamed the place down. But no, not a sound. I hate myself for that.

'Of course my period didn't come. I willed it to come, just as I'd willed it not to come every month for years.

'I've only ever told one person what happened – my friend Bernadette, although I didn't mention who did it. She said I should get rid of the baby, that I'd never be able to look at him without seeing that man. "How will you be able to love him?" I even booked an appointment at the clinic, but I knew I couldn't go through with it. It wasn't the baby's fault. He was innocent. I promised myself that no one else would ever know. That I would always protect him. I knew he was going to be perfect.

'And now he is dying and Curtis is the only one who can save him. But there are conditions . . .'

Love, that's what she told me. She said our foundation was based on love, not lies.

But I chose not to believe her. I held on to my pain instead, rocked it and nursed it, allowed it to bloom and grow.

I traced the roots of her decisions back through the years, and blamed her for what they produced, the lives they strangled and suffocated.

Now I see the whole picture and the force of her love belittles me.

This is not about forgiveness. That is an arrogant concept. I have nothing to forgive.

But I hope she forgives me.

The shame is all mine.

I didn't trust her or believe her.

I chose to think the worst before the best.

No one is perfect.

Not me. Not my mother.

Love is flawed.

But I know I am better with it than without.

## Linda

It is Jonathan's funeral today and I'm pulling out all the stops. I've dragged a comb through my hair, to little effect, it has to be said. It's gone feral over the years and now resists any attempt to tame it. An old suit at the back of the wardrobe has been resuscitated for the occasion, although I'm regretting my decision not to send it to the dry cleaner's. It's giving off a whiff of dampness and I'm concerned I smell like a fusty old woman. I was hoping the wash of colour on my lips would be the final flourish, as it used to be back when I was young. But sadly, it has done little to brighten my pallor. Never mind, I tell myself, this is all about effort. If Jonathan can die in a shirt and tie, I will damn well go to his funeral looking the part.

The church is packed full. Standing-room only. I can't say why I'm surprised, he was a popular man. I suppose I liked to think he was my friend and mine alone. I take a seat in the second row. In front of me I notice his ex-wife Jan holding hands with Vanessa, her old neighbour.

When Gabriel stands to read the eulogy, I don't know who

I'm crying for any more. Gabriel, who talks so eloquently about my old friend and his godfather, or Jonathan who should be here, should never be gone. Gabriel's voice clogs with tears but he marches through, without recourse to profanity, which is something of a relief, let me tell you.

Towards the end, he says Jonathan taught him that the truth can repair and heal, and while I don't necessarily agree, I have to admit it has a nice ring to it.

His last words are: 'Jonathan, if you're listening, you didn't fail.'

I have no idea what he's talking about, but when he makes his way back to his seat, I give him a smile as if to say, *Well done*.

The day is a sullen affair. Grey clouds glower and threaten, though mercifully hold back the rain. At the cemetery, there is only a smattering of close friends and family evenly dispersed around the grave.

I'm standing alone, giving Jan and Vanessa a wide berth lest they try to tempt me back to theirs for a prawn sandwich and warm wine, when a hand takes mine.

I know the touch of that hand. I've held it since he was born.

My boy.

He pulls me into his chest and I yield to his embrace. I can't hear a word the vicar is saying above the throb of my heart, my sobs.

'I love you, Mum. I thought you should know.'

I hope Jonathan wouldn't mind me saying this on the day of his funeral, but I can't remember being happier.

Later, Gabriel and I find ourselves alone. The sun has poked out from behind the clouds and brushes the sky pink and orange.

'I'm not like him, you know,' Gabriel says.

This is it. The fear that has stalked me and coloured our

relationship, the one we've been too terrified to voice in case it becomes real.

But it is out there now and we let it sit for a while between us, so we can see it is not real. It is nothing.

'I know,' I say, because this is the truth.

He never was.

# Acknowledgements

My thanks to the following;

Kate Stephenson, my editor at Wildfire, for pushing, pressing and helping me untangle and streamline. The book is all the better for your input.

To Alex Clarke and Ella Gordon.

To Imogen Taylor for her enthusiasm and support.

To Millie Seaward and Georgina Moore.

To my agent, Nicola Barr, for knowing how to make it better.

To Dr Raj Bathula for helping me with medical questions. Any mistakes are my own.

To Tom Andrew for advice on sailing in the Kyles of Bute. It is a stunning place and I will return one day soon.

To the group of fellow crime authors who make me laugh out loud when I should be writing. Thanks for the fun, support and showing me how to take procrastination to new levels.

To readers and book bloggers who take the time to tweet, email and leave reviews, I am eternally grateful.

To my friends for keeping me sane and feeding me wine when necessary.

To my family, Liz and Danny McBeth, Jacqueline McBeth, John and Margaret Curran for their enthusiasm and child care.

To Finlay, Milo and Sylvie; the book would have been finished in half the time without your input but life would be so much emptier. I think that means we're quits.

To Paul, my love and thanks as always. I suppose you should read it now.

*An Act of Silence* deals with difficult issues and I thought long and hard before I decided to delve in to them. Every survivor's story is different and I don't claim to represent all or any, only the experience of the characters in the book. What I hope I have shown however, is that the silencing, the choosing not to act or listen, is a form of violence in itself. Also, that the damage doesn't repair when the abuse stops, but its ripples and currents run down through the years.

I read many testimonies of abuse in the course of my research, but two works I found particularly helpful were *Chosen*, a documentary by Brian Woods and Chris Eley about boys who were groomed and abused at Caldicott Prep School, and *Victim Zero*, Kat Ward's account of her abuse at the hands of Jimmy Savile.